Dying To Be Heard

Margaret Demeray Book Four
Paula Harmon

January Press

Dedication

This book is dedicated to every single person, of whatever nationality, race or gender who has fought, or continues to fight so that everyone has an equal voice.

One

Sunday 4th May 1913 London

Margaret's short speech outside Marylebone police court was nearly over, but the drivers, cabbies and pedestrians whose progress had been halted by the procession were not in the mood to listen in silence, even if it might speed things up.

'Get back in the kitchen where you belong, you hoyden! Get off the bleeding road.'

'Women ask only what monied men take for granted,' Margaret stated. 'The right to a voice, to choose for themselves. We call on those men who cannot vote to join us. Aren't you angry that richer men with no idea of your lives control you?'

'Someone oughta be controlling you. Here, you coppers, why ain't yer nabbing them for blocking the traffic?'

'Let every voice be heard. Let—'

'I've had enough o' *your* voice. Shut yer trap!'

'Stow the potato pie! Your old man oughta be ashamed!'

'Old man?' bellowed a wagon driver. 'What sort of flaming maniac would marry one of this lot and not drown her?'

'Women could bring so many qualities to parliament: compassion, nurture—'

'Get home and nurture your baby, you nagging bint!'

'That hinchinharfer's ole man probably can't give her one. That's the trouble. Come down here, missus. I'll give you something worth squeaking about!'

Loud guffaws and jeers. A policeman next to Margaret sniggered and shifted position. She wasn't sure if he had made a crude gesture, or whether he intended to 'accidentally' let the hecklers drag her off the stool and see what happened next.

She took a deep breath. 'They demand taxes from every adult, yet some of you men cannot cast a vote to choose the government which takes their money! Support us! Women demanding your rights as well as their own are being imprisoned—'

'Because they keep bloody smashing windows and setting fires.'

'Yeah, and trying to blow up Piccadilly tube station on Friday! Did one o' *you* do that?'

Margaret had prepared for that question. 'No one has claimed responsibility for that incident. Nothing suggests anyone here was behind it.' She looked into the faces of the suffragettes before her: militant and non-militant alike, they smiled up in support.

'Have they got a permit for this?' demanded the cabbie.

The constable didn't answer, and Margaret risked a glance. Phoebe would have obtained a permit, but it might have been revoked after the incident on the tube. The constable had turned aside to talk to another policeman.

'What you need is a smacked backside!' Someone gave Margaret a swift, hard punch in the kidneys. She wobbled on the stool, feeling every muscle tense, and her heart raced.

'Steady now, sir!' said the constable, paying attention again. 'If you break her ankle, she'll be slower moving off. Hurry up, missus. We can't hold them back much longer.'

'Just let me at her! I'll bleeding well lock her up myself!'

'What's the point?' snapped another man. 'Soon as she went off her rocker they'd let her out, which is more'n I would!'

'Off her rocker? She's starving herself! Let 'er sodding starve. Save the taxpayer a bob or two.'

Margaret forced herself not to look at Maude. 'The Cat and Mouse Act shows the true mettle of this government: bullying and sneaking. But we will not be overcome. Justice *will* prevail. We *will* have universal suffrage! Support us, help us, speak out for justice! Votes for Women! Votes for All! Ladies, about turn!'

Margaret stepped down from the stool, which was snatched up by a supporter. The suffragettes turned and began to sing 'The March of the Women'. She took her place alongside Maude, heart thudding and stomach clenching. She kept looking forward, but at the edges of her vision were the faces of hecklers, now above her rather than below, their fingers jabbing and gesticulating, their words forming an obscene chant.

Home-breaker, fishwife, henpecker, hag, shameful, barmy, witch.

Vandal, bitch, hoyden, drab.

Regardless, one hundred women, bright and feminine in the spring sunshine, marched down the centre of the road. Their neat white dresses were crossed with sashes of green and purple, their white hats adorned with lavender. Heads were high, backs straight, faces determined. The traffic steered round them, most drivers yelling curses as they passed.

Margaret quavered inwardly, and she suspected others did too, but like them, she refused to show it. Even timid Miss Tabor managed to convey indifference and detachment – if one ignored her tight grip on the banner's pole and looked only at her face.

They marched as equals: women of independent means, university women, professional women, shop-women and maids on their half day, housewives, mothers, spinsters. Grouped by locality, profession or friendship, they marched in blocks. Within each block, one woman bore a standard, or two shared a banner:

Votes For Women
We Will Fight The Good Fight
Deeds Not Words

Senior officers and marshals flanked them, protecting their members from being jostled by the line of police who marched alongside, themselves jostled by irritated drivers and pedestrians.

On the way to the police court, Margaret and Maude had borne the banner that Mrs Nutford and Miss Tabor now bore. Margaret's arm and shoulder muscles still throbbed from her earlier effort to keep the pole from tipping or twisting.

'Did that man hurt you?' said Maude, as the song ended and another began.

'A little. I'll be all right. He didn't have enough space to put much power into it.'

'You should have dropped the script and used all the bad language you learned in the East End.'

'Waste of breath, and it wouldn't help the cause.'

'Sadly true.' Maude's voice faded into a cough.

Margaret turned as much as she could without losing rhythm and regarded her friend. In the harsh sunshine, the hollowness of Maude's cheeks appeared unhealthy rather than elegant, her wrists were thin and her outfit seemed loose. The white strands streaking her dark hair had not been noticeable the night before. She looked older than forty.

The sun caught on the Holloway badge pinned to Maude's sash. 'I could kill for a drink,' she said.

'There'll be tea soon.'

'I wasn't thinking of tea.'

'You shouldn't be doing this,' said Margaret.

'What's the point of marching to the police court and making speeches if the women it imprisoned aren't with you?'

'You're—'

'Get these harpies off the street!' yelled a man to their right. 'I don't pay my taxes for coppers to nursemaid a load of harridans. I've got fares to pick up. Whose side you on?' He shoved the policeman, who stumbled into the marshal, who knocked against Miss Tabor. She broke her stride, trying to manage her tipping pole, and Maude and Margaret marched into her and Mrs Nutford before they could stop themselves. The policeman broke ranks to remonstrate with the cabbie while the banner carriers regained control and resumed their march.

'Are you all right, Miss Tabor?' called Maude. 'Have you hurt your wrist?'

Margaret heard the pain in her answer. 'I shall be fine. If *you* can go on, Mrs Holbourne, so can I.'

In the moments when they'd been pushed together, Margaret had felt the trembling in Maude's frame, seen her falter, then swear, her clenched hands pressing her stomach before breaking free to swing again. 'You're not well enough to march, Maude.'

'Stop fussing, Demeray.'

'I'm not. You're on licence. If a policeman recognises you and sees you apparently fit and healthy, he'll put you back in prison to serve another six months of your sentence, and—'

'Not without a fight, he won't.'

'Oh, Maude.'

'Do shut up, Margaret. I'm in the mood for blacking someone's eye. Stop nannying me, or it'll be yours.'

'I don't know why you're annoyed. I was the one trying to talk over all that yelling.'

'You should be taller.'

'I'll bear that in mind for next time.'

They had nearly reached the church rooms where the rally would continue. The blocks were breaking up into individual women, most of the police backing off to let the traffic move. Phoebe was waiting at the door.

'I don't suppose there's brandy,' said Maude, wistfully.

'Only if you show signs of fainting,' said Phoebe. 'But we were a little behind schedule, so no doubt the tea will be stronger than normal.'

'If it's not as thick and strong as paint, it won't help,' said Maude, gloomily. 'And Margaret could do with something to drag her out of self-pity. Look at her. Since when did any of us care what men shouted at us? Chin up, Demeray. Motherhood has made you soft.'

'No it hasn't,' said Phoebe. 'It was a good speech. You always say that we only need to persuade one person. I'm sure she persuaded more than one today.'

Inside the hall, Margaret refreshed herself with tea and settled to listen to the speeches. The police were keeping hecklers out and evicting any who started up within, so the audience was at least interested in what was being said.

All the speakers were passionate, but none more so than Maude. For a woman who ought to be recovering in bed from hunger strike and forcible feeding, she gave an impression of mesmerising power. Even the most genteel women were on the edge of their seats as she described what she'd endured as an active member of the Women's Social and Political Union.

As her voice grew louder and her words more forceful, the atmosphere began to change. Maude left no doubt that the government couldn't be trusted and militancy within the WSPU was utterly justified. Miss Tabor had a look of near-rapture on her face and her hair was coming down and tangling in the old-fashioned ruby earrings she always wore. She readjusted a tortoiseshell comb, then snatched at Margaret's hand. Margaret shifted sideways: the level of passion made her deeply uncomfortable. She felt as unnerved by Maude as she had been by the hecklers, detached from the rising emotion, threatened by it and desperate to leave.

'We desire peace,' concluded Maude. 'We want to protect those whom the police disregard. Without the vote we cannot act, therefore we demand the vote. The government, in its constant deceit, is responsible for every act of ours which they choose to call an outrage. If they kept their promises, if they gave us that to which we have a right, all militant action would cease. Our opponents will stop at nothing. One of our supporters, Jeremiah Stokes, was murdered just the other day. They say it was a burglar, but how can one be sure? Be on your guard, but do what must be done! Make no mistake – if you do not take direct action, if you shirk your responsibility, then not only do you prolong the campaign, but you side with Mr Lloyd George and his minions. You betray your sisters as they suffer in prison! Women – know your duty and do it!'

'Oh yes,' breathed Miss Tabor. 'Oh yes.'

Outside, Phoebe drew Margaret aside. 'Maude shouldn't have mentioned Jeremiah Stokes,' she said. 'It's got people's blood up. I didn't think his death and his support of universal suffrage were connected. Wasn't the autopsy done at Dorcas Free? Does Fox—'

'It's nothing to do with Fox,' said Margaret. 'But yes, Dr Naylor and I undertook the post-mortem. Dr Gesner was away. Stokes was shot at close range, but it wasn't suicide. The reputable papers all reported that.'

'Yes, and that it was almost certainly a disturbed burglary. I don't know why Maude is referring to what the sensational press say.'

Margaret turned to see if Maude had emerged and gasped as a jolt of pain went through her. 'Did that ruffian really hurt you?' asked Phoebe.

'Sitting on a folding chair for an hour hasn't helped.' Margaret rubbed the small of her back. Miss Tabor, grey-faced, was standing by the gate, nursing her wrist. 'I'm more worried about Miss Tabor. I'll take her to the first-aid position.'

The policeman on the gate reached Miss Tabor first, his disdain replaced by concern. 'Here, madam, don't faint. Let me—'

Miss Tabor recoiled, horror on her face. 'Don't touch me, you beast!' She stumbled and let out a squeak. 'Look what you've done! My ankle!'

The constable's sneer returned. 'Suit yourself. Get the coven to help you.'

Supported by Margaret, Miss Tabor turned towards the hall. 'Please don't fuss, doctor,' she bleated. 'I shall be all right. That awful man...' She peered over her shoulder and stiffened. 'Oh no!' She buried her face in Margaret's shoulder.

'Once you're bandaged up you'll feel better,' said Margaret.

'I need to go home. I've just seen Mother's friend. She and Mother were supposed to be in Town till late, but she's here, staring! That means Mother might be on the way home. She mustn't know I'm doing this!'

Margaret looked past the police, suffragettes, supporters and detractors milling about. People stared as they drove slowly past in their vehicles, including an elderly lady glaring through her pince-nez.

'I *must* go,' whined Miss Tabor, her face still buried. 'Could Miss Pendleberry take me?'

Margaret glanced towards the hall. Phoebe was going inside. At that moment, though, she saw what she'd been hoping for all afternoon: the familiar sight of Fox's driver, Bert, pulling up in the car. She waved discreetly and Bert touched his cap, which meant she could approach. 'No, but my husband's driver has arrived. He can take us.'

Miss Tabor peeked under the brim of her hat. 'But Mother doesn't know *you*. She only knows Miss Pendleberry. What will the neighbours say when I turn up in a strange car with a strange man?'

Margaret counted to ten under her breath. 'Then let me escort you to the hall. Phoebe will be free in an hour or so.'

'I have to go home *now*.'

'Is everything all right?' asked Miss Stevens, a younger suffragette wearing an undergraduate gown.

Miss Tabor pointed. 'We have to move from here to there without being seen.'

'You need a distraction?'

'Yes.'

'Good-oh,' said Miss Stevens. She moved towards the gate, snatched the constable's helmet from his head, threw it over a wall, then ran in the opposite direction. Everyone turned to watch the policeman as he stood swearing and looking about him in confusion.

Under cover of shouts and laughter, Margaret grabbed Miss Tabor by her uninjured arm and marched her to the car.

Two

M iss Tabor insisted throughout the journey that while some people said her home was in refined Tyburnia, it was unquestionably in even more refined Marylebone.

The house was, in fact, in Paddington. The confusion added ten minutes to the journey.

By the time they arrived, Miss Tabor had given her WSPU sash to Margaret, to pass to Phoebe for safekeeping, and buried her hat's suffragette decoration in her handbag. She now appeared to be simply a woman of nearly fifty in a white summer outfit.

The Tabors' home was one of several large, stone-faced terraced houses surrounding a small park. When they were new, each would have been creamy and fresh, containing just one family and its staff, every visible window dressed with care and cohesion. But over the sixty years since, London soot had streaked all of them with grey. Several had been turned into flats with a mishmash of curtains and window-boxes, and varying levels of effort were put into outer cleanliness, giving them rather a slatternly look.

From the outside, however, the Tabor household was as pristine as possible, and Miss Tabor was proud to relate that she, her brother and her mother had a staff of five, four slept in the attics and the boot boy slept in a room off the kitchen, below street level.

'I hope the boot boy's room is dry, warm and well-ventilated,' said Margaret.

Miss Tabor stared. 'You really needn't worry. The working classes are very robust.'

Bert handed Miss Tabor out of the car and Margaret made to follow, but Miss Tabor shook her head. 'No need, Dr Demeray. If Mother's home, I shall explain that I tripped while I was out, visiting the shops in Marylebone. You were passing, saw to my injuries and had your chauffeur bring me home, but are unable to stay.'

'Absolutely none of that is true,' said Margaret, frowning.

Miss Tabor pursed her lips in disapproval. 'I do *not* tell false-hoods. I *did* visit a shop earlier and I *did* trip, because I was assaulted by a police officer. You've passed me several times today, your chauffeur *has* brought me home and you *must* be keen to return and speak with Mrs Holbourne. She is an utter inspiration. I *so* wish I could have stayed.' A startling glow of adoration crossed Miss Tabor's face, then disappeared as the shining black front door of her house opened.

A man in his forties whom Margaret vaguely recognised stepped out.

'Oh!' Miss Tabor breathed, in evident relief. 'It's my broth-er, Hedley. You may have seen him collecting me from Miss Pendleberry's meetings. Mrs Holbourne has kindly invited him to dinner on Saturday, to encourage him to support the cause.'

'Has she?' said Margaret, as Mr Tabor made his way down the steps. 'I'll be there too. As, presumably, will you.'

'Oh no, I couldn't leave Mother. Men are so much freer, aren't they?'

Margaret restrained a sigh of relief that she wouldn't have to endure Miss Tabor's chatter and nodded in greeting to Mr Tabor. His face, a male version of his sister's, was unremarkable: mousy hair, small dark-blue eyes, podgy cheeks, a fuller than average beard. He put out an arm for his sister. 'I wasn't expecting you back so soon, Rhoda.'

'I've hurt my ankle, Hedley. Dr Demeray here has been of assistance, but if you'll help me up the steps I'll have Sarah bandage it. Is Mother back?'

'Not yet. I believe I'll see you next Saturday at Mrs Holbourne's, Dr Demeray. I look forward to making your acquaintance properly.'

'That'll be lovely,' said Margaret. 'Are you sure you wouldn't like me to—'

'No, thank you,' said Miss Tabor. She turned, took her brother's arm, climbed the steps and with the tiniest wave, slipped inside.

'Cor blimey, what a street,' said Bert. 'I've never seen so many curtains twitching at once. It was like being surrounded by an entire chorus line doing the can-can, only with nothing under the frilly lace that anyone would want to see. I only came to see you were all right. The anti-suffragette crowds are getting uglier.'

'I'll survive,' said Margaret. 'It takes my mind off things.'

'Are your father and sister still in Madeira?'

'Yes. My stepmother's funeral took place last week, but I don't think Father wants to leave her behind.' Margaret felt tears well up and once again wasn't sure if it was grief, guilt that she hadn't been able to help, or both.

'We're all ever so sorry, Mrs F,' said Bert. 'There was nothing you could have done differently. The climate there's a million times better than London, but...'

'But she had one bout of pneumonia too many,' said Margaret. 'I know. And maybe even Madeira was too wet, though they loved it so. I still wish I could have been there, but it was all over before I could even arrange leave and book my passage. I probably wouldn't have got there in time and as you say, there was nothing I could do that the local doctors couldn't. Only ... I was so fond of her, and she made Father so happy.'

'One day you'll find an effective cure for those sorts of infections.'

'Maybe not me. But by God, someone must.' Margaret cleared her throat. 'Is all well with Fox?'

'He'll finish eating scouse and be back on Thursday.'

'I don't believe for one moment he's in Liverpool,' said Margaret. 'But I'll be glad to have him home.' She paused. 'Do you think the war in the Balkans can definitely be stopped?'

'You're getting the Danube muddled with the Mersey,' said Bert. 'But if negotiations here in London go well I don't see why not, provided no one mucks things up. Not that it's anything to do with Fox.'

'Of course not,' said Margaret. 'I've told everyone he's in Liverpool as instructed.'

Bert chuckled. 'Good girl. Where to next?'

'I can take a cab. Haven't you something more important to do?'

'You're important.'

Margaret checked her watch. There was no point in returning to the hall now. 'Do you know anything about the death of Jeremiah Stokes?

Bert blew out his cheeks and considered. 'Sing me the first line and I'll join in if I know the chorus.'

'He was shot in lodgings in St John's Wood.'

'Oh, him. One of the illustrated papers had a sketch of him hunched over explosives looking sneaky, then lying dead with a pistol beside him. Not our concern.'

'I'd have thought you'd be interested in people with explosives.'

'Someone checked and it was nothing to do with us. Why? Does it make a difference to where you want to go now?'

'Could you take me to Dorcas Free? I'd like to collect his file before taking the tube home.'

'I'll take you there *and* home,' said Bert. 'Do you fancy driving?'

Margaret glanced up at the house. A worried face peeped round a lace curtain and a dainty hand flapped. 'Let's get away from here first,' she said. 'If the curtains twitch any more, they'll disintegrate.'

Margaret went to her office in the deserted mortuary wing.

She was surprised to find Dr Ruth Naylor sitting at her desk, reading Jeremiah Stokes's file. Dr Naylor was a Quaker and as much as she could, kept Sunday as a day of spiritual contemplation and charity work.

The older woman looked up and grinned. 'I thought you'd come the moment the rally disbanded.'

'I didn't see you there!'

'Matron and I were observing two off-duty nurses to make sure they conducted themselves with the dignity Matron demands. Which they did.' She grinned. 'My parasol, however, inexplicably jabbed anyone employing bad language. I enjoyed your speech: it was passionate but rational, which is more than can be said for Mrs Holbourne's.' Dr Naylor closed the file and handed it over. 'I gather she was recently released from prison, three months into a term of imprisonment for criminal damage. Hunger strike, I presume.'

'They force-fed her and it's taking her time to recover. She's angry. *I'm* angry. If they'd listen to what we want, the militants among us wouldn't act with so much force.'

'I take it you're not a militant,' said Dr Naylor.

'I did my share of throwing bricks at windows when I was younger.'

'But no longer? Don't you keep a hammer in your bag, as Mrs Pankhurst says you must?'

'I'm not convinced about recent tactics,' said Margaret. 'I just wish the government would listen. What threat do they honestly think women pose as voters?'

'Letting women leave their natural realm and mire themselves in politics would destroy society, my dear,' said Dr Naylor, impersonating a stuffy male voice. 'You should rely on your menfolk.'

'What if my menfolk are fools?' said Margaret. 'It's a ridiculous argument.'

'I know,' said Dr Naylor. 'But things are changing. I'm glad you decided to leave St Julia's and join us at Dorcas Free. We can prove that more women on the medical staff does not mean less clinical excellence. Dr Gesner is very glad that you're working with him.'

'He's never said so.'

'It's not in his nature to gush – but he's left you in charge till Thursday, hasn't he? That would never have happened a few years ago in a hospital with male and female staff. This is *my* way to fight for women, Margaret,' said Dr Naylor. 'Not with hammers or bricks, but gentle persistence. And I've wanted to work with you ever since you were an argumentative student back in the nineties. Let's fight the good fight together. You needn't follow Mrs Holbourne's example.'

Margaret sighed. 'She and I have been friends more than half our lives. I trust her to be...' She stopped, feeling treacherous.

'Wise?' suggested Dr Naylor. 'Then why mention the death of Jeremiah Stokes? It roused her audience in an alarming manner.'

'He was a suffrage supporter with the means for making bombs.'

'What has that to do with anything?'

'Some speculate that his killer wanted to punish him for his views.'

'Some? Who?

'The sensational press.'

'Surely a respectable journalist like Mrs Holbourne wouldn't use that sort of misinformation to drive an argument. And surely her audience is in the main too well educated to read the sensational press – or believe it if they did!'

'People read what's interesting and believe what they want, in the face of duller accuracy,' said Margaret. 'But Maude using his case in her speech makes no sense. Unless...'

'Unless the police are wrong.'

'If so, how does Maude know?'

'Maybe she doesn't. I taught you to go to the facts.'

Margaret shifted in her seat and perused the file. 'Mr Stokes was shot at close quarters, but not close enough for him to have shot himself. Suicide was initially suspected because the oven in his room had been turned on but not ignited. The room was full of gas.' She pointed at a paragraph. 'Yet there was no evidence that he'd inhaled any of it before death. And the police photographs show his body just inside his doorway. That suggests he'd been disturbed while lighting the oven, gone to the door and was then shot. The burglar left the scene without turning the gas off, since why would he?'

Dr Naylor sat back. 'I suppose that doesn't preclude a deliberate murder.'

'No,' said Margaret. 'But Stokes was an obscure clerk living in a flat. At the inquest, it appeared that neither his colleagues nor family knew of his views, and he had no particular friends.' She closed the file, rubbed the small of her back and winced.

'You know what to look out for in the event of kidney damage,' said Dr Naylor.

'Yes, doctor.'

'Make sure you do. I can't have you being sick.'

'No, doctor.'

'Now, take the file if you must – but go home.'

'I generally spend Sundays at my sister's with my father and stepmother. It doesn't seem the same now.'

'I know,' said Dr Naylor. 'And I understand your grief. But now you must make your own traditions for your own family, and enable your stepmother to live on through them somehow. Let us both enjoy what remains of the Sabbath.'

After rereading the Stokes file that evening, Margaret telephoned Maude to discuss the rally and asked, as nonchalantly as she could, why his murder had been brought up.

'Because there's something very odd about his death,' said Maude. 'Why burgle those flats? They're rented by people like Stokes. What would any of them have worth stealing?'

'Most people have something. The burglar just has to want it.'

'You may be right,' said Maude. 'But I know someone who was in the same small suffrage group as Stokes and *she's* convinced it was more than just bad luck. Besides, he's a loss to the cause, and deserves to be remembered for what he wanted to achieve.'

It was tempting to say 'Bombing things?', but Margaret knew that wasn't what Maude meant. 'You should tell the police or hire a private detective.'

'No evidence yet,' said Maude. 'Phoebe said you had to take Miss Tabor home. Have your ears recovered from all that dreary twittering?'

'More or less. I met her brother. He said he would be at your dinner party on Saturday.'

'Oh yes, I meant to tell you. You weren't at Phoebe's meeting on Friday, but he came to collect his sister a little early and Phoebe's maid admitted him. It appears that he and I have a mutual acquaintance, a Mrs Philbrook, in the movement, which he broadly supports. So I decided to invite both of them, if only in case Fox couldn't come and you needed help to dilute the Bryces.'

'The who?'

'Geoff's guests. Theatricals. Anyway, Miss Tabor kept butting in, saying that her brother's a war hero like their dear father. Hedley was embarrassed, and said that while their father died in the Afghan campaign, he was invalided out as a cadet before he could serve. He'll be interesting to Fox, I hope, given the military connection.'

'The what?'

Maude made an exasperated noise. 'Oh honestly, Margaret. I haven't forgotten that Fox was in South Africa in '02. The army is common ground, surely. Will he be back from Liverpool?'

'Yes.'

'Good. Well, I'll see you next Saturday, Demeray. Goodbye.'

Three

On Thursday morning, Fox sent word that he'd be home before ten p.m.

By eight thirty, the sun had set. Outside, the northerly breeze had dropped but the house felt cold.

Margaret turned on the lamps and lit the fire. Using the day's newspapers as kindling, she watched articles about the Balkan conflict flare up then crumble into ash, and willed it to be prophetic.

The war was surely near its end. And Fox – if he'd been there, as Margaret suspected – was back in Britain and safe. Everything was ready for his return. Freda, their new cook-housekeeper, had made sure of that. At twenty-two, Freda might be young, but her cooking was excellent and she was good company for seventeen-year-old Nellie Pinter, the nurse-maid.

Margaret settled by the fire with her cat Juniper and the embroidery she'd started in April, with a view to giving it to her sister as a birthday gift. It had been abandoned while they dealt with the flurry of telegrams from Madeira about Thirza's worsening health. Then Katherine went out to help their father, having neither small children nor paid employment to keep her back.

Margaret had never particularly enjoyed sewing, but the intricacy of embroidery kept her fingers supple for surgical work and stopped her mind churning over problems she couldn't solve. Her mind was fully engaged in forming a French knot, so when the sitting room door was flung open, she jumped and drove her needle deep into the finger she'd forgotten to put a thimble on.

Nellie, her face red, burst in. 'Come quick, ma'am!' She was smiling, almost bouncing. Nothing serious, then.

'What have the twins done now, Nellie?' said Margaret, sucking her finger.

'Nothing, ma'am. They're fast asleep.'

'Then what's wrong? Anyone would think the house was on fire.'

'*Ours* ain't.'

'What? Whose? A neighbour's?' Margaret dropped the needlework on the side table and stood up, dislodging Juniper.

'No, ma'am, it's Paddington way. We're in no danger. You can only see from the top of the house, ma'am. Come quick!'

Margaret followed Nellie, wishing there were fewer floors in the house and wondering whether Maude was right about her staff being too familiar, until she stood with Nellie and Freda, peering towards a very definite conflagration a mile or so northeast. Freda seemed even more excited than Nellie.

Margaret had limited experience, but she suspected by the size of the fire that something smaller than a house was alight: a garden outbuilding, perhaps. It was far enough away not to worry about, and hopefully the fire brigade would extinguish it before it reached any neighbouring buildings.

'Ain't it scary-beautiful, ma'am?' breathed Nellie.

'Go on with you, Nell,' said Freda.

'The missus gets my drift. Don't you, ma'am?'

'I do,' said Margaret.

Even at a distance, the orange flames against the dark buildings and sudden bursts of golden sparks in the night sky were like an exotic flower, lethal but mesmerising. It was lovely, even as it devoured and destroyed, but Margaret felt an unease unconnected to the loss of someone's property or a potential risk to strangers' lives. She told herself that perhaps this was what it had been like when the Great Fire of London started: people watching from a distance, as if it were a conjuring act or an illusion, not something that could consume anything in its path until the city was aflame. Surely nothing like that could ever happen to London again.

'It's getting smaller,' said Freda, a hint of disappointment in her voice. 'I suppose the fire brigade's putting it out.'

'It'll all be over soon,' said Margaret. She stepped back from the window, but her sense of unease persisted.

From the ground floor came the sound of the telephone. Freda scurried off to answer it.

'Are you all right, ma'am?' said Nellie. 'You look pale. Are you afraid there'll be casualties at the hospital tomorrow?'

'I'm sure there won't be and I wouldn't be worried if there were. A goose stepped on my grave, that's all.' She smiled. 'Go and see that the twins are all right. I'll find out who's telephoning.'

Margaret had just reached the hall to take the receiver from Freda, who'd mouthed *Miss Pendleberry* at her, when there was a loud, rapid thumping on the front door.

'Just a moment, Phoebe,' Margaret said into the receiver.

'But—'

Margaret and Freda exchanged glances. The door rattled under a fresh onslaught.

'Who is it?' Margaret called, taking an umbrella from the stand.

'Just open up before I break it down!' The voice was that of Maude's husband, Geoff. But instead of sounding vague and friendly as usual, he seemed furious.

Margaret opened the door and he barged past her. 'Where is she?'

'Who?'

'Maude.'

'I don't know.'

'Don't fib, M.'

'Why would I fib, Geoff? And why would Maude be here? She knows Fox is coming home tonight, after being away for ages, and we're coming to your house for dinner on Saturday.'

There was a squawk from the telephone and Margaret lifted the receiver. 'Phoebe, are you still there? Do you know where Maude is? Geoff's lost her.'

'Or you're hiding her,' snapped Geoff.

'Why on earth would I—' Margaret sighed, then beckoned Freda, who was gawping. 'Could you make some tea, please, and take it to the sitting room.'

'Wouldn't Mr Holbourne prefer whisky, ma'am?' Freda whispered.

'He's getting tea first.' *Even if it's just to get you out of earshot.*

'Oh Lord,' said Phoebe over the telephone. 'Geoff was here half an hour ago. That's why I was calling you. I think it's to do with a fire nearby, in Nelson Avenue.'

Margaret gasped. Of course: both Phoebe and Maude lived in Marylebone, to the northeast of Bayswater. 'I saw it from upstairs. I didn't realise it was near you.'

'It's not close enough to worry about,' said Phoebe. 'Tyburnia ... Paddington, really. I only just heard myself. That isn't the point. Let me talk to him, it'll save time.'

Margaret offered the receiver to Geoff, whom she knew as indolent and gentle. He snatched it from her. 'A telegram? ... Where from?... When was it timed?... But that's before...' He deflated a little. 'Of course I'm bloody worried. Aren't you? If you can, tell her to come home. No matter what.' He slammed the receiver on its rest. 'I'm sorry, M. I shouldn't have been so rude.'

'What's going on?'

'Is Fox here?'

'Not yet. Did you want him?'

'No.' Geoff swallowed. 'You know the MP who wrote that filthy letter to the *Times* about suffragettes recently?'

'Yes.'

'He lives in Nelson Avenue. Some sort of fancy pagoda thing in his garden caught fire earlier. It spread to all the other wood-work too – arches, and so on – and nearly reached the former stable where he keeps his car.'

'I saw it. But what—'

Geoff drew her into the sitting room and closed the door. 'The last time anyone saw Maude she was in a shed in *our* garden, though she barely knows one end of a spade from another. I was at my club. If I had known, I'd have thought she was research-ing for some article or other. But now the gardener's boy says there's been a box there for some weeks, getting fuller every day. Rags, a paraffin can, kindling. God knows why he never told the gardener, or me: the whole place could have gone up. Anyway, now it's all gone – and so has Maude. She didn't leave word with the servants as to where she was going. I'm not a fool, M, and nor are you. I'm sure she's behind the arson. She's been building up to something for weeks. Surely you've noticed.'

Margaret frowned, but didn't answer.

'The thing is, where is she now?' Geoff continued. 'The fire started perhaps an hour ago and there's been no word from her. Nothing. I thought maybe she was here or at Phoebe's – that you both knew what she was doing. But clearly you don't. And... what if she was caught in her own act of destruction? What if—'

'Maude is nothing if not competent,' said Margaret. '*If* she did it, I repeat *if*, she'll be making a false trail and brushing off any soot before she goes home.'

'Will she?' Geoff slumped. 'What if she got something wrong? What if—'

'Sit down by the fire,' said Margaret. 'Breathe deeply. I heard you ask Phoebe about a telegram.'

Geoff dropped into the armchair, picked up Margaret's embroidery and stared at it as if the stitched flowers might convey a message. 'Maude wired Phoebe to ask if she'd like to join her at the University Club, but the telegram was delayed.'

'There you are, then. She's been there all along.'

'It's hardly any distance between the club and Nelson Avenue. Maude could quite easily have taken a cab there, sent the telegram, then gone out again and set that fire.'

'And then she could have returned,' said Margaret. 'Or, more likely, she's been there all along, as innocent as a daisy. Why not telephone the club and speak with her?'

'They won't speak to a man.'

'Provided you don't make them think you're an overbearing husband disturbing his wife's peace, they will. Now, please put that embroidery down. It's a gift for Katherine.'

'Good God, is it really?' said Geoff, staring at the tangle of knots and colours within the hoop. 'I thought you liked her.'

'You're looking at the wrong side.'

'Oh. Yes. Though this white flower seems to have blood on it.'

'It'll have a good deal more if you don't put it down.'

Geoff dropped it on the table. 'When is Fox due home?'

'Any moment.'

'Mmm. Well...' He stood up, looked round for his hat, then realised he'd never removed it. 'I won't disturb your reunion. I'll go home and telephone the club from there. No doubt you're right, and she's been there all along. I'm, er... I'm sorry to have been such a bore. All the best to Fox, but, um, don't bother him with this. See you both on Saturday.' He tipped his hat, shook her hand and left the room, almost bumping into Freda with the tea tray. Margaret heard him let himself out.

'Thank you, Freda,' she said, 'Mr Holbourne couldn't stay after all. You can go off duty now. When the master comes home, I'll make his supper.'

'Very well, ma'am.' Freda bustled away, presumably to join Nellie and discover if there was anything more to be seen of the fire in Nelson Avenue.

After a moment's hesitation, Margaret put through a call to Phoebe, reasoning that the chill she felt was caused by the cold hall.

'Is Geoff still there?' asked Phoebe.

'No. He's gone home to telephone the University Club.'

'Why didn't he do that in the first place, instead of barging round to yours and mine? Maude often hires a room there to get away from domestic woes. I've spoken to her now. She seemed quite as normal.'

'You know why he barged round. He was worried that she hadn't been there the whole time.'

'Maude says she's spent the evening working on a speech and she'll go home when it's finished. I hope Geoff's calmer when he speaks to the club staff than he was when he spoke to me, or they won't let him speak to her. And if he speaks to Maude like that, she won't go home at all.'

'Do you...' Margaret wouldn't put her doubt into words over the telephone, and Phoebe didn't answer her unfinished question. If they'd been in the same room, they could have asked and answered without speaking at all.

Phoebe let out a sigh. 'On *quite* another matter, the fire in Nelson Avenue is completely extinguished and no harm has been done. Other than to some pretentious garden constructions, including one shaped like a Chinese pagoda.'

'A pagoda in Tyburnia?'

'I know. Ridiculous,' said Phoebe. 'Anyhow, let's go back to minding our own business. Have a good evening, and say hello to your better half when he comes home.'

Four

Margaret was turning the bloodstained daisy into a red peony when Fox walked in.

'Hello, wife.'

'I wish you wouldn't sneak in like that,' she said. 'I nearly stabbed myself again.'

Fox bent down to kiss her. 'Could you put that needle down, or do you want to skewer me for being away so long?'

She dropped the embroidery and rose into his embrace. 'I'm so glad you're home safe. The place sounds so ominous.'

Fox tipped his head on one side. 'Liverpool?'

'You wouldn't have taken a cholera belt to Liverpool. I mean the Balkans.'

'Shh.'

'Nellie and Freda are upstairs, watching a fire.'

'A what?'

'A garden shed was on fire in Tyburnia. We could just see it from the maids' bedroom. It's probably out now.' Margaret paused, wondering whether to mention Geoff's suspicions about Maude – *her* suspicions, come to that – but Fox pulled her closer.

'I'm surprised there's room in the papers for anything about the Balkans,' he said, 'considering every second article is about the suffragette menace. I presume they don't mean you.'

'I've been too busy keeping your slippers warm,' she said, relaxing into his arms. *What kind of friend would I be if I implicated Maude without evidence?*

'It was worth coming home, then,' said Fox. 'Even if it meant leaving a truly beautiful part of the world.'

'You're definitely not talking about Liverpool.' She stroked his cheek. 'The papers say the Balkan League will agree a treaty with the Great Powers in London soon.'

Fox kissed the top of her head. 'The whole thing's as stable as a bridge made of meringues. *If* it's signed, one can only hope it'll hold long enough for someone to replace the meringues with concrete.'

'If?'

He released her to look into the hallway before shutting the door and returning to the fire. 'I had to find a man who works for the diplomatic corps. Unimportant in himself, but with enough knowledge to write a highly inaccurate book which would make him a fortune if published. The problem is that it would be as dangerous as it is inaccurate, and could destabilise all the negotiations.'

'So you've been tracking him and the manuscript down?'

'Yes. He'd taken a leave of absence for a tour in Italy, but his senior had concerns and told Hare. I found him in Sarajevo, talking to various questionable people.'

'Sarajevo!' Margaret gulped. She'd hoped Fox was safely in Vienna, a long way from battlefields and political turmoil, winkling out what he needed in cafés and restaurants. 'But isn't it under military control? Wasn't it—'

'Dangerous? Perhaps. All the more reason to extract the fool before the Austrians discovered what he was writing and confiscated his passport. So I apprehended him and brought him back.'

Margaret forced a smile and patted his waist. 'Now you can put your cholera belt in the laundry.'

Fox chuckled. 'I never wore it. I like to keep my slender figure and I've never understood how it's supposed to work.'

'Nor I. And the book? I assume you have it. Was there just one copy?'

'Fortunately, yes, and the wretch had only approached one London publisher with a vague proposal. It's Hare's job to encourage them to drop any interest they have, while we go through the manuscript for anything we're unaware of and tackle it.' Fox went to the mantlepiece and patted the doglike plaster creature which Margaret had once won at a fairground stall. In the intervening three years it had lost an ear and its orange glaze was cracked, but this had somehow added to its charms. 'Have you been looking after your missus, Mr Tod?'

'He has.'

'And have you been lonely, Clever Bear?' said Fox, touching a small, rather stern wooden carving at the other end of the mantlepiece.

'Yes, she has,' said Margaret. 'Very.'

Fox took a similar bear from his pocket and placed it beside its mate. 'Never mind: Naughty Bear's back and ready to tell the children all about his adventures tomorrow. Or he'll tell them about *some* adventures.' He turned to Margaret. 'I take it they're well?'

'They're very well indeed.'

Fox took her hand. 'Let's go to the nursery. I won't wake them, but I want to see them. And how have you been? I was so sorry to hear about Thirza.'

'She deteriorated in her final illness so quickly. Three days' sailing doesn't sound much when one is on holiday, but I would have arrived a day too late. I should have gone with Katherine when she went.'

'It wasn't that simple,' said Fox.

'Let's talk about something else.'

'Very well. How's Dorcas Free?'

'I'm still getting used to it,' said Margaret, as they left the room. 'But it's all right.'

'It's been nearly six months. If you're miserable, go back to St J's. I'm sure Dr Jordan would greet you with open arms.'

'One can never go back. And I'm not miserable: it's just different. I miss the East End.'

'You know what I think, but it's your decision,' said Fox. 'Is there anything I need know about?'

'We're invited to a dinner at Maude and Geoff's on Saturday. If you don't want to go, I can decline. They won't mind.'

Fox paused at the bottom of the stairs. 'Don't do that. How are they? Have things settled down now Maude's been out of prison for a while?'

Even in the soft lamplight, Margaret could see how exhausted he was from his mission and his long journey home. 'Everything's fine,' she said.

It was good that the next day was one when Margaret didn't work at the hospital. Hare had given Fox some leave to recover from travelling and they had planned a drive in the country. She got out of bed, stroked Juniper, who was asleep on the chair, then opened the curtains. It looked warmer, as if summer was finally on the way. Above, she heard the children chattering while Nellie gave them breakfast.

Juniper opened an eye. There was a reasonable chance that Margaret might go back to bed and her lap would be free for a while. On the other hand, it might soon be occupied by the twins. From Juniper's point of view, they were more bearable at seventeen months than they had been as infants, but they were still not to be trusted with a tempting tail. She stretched, then sprang to the windowsill and slunk under the sash to claim sanctuary on the roof of the extension below. It was too early for her dignity to be affronted by the heavy-handed caresses of small children.

Margaret climbed the attic stairs. Nellie was feeding the children porridge. She looked wan, and after some prompting, admitted she had stomach cramps and wished she was in bed with a hot-water bottle.

'Go on, then,' said Margaret. 'I'll bring you some aspirin in a bit. Freda and I can manage till later.' She waved Nellie out and turned to the twins. 'Guess who's home, children!'

'Daddy!' crowed Edie, banging her spoon and sending little blobs of porridge flying.

'Naughty Bear!' cried Alec, jiggling in his seat. 'What he do?'

Margaret laughed. 'You'll have to wait and see.'

Mid-morning, after he'd related the implausible but exciting exploits of Naughty Bear to the twins, Fox telephoned Hare, his senior officer, then helped Margaret and the twins settle in the front seat of their Ford for a day in the countryside. Without Nellie, it would have made more sense for Margaret to sit in the back with the children, as they were apt to snatch at the steering wheel, but after nearly a month without Fox she didn't want to. As she'd hoped, the time of day and the motion of driving made them both fall asleep within five minutes of leaving. She tucked them within her shawl, one on either side, and relaxed.

'Has Hare succeeded with the publisher?' she asked.

'He will.'

'May I ask what your budding author planned to say in his book?'

'Are you looking for ways to make your essay for Dr Naylor's next tome more interesting?'

'That would be helpful, but no. If you can't say…'

Fox shrugged as he turned south. 'As you know, the Balkan League may split at any moment. We, France, Germany and Russia believe that the treaty being negotiated will calm things down. At the same time, we each want to make sure the individual Balkan countries are allied with the right Great Power. Everyone wants access to the sea; no one wants to be locked in by potential enemies. It's very delicate.'

'But no one among the Great Powers is anyone else's enemy, in theory.'

'No. But Germany would be happier if Russia and France hadn't made an alliance that surrounds them and Austria-Hungary to the east and west. If Russia gains control of Romania, Bulgaria and Serbia, Austria-Hungary will feel threatened to the south, too. Then again, they know Russia and France aren't easy bedfellows.'

'There are three in the bed: we're there, too,' said Margaret. 'It's not natural for Britain, Russia and France to be allies. There are people still alive who remember the Crimea, and whose grandfathers fought Napoleon's army. And there are definitely men alive who fought the Russians in the Afghan war. In fact— Watch out!'

A delivery boy on a bicycle veered across their path and that of an omnibus, then disappeared down a lane.

'Little…' Fox managed not to stall the car and started to accelerate again. 'Yes, we're all old foes, and I imagine Germany is hoping allegiances might weaken for that reason. I doubt they're scared of France alone. They trounced them forty years ago and no doubt think they could do it again. But if France is protected by Britain and Russia, it's a different matter.'

'If the book said all that, it's not so scurrilous, surely. Or even new.'

'It didn't say that.' Fox slowed as they met a horse-drawn wagon, the horse flicking its mane and the driver pulling the reins to retain control. He waited till they'd passed before continuing. 'It delved into all the negotiations and plotting behind the scenes that no one is supposed to know about. It hints at allegiances being undermined while secret agreements are made between opposing sides.'

'I can believe that.'

'Quite, but revealing them could threaten the treaty. Otherwise, it's full of theories based on nothing. He says the Russians and French will steal British territory while we're trying to support them, because they don't know how to behave like gentlemen.'

'What? Where?'

'He's unspecific, but hints at Russia aiming for India via Afghanistan and France stealing Egypt from Britain.'

'Egypt isn't in the Empire.'

'We're holding it as a protectorate, though, and it would be useful to the French. They'd have control of almost the entire north coast of Africa. The real worry is that he wrote that there's a plan for Britain to colonise the Balkans, bring them into the Empire, and civilise them under Pax Britannica.'

'That's ridiculous.'

'A certain type of person would believe it, and clamour for the government to act on the threat to our existing empire. If Italy thought France was trying to gain control of north Africa, threatening their colonies, and Germany thought there was an ounce of truth in a plan to annex the Balkans, which would threaten Austria-Hungary, it would be a diplomatic catastrophe.'

'But the book will be suppressed, so it's all right.'

'Hare says the man can't produce some of the letters he based the book on, most of which he stole from official files. He said he'd destroyed them, but ... he seems panicked. He begged to be kept under house arrest rather than remanded in custody. Hare thinks he's lost them and is trying to find them.'

'So...'

'So we'll turn his house inside out then let him return home, but provide him with two – shall we say - house-guests to keep him company, then keep him on a long leash, to see where he goes.' Fox nudged her. 'It's a simple enough job, nothing for you to worry about.'

Alec half-woke and nearly slipped from Margaret's arm. It was an effort to tuck him back in without letting go of Edie. 'On the way back, perhaps you could look after the children while *I* drive.'

Fox snorted. 'With your sudden braking and gear changes, they'd be flying out in all directions.'

'You're a very rude man.'

'Yet overwhelmingly lovable and thoroughly irresistible.'

'Huh.' She opened her mouth to argue, then saw the weariness in his eyes that she thought he'd slept off. 'You say you aren't worried – but you are, aren't you?'

Fox wrinkled his nose. 'I'll be glad when Hare's arm-twisting has paid off, certainly. But there's always something to be concerned about.'

'The suffragette menace?'

'You're the only suffragette who can menace me,' said Fox, with a grin which faded quickly. 'Anyone who believes I'm Special Branch might think the latest activities are my concern, but they're not. As I've said before, I can't stop you being arrested: I can only get you the best lawyer we can afford.'

'It's over two years since I've done anything to be arrested for,' said Margaret. 'Mau— Phoebe thinks I'm terribly slack.'

'Mauphoebe? She sounds dreadful.' Fox's grin returned. 'Don't worry, I'm not remotely interested in the burning of a ridiculous pagoda in a reactionary fool's garden. As long as you didn't do it, I don't care at all.'

Five

At Maude's dinner party, Mr Bryce sat on Margaret's left expressing his disapproval of moving pictures. He appeared around fifty, his Dublin accent neutralised by eleven years in London. His sister, perhaps fifteen years younger, had been placed beside Fox, across the dining table. She spoke proudly of her early years on the Dublin stage, before moving to Paddington with her brother to take on Theatre Valerina near Carmelo Street.

'I gather you work in St Julia's Hospital near Aldgate,' said Mr Bryce.

'I left six months ago. I work at Dorcas Free in Marylebone now.'

'Bet you miss the East End,' he said, and nudged her. 'Go on, tell us a story about a funny cockney. I might use it in a show.'

Margaret was grateful for Fox, who raised his voice a little as he told Mrs Philbrook about the week-long motorcycling tour he and Geoff had undertaken the previous autumn, 'to get away from domestic drudgery'.

'A week is nothing,' said Maude, straight-faced. 'Margaret and I shall visit Egypt for six months and leave you men minding the children.'

Mr Tabor and Mr Bryce looked shocked. Mrs Philbrook smirked in approval, her hazel eyes crinkling behind their spectacles. Until that point, it had been hard to read Miss Bryce's face, which under her coppery hair was so pale and expression-less that she might have been made from folded paper. But now her black-rimmed eyes flickered from Maude to Geoff, then Margaret to Fox, and her sandy eyebrows dropped in a quizzical frown.

Margaret, wondering if Miss Bryce was memorising expressions for acting, giggled into her wine and glanced at Fox just as he glanced at her. Despite the elaborate candelabrum and floral displays between them, she saw his subtle wink before he turned to speak with Miss Bryce again. Margaret had known him three years almost to the day and knew all his annoying habits, yet he still made her blood throb. She turned to speak to Mr Tabor, but could hear Mr Bryce telling Maude his views on moving pictures. She was half-poised for Maude to mention Margaret's connection to a film-maker in Glassmakers Lane, but it seemed as if Maude either couldn't get a word in edgeways or had chosen not to try.

'I keep meaning to ask you, M,' said Geoff, as the cheese course arrived, 'how is it working for a German? Does he see conspiracies everywhere, as the press reports?'

'That's not a national personality trait,' said Margaret. 'Just a current political one. I suspect it's why Dr Gesner took a job in London, though I can hardly ask.'

'What if he's a spy, like that dentist in Portsmouth who was in the papers?' asked Mr Tabor.

Margaret made a noncommittal noise, restraining herself from saying that Fox had hinted the same. 'He'd lose interest trying to uncover anything useful from our patients. The ones we get whole are dead.'

'Whole? Dead?'

'Dr Gesner and I are pathologists. We undertake tests on tissue and amputated limbs, and we also do post-mortems.'

'Good Lord,' said Mr Tabor, pushing the Stilton to the edge of his plate.

Geoff chuckled. 'Dead women tell no tales, eh?' He glanced at Fox, who was listening to Miss Bryce explain something with a lot of hand-waving. 'One or two military types at the club seem to think there's a risk of getting dragged into a war.'

'It's the same at mine, too,' said Mr Tabor. 'Can't see it myself. We're more like Germans than French: a chat is all that's needed. The Balkans are a long way away and they'll soon be sorted out.'

'Carved up, you mean.' said Margaret.

Mr Tabor raised his eyebrows. 'I imagine that when you're busy with suffrage, working and running a home, you might not grasp—'

'Don't argue politics with Dr Demeray,' said Geoff. 'She'll tie you in knots, which may be why Fox is always rather vague when I ask him his views.'

'He loathes war,' said Margaret.

'Is your husband a pacifist?' Mr Tabor looked aghast. 'We can't let another country get above themselves.'

Geoff laughed before Margaret could answer. 'He was in the army before joining Special Branch, Tabor. I've known him three years and I wouldn't describe him thus. One doesn't have to be a pacifist to want peace.' He raised his glass and turned to Miss Bryce. 'How—'

'What do *you* think, Mr Holbourne?' boomed Mr Bryce. 'I've been discussing Chekhov, the Ballet Russe and Russian peasant art with your lady wife, and I say don't be fooled by set and costumes. Look at the management.'

'I'm sorry, I don't follow?'

'I mean that the country's art is distracting everyone from what the government is doing. Mrs Holbourne thinks their failed attempts to send ships across the top of the globe are to find an easy route to Siberia. Ha! She takes the romantic feminine view, of course.' He drained his glass and held it up for a servant to fill it.

Margaret looked at Maude. Her face was a study of well-bred insouciance, but the twinkle in her eye suggested the dangerous look of a cat pretending indifference while a foolhardy mouse runs into its line of sight.

'Now what *I* think,' said Mr Bryce, 'is that Russia's after Canada. Possibly the territory of Alaska too, but...' He waved nearly seven hundred square miles of land away with his refilled glass, spilling a little. 'Firstly, that's no longer British. Secondly, it comes after they've trawled all round *our* land. Now I may not be a romantic, but I'm not a military man either. What's your view, Superintendent Foxcroft?'

Fox sipped his wine. 'It could be either, I suppose. What makes you think it's not simply an adventurous challenge, as Mrs Holbourne says? They've lost, what, two or three ships in the attempt and hardly kept it a secret.'

'Risking life and limb is romantic,' said Mrs Philbrook. 'I don't know why, but it is. To both women *and* men, Mr Bryce.' She stared into the distance as a dark-blonde curl came loose and coiled on her cheek. 'The search for Timbuktu! Attempting to climb Mount Everest! Flying the Channel! One's imagination is captured by the bravery of the men – and indeed the women, who receive less press – fighting against the odds to bring honour on their country.' Her expression became serious. 'Aren't we all mourning brave Captain Scott and his men? What courage they displayed till the utter end, and all to the glory of Great Britain if they'd reached the South Pole first.'

There was a collective murmur of agreement, but Mr Bryce grunted and raised his eyebrows. 'I'm a simple man, Mrs Philbrook. If the show costs more to put on than you get back in tickets, I find it foolish, not romantic.'

'Men have been trying to sail the Northwest Passage since time immemorial,' Geoff pointed out. 'It's not necessarily aggression.'

Mr Bryce drained his port. 'Amundsen did it, what, seven years ago? Why do the Russians need to? You can't trust them.'

'I'd agree with you there,' said Mr Tabor. 'Although I think they're more interested in India. If we're not careful, they'll sneak down through Afghanistan and...bang! I wish I were fit enough to fight.'

'Do you think so, Tabor?' said Mr Bryce. 'Well, it's all a bloody mess whichever way you look at it.'

A sharp intake of breath came from Miss Bryce, who then cleared her throat. The weight of her disapproval was enough to fell an ox.

'Sorry, ladies.' Mr Bryce grinned.

Margaret watched Fox. His expression was friendly but she knew he was on the alert: listening, watching, finding mysteries in innocuous conversation. She wished he could rest.

'Perhaps we ladies might retire,' said Maude, rising. 'We'll have some feminine, romantic conversation while listening to sentimental records on the gramophone. Do join us when you feel strong enough to endure it, gentlemen.'

The drawing room was bright with lamps, light sparkling off ornaments, pictures and flowers. Chairs were arranged round the fireplace for conversation and card tables were set out for bridge, while an area of the floor had been cleared for anyone who wanted to dance. The French windows were open onto the garden.

Maude put a recording of 'La fille aux cheveux de lin' on the gramophone and offered more port.

'Do tell me about your work, Dr Foxcroft,' asked Miss Bryce.

'Demeray,' said Margaret.

'I apologise, Dr Foxcroft-Demeray.'

Maude grinned as Margaret held in a sigh. 'No, I kept my name after marriage, so I'm just Demeray. Fox is just Foxcroft – well, sort of. The children are Foxcroft-Demeray to keep my family name alive.'

'How interesting,' said Miss Bryce. 'Our cousin has registered his children under the Irish spelling of our surname: Brisleáin. But that's another story for another time perhaps. Do you enjoy pathology?'

'Yes, I do. It's very interesting and doesn't involve too much bedside manner.'

'Dorcas Free is an admirable institution,' said Mrs Philbrook. 'More women on the staff than usual, without detriment to anyone. That'll prove something.'

'It will prove more when the adult patients are mixed, too,' said Margaret. 'But that's not till next year. Small steps.'

'Indeed. My late husband invested when it was first mooted, you know, so I have an interest in the place. He's been gone five years, but hopefully his investment made a difference.'

'That was good of him, Mrs Philbrook,' said Margaret. 'I'm sorry he was unable to see it come to fruition.'

'Sabina, please,' said Mrs Philbrook. 'And I'm sure he has his reward. Is pathology all you do?'

'I work four days a week, including teaching and writing up research at home, as well as giving talks. And then, of course, there are the children. Perhaps that's in the wrong order...'

'Twins, I hear, and one of each.' Mrs Philbrook twinkled. 'Saves time, I suppose. But double the trouble?'

'Twins are small, of course,' said Miss Bryce, staring into her port.

'I didn't notice,' said Margaret, with a grimace.

'What sort of talks do you do?' asked Mrs Philbrook.

'I speak to women's social groups about good health practice, and to residents' associations about how to secure improvements to the conditions there.'

'And when you're not doing all that, I believe you take part in suffragette rallies. Excellent.'

'Yes, I do.'

Miss Bryce sniffed. 'I have to confess that current suffragette activity worries me. Quite unladylike.'

'Don't you understand the aim?' said Mrs Philbrook. 'Even Mr Tabor's sister, who's shy and very ladylike, is interested.'

'She even goes to your group, Mrs Philbrook,' said Maude.

'Only the once, as far as I'm aware,' said Mrs Philbrook, with a smile. 'And I don't run the group. I simply attend.'

'Of course I understand the aim,' said Miss Bryce. 'But it seems to have become so, well, anarchic.'

'The government has repeatedly made promises which it's then reneged upon,' said Mrs Philbrook. 'They must be made to listen. Don't you want your own voice?'

'Yes,' said Miss Bryce. 'But as an Irishwoman, reports of using bombs to make a point make me disinclined to be tarred with the same brush as arsonists and rebels.'

'It's quite a different brush,' said Maude. Only a close friend would have realised there was irritation beneath her smile.

'If the government does not want to be met with force, Miss Bryce,' said Mrs Philbrook, 'they should keep their promises. We will lay down our arms immediately. But let's change the subject somewhat. I do so love the theatre, and perhaps a suffrage play might help you and others understand our passion in a gentler way. Would your brother consider putting on *Votes For Women* and *How the Vote Was Won,* for example?'

'Mr Holbourne has mooted that already,' said Miss Bryce, her expression still doubtful. 'I'm concerned that our theatregoers would associate Theatre Valerina with negative public opinions. What other plays do you enjoy, Mrs Philbrook? We've done quite the run of Shaw recently.'

'Oh, how wonderful!'

Miss Bryce's face cleared. 'Which is your favourite? I do love *Major Barbara*.'

As the conversation turned, Margaret excused herself and stepped into the garden.

Maude joined her, lit a cigarette and drew on it. 'Are you going to lure Fox into the garden later? You'll scare the wildlife.'

'Just getting some fresh air,' said Margaret, wafting Maude's smoke away. 'It was a lovely dinner. Thank you for not mentioning to Mr Bryce that I have connections with a moving-picture company.'

'"My Nemesis, dear Mrs Holbourne",' said Maude in a deep growl, and giggled. 'I shan't throw you under that particular omnibus, I promise. Come back inside, Demeray. It's far too chilly, and the air is full of smoke.'

'Yours?' Margaret frowned. Was Maude trying to tell her something?

But Maude simply waved a hand at the surrounding houses. Their chimneys were just visible, black against the night sky, and it was possible to make out smoke drifting into the clouds that half-obscured the moon. Then she frowned, put the cigarette in the hand holding the glass and pressed her free fist into her stomach.

'If the pain is so bad...'

Maude released the pressure. 'It'll pass. I ate too much.'

'You hardly ate a thing.'

'You're neither my mother nor my doctor, thank God, so it's not your concern.' Maude took a gulp of port. 'Did you tell Fox Geoff was pestering you that night?'

'I had to, since Freda might have mentioned it. I said he came looking for you because you'd forgotten to tell him you'd be at the University Club.'

Maude shivered a little. 'That's all you said?'

'What else is there to say, Maude?'

'Nothing.' Maude tucked her arm into Margaret's. 'Nothing whatsoever.'

Six

It was drizzling on Tuesday morning and Margaret decided to take the tube from Bayswater instead of walking or cycling. She still had to remind herself to head north instead of east.

The last person she expected to see at ten to eight, when she arrived at Edgware Road underground station, was Maude.

Maude seemed equally startled to see Margaret. 'Hallo Demeray, you're rather early.'

'I didn't think you knew this time of day existed.'

Maude patted her capacious handbag with a damp copy of the *Suffragette*. 'Things to prepare for the next rally.'

'You should have arranged it by post or telephone.'

'Needs must,' said Maude, checking her watch. 'I'm only going to Paddington, but Geoff has the car. Besides, I could leave some leaflets in the carriage. Why are *you* so early?'

'Just to warn you, the carriages will smell of damp dog, and I'm only half an hour earlier than normal. I'm buying cakes for the pathology wing.'

Maude brightened. 'Are all those promises of career advancement coming to fruition at last? Will you be in charge of pathology?'

'No, Dr Gesner's still chief.'

'You're older and more experienced.'

'I'm only older by four years and I don't work every day. It's perfectly reasonable for him to be senior to me.'

'So why buy cakes?'

'To celebrate being there for exactly six months.'

'You'd better start looking celebratory, then,' said Maude. 'At the moment you look as if you're going to a funeral. Cheerio.' She gave Margaret a quick kiss on the cheek and slipped into the rush of people entering the station.

Margaret had just laid the cakes on her desk when Dr Gesner came in and told her that all available doctors were needed urgently in the boardroom.

She flung her coat and hat onto a chair and rushed along with him. 'What's happening?'

'I wish it were to celebrate that you have not fled back to St Julia's, but I fear not.' The English humour sounded odd in his soft German accent, but his expression was deadpan. 'It's six months today, isn't it?'

'Yes. I didn't think anyone would remember.'

She had to half-run to keep up with his long-legged march through the corridors. 'Have the ambulance people delivered a dissection body to the wrong hospital again?

'I doubt Dr Innes would call a meeting for that,' said Dr Gesner. 'Irritating as it is.'

The boardroom was full of standing, silent doctors. Including Margaret and Dr Naylor, there were four female doctors to twelve male. Dr Naylor nodded a welcome, but there was no accompanying smile.

'I'll come straight to the point,' said Dr Innes, the senior physician. 'There's been an explosion at the post office in Carmelo Street. For any who don't realise, that's between here and Paddington Station.' He scanned the room. 'Has everyone arrived who might travel that way?'

Gasps, mutters, craning to look round the room.

'I did,' said Dr Gesner. 'It seemed normal at seven thirty.'

'I normally come that way, too,' said one of the junior doctors, 'but I was running late today and took the tube. What time did it happen? I'd normally pass at quarter to eight.' His face was pale, his eyes wide.

Everyone turned to the clock. It was nearly half past eight.

'About fifteen minutes ago,' said Dr Innes. 'For once, your tardiness has been a blessing.' He gave the doctor a reassuring smile. 'Take a seat if you need to.'

The junior doctor shook his head, but gripped the back of the chair in front of him.

'I often cycle along Carmelo Street,' said Margaret. 'But I also took the tube today.'

'So everyone's here who should be here.' Dr Innes scanned the room. 'Good.'

'I assume people have been injured,' said another doctor. 'Was it a gas leak?'

'The cause is unconfirmed,' said Dr Innes. 'No reported deaths, though there are several casualties, including three very serious ones. Outside, a railway porter on the way to Paddington. Inside, a postman who was emptying the box and a female clerk who was nearby. The postman and passer-by have been taken to St Mary's. Regrettably, the former is likely to lose a leg, and both have severe facial wounds. The clerk is being brought here. Other female casualties will also arrive, but Miss Lewin needs immediate attention. Her lower left arm was trapped by rubble and her hand badly damaged. She has been rendered deaf, although this will hopefully be temporary. As you can imagine, she's highly distressed and not entirely rational. This is a surgical job, therefore either Mr Baggott or Mr Dupré must put aside scheduled surgery to assist, but the report sent through said that she is terrified of being operated on by a man. Therefore—'

'How absurd!' exclaimed Dr Southern, a blond man in his late twenties. 'There are very few qualified female surgeons in the country and none here. Just sedate her and have done with it.'

Dr Innes frowned. 'Miss Lewin will fare better if she cooperates, Dr Southern. I hope you show more consideration to the patients on your ward.'

'If they're that ridiculous,' said Dr Southern, 'I get Dr Howe to deal with them.'

Dr Howe, a tall woman in her forties, rolled her eyes. 'Often, they fear a surgeon seeing them naked, although more recently women are reluctant because they've heard about the forcible feeding of suffragettes by prison doctors.'

Dr Innes nodded. 'That's Miss Lewin's concern. We must make her understand that I forbid any doctor here from practising forcible feeding. While I know any one of you ladies could encourage her, I shall ask Dr Demeray to assist, due to her experience.'

'Of course,' said Margaret. She wasn't sure if she was more alarmed than honoured, and for a moment feared the other women would resent her, but even ambitious young Dr Callendar's face registered nothing but relief.

'Due to your role, Dr Demeray,' Dr Innes continued, 'you have the best direct surgical expertise of the women here.'

'Dr Demeray takes bodies apart,' countered Mr Dupré. 'She doesn't put them back together.'

'She has to know where things belong in the first place,' said Dr Innes.

'Ridiculous,' said Mr Dupré.

Mr Baggott inclined his head. 'I shall undertake the operation. I am glad to accept Dr Demeray as observer, and as assistant if I need one.'

'I'll be glad to do so.'

'Have you any idea what to expect?'

Margaret nodded. 'Among other things, I assisted at the train crash at St Johns in 1898, and when a gas leak ignited in a Farringdon house in 1901. I helped treat the living, including some of the emergency surgery. I helped make the dead as presentable as possible for their loved ones. You?'

'Among other things, a colliery collapse in Cheshire, 1889. Aldersgate bombing, 1897.'

Across the table, they exchanged grim smiles.

'Very well,' said Dr Innes, consulting his pocket watch. 'Let's get to work.'

Miss Lewin's bandaged left arm and the stretcher on which she lay were the only clean things visible. Her clothes and hair were dust-saturated. Her face and ears had been hurriedly wiped, leaving smears. Tears had made streams through the swirls of dirt, then dried. Her low moaning was punctuated by sobbing pleas for someone to stop the ringing in her ears. According to the notes, she was in her mid-twenties, engaged to be married, an exemplary employee, calm and cheerful. At the moment, she looked like an ancient, grey-haired madwoman.

Margaret lifted a slate which the nurses used to communicate with literate deaf patients. On one side, she'd written: *I'm Dr Margaret Demeray. You need surgery on your hand. Don't be afraid. I shall stay with you.*

'Are you a surgeon?'

Margaret shook her head. She'd anticipated the question and turned the slate over. *This is Mr Baggott. He is highly skilled and will do everything to save your hand.*

Miss Lewin's gaze flicked to the surgeon, the theatre nurses, the anaesthetist, her arm, then back to Margaret. 'M-might I l-lose it?'

'Hopefully not, if we're quick.' Dr Baggott enunciated slowly.

Miss Lewin frowned and looked back at Margaret. 'What's he saying?'

Margaret wiped out her messages and scrawled as neatly as she could: *He hopes not if we operate now. Will you consent? I shall stay with you.* She reached for the other woman's right hand and touched it gently, certain of bruises under the dust.

Even if Miss Lewin consented, the blood flow to her hand might have been blocked while her arm was trapped, and blood poisoning might still kill her. But there was no way of being certain if Mr Baggott couldn't operate. They could assert that she had been rendered temporarily mentally unfit and force the issue. But she had a much better chance if she consented.

Miss Lewin closed her eyes briefly, then nodded.

In the operating theatre, Mr Baggott worked in near silence as Margaret stood beside the anaesthetist. Miss Lewin lay under a sheet with only her face and left arm exposed. Her hand was swollen. Most of its bones and three of her fingers had been broken. A narrow dent indicated where her engagement ring had been.

'There's no sign that blood flow stopped,' said Mr Baggott, with relief. 'I won't have to sever the hand, but it may never be much use.' He looked at Margaret. 'If all I could give you was a hand that looked odd and would never work properly again, would you prefer that over a false hand?'

Margaret considered. 'I think so. You?'

'Probably.'

'Do you think you can save any function?'

Mr Baggott indicated with his head that she should come closer and look. 'I will remove as many of these bone fragments as I can: there's too much risk of damaging the tendons further by prodding about for the smallest ones. Over time, they will dissolve naturally. I will straighten the other bones so they can heal themselves, and mend these tendons. Tell me, what would you say the risks are?'

Margaret looked at the inner parts of Miss Lewin's shattered hand and then at her own, flexing and straightening her fingers, visualising the tendons, muscles and bones working together to do what she needed. 'If her hand doesn't return to normal but is set to heal completely straight, she will be very limited in her work and daily life. It would be little different to a false hand. But if her hand heals slightly flexed and can't quite straighten, she would probably be able to work at the post office or at home, pick things up, and use utensils.'

'Exactly what I was thinking,' said Mr Baggott. 'Will you explain that to her afterwards? Thank you. Now step back, please. Nurse, will you swab?'

He continued, only beckoning Margaret forward once more when he worked out his approach to a ligament.

Miss Lewin was still deaf when she came round, but she seemed to accept Margaret's assurances and slipped into a natural sleep.

Margaret returned to the pathology wing and found Dr Gesner in her office. 'I was going to leave you a message – I am about to return to C ward,' he said. 'Mr Baggott telephoned to say he's impressed by your knowledge and presence of mind. I'm not sure why either should surprise him: I have told him often enough. Did you ever think of going into surgery yourself?'

Margaret shook her head. 'I heard some lectures by Dr Aldrich-Blake when I was training and have met her a few times since. She is inspirational, but I very much enjoy what I do.'

'It's a wise person that sticks to what they love,' said Dr Gesner. 'Although sometimes it takes time to learn to love the place where they do it.' Did he mean her, or himself?

'What's the latest situation? Have many more come from Carmelo Street?'

'Two children, not too badly hurt,' said Dr Gesner. 'Five women, two pregnant. So far all is well with one of those, but unfortunately the other has since given birth. The child is around six weeks early. Everything is being done that can be done, but...'

Margaret nodded. Her twins had been born six weeks early. It had been touch and go whether either would survive, and that had been under much less stressful circumstances.

'Cuts, bruises, concussions, in the main,' Dr Gesner continued. 'No operations are necessary. But that doesn't account for the effects of shock. Dr Naylor has asked if you can assist on D ward: one of the casualties is elderly and has a weak heart. You have knowledge which Dr Naylor could use.'

On D ward, there was little Margaret could do. The old lady faltered between life and death, her lips blue, her breathing shallow, occasionally catching, then growing quieter. Someone had found her husband and daughter, but hospital protocol meant they had to remain in the corridor while the old lady passed away under the gaze of strangers: a nurse and Margaret holding her hands while the chaplain recited prayers.

Afterwards, Margaret spoke with the bereaved then visited Miss Lewin. She struggled to explain on the slate that Mr Baggott had saved her hand, but that it might never work as it had before.

'What if Henry thinks I'm a cripple and won't marry me?' Miss Lewin whispered. 'What if the post office says I'm no good any more?' Now that her face was clean, the cuts and bruises on her face stood out. Her exhausted tears trickled into the hair that was still dusty under a hospital cap. 'What a wicked thing to do.'

'Wicked?' said Margaret, forgetting she needed to write on the slate.

But Miss Lewin understood. 'It was a bomb.'

Not gas? Margaret scrawled.

'I couldn't smell gas, just something like almonds. Alf said, "That parcel's a bit greasy. Not sure I fancy touching that," and I turned to look. There was a flash and a bang and next thing I know... Is Alf all right?'

Margaret scribbled on the slate. *He's at St Mary's. He's alive.*

Miss Lewin nodded, the tears still trickling. 'What a wicked thing to do.'

Margaret returned to her office once more. It was lunchtime but she had no appetite. An orderly brought her a pot of tea and a special edition of the local newspaper.

Bomb attack at Paddington Post Office. Who is to blame?

The front wall of the post office on Carmelo Street in Paddington was destroyed this morning when what appears to have been a parcel filled with explosives detonated at a quarter past eight. Twenty casualties have been reported, one of whom is in a grave condition in St Mary's Hospital. It is not yet clear whether the post office was the intended target, nor has anyone so far claimed responsibility. However, given the outrage at Sir George Riddell's house in Walton-on-the-Hill just three days ago, and last week's arson attack in Tyburnia, both claimed by the WSPU, is it unreasonable to assume that this is another despicable act by one of Mrs Pankhurst's followers in the name of female suffrage?

Margaret put the paper down with trembling hands. Maude would smash windows, she'd assault a policeman, she'd do almost anything for the cause. Maybe she'd set fire to a pagoda, but surely she wouldn't plant a bomb?

But Maude never travelled by tube. If she needed to get to Paddington, she'd take a cab.

The cakes Margaret had brought in earlier that day lay forgotten, growing staler and more irrelevant by the second.

Seven

'There's no certainty that it's suffragette activity,' said Fox, refilling Margaret's cup from a thermos flask.

They were huddled in a shelter within the grassy park at the centre of Dorset Square. The hospital was only a few hundred yards away but it felt a million miles, in terms of wealth. The square's residents preferred not to imagine that anyone poor lived in or near Marylebone, let alone that they might become ill.

'Who else?' said Margaret. The sandwich Fox had brought her remained uneaten. 'The only outrages the papers report these days are by suffragettes.'

'That doesn't mean that only suffragettes are vandals, just that their exploits sell newspapers.'

'A bomb in a post office on a working day isn't vandalism: it's attempted murder. In fact, maybe it's murder, now that poor old lady has died.'

Fox reached for her hand. 'Amateur bomb-makers often make mistakes. It's possible the device wasn't supposed to explode until it reached its destination, which might have been an empty building, like the Riddell house. The intent might have been pure vandalism.'

'What you mean is that Maude could have done it. She studied chemistry at Oxford. She's not stupid.'

'A good many people could have done it,' said Fox. 'Why would I suggest Maude? My instinct tells me she wouldn't. What does yours say?'

'The same.'

'Besides, would she put her best friend at risk for the cause?'

'How do you mean?'

'She knows which way you cycle, doesn't she?'

'I don't often go that way.'

'Well, whoever was responsible, and whichever route you normally take, I'm glad you took the tube today.' Fox's hand tightened on hers, then he pulled her into a one-armed hug. He had arrived at the hospital with Bert, ostensibly on behalf of Special Branch, and taken her out for fresh air while he took her statement.

'I need to go back to work. There may be more casualties,' said Margaret, without moving.

'There won't be.' Fox squeezed her gently. 'Everyone injured is at a hospital. The front of the building is being stabilised. All valuables – stamps, postal orders, cash and so on – have been taken to another post office. All the mail, damaged and undamaged, has been taken in the hope of finding evidence, and with a view to delivering anything that can be delivered afterwards.'

He scanned the park. The only other people enduring the weather were a young couple sitting close on a bench, enjoying the excuse to cuddle up behind an enormous umbrella, and two elderly ladies with walking sticks, doddering along with an ancient, bow-legged terrier. The dog peered down at the sodden gravel, only lifting his disconsolate head to shake off the rain and eye the walking sticks, possibly because he wanted one of his own for his arthritic hobble.

Margaret stole a glance at Fox. How far could you trust your instinct about strangers? How would Miss Lewin, assuming she recovered sufficiently, feel when she returned to work, wondering which of the people approaching the counter or dropping things in the postbox might want to harm her? Did Fox assess everyone he met as innocent or guilty? It must be exhausting.

He looked down at her. 'I'm not letting you go back until you've eaten at least half that sandwich.'

'How will you make me?'

'I'll ju-jitsu you.'

Margaret had neither the energy nor the humour for a witty retort. She took a reluctant bite of the sandwich and realised she was hungry after all. 'It's no good being glad I took the tube. Who's to say the underground won't be targeted again? Mr Baggott helped at Aldersgate in '97. Sixty people were injured; one died, if you recall. That was Russian anarchists, wasn't it? Could this be?'

'Maybe. Maybe something else. Smith has had some intelligence.'

'Smith? I thought you thought he was either an idiot or a double agent.'

'Either way, we have to follow it up. It's to do with an old friend.'

Margaret heard the tone of his voice change. 'Whose friend?'

'He was very fond of you, as I recall. A Mr Abney. Remember him?'

'How could I forget?' Margaret's mind stopped revisiting the injuries she'd witnessed that morning and went back three years to when she'd first met Fox. Then, Mr Abney had been a visitor to the hospital. He'd seemed little more than a nuisance - a leering, lascivious, patronising man who stared at her bust and implied that she should be honoured to be allowed to speak alongside men at a symposium. Maybe he was all those things, but he also possessed a mind of greed and evil which had led to the death of numerous men and could have led to even more.

But cunning as he was greedy, Mr Abney had escaped justice. 'He should have been hanged.'

'Yes,' said Fox. 'And I promised that one day I'd make him pay for what he did. Maybe that time has come.'

'You mean he's involved in a similar enterprise?'

'If there's money to be made, I wouldn't be surprised,' said Fox. 'He slinked off to Flanders, apparently washing his hands of all dirty work – but appearances can be deceptive. We've had him under surveillance ever since. I'm determined we'll find the evidence to convict him.'

It had disgusted Margaret when Abney managed to elude arrest. She had vaguely hoped that he'd mended his ways, unlikely as that seemed, as it was the only way she could stomach the reality. Clearly she'd been wrong. 'So there might be some evidence?'

'Smith thinks he's buying and selling information. Not with any loyalty – simply to make money. We're not clear how things are crossing borders.'

'That's not new, and it's cleaner than the last thing he did.'

'Until it leads to war,' said Fox. 'The papers I'm after are exactly what he wants, which means he could be instructing someone. He, or whoever he's instructing, could be putting the frighteners on whoever has them. If there's anything left of the address on the parcel, it might help.'

'How could there be?'

'You'd be surprised.'

'Disgusting as he is, that has nothing to do with today's bomb,' said Margaret. 'I've lost count of how many suffragette arson attacks and potential bomb attacks there have been this month. Why should this be different?'

Fox sighed. 'I'd have expected the WSPU to have sent a message to Scotland Yard saying it was them by now. They're usually very honest.'

'Even with so many injured?'

'Even with so many injured. Mrs Pankhurst may shield her perpetrators, but she doesn't pretend they haven't acted. I'm concerned it's something else.'

'Like two years ago?'

Fox shook his head. 'Both the intelligence and the device seem a good deal more amateurish than that. One home-made bomb is hardly an attack on the capital. But something's making me tingle and I swear it's not suffrage. I doubt it'll come clear today so I shan't be late home tonight.'

'Even though you're investigating this?'

'I don't investigate suffragette activity, unless there's something else going on,' said Fox 'While I have my views on Mrs Pankhurst's incitement to violence, I think Mrs Pankhurst herself, and the vast majority of her followers, only want the vote. I can't imagine anyone coercing Mrs Pankhurst, Maude or you into treason, under cover of the fight for suffrage. But someone suggestible...'

'Maude isn't suggestible.'

'I don't suspect Maude.'

'Nor do I.'

'Sounds like you do to me. Why?'

Margaret shrugged and swallowed another bite of sandwich, her appetite gone again. 'I'll visit her after work and see if she's heard anything. But that'll make me even later home than I might be anyway. Could you let Nellie know? It's easier for you to send messages.'

'Of course,' said Fox. 'I have to trust someone else to follow up on Abney for the moment. Assisting with the twins' bedtime and disrupting Nellie's routine makes things unravel in my head sometimes.'

'Is there anything I can do to help?'

Fox stared out across the park again, then looked at her, gave her another squeeze and removed his arm. 'You can tell me what's been on your mind for the last couple of days.'

'It's really not—'

'Not important? I'd still rather know.'

'It's supposition, not fact. And none of my business, anyway.'

'I'd still listen, but if you won't say, perhaps see if Miss Lewin can recall anything useful. The size of the parcel, the writing on it, anything at all. But if she's deaf and talking loudly, ask her to write it down.'

'Is the postman able to recall anything?'

'I've no idea,' said Fox, rising and offering Margaret his arm. 'He's lost the use of a leg and an eye and is heavily sedated. Who knows if his mind will have blotted it all out when he comes round. And the passer-by isn't in much better condition. Though of course...'

'Of course what?'

'He might have been the one who'd posted the parcel.'

Margaret didn't need to make arrangements with Maude. When she returned to the pathology wing, a telegram from Maude had arrived, asking her to visit after work because she wanted to request a favour.

A little before six, Margaret was ushered into Maude's personal sitting room and office, wondering what on earth she would say.

It was a well-designed room, the two halves – one businesslike and efficient, the other softer and more comfortable – blending in the muted greys and greens on the leather of the desk, the upright chairs and the curtains at either side of the long windows looking onto the garden.

It didn't have the femininity of Phoebe's drawing room in another grand Marylebone home, but there was no doubt that it was a woman's domain, from the prints to the books to the cushions that Fox and Geoff would have thought pointless in the extreme. The only thing missing, in Margaret's view, was a cat or two, and the only thing she wished were absent was the faint odour of Maude's cigarettes.

Maude greeted her with a kiss, then contemplated her. 'You look worn out, Demeray. Have the corpses been trying today?'

'The corpses have had to wait,' said Margaret. 'Some of the casualties from the explosion in Carmelo Street came to Dorcas Free, including a clerk who was badly injured and an old lady who died. It was all hands on deck and it's been an awful day.'

'Oh goodness!' Maude's reaction seemed natural, her face paling, her expression grim. There was no evidence of guilt, or any sign that she was about to justify what had happened. 'I heard one woman was badly injured but I didn't realise she'd been taken to Dorcas Free. How is she?'

'Deafened, for the moment at least, and a badly damaged hand. Worried she might lose both fiancé and job. An old lady's heart gave way and I couldn't stop her dying. The post-mortem couldn't prove the blast had brought on the attack, but it's hard to believe otherwise.'

'I prescribe brandy,' said Maude. 'You look quite drained. Sit down and let me pour you some.' She went to a side table and quarter-filled a small glass. 'You usually cycle to work via Carmelo Street, don't you? Thank God for the rain this morning.'

'It feels selfish to be glad I'm safe when other people weren't.'

'I can understand that.'

'I hope you weren't anywhere near,' said Margaret. 'You said you were going to Paddington.'

Maude looked startled. 'Me? I meant Paddington Station, not the area. The Reading train, you know. I didn't even hear the explosion.' She tapped ash from her cigarette. 'I assume you know it was a bomb. Have you heard if anyone's taken responsibility yet?' She was pale and thoughtful, inhaling deeply. A journalist's curiosity sparked from her eyes, but the question seemed genuine enough.

'No.' Margaret took a breath, watching her. 'I'll be honest: I wonder if it was something to do with suffrage.'

'Well, I don't know anything about it, if that's what you're hinting at,' Maude snapped. 'Why should I? I've made my views plain enough at our meetings. I am unapologetic about vandalism, and I will fight any man who tries to beat me or assault me till my fists bleed. But I wouldn't endanger life unless it was to protect my own or that of someone I loved. And even then, I wouldn't find it easy.'

'One wouldn't.' Margaret glanced away, then back. 'I wondered if you thought we'd be blamed for it somehow.'

'I don't see why,' said Maude. 'A WSPU member would have admitted it.'

'As they did the burning down of the Tyburnia pagoda.'

'Yes.' Maude stared at her cigarette for some time. 'That evening – the evening when I was at the University Club and Geoff came looking for me. Where did he say he was before he went home and found I wasn't there?'

Margaret considered. 'I can't recall if he said. I had the impression he was at his club.'

'I thought he might have been at the Bryces'.'

'Maybe he went to both,' said Margaret. 'It's possible to visit more than one place in an evening.'

Maude looked up. 'When was the last time you smashed a window or a streetlamp in the name of the cause, Margaret?'

Margaret felt herself tense. 'December 1910? January 1911? I'm not sure, exactly.'

'Don't you believe in it any more?'

'With all my heart,' said Margaret. 'But I don't seem to have had time for window smashing. And now things have moved on and it's just ... violence.' She closed her eyes, recalling her work at the aftermath of the St John's train crash, aged twenty-four: the broken limbs, the blood, the terror. She wondered what Maude would do if she looked into the eyes of someone she might hurt – not the silly owner of a sillier shed, but someone desperate for a letter which would never come because it was burnt to cinders in a post-box, or someone who might be engulfed in a house fire... Was it like looking into the eyes of someone at whom you were pointing a loaded gun? Could you ever justify it? 'It's the violence. I'm a doctor.'

'If the government did as they promised, it would all stop.'

'I know.'

'I have other things I want to do in life,' said Maude. 'But I want to know that Becca and Edie will be equal in law with their brothers by the time they're grown up. Don't you?'

'Very much so.'

Maude drew a breath and pressed her stomach. 'My doctor prescribed laudanum for the pain. I took some once, but I'm not sure whether to continue. I've met women who've taken it and they're very strange... I never know quite what to believe when they tell me things.'

'Oh, Maude,' said Margaret, 'please don't. It's addictive, and after a while, it stops working. I know it's easy for me to say, but please don't. I'm worried about you.'

'Stop fussing, Demeray. Some fresh air will do me good. I'm off to Oxford after a story for *Athene's Gazette* this evening.'

'Is that what the favour's about, or was it the laudanum?'

'Neither,' said Maude. 'It's about Becca. She's at an impressionable age.' Maude swallowed then continued, her voice steadier. 'If I weren't here to mother her, would you do it? Phoebe's a little too schoolmistressy. My sister's too busy. My parents and Geoff's...' she shuddered.

'Do you mean while you're in Oxford?'

'Hardly: I'll be back on Friday. This would be quite a different situation.'

'Why wouldn't you be here, Maude?' Pushing aside the thought of managing Maude's unruly children as well as her own, Margaret's mind whirred with possibilities.

'Would you do it?'

'Of course I would. But please tell me it won't be necessary.'

'I can't promise anything, Demeray.' Maude squeezed Margaret's arm and smiled a more natural smile. 'Hopefully it won't come to that. But Margaret: don't tell anyone until you have to. Not even Phoebe. Not even Geoff.'

Eight

At nine thirty the following morning, Margaret went to visit Miss Lewin. She was still pale, sleepy from medication and the after-effects of anaesthetic. With her brown hair cut to shoulder length for ease of washing, she looked younger than twenty-three. She was still unable to hear and gave Margaret a wan smile, then read the slate, on which Margaret had written: *An expert says that all being well, your hearing will be normal within six weeks.*

Miss Lewin smiled. 'Everything hurts,' she said, her voice hoarse but no longer loud. 'Even the bits that shouldn't.'

You're young, wrote Margaret. *Just follow the doctor's orders.*

'I'm used to following rules. Postmaster General, you know. How's Alf?'

Getting better every day.

'Thank the Lord.'

Margaret nodded. Then she wrote: *If it isn't distressing, can you recall what was written on the parcel? Don't worry if you can't.*

Miss Lewin frowned. 'Four? Six? A name that made me think of hogs.'

A butcher?

'No, a name. Can't remember why it made me think of hogs.' Miss Lewin's voice was hoarser and her eyelids were drooping.

Margaret mouthed 'Thank you'.

She returned to the mortuary wing, hoping to find something easy to deal with. Instead she found her star pupil, Polly Buckram, face wet with tears, fretting about whether an 'utterly failed' essay meant she should give up medicine and study art instead. She'd missed five marks.

It was hard not to compare her with one of Margaret's previous assistants, Algie. He hadn't even flinched on the day Margaret deducted twenty marks. He'd grinned like a guilty puppy and promised to do better next time, while clearly planning to drown his sorrows with his classmates and forget the whole incident. Polly, though, wanted to prove herself every bit as intelligent, earnest and serious as any male student, while being infinitely more empathetic and therefore infinitely better. Every now and then, her fear of failure pushed her to tears.

Worried about Maude, and frustrated that she couldn't help Fox identify the parcel's recipient, Margaret snapped, 'Please restrain the melodrama, Miss Buckram. It's only five marks.'

Polly drew in a wet-sounding breath and dabbed her eyes. 'It's not easy being a female student.'

It was an effort for Margaret to feel pity: she and Polly were so dissimilar. 'You should have been one in the nineties, or worse still, in the eighties like Dr Naylor. *Then* you'd have something to complain about.'

'No one told you to do art instead, Dr Demeray.'

Margaret felt her hands clench. 'Didn't they? I had to argue with the relation who paid the fees in order to go to Oxford at all, let alone read science. I had to argue even harder when I left after a year to study medicine. Half my cousins mocked me, and one has snubbed me ever since.'

'Didn't it make you want to give up?'

Margaret shook her head. 'It made me angry. My older sister fought for her independence without flinching and ensured my education meant I could go to university. If she didn't flinch, *I* wouldn't flinch, and I wouldn't let her efforts go to waste.'

'Nothing I achieve is good enough for the male students. Even if I beat them.'

'It's enough for me.' Margaret sighed. 'Stop trying to compete with them: compete with yourself. And they're not *all* like that. Buck up, Polly. Crying won't change anything. You are an excellent student – I wouldn't have you as my assistant otherwise – but you need to develop a thicker skin.'

Polly scrubbed her eyes with her handkerchief. 'Could I do something extra? Just me? A study, I mean.'

'Perhaps.' Margaret, discouraged from crying since childhood, considered the streaked face in front of her with mild disgust. She sifted her correspondence for inspiration. It consisted largely of brochures, bills and requests for a doctor's testimonial. She picked up one of the latter. The company sold patent medicine containing opiates, and she thought of Maude.

'Here's something,' she said. 'Laudanum: its addictive quality, that is. How long it takes to become addicted, and if addicted, what happens if you stop. How long it takes to come out of your system, and so on. To make myself clear, I am categorically *not* asking you to do experiments, I'm asking you to research. Do you understand?'

A rare look of sneaky rebellion crossed Polly's face. 'Of course, doctor.'

'I mean it, Miss Buckram. If you experiment – and I *will* find out – I'll fail you.'

'Fail me?' Polly was aghast. 'Oh I promise not to! Honestly, I promise!'

There was a knock on the door and the clerk, Miss Upton, put her head round it. 'The police have brought in a body, doctor. Dr Gesner would like you and Miss Buckram to join him in the laboratory.'

Margaret gasped. 'Is it from the explosion? Has someone only just been found?'

'No,' said Miss Upton. 'It's an alleged murder victim who was found last night. The police kept it till this morning.'

Inside the laboratory, a police sergeant stood next to Dr Gesner as they looked down on a woman's body, a sheet pulled up to her armpits. Her face, framed in auburn curls, was mottled, and there was a gunshot wound above the left breast.

'Ah, good morning, Dr Demeray, Miss Buckram,' said Dr Gesner. 'Here is a peculiar case.'

'Murder by gunshot?' said Margaret.

'Or is it?' said the sergeant. 'My inspector's not convinced and they've called in the Yard, and their Inspector Silvermann's not convinced either.'

'Silvermann?' said Margaret. 'I met a Silvermann from N division last year.'

'That's him,' said the sergeant. 'Dunno what he did or didn't do to get in the Yard, but there he is. Anyway... This is Miss Lois Halpin, aged thirty-six, former actress, living on a tiny income in her own little house in Paddington. It's a bit like the Stokes case, and then it's different.'

Dr Gesner looked sideways at Margaret, then frowned at the sergeant. 'How?'

'Similarities: household gas, bullet wound doesn't appear self-inflicted, women's-suffrage supporter, maybe a disturbed burglary.' The sergeant ticked off the points on his fingers. 'Differences: no bomb stuff, two witnesses rather than none, and the thing that's strangest of all – hardly any blood. Mr Stokes, if you recall, was soaked in it. Can you find out what's what?'

'We can gather evidence on what appears to have killed her,' said Dr Gesner. 'It will be for an inquest to decide what the evidence means. Miss Buckram, you have a notebook for your observations? Good. If you wish to ask a question, please do. Now, let's remove the sheet. Sergeant, will you stay?'

'Yes, doctor. My breakfast's nicely settled and the inspector wants me to take notes.'

'No bomb-making equipment in the house?' asked Margaret, as she prepared her instruments.

'Not so far,' said the sergeant. 'But there was an empty laudanum bottle. I know that's not unusual, but the inspector wonders if it's relevant.'

'Laudanum,' breathed Polly. 'It's a sign.'

'A sign of what?' said Dr Gesner.

'I'll explain afterwards,' said Margaret, trying not to roll her eyes. 'Let's see what killed this poor woman.'

At home that evening Margaret took a telephone call from Phoebe, who told her they'd both been summoned to afternoon tea with Mrs Tabor on Wednesday afternoon at four thirty.

'But I'll be working.'

'So shall I,' said Phoebe, her voice irritated. 'But it's her At Home afternoon for acquaintances and she particularly wants to meet you, since you assisted her daughter when she sprained her ankle.'

'Oh my.'

'It doesn't do to refuse Mrs Tabor, she'd take it out on Rhoda if one of Rhoda's friends declined. Fortunately, as headmistress and owner of a school, I can do as I please. I appreciate it might be harder for you, but I have no idea how to explain that to a woman who believes it undignified for ladies to work at all, let alone in medicine. Can you manage? I'd rather not endure it alone.'

'Hasn't Maude been invited?'

'Thankfully not. They would agree on nothing.'

'That would be entertaining.'

'Not for Miss Tabor afterwards, I fear,' said Phoebe. 'My grandmother gave rather dark hints about discipline in that family.'

'Miss Tabor is nearly fifty.'

'In my experience, people who were regularly locked in cupboards as children never quite come out. You must have noticed how on edge the woman is.'

'She's a shocking fibber.'

'Of course she is,' said Phoebe. 'Any good teacher will tell you that a child who's never allowed to do anything will learn how to lie convincingly very early. The skill is to work out the truth within the lie. There's always something, as that's how they justify the lying. Will you come?'

'I'll do my very best.'

After the call, Margaret sat in the nursery with the children, reading to them from a picture book, while Nellie darned and mended in the corner.

'Daddy read?' said Alec.

'Daddy's not home yet.'

'Naughty Bear away?'

'No, Naughty Bear's on the mantlepiece with Clever Bear and Mr Tod. Daddy's just late at work.'

'Mumma, Edie sad,' said Edie.

'Don't be sad, darling. Daddy's just busy.'

'Mumma busy. Daddy busy. Busy busy.' Edie pouted and rubbed her eyes.

Margaret hugged her, wondering as ever which was worse: leaving the children while she worked, or being frustrated while she cared for them instead of working. At least work kept her mind off what Fox was doing. 'You and Alec are busy with Nellie, having lots of fun. Mummy's day wasn't fun at all and I don't know about Daddy's. But I'm taking you to the park soon with Auntie Maude.'

'And Sam-Sam?' asked Alec, hopefully.

'Oh gosh,' said Margaret, wondering what Maude's five-year-old son would teach Alec this time. 'I suppose so.'

'Amorrow?' said Edie.

'Not tomorrow. Soon.'

'Wanna Daddy,' said Edie.

'And hey presto! Here he is!' said Fox, appearing in the doorway.

'Oh, sir...' said Nellie, with a cross frown.

'I'm not here to play,' said Fox. 'Daddy is very very tired and needs to sleep, just like you do.' He rubbed his eyes and stretched his mouth in a big yawn. The twins followed suit. 'So let Mummy and Daddy kiss you goodnight, then you must settle down and say your prayers with Nellie.'

The twins squeezed their eyes shut and gabbled, 'Gobbess-mumandadanelli—'

'Wait till we've gone!' said Fox, kissing Edie's head and putting out a hand to pull Margaret to her feet. 'Mamma and I need all the bessings we can get.'

Closing the nursery door, he led Margaret to the sitting room and closed the door. His face was solemn. 'I'm being pulled every which way, Margaret. My manpower is reduced because we need to watch the delegates for the London treaty, and Hare's on my back because I can't provide definitive proof that the letters won't emerge and cause diplomatic chaos. Our man's now admitted that the letters are in someone's safekeeping, and he's asked her to destroy them. He's confident she has: I wish I were. He won't give her name as it'll compromise her.'

'A mistress.'

'Presumably, which makes him even more of a dark horse. He doesn't seem the type to have a mistress. We suspect she's in West

London but that's only from following him. He mentioned Dorcas Free in an unguarded moment when we were asking about her, then got flustered and said it was near where he lived – which isn't true. When we asked whether his friend was a nurse or a doctor he looked blank. When I suggested a patient he looked affronted, as if we were suggesting he'd have a liaison below his status, though he's likely to go to prison and has nothing to be snobbish about. So it's either a misunderstanding, or something else.'

'Have you established that the parcel bomb definitely wasn't a suffragette?'

'There's no *definitely*,' said Fox. 'There were burnt copies of *The Suffragette* at the scene, but they seem to have come out of an envelope. My instinct says it's something to do with our man but I can't prove it. Those kinds of letter bombs almost always go off long before they reach their destination. What if someone was sending it to the mistress to threaten her? It's a shame we don't know the address.'

'I asked Miss Lewin,' said Margaret, 'but she's still very much in shock. All she said was that the name made her think of hogs and there was a number four or six.'

'Hogs?' Fox sighed.

'I'll let you know if she remembers more.'

'Thanks.' He put his arm round her and she could feel his tension. 'Hare's given Smith a good deal of responsibility and I'm not sure it's wise.'

'You've felt that way for two years.'

'I know. Perhaps it's simply prejudice against him for sending me on wild-goose chases before.' Fox rubbed his temples. 'Why do I do this job? I'm working for a government with an internal policy which it can't even apply consistently, whether it's suffrage or Irish independence. I can never decide if it's incompetence or deliberate intent to confuse the electorate. And then there's its foreign policy, which promises loyalty to new allies while doing the diplomatic equivalent of whispering behind a hand about them to potential mutual enemies.'

'It's like being back at school.'

'Only with deadlier consequences,' said Fox. 'Enough about my day. How was yours?'

'Odd,' said Margaret. 'I'll be addressing an inquest into the murder of an actress in a few days.'

'Isn't that Dr Gesner's job?'

'He has to go back to Germany on family matters.'

'That is odd.'

'I didn't mean that: his father-in-law is ill. I meant that the post-mortem was odd. We don't think the woman was murdered, yet the witnesses say she was.'

'Witnesses are as unreliable as letter bombs.'

'Yes, but these two were injured in the alleged attack. It won't be the easiest inquest.'

'Never mind,' said Fox, kissing her. 'It can't be worse than a suffragette rally. At least the coroner won't thump you.'

'Probably not,' said Margaret. 'But Inspector Silvermann might.'

'Dear God, not him again.'

'Apparently so.'

Nine

The witness box in the centre of the coroner's court made Margaret feel as if she'd been hauled up before the Witchfinder General to explain her fondness for dancing and cats. When a shaft of sunlight struck her, she wondered whether it meant divine support or judgment, and if so, how to tell which.

She had given evidence in police courts over the years, and once in a closed hearing at the assizes, but this was the first time she'd addressed the coroner. It was one thing having her evidence picked over by a lawyer; it was something else having it picked over by a fellow medical professional. A barrister might think himself superior to a mere doctor from a hospital for the poor – particularly a woman – but though he might know the law inside out, he only had a layman's grasp of medicine.

Dr Augustus, on the other hand, knew both law and medicine. She had met him once, through Dr Jordan. She knew he objected to female doctors on principle and would give no quarter if she was vague or inaccurate.

The police sergeant, like the coroner, knew what the post-mortem report said. He sat, expressionless, watching for witnesses' reactions. Observers fidgeted on their hard seats, staring at Margaret as she waited for the coroner's questions. She stared back.

She was unsurprised to see Miss Bryce among the spectating public, because the sergeant had droned in his opening statement that Miss Halpin occasionally acted at Theatre Valerina and was well known to the proprietors, who knew of no reason why she should harm herself or be harmed by others. Margaret was, however, surprised to see Mrs Philbrook in the shadows at the back. Perhaps the impression that Miss Halpin had no friends, other than perhaps Miss Bryce, was untrue, though Mrs Philbrook was from quite a different class. It seemed more likely that Mrs Philbrook was curious.

The victim's sister, Mrs Bessemer, dabbed at damp eyes with her right hand, her bandaged left hand resting on a large handbag. Beside her, Mr Bessemer rested his chin on a pair of crutches. They said they had seen Miss Halpin shot.

Various other witnesses from the neighbourhood, who under earlier questioning had proved they'd seen nothing worth knowing, shared sweets and sat back for the entertainment.

The jury wriggled in the pew-like jury box, licking their pencils, ready to make more notes.

A large contingent of journalists sprawled over the press benches, jabbing each other with elbows and knees to gain more room. A few female reporters did too. One of them was Maude. A murder trial wasn't usual fare for *Athene's Gazette*, so Margaret assumed she was there in support of her, and perhaps also to write an article about a female pathologist giving evidence. Despite everything that had happened recently, Maude was a reassuring presence: professional, straight-backed and confident, spreading out her things on the narrow table to cramp the young men on either side. They appeared disinclined to argue. Perhaps they'd spotted the Holloway badge pinned to her jacket and wondered what she'd done to be put in prison, or perhaps they thought her elbows were too sharp to dispute with.

The journalists were about to become even more irritated. The cause of Miss Halpin's death had yet to be determined by the coroner's court, but the press had been describing it as a crime of passion ever since the shooting. The more lurid papers had conveyed the probability that Miss Halpin's suitor, Mr Carter, was to blame, though he was quite legitimately abroad. It made a wonderful story in a dull neighbourhood, so no one would be happy that Margaret wasn't going to confirm their assumptions.

Mr Bessemer had given his evidence. He and his wife had come for a meal. Having a key, they had entered the house around seven p.m. Almost immediately, they heard what sounded like a shot in the kitchen. They rushed in to see Miss Halpin collapsed at the table, bleeding from a chest wound. A man muffled to the eyes, whom Mr Bessemer swore was Mr Carter, stood nearby. On seeing them, the assailant fired a second shot at Mrs Bessemer, striking her hand, a third at Mr Bessemer, striking his leg, then fled.

Mr Bessemer, his wound notwithstanding, pursued him. It was no later than ten past seven. Many of Miss Halpin's neighbours were out or not answering their doors, and Mr Bessemer was hampered by the wound to his shin. It took him a further ten minutes to find a constable and return, by which time Miss Halpin was dead. Mrs Bessemer, giving almost identical evidence in a soft Belfast accent, said all attempts to rouse her sister had been in vain.

Now it was Margaret's turn. She gave a brief description of the receipt of Miss Halpin's body at Dorcas Free and the technical aspects of the subsequent post-mortem.

'Thank you, Dr Demeray,' said Dr August. 'Now, you've heard Mr Bessemer's statement, which was broadly reiterated by his wife. In your view, during the twenty minutes between the first shot and Mr Bessemer returning with a policeman, was the injury sustained by Miss Halpin sufficient to cause her death?'

'No, sir.'

The press muttered and the jurymen cleared their throats in disbelief. Margaret couldn't see Mr and Mrs Bessemer without turning her head, but she heard a squeak like a ferrule slipping on the wooden floor.

'Could you explain your assertion?' said Dr Augustus.

'Under normal circumstances, the injury was unlikely to cause death at all,' said Margaret. 'Certainly not within twenty minutes. The bullet struck Miss Halpin's upper left chest, missing all major organs, and was stopped by the collarbone. It *would* have caused a lot of pain and internal bleeding, but she ought to have survived. The injury itself would only have killed her if she contracted an infection. If she had, she would still have survived for several days.'

'Yet she died.'

'Yes, sir. But before the gun was fired, she'd already been asphyxiated.'

'In layman's terms, please, doctor.'

'She had suffocated from inhaling household gas. Then, after she'd died, she was shot.'

The word 'after?' echoed round the room as spectators and journalists alike wondered if they'd heard right.

'Silence in court!' called the usher.

'The police evidence is that Miss Halpin was sitting at the kitchen table by the stove,' said Dr Augustus when the noise had settled down, 'so it's possible she inhaled the gas deliberately. However, there was no note, as is usually the case. Could it have been suicide?'

'There is no evidence to prove or disprove the possibility.'

'Did you discover any reason why she might have harmed herself? A fatal illness, perhaps, or a shameful pregnancy?'

'No, sir. Apart from one particular, Miss Halpin was fit, healthy and young, but—'

Shuffling interrupted her: an elderly juryman had risen to his feet.

'Have you a question?' said Dr Augustus.

'An observation, your honour ... sir ... doctor... Miss Halpin wasn't young. She was near enough an old maid who, gawd rest her, accepted the advances of the only man willing to marry her. And that man murdered her. He should swing for it.'

'This is an inquest, sir,' said Margaret. 'I'm here to provide medical evidence about the cause of death, not discuss perceptions of youth or someone's guilt or innocence.'

'Pshaw. Where's a proper doctor when you need one?'

'You're looking at two of them,' snapped Margaret.

Dr Augustus harrumphed, then waved at the juryman. 'Please be seated and let me ask the questions. Jot your thoughts down, and at the end of proceedings when I sum up, let's see if they haven't been covered. But please do bear in mind that Mr Carter sailed to Australia in February and left there to come home four weeks ago. Only in the most fantastic fiction could he have returned here in time to commit a murder, then somehow returned to a steam ship which was then still more than a week away, on which he was given the telegram informing him of his fiancée's demise. Now then, Dr Demeray,' Dr Augustus scratched his nose and perused his notes. 'One final thing: you said "Apart from one particular, she was fit and healthy". What was the exception?'

'Miss Halpin's hair and nails show clear evidence of morphia. Her stomach contained a dangerous amount of laudanum. It appears that she had been ingesting with great regularity.'

'It's not illegal,' mused Dr Augustus, making another squiggle in his notebook. 'A great many women take it, despite its addictive tendencies. But the gunshot changes things. Poison, gas and gun. Someone very much wanted her dead.'

It was good to be out in the sunshine. Margaret approved of the verdict – unlawful killing by person or persons unknown – but sensed the journalists' disappointment as they filed past. Unable to report murder or name a suspect, they huddled in an aggrieved pack waiting for the Bessemers to emerge, apart from two female journalists who nobbled Maude as she was making her way towards Margaret.

'That was nice and discreet, doctor.'

Margaret jumped. Inspector Silvermann was behind her, lighting a cigarette. He threw down his match and pocketed the box before tipping his hat.

'Discreet?' said Margaret.

'No frills. No speculation.'

'It's not for a pathologist to speculate.'

The inspector snorted. 'That didn't stop you last year.'

'Drawing possible conclusions in a mortuary and stating them as facts to a coroner are two very different things, especially in this instance. Did someone poison her, then gas her, then shoot her? Without meaning to sound callous, what a palaver. I can't imagine that whoever shot her didn't know she was dead, even if the Bessemers didn't realise.'

'Rum case, isn't it?' The inspector drew deep on his cigarette and fixed his gaze on Maude. 'She was one of your lot. Did you know?'

'Who? What sort?'

'Miss Halpin. Suffragette.'

'The sergeant said she might be, but that has nothing to do with my work.'

The inspector scrutinised her. 'Given up the fight, have we? Shall I take you off the list?'

Unease coiled in Margaret's stomach. She forced her voice to sound calm and detached. 'Is it relevant?'

'Could be. If you *were* going to speculate... Any reason why she took laudanum?'

Margaret returned his cold stare. 'There were deep abrasions in her oesophagus and damage to the duodenum. In layman's terms—'

'Sores in her throat and stomach. I told you before, I'm not H division. I can spell my own name, count to ten and everything.' Light words but no smile. 'You didn't mention the abrasions in court.'

'They weren't relevant to her death: the damage was from some time ago. Was she ever imprisoned and forcibly fed?'

'Three times. She always put up a fight.'

'How thoughtless of her not to lie back and let them shove tubes up her nose.' Margaret looked at Maude, who had managed to shed the female journalists and was in conversation with Mrs Philbrook. Maude glanced at her, face impassive, gaze flicking between Margaret and the inspector.

'Well, if a woman doesn't want that,' said the inspector, 'firstly, she shouldn't break the law, and secondly, she shouldn't starve herself.'

'This is a fruitless conversation. I have to go back to Dorcas Free and you have to work out who's responsible for Miss Halpin's death.' She took a step towards Maude.

'I think it's to do with the suffrage movement.'

Margaret paused. 'What?'

'This crime.' Inspector Silvermann took another long drag on his cigarette, watching Margaret's impatience peak. 'When we got there, the corpse's face was pink. Classic. We knew straight away. The jets on the stove and the wall lamps were turned off, but the kitchen had been full of gas. The Bessemers said they hadn't touched the stove and couldn't smell anything, and of course the back door was wide open as they said matey-boy had legged it. But it was there. The gas, I mean.'

'So he must have gassed her then turned the gas off.' Margaret shrugged. 'Then shot her to make certain she was dead, even though it risked raising the alarm.'

'Or he killed her then fired into a room full of gas. Hitting her was incidental.'

'Why would he do that?'

'What could a spark from a pistol do in a room full of gas?'

'A spark?' Margaret frowned.

'Ever read a penny dreadful? What would happen in one of those if someone fired a gun in a room full of gas?'

Margaret thought of the stories her nephew Ed enjoyed, which he occasionally lent her. 'In a *book* it would trigger an explosion. But in reality?'

'You're a scientific woman,' said Inspector Silvermann. 'You know it's highly unlikely. But for someone who believes what passes for fact in sensational novels, it might seem like a dead cert.'

'Is Mr Carter, the missing suitor, that sort?'

'Dunno yet: he's on his way back from Australia. We'll talk to him, but I don't think he's responsible. It's someone wanting to give her a taste of her own medicine.'

'Like Jeremiah Stokes?'

'You've heard that rumour, have you?'

'Yes. Well, good luck, Inspector. My part in this case is over.'

'Maybe.' Inspector Silvermann dropped his cigarette and ground it out. 'But it'll nibble away at you now, won't it?'

'No. I can't see any link to suffrage.'

'Perhaps you should look harder.'

'Why are you telling me this?'

'It's a warning. There's a lot of respect for you personally in the force, but times are changing. There's more than one list, Dr Demeray. You're on the "keep an eye on" one. Miss Halpin was on quite another.'

'I don't know what you're talking about, Inspector, and I have to go.'

The inspector lowered his voice. 'Have you heard the latest about Alf Emery, the postman injured by the Carmelo Street post-office bomb? He might never work again. He's got a young family, who might have been better off if he'd died and they'd got the insurance. There was another kiddy on the way, but when his wife heard she lost it. Little girl it was, so I hear. Whatever happens, she'll never get the vote, will she?'

'That's terrible.'

'Everything points to it being a suffragette who planted that bomb. Miss Halpin was under investigation for it.' The inspector leaned close, as if whispering an endearment. His breath stank of cigarettes. 'Is the vote that bloody important to you? 'Cos it wouldn't be to me. And remember, it's not just the police who keep lists. If you think a bit of manhandling by a copper when you're obstructing a road is an affront, or someone being force-fed to save her life, let me tell you – we're positive pussycats compared to others I could mention.'

'Are you threatening me?'

'Let the lady pathologist speculate.' The inspector straightened up. 'See you round.' He stalked off.

Margaret swallowed, shook herself, and turned to join Maude and Mrs Philbrook. But they had gone.

Ten

With a morning spent at the inquest, work had piled up. Margaret rushed out for something to eat at one fifteen, but was stopped at the desk by Miss Upton, who handed her a message from Miss Lewin. The message said that after racking her brains, all she could recall of the parcel was *S Queale, Russett House,* and perhaps *St J—. S Queale* had made her think of pigs, and *Russett* of apples, and she wasn't sure which saint was indicated by the J, or even whether any of it was right.

'Come along, Demeray, it's your lunch time.' Maude's voice made Margaret turn.

'I don't have long, and I need to send a telegram to Fox,' said Margaret. 'Do you mind?'

'Not remotely.'

A short while later, they sat in a small café eating sandwiches. 'I wish you'd stayed after the inquest,' said Margaret. 'I wanted to say how good it was to see you there.'

'You seemed happy enough with your policeman.'

'I'd rather eat my own hat.'

Maude chuckled. 'I had to telegraph my editor, and I was certain I'd catch you now.'

'I was surprised to see Mrs Philbrook. Did she know the victim?'

'Miss Halpin attended the same suffrage group.'

Margaret sipped her tea. 'Inspector Silvermann suspects Miss Halpin was militant, although I suspect embroidering a banner is enough to get his goat.'

'Is it now?' said Maude, swallowing a morsel of sandwich with an effort. 'I knew Miss Halpin, too. I made her acquaintance – if you can call it that – in Holloway after the Oxford Street window smashing last year. Could you tell she'd been forcibly fed?'

'There was a lot of damage.'

'She was the one whose reasoning I thought was affected by laudanum,' said Maude, shuddering. 'I didn't know her well, so I can't say if she was suicidal, but I doubt it somehow. She was anxious to ask me about something; I intended to visit after returning from Oxford. The next thing I know, her death is in the papers, looking very like Jeremiah Stokes's. What if someone killed her before she told me what was on her mind?'

'Had she told anyone else?'

Maude shrugged. 'No idea. But there's something wrong about it all.'

'Despite not liking militants, Inspector Silvermann is fair and will do his best to find out what happened. But I'm not sure it's the same as the Stokes case, unless he and Miss Halpin shared the same concern.'

'I think it's a different connection.' Maude brushed crumbs from her fingers, the sandwich half-eaten. 'Someone sent *Athene's Gazette* some cuttings about their deaths with a typed note saying *Death to the militants. Who will be next?* It's rather wearying.'

'It's worse than wearying.' Margaret reached for Maude's hand, her heart chilled. 'Tell the police.'

'They won't care,' said Maude. 'There's a better than average chance a policeman sent it. But there's a connection between those deaths, and I'm going to keep them in *Athene's Gazette* until someone does something about it.'

Dr Southern assisted Margaret in the afternoon. 'I gather Mr Baggott appreciated your assistance in that operation,' he said, as they compared notes on samples. The words were light, but there was a twitch of irritation at the corner of his mouth.

'Any one of us could have done it,' she answered. 'Miss Lewin's need was paramount.'

'Ridiculous woman.'

'Scared woman.'

'Whatever happened to enduring one's lot?'

'As you endured not being chosen to assist?'

Dr Southern looked up from his notes. 'Touché, doctor. I had no particular desire to watch the operation. It was the insistence that one sex was better than another which I found annoying.'

'Isn't it?' said Margaret.

Dr Southern's mouth twisted into a rueful smile. 'I surrender. You can twist my words more effectively even than my wife. I fear to introduce you at the fundraising soirée on Saturday.'

'Do you know, I'd quite forgotten the soirée,' said Margaret, contemplating him. She hadn't realised Dr Southern was married. Under thirty was young to marry for a professional man who hadn't yet made his name, but she could hardly say so.

'We doctors at Dorcas Free are quite the mixed bag, are we not?' he continued, twiddling his pen. 'I gather your husband is a policeman, if a few rungs above the usual. He must turn a blind eye to your suffragette activities and friends.' His expression goaded her to make a witty retort, but she wouldn't rise to the bait.

'Why not ask him?' she said, then tapped her notes. 'For now, shall we discuss this?'

Leaving the hospital later than usual that evening, Margaret made for the underground.

It was hot and busy. She was swept along in a tightly bunched throng of people of every size and shape, elbows and handbags knocking into her, and blinded when someone taller squeezed in front. Her view opened out, then a tallish man with sloping shoulders slipped in front, hurrying, stumbling, squeezing through with apologies, his brown fedora slipping. The flow of people parted and re-formed behind him, then a shorter, stockier man pushed through in a similar way. Margaret was knocked off-balance and trod on someone's foot, then someone trod on hers.

Another man passed, slipping gently through gaps in the commuters. She sensed it was Fox without seeing him properly. If he sensed her, he gave no sign. Her hand reached out and was knocked back by a stout woman in mourning black who bumped into her. A broad-hipped woman in a pale summer dress moved quickly by, colliding with a short man with a limp, whose twisted face was barely visible between collar and hat brim. He caught sight of Margaret watching and his eyes flickered over her in an unnerving manner. But as he bent his head and hurried forward, Margaret forgot him: she was more interested in Fox. There had been something very focused about Fox's stride. Perhaps he was on a trail and she shouldn't try to catch him.

Some of the passengers veered towards different platforms, easing the volume. Margaret could make out Fox ahead of her, and in front of him a sort of eddy as people swerved around something.

There was a shout: 'Bomb!'

And another: 'Parcel bomb! Run!'

People turned and pushed against those still moving forwards. 'Bomb! Run!'

The cry echoed off the tiles of the tunnel and was repeated, passengers unsure whether to run forwards or go the other way. Cold sweat trickled down Margaret's back and her clammy hands trembled inside their gloves. She forced herself to push Miss Lewin's dusty face and shattered hand from her mind while she worked out what to do. She strained to see Fox and thought she could just make him out, standing near the place where the people swerved. She opened her mouth to call out but a man barging past snatched at her arm. 'Run, madam, run!' She shook him off.

Two young women ran hand in hand until one stumbled and fell, then staggered up to limp on. A man swept a child into his arms as he hurried, pushing a woman and baby ahead of him.

The tall, stooped man she'd seen earlier straightened up from a crouch and looked about him in surprise and confusion.

'Him!' shouted someone. 'He's planted a bomb! Get him! Police!'

'Which way? Which way's safest?' shrieked a woman. 'He might have been dropping them all along. Make for the train!'

The man backed away with his hands raised, shaking his head, but was caught up in those pushing towards the tracks. Fox followed, with the merest glance at the place where the man had been crouching, and both disappeared from view. The crowds, swirling and weaving, had thinned a little.

'Make way! Police!'

Margaret stepped away from the wall as two policemen pushed past. She imagined the brickwork collapsing and engulfing her but she couldn't leave Fox to die alone. Above the shouts came a thin wail of panic. As Margaret passed, she realised it came from an old man standing motionless with his hands over his ears. A woman in her middle years pulled at him. 'Papa, please! It's not Boers. We must move.'

Swallowing hard, Margaret pressed on. A policeman stood where the man had crouched, peering at something on the floor. A copy of *The Suffragette* had been kicked across the floor and now lay against the wall, trampled and ripped. He bent to retrieve it, then rolled it up and prodded the parcel. Holding her breath, Margaret hurried onto the platform. It was overcrowded, and passengers ebbed and flowed towards the edge as the second policeman called for them to make way.

'It's him!' shouted several voices, fingers pointing in various directions.

Margaret could see the tall, sloping-shouldered man, and Fox among those closing in on him. She was too short to be certain, but surely they were dangerously near the edge?

There was a whistle and a bellow. 'Stand back! Stand back! Train approaching.'

The passengers ebbed, then lurched forward again.

'I've got to get on! There's a bomb in the station!'

'Let me through!'

'Arrest that man!'

In the push of people, Fox and the man appeared to be about to overbalance. The policeman was yelling for people to stand back as the train approached with a squeal and a rattle. It screeched to a halt and the bulge of passengers pressed forward again. The tall man disappeared from view with a yell, followed by Fox.

There was a scream, then another, and a third, deafening scream nearby. Margaret realised it was her own. She pushed forward but someone pulled her back. It was Dr Southern.

'What are you doing?' he shouted over the din.

'What are *you* doing?' she cried, shaking him off. 'Someone's gone under the train! We have to help! It could be—'

'Let the police clear the way.'

'But—'

'You're no good hysterical.'

'I'm not!'

A policeman's whistle sounded long and loud, silencing the passengers. Another whistle behind Margaret joined in, then both stopped.

'This is the Metropolitan police,' bellowed the policeman on the platform. 'Please listen! Two people have sustained injuries. Are any doctors or nurses here?'

Margaret and Dr Southern raised their hands, along with one other.

'Come through, please. Everyone else, make way.'

'But the bomb!' someone cried. 'We have to get on the train. If it's the bomber, who cares if he's under the wheels?'

'There is no bomb!' yelled the policeman behind Margaret. 'It's an empty box. Anyone who saw anything different, make an orderly queue and speak to me. No one's dead, but please let the medics through.'

'But I'll miss the train!'

'The train's not going anywhere until we say so, sir. Now, make room for these injured parties.'

Margaret's heart thudded as she neared the platform edge with the second policeman. Grumbling and arguing, some passengers turned and made their way towards the entrance. Among them limped the tall man, wearing a straw boater instead of the fedora. Beside him was Fox, close enough to suggest they were arm in arm.

Fox caught sight of Margaret and blinked, the colour draining from his face, then gave the tiniest shake of his head as he passed by.

On the platform edge lay a man and a woman, a little apart from each other. The woman was gasping for breath, the man grey-faced, his arm twisted into an unnatural shape.

'I thought someone had gone under,' said Margaret, kneeling by the woman as Dr Southern and another man bent to the other casualty.

'Luckily not quite, madam. This man tripped but was pulled back in time. His arm was struck by the train, but it was nearly at a halt. It could have been much worse. As for the lady, she nearly suffocated in the crush and it's a wonder she's the only one. Fools.'

'And the bomb?' said a bystander. 'A hoax, you say? That man planted something. Where is he? He needs arresting!'

'Don't you worry about that, sir,' said the policeman, looking up from where he knelt helping Margaret. 'Plain-clothes officers arrested him. You can rest easy. It's all under control.'

Fox returned home at eleven, pulled Margaret into his arms and held her tight. 'I can't tell you how I felt when I saw you there. For all of five minutes, I'd thought there was a bomb.'

'You don't need to tell me – I felt the same about you. Who was the man who planted the box? Was it the tall man in the fedora?'

'The tall man with the fedora is called Silas Queale.'

'So it was his name on the letter bomb?'

'If it was, someone made a mistake,' said Fox. 'Queale's home isn't Russett anything and it's in Hammersmith, but Silas Queale is the man who stole the letters. He didn't plant anything, though. He didn't have time, and he was under my watch and Smith's. Queale says he heard someone say there was a box of abandoned kittens and crouched to look. The next thing, someone was shouting about a bomb. He didn't realise people meant him until the panic started.'

'Weren't you escorting him?'

Fox shook his head. 'Smith and I were following him to see what he did. I'd actually lost sight of him: I only spotted him again when all the commotion started.'

'It was terrifying how quickly everything went from normal to utter chaos.'

'Too quickly,' said Fox. 'Who left the box? Who knew Queale had a soft spot for animals and a man whispered to Queale there were abandoned kittens? Where did the first yell about the bomb come from?'

Margaret pondered. 'I'm not sure. Thinking back, I swear I heard a woman's voice behind me before anyone's ahead of, which is odd but it was so chaotic, I couldn't swear to it. Was *The Suffragette* left deliberately, or dropped?'

'Impossible to know,' said Fox. He released her and sank into an armchair. 'No one saw this coming. I thought Queale would lead us to the letters if he thought he was off the leash for long enough. Smith kept closer than I did but couldn't say who spoke to him. Queale seemed composed earlier, but at the station he was running as if he intended to throw himself under the train. Now he's too frightened to talk, because he thinks we'll bring danger to his mistress. Hare is fuming. The documents are even further from our grasp now.'

'It's not your fault.'

'Tell Hare that.' Fox rubbed his arm. 'I expect I'm black and blue. I grabbed Queale and someone grabbed me, or we'd have gone under the train. I think someone's trying to stop Queale giving up the documents. The hunt for his mistress starts again tomorrow.'

'How, if he won't talk?'

Fox stared into the empty fireplace, then at Margaret. 'Since arrest, he's written a sort of diary on scraps of lavatory paper, which he hides under the bathroom floorboards. He really is a very amateur secret agent. It's retrieved daily and put back, so he doesn't know. It's mostly a record of our iniquities, his romantic longing for Paddington theatres and his need to communicate with someone via a newspaper, which is why we let him out today to see what happened. We'll do it again – if he'll leave the house unescorted, that is. His favourite newspaper or journal starts with D. Where does one even start?'

'Are you certain that Queale left the documents with a woman?' said Margaret. 'If his lover is a man, there would be even more reason not to admit it – he'd risk being tried for that as well.'

'He refers to her as his brave little suffragette, so it's unlikely. We need to find her and secure the documents.'

A cold thought came over Margaret as she stroked the thin scar on his temple. 'Fox, are you sure the person who hurt your arm was pulling you?'

'No,' said Fox. He looked up at her. 'And I have a question.'

Margaret swallowed. Memories of the previous year still haunted her dreams, images of what had happened and what might have flickering like a faulty moving picture. They'd moved house, she'd changed job, she'd hired a new maid, she'd sworn she'd let Fox do his work without asking questions or offering to be involved, but she couldn't erase the events she wanted to forget. 'What is it?'

'Lois Halpin, whose inquest you attended today, is the person alleged to have posted that bomb, isn't she?'

'Yes. But Maude says—'

'And Miss Halpin was a suffragette actress living in Paddington.'

'Yes.'

'Will you visit her house with me tomorrow evening, to see if there's any evidence linking her to Queale? If Miss Halpin was the mistress, perhaps the papers are there. If she wasn't, no harm done. If anyone asks, you can say you wanted to see the crime scene for yourself, in case any medical information had been missed.'

Maude had been certain that Miss Halpin was murdered, like Stokes, for what she believed in. Maybe Margaret could prove it, one way or another, and stop it happening to anyone else. To Maude.

'It'll annoy Inspector Silvermann,' said Fox.

'Then I shall.'

Eleven

Bert collected Margaret from the hospital at six the following evening. Fox read aloud from the newspaper as they rode in the back of the car.

'"Dr Deverill, the lady physician, speaking on behalf of Dr Genser of St Dorcas Free Hospital, made an attractive presence in the witness box and remained calm under questioning, although due to female verbosity, perhaps some of Dr Genser's findings were not reported as clearly as they might have been, since the jury was clearly confused." What drivel. If it helps, every single surname is spelt wrong.'

'I'm reasonably sure I wasn't verbose,' said Margaret. 'And the jury reached the correct verdict, in my view. Though the press didn't think so, as you can tell.'

'Do you know Inspector Silvermann's hypothesis?'

'That someone with a detective-novel fixation tried to blow Miss Halpin up by shooting into a room full of gas.'

'Implausible.'

'He'd agree, but he also thinks the depths of the stupidity of the general population have yet to be plumbed.'

'True,' said Fox, 'but why?'

'Revenge for Carmelo Street, which he considers a reasonable response. He really doesn't like suffragettes.'

'A lot of people don't.'

'He says there are lists and Maude's on one.'

Fox raised his eyebrows. 'In March, Maude was imprisoned for taking an axe to an MP's cricket bat and golf clubs, scattering the fragments among his prize roses and setting them alight, then using the axe on the tyres of his car. Of course she's on a list.'

Margaret looked out of the window for a while. 'He says I'm on another list, Fox. Am I?'

'Of course,' he said. 'How do you think I found you?'

She turned. His expression was serious. 'As an agitator?'

'I wasn't looking for an agitator. Just someone in the right field with strong views who might have access to the right things.'

'I mean, am I on a list as an agitator?'

Fox shrugged. 'Suffragettes, like any political activists, are potential agitators, and therefore a possible threat to national security. But being on a list doesn't mean being a target or under observation. It just means that if anything happens, we will cross reference and look for connections. That's assuming it's possible to cross reference. It's amazing how often funny surnames get misfiled, Dr Deverill.' He grinned, but she didn't respond in kind.

'Is Maude on one of your lists?'

'Yes.'

'I see.'

'I hope so. It's not personal, and I'm not interested in tracking suffragettes down unless they plan to disrupt the treaty or hand documents to potential enemies. And since she and Geoff are friends of ours, I keep my distance as much as possible. I trust your faith in her, Margaret. But I also hope you'd tell me anything I needed to know, so that I could head it off at the pass somehow – or you could.'

Margaret sighed. 'Maude knew Miss Halpin a little, and thinks she and Jeremiah Stokes were selected for murders because of their views, not because of anything they'd done,' she said. '*Athene's Gazette* received a threat. I hope it's general rather than personal, but she won't go to the police.'

'She should.'

'I know. But she's never once mentioned the treaty.'

Fox tapped the paper. 'How about the German royal wedding? There's a list of suffragettes we're watching who want to interfere with the King and Queen's attendance in Berlin. I hope we haven't missed one.'

'I don't think so,' said Margaret, without certainty. 'I think she'd struggle to leave the country while on licence. And just now, as I say, she's concentrating on obtaining justice for Mr Stokes and Miss Halpin.'

He relaxed a fraction. 'I'm glad to hear that, but it's another thing those letters could affect if they get into the wrong hands now. Every reigning monarch in Europe will be at Princess Victoria Louise's wedding. The King would be put in an impossible situation with the Emperor and the Tsar at the very least, let alone anyone else. And even if the documents turn up afterwards, they could stop the treaty being signed. The delicate allegiances already in place will crumble, and ultimately… I can't see anything less than war breaking out.'

'It broke out last year.'

'I don't mean the Balkans, Margaret. I mean Western Europe. I mean us.'

'You keep saying it, Fox, but do you really believe it? The King and Queen are going to Germany quite happily. Last year, the German Emperor and Empress came to Britain. Germany might want greater control in the Balkans, but surely rumours that they're trying to annexe land in France and the Low Countries again are pure speculation.'

Fox scowled. 'No one wants to believe the signs before them. They'd rather believe the King, the Emperor and the Tsar will chat like chums while another princess has an extravagant wedding.'

'They're cousins.'

'You have a million cousins,' said Fox. 'Can you trust all of them?'

Margaret wrinkled her nose and shrugged.

'The reality is not that war is unlikely, it's that no one is ready. Not even the Germans. Definitely not us.' The car slowed. 'Here we are. Bert will come back for us in an hour.'

Lois Halpin's home was halfway between Carmelo Street and Theatre Valerina, at the junction of a pleasant road of red-brick buildings and a narrow lane. There was a large blue and white advertisement for Cadbury's Chocolate on its gable end, above a side door. The front window was larger than its neighbour's, with net curtains beyond a deep sill.

'I didn't realise she ran a shop,' said Margaret.

'This hasn't been a shop for at least twenty years,' said Fox.

'Did the police obscure the glass?' said Margaret, peering in. The panes were smeared with streaks of white and paint had gathered in the corners of the black frame.

'You wouldn't be able to make out an elephant through that net,' said Fox. 'But presumably, yes, they did.'

Margaret pointed at the lintel above the window. The black paint had peeled and faded to reveal old lettering in gold: C. Bythell, Costumier, Haberdasher. 'Not another haberdasher.' She grimaced.

Fox chuckled. 'It's irrelevant. Let's go in.'

He unlocked the door and ushered Margaret through. Despite the net curtains and smeared windows, the space was light. The shop counter had been removed to create a large, airy sitting room. Comfortable chairs faced the fireplace, surrounded by low bookshelves and a couple of tables. The walls were decorated with framed Theatre Valerina playbills from the 1890s and watercolours of bright theatrical costumes.

'It's not what I'd expected,' said Margaret. 'It seems modern, somehow. Calm, pleasant, homely. I expected it to show signs of Lois's illness. Healthy people don't take that much laudanum.'

Signs of a life arrested were everywhere. An open copy of *The Tempest*, scattered novels, a copy of *The Suffragette*, a dish of humbugs. In a photograph on the mantlepiece, Miss Halpin walked down a seaside promenade arm in arm with a man. She was grinning at the photographer: a snapshot of radiant joy. Margaret found it almost impossible to reconcile this woman with the blotched face at the mortuary a few weeks ago.

It seemed an unforgivable intrusion to go through Miss Halpin's things. But an unexplained death obliterated any right to privacy and secrecy, even for the victim.

'Surely the police would have found anything odd.'

Fox shook his head. 'They were looking for things in plain sight: a threatening letter, perhaps, and three bullets. They found no letters and only one bullet. If what I'm interested in is here, it's hidden.'

'Or destroyed, or it wasn't here in the first place.'

'It's worth trying. Shall we start searching?'

'Let's start here, then go to the kitchen.'

'Is that where a woman would hide documents?'

Margaret put her head on one side. 'I can't speak for all women. I'd destroy them in a fireplace or the oven, but presumably the police would have spotted burnt paper. If I were hiding them, assuming there's not a safe or a strong box or secret cupboard anywhere, I'd either hide them inside other documents like newspapers, or large volumes like cookery books. Or there might be a place in the chimney where they could go.'

She picked up *The Suffragette* and shook it. Nothing except a cutting about fashion from a different paper fell out. 'How did Lois come to live here? I had the impression she wasn't working much. How could she afford it?'

'Thanks to Miss Clementina Bythell, whose name is on the lintel outside,' said Fox, applying his penknife to the gummed paper which sealed the frame holding Lois's photograph. 'We're looking for any link we can, so we found out that much. Miss Bythell joined her father in making theatrical costumes in the 1860s, chiefly for Theatre Valerina. After her father died Clementina moved into selling haberdashery before giving up entirely in 1898. She would have been in her late sixties by then. She owned the property and she must have put enough away to retire. It's hard to get hold of censuses officially, of course, but Elinor has her own special way. Lois Halpin, born in Belfast, is recorded on the census as a general servant here in 1891, aged fifteen, then ten years later as an actress. Neither are on the census of 1911. Miss Bythell had been involved in feminist endeavours long before they became, shall we say, fashionable, and was an associate member of the Actresses' Franchise League. She almost certainly introduced Lois to the suffrage movement. Anyway, she died a year ago and left the house to Lois. It hasn't a great deal of value, but a house is a house.'

The sitting room led directly into a good-sized kitchen with a large table in the middle, two dressers, and a gas stove lurking under the chimney. Another door opened into a narrow passage which contained a larder. On the marble shelves were a piece of cracked, hardened cheese wrapped in greaseproof paper, a dish of runny, rancid butter and a jug of sour milk. On the other side of the kitchen, an archway led to a scullery with a tin bath hanging on the wall, and beyond that a door to the backyard and WC. The kitchen was as Margaret recalled from the photographs, but the perspective seemed different, the room larger.

'Would you sit in that chair, Fox, so that I can compare it with what I remember of the police photograph?' said Margaret. 'Or would it worry you to sit where she died?'

'I've faced worse things than haunted chairs,' he said, taking his seat and watching her pace. 'You tell me how she sat, and I'll tell you where to stand if you were going to shoot me. Then maybe we can swap places – or will that worry you?'

'I'd like to say it won't,' said Margaret. 'However, if I smell coal-gas, cordite, laudanum or even Miss Halpin's perfume, I'll be out of that chair before you can say ghost.'

'Call yourself a scientist?'

'No one can explain everything. Not even you.'

They took it in turns to pretend they were Lois, the assailant or the Bessemers, and searched for anything to indicate if they were standing or sitting in the right place. Then they hunted for documents. There was nothing.

Upstairs were three bedrooms. The largest, with a double bed, seemed to have been Miss Halpin's. The drawers and wardrobe doors were partly open. The others, with single beds and bare washstands, were neglected and dusty.

There seemed to be nothing relevant anywhere. There were a few library books, a basket of mending, a half-finished dress on a mannequin and a scrapbook of cuttings from various journals, covering suffrage, theatre and fashion.

'It's a wild-goose chase,' said Margaret, lifting the neatly folded clothes in Miss Halpin's bedroom drawers. The scent of lavender rose, then cedar, as the lining paper shifted to reveal the wood below. 'Though it's odd there's no bottom drawer. You know – new underwear and nightgowns ready for a wedding.'

'Maybe she was too addled with laudanum to prepare one,' said Fox, picking up a copy of *A Room With a View* from the nightstand and flicking through it.

'These drawers seem very neat, if that's the case. The lining paper's fresh.'

'Lining paper?' Fox put the book down. 'Wallpaper?'

'Newspaper.' Margaret lifted a pile of clothes out and put them on the bed, then extracted the lining and unfolded it. 'Not letters or documents, if that's what you mean.' She perused it. 'Advertisements on this side, and on the other, articles about mending and a charitable club sewing to clothe the needy. The paper's called *The New Dorcas*. I've never heard of it.'

'It's a means of communication with a D in it that doesn't start with *Daily*,' said Fox. 'Let's get the linings out.'

They removed and refolded all the paper, replaced the clothes and went downstairs. 'Has anything else struck you as odd?' asked Fox.

Margaret frowned. 'At the inquest, the Bessemers said she was preparing dinner but there's no evidence of it. The police have left everything, but there's not even a potato peeling.'

'Perhaps she turned the gas on, intending to light it, then—'

'Who puts an oven on before they've started preparing the meal?' said Margaret. 'It would be a waste of gas. Anyway, I can't think of any other place to look without taking things apart.'

'I agree,' said Fox. 'I'll take these papers to the office and arrange for someone to search under the floorboards, and so on.'

A clatter against the window, followed by a squawk, made them jump. Fox unlocked and pulled open the door. A young boy with a paint pot and brush was standing outside. A small group of youths stood a few feet away.

'Stop it!' Fox shouted.

'It's the truth!' the boy shouted back.

'I'm the police,' snapped Fox, showing the boy his warrant card. 'There's no evidence Miss Halpin set a bomb anywhere. Nor that she's ever killed anyone.'

'All suffragettes is the same!' yelled the boy.

'Miss Halpin is dead. This is her sister's property now. What do you expect to achieve by vandalising it? Do you expect her to come back and see what you're painting?'

There was a tiny gasp. 'Yer what? The other lads did it. Someone keeps cleaning it off. You gonna arrest me? Arrest them suffragettes instead. Stop them blowing anything else up.'

'I'm not arresting anyone,' said Fox. 'Fetch a bucket of water and a mop. I'll have a word with the beat bobby and if that paint is still there when he does his round, he'll arrest every boy in the street. Now skedaddle.'

He and Margaret stepped outside and looked at the window. Its glass was daubed with an *M*, followed by a trickle of paint that might have been the start of a *U*. 'What it is to be innocent until proven guilty. Here's Bert, not a moment too soon.' Fox locked the door, handed Margaret into the back of the car, had a word with Bert then joined her, his face solemn.

'I'm doubtful the documents were ever here, Fox,' said Margaret. 'Miss Halpin was killed for another reason: possibly one of the two Maude suggests. I can't see any connection with Queale. You can stand easy.'

'I wish I could,' said Fox. 'Bert just told me the police are saying that Alf Emery, the postman, gave a different address to the one Miss Lewin said. He also said Queale, but he's sure it was Russell House, and there's a Russell House in St James's. It's where we've been keeping him. Someone has found out.'

Twelve

On Wednesday, Margaret found Dr Gesner in the laboratory, peering into a microscope.

He looked up. 'Good morning, doctor. Thank you for the report on the inquest. I'm sorry to have left you with such an unusual case.'

'Please don't be sorry,' said Margaret. 'I had to do it sometime. I hope all is well at home.'

'Nothing has changed,' said Dr Gesner. 'There was no need to stay longer. You must find me heartless, when you longed to be with your stepmother when she died, but my father-in-law is very much a creaking door, as you say. He may yet outlive me, and our mutual affection is not strong. I find Germany rather fretful at present. It seems calmer here.'

'Is there much excitement about the royal wedding?'

'Ach, too much fuss. I confess that I'm not interested. Who can imagine the cost of protecting them all? I'd rather it was spent on hospitals and schools.'

'I agree,' said Margaret. 'But perhaps it'll help negotiations over the Balkans.'

Dr Gesner frowned. 'Will it not be like any family wedding, where old resentments bubble under the surface, but with more expensive clothes and better food? Who was the favourite grandchild? Who offended whom in 1870? Who was given the best inheritance – or in the case of the Tsarevich Alexei, the worst? Who still wants to steal someone else's lands?'

'Perhaps, but they are too refined to scrap in a public house about it.'

'Better a public house than a battlefield.'

'Do you think it will come to that?'

He shrugged. 'My country is sending zeppelins to fly over your country's fleet, while your country is building the means to shoot down zeppelins from the decks of its destroyers. Is that pure scientific curiosity? Have British men been released from German prisons to celebrate the royal wedding purely because the authorities now recognise that they were tourists and not spies? I don't believe it.'

'I hope you're wrong.'

'So do I.' He contemplated her. 'You seem distracted. Were you caught up in Monday's regrettable incident on the underground?'

Margaret tried to work out what Dr Southern might have said, but Dr Gesner's expression was simply concerned. 'I was, but it turned out to be nothing, as I'm sure Dr Southern mentioned.'

Dr Gesner looked confused. 'He has said nothing about it. Was he there?'

'Oh! Yes, he was. We treated two injured people. Ummm...' She squirmed a little under his steady gaze. 'Might I ask an indulgence? Could I work during my lunch hour and leave at four o'clock? I've been invited to a tea party, and the old lady who invited me is rather didactic and doesn't understand women with careers. It's rather complicated and I'd rather not go, but... It's really hard to explain.'

'Social politics?'

'I'm afraid so. The rules are worse than those of cricket.'

'I don't understand either,' said Dr Gesner. 'But take your lunch hour and also leave at four, or take half an hour at lunchtime and leave at three, so that you can go home to change if you wish. You have been burdened in my absence.' He returned his attention to the microscope, his voice a little muffled. 'By the way, we have received a communication.' He nodded at an envelope on the side. 'Perhaps you should read it before giving me your opinion on this sample taken from Mrs Singer on D ward. She is very ill, but perhaps there is hope.'

The communication was a letter from Inspector Silvermann, asking for more detail from Miss Halpin's post-mortem.

Is it possible to tell whether Miss Halpin was unconscious from laudanum before she was gassed?

Was the amount of laudanum in her body enough to kill her if she hadn't been gassed?

Apart from the actual injury, what would happen to a person mentally and physiologically if they were shot with the intent to injure but not kill?

'The last question is interesting,' she said. 'He was following a very different tack after the inquest.'

'So I gathered, from your report. Perhaps he's talking about the Bessemers. They were shot too.'

'I hadn't thought of that.' Margaret considered. 'Anyway, I've pre-empted the inspector to some extent. I have Polly Buckram researching the effects of laudanum and it's possible she'll discover something I don't know. As for the Bessemers he'll have to ask the doctor who treated them. The simple answer is that they'd suffer shock, they'd risk infection and they'd fear that risk. Apart from the obvious physical effects, the main impact would be mental, which is very much outside my remit.'

'And mine,' said Dr Gesner. 'Let's work on a response after this morning's laboratory work. Inspector Silvermann can wait. Or can he?'

'Definitely,' said Margaret. 'Mrs Singer's life, in my view, is of much higher importance. We need to get on with our job, and Inspector Silvermann can get on with his.'

On the dot of four thirty, Margaret and Phoebe arrived at the Tabors' house. Margaret had changed into her pale-blue costume with daisy embroidery, while Phoebe was un-schoolmistressy in dusky mauve. Until the door opened Margaret felt energised and summery, but in the dark hall, under the gaze of gloomy oil paintings, then in a drawing room decorated in the style of forty years before, she felt dimmed and weary. The room, in theory, was no worse than her father's drawing room, which was cluttered with ornate furniture and more ornaments than a market stall, but while the room in Clapham exuded welcome and pleasant chaos, the Tabors' felt like a deliberate attempt to make extra work for the servants.

Miss Tabor was the only person there, rigid on a straight-backed chair. She rose to greet them with a kiss, hands fluttering, face pink. 'It's so good of you to come – what a delight! I was so glad that Mother agreed. Mrs Philbrook is coming, too. Dr Demeray...' Miss Tabor blushed even pinker and murmured, 'Mother may call you Mrs Foxcroft. Please don't be offended. It's just her way, and she is rather frail.'

Margaret forced her mouth into a polite smile. She had just seated herself beside Phoebe on an overstuffed sofa when Mrs Philbrook entered, greeted them and sat beside Margaret. 'How is dashing Superintendent Foxcroft?' she said.

'Dashing,' said Margaret. Her false smile threatened to stick permanently. This visit felt interminable already and she had only been there for two minutes. She would rather be in the lab dissecting a diseased bowel. 'Dashing about, that is.'

'Ah, yes. The suffragette murder.'

Margaret blinked. 'Excuse me?'

'Miss Halpin, cut down in her prime for her beliefs. Tragic.'

'It was,' gabbled Miss Tabor. 'And poor Stokes, too. Most troubling. They weren't our sort, of course, but he was so fretful, and I—'

Mrs Philbrook gave her an indulging smile though her brows furrowed. 'Poor Stokes was killed by a burglar.'

'Why would anyone burgle Stokes?' Miss Tabor's fingers threatened to break under the pressure of her hand-wringing. 'It's such a wicked world.'

'Don't worry, dear Rhoda,' said Mrs Philbrook. 'The police, apart from their persecution of suffragettes, are generally very efficient. And since Dr Demeray dealt with both post-mortems and her husband is investigating, it's a family affair.' She gave a girlish chuckle.

'I did, but he isn't investigating,' said Margaret. 'Miss Halpin's case is Inspector Silvermann's entirely.'

'That's a shame, as I'm sure your dear husband would find the culprits much more quickly. But I suppose sordid murders aren't really the business of Special Branch. They're generally concerned with Fenians and anarchists, aren't they? So whom is he seeking?'

'Fenians and anarchists.'

Mrs Philbrook sighed. 'Well, one can only hope that Inspector Silvermann finds the culprits soon. Oh, and Dr Demeray, on Monday, I thought you dealt with those poor injured people on the underground with admirable calm. I confess I was quite terrified.'

'I'm sure you were,' said Phoebe. 'I read about it in the newspaper but hadn't realised either of you were there.'

Mrs Philbrook was slightly pink. 'I was a little way behind Dr Demeray when someone shouted that there was a bomb, and then I was swept past by people rushing for the train. I thought you saw me.'

'I'm afraid I didn't.' Margaret frowned, trying to recollect the scene. The only faces she could recall clearly were Fox's, Queale's, the old soldier sobbing with fear, and a sense of shared fear which seemed like an entity in itself. 'I was terrified too – it was such pandemonium. At least there was no bomb in the end. It was wicked of someone to say there was.'

'I imagine people are oversensitive just now.'

'People should listen to our pleas and it will stop,' said Miss Tabor, with a small smile.

The door began to open and Miss Tabor sat up straighter, which Margaret would have thought impossible. She half-expected someone to call 'Court rise!'.

In walked an elderly woman in grey, with a stick. She was a dried-up version of her daughter, except that the hint of whimsy in Miss Tabor's mouth was replaced with the look of someone who'd unexpectedly found themselves eating a particularly sour lemon. She was followed by Mr Tabor, who nodded to the ladies, guided his mother to the only comfortable-looking chair in the room, then stepped aside for her to be tended by an equally elderly woman in a black uniform and neat white cap.

'That will do, Eddison. Find out why the tea hasn't been brought in. Good afternoon, ladies. Hedley, introduce me.'

As Mr Tabor did so his mother's gaze rested on each woman in turn, lingering longest on Mrs Philbrook, who shifted awkwardly, making the unforgiving sofa lurch.

'I have known Miss Pendleberry since her childhood, of course,' she said, when the introductions were complete. 'I invited her as a mutual friend of Mrs Foxcroft, who kindly tended my foolish daughter's injury, and of Mrs Philbrook, who I believe goes to the same prayer group as Rhoda. I like to meet Rhoda's friends. I hope none of you are as frivolous as Mrs

Nutford, though judging by those girlish clothes, one can't be too sure.'

'Actually—' said Phoebe.

'Mrs Philbrook likes *The New Dorcas* too, Mother,' said Miss Tabor.

'It was introduced to me by Mrs Holbourne,' said Mrs Philbrook.

'Ah!' breathed Miss Tabor. 'I thought a woman like Mrs Holbourne would share my interest in clothing the deserving poor and the heathens!'

'Heathens are never deserving, Rhoda,' said Mrs Tabor. 'And the poor should shift for themselves. If they want better conditions, they should work harder. However, I would rather you wasted your time knitting and sewing than shrieking for the vote like a harridan. The name Holbourne is familiar. Why is that?'

'The Holbournes have a house near Portland Place, not far from me,' said Phoebe. 'They invest in a good deal of local enterprise and are benefactors of charities like Dorcas Free. Mrs Holbourne, Dr Demeray and I have been friends for many years. Grandmama was very fond of both.'

'Mmm.' Mrs Tabor scanned her guests again, something in her flinty eyes suggesting a cobra swaying as it watched its prey.

'I've only recently heard of *The New Dorcas*, Miss Tabor,' said Margaret. 'Have you a copy you might lend me?'

'I shall give you one before you leave.' Miss Tabor smiled but remained rigid, her white-knuckled hands clenched in her lap.

'Why are you just sitting there, Rhoda?' said Mrs Tabor. 'Pour the tea, please.'

'Sorry, Mother.'

'Eddison, why have you not passed the plates and offered the food?' She turned her gaze on Margaret. 'I understand your husband is a senior officer in some branch of the police force, Mrs Foxcroft. I assume he is tracking down Russians.'

'He hunts out anarchists, Mrs Tabor,' said Mrs Philbrook, before Margaret could respond.

'All anarchists are Russian,' said Mrs Tabor. 'Russians killed my husband in the Afghan campaign in '79. We had to leave India after that.' She turned her head towards a dark portrait of a man in an officer's uniform, glaring at the room down a large nose. Behind him were a hot sky, an impression of Indian edifices and a mountain range. 'Enoch died a hero while defending India from the Russians, but mark my words, they will try again. This government is a fool to be courted by them: a leopard does not change its spots. And India needs a firm hand, just as Ireland does. Why independence? Why Home Rule? What is so terrible about being British? Do they not share our glories? Our knowledge, our superiority, our rich culture: Ovid, Virgil? What do *you* think, Mrs Foxcroft?'

'The Irish, Scots, Welsh, Cornish and Anglo-Saxons all have myths and stories that beat Ovid and Virgil – who weren't British – hands down,' said Margaret. 'Indian poetry was being written when Britons had no written language at all.'

'We have done wonders for India.'

'India's done significantly more for us with little in return, Mrs Tabor,' said Phoebe.

'Nonsense!'

'The ladies have a point, Mother,' said Mr Tabor. His palms were flat on his knees, his fingers a little curled. 'Imagine someone walking in, sitting in your chair and telling us and our servants what we should eat or wear and whom we should worship, while taking our most precious belongings away and treating us as if we were second or third rate. Imagine if I were allowed to join the army or police force but never rise beyond a certain rank, even if I was more capable than the officer above me.'

'Really, Hedley. Where has all this come from? No native can be better than a Briton. It is impossible.'

'A maharaja would outrank me by miles.'

'Ridiculous.' Mrs Tabor gave a low chuckle and smiled an unnerving smile. 'Ladies, I apologise: this conversation has taken a peculiar turn. I shall explain the requirements for polite conversation to the children later. Now, let us talk of something else. Do you know if the dear King and Queen have left for Germany yet? What do you imagine the royal ladies will wear at the wedding?'

An hour later, clasping a copy of *The New Dorcas*, Margaret climbed into a cab with Phoebe and let out a groan. 'That was dreadful. It's not as if either of us is really Miss Tabor's friend.'

'Poor woman,' said Phoebe. 'Hedley will get short shrift for contradicting his mother.'

'I don't understand why he hasn't long gone.'

'It would be easier for him, I agree,' said Phoebe. 'But maybe not much easier. Grandmama said that Lieutenant Colonel Tabor left the money in his wife's control during her lifetime. I suppose at the time of his death the children were still young and he hadn't anticipated dying – which seems rather remiss of a soldier – but there you have it. And Mrs Tabor shows no sign of relinquishing control.'

'Frail, indeed,' said Margaret. She rolled her shoulders. 'I can't wait to tell Maude about it tomorrow over lunch. It's a shame you can't join us. We're meeting at the café attached to Theatre Valerina. I've never been.'

'I shan't be able to attend the soirée tomorrow evening either,' said Phoebe. 'But I'll join you both and the children on Saturday, at St James's Park.' Phoebe nodded at *The New Dorcas*. 'Why did you borrow that rag? Miss Tabor will corner you at suffrage meetings to discuss tatting.'

'That will be a short conversation,' muttered Margaret. She glanced at the cover, with its picture of a smug housewife wielding a needle, and opened the journal.

No wonder the woman on the cover looked smug. The first articles covered sewing or general do-goodery, but the rest was about suffrage. A husband, or didactic mother, would dismiss the journal as feminine drivel, so the reader could read and plot in peace. On the other hand, there was nothing militant which might lead to publication being suppressed, as was happening to *The Suffragette*. No wonder Maude and Mrs Philbrook disdained it. No wonder Miss Halpin had lined her drawers with it. Unless one liked sewing while being mildly agitated about politics, it was of no interest at all.

Thirteen

T he café attached to Theatre Valerina was fresh and busy.

'I thought you didn't like the Bryces, Maude,' whispered Margaret.

'I don't,' said Maude.

'Then why patronise their establishment?'

'I'm observing.' Maude cut a morsel of omelette. 'It's all good copy.'

'For what?'

'Whatever looks interesting.'

Margaret scanned the room as covertly as she could. Posters on the walls declared that the theatre's current programme comprised vaudeville turns followed by a performance of *Little Miss Llewellyn*, starring Miss Bryce. The tables were full, some occupants familiar for reasons Margaret couldn't place, other than perhaps she saw them on her journey to Dorcas Free.

The profile of one short man made her briefly very anxious, until with a shock she recognised him from the underground station on the evening when Fox had nearly gone under the train. A small group of women on one table talked intently. Two young men sat back, plates empty, seemingly lost in thought, until one spoke and the other shrugged, then leant forward to answer. On another table, a thin young man in a threadbare suit held his cup in both hands, a distant, desperate look in his eyes.

Trying not to be obvious, she leaned back to see round a pillar and stifled an exclamation. Dr Gesner was there, consulting a notebook propped against the cruet while eating a slice of pie. He had as much reason as she did to be there. It was as good a place as any for him to lunch.

'Oh!' The waitress's voice made her turn. 'Sorry, sir, I thought...' She was serving the short, stout man, who appeared to have moved seats to the opposite side of his table.

'All the world's a stage, and all the men and women may be players,' said Maude.

'Merely players.'

'I know what I mean. Eat up: chicken aspic looks revolting when it melts.' Maude ate a morsel of omelette, put her cutlery down and dabbed her mouth with the napkin. 'I wondered if Geoff would be here.' She was looking round the room with a good deal less subtlety than Margaret hoped she'd managed, her shoulders tense. 'Lois Halpin used to meet Stokes here occasionally, I think.'

'And Geoff?' said Margaret.

'No, of course not. Anyway, how was afternoon tea with the Tabors?'

'Torture.' Margaret described the event, to Maude's amusement. 'Mrs Philbrook was there. She seems friendly with the family.'

'I've occasionally seen Mr Tabor driving her about. He must always be in the right place at the right time.' She winked.

'She doesn't seem as militant as you. What is the meeting like?'

'The talk is more militant than at Phoebe's, but I initially went because Lois Halpin asked me. She had seen an advertisement in that *New Dorcas* magazine. Such a funny journal.'

'It seems deathly dull.'

Maude nodded. 'The advertisement invited those interested in freedom but daunted by groups dominated by propertied women to meet up. It piqued Lois's interest, so she went. Afterwards, she sent me the advertisement and it piqued mine.'

'Even though you're a propertied woman who dominates groups.'

'You can't talk, Demeray,' said Maude. 'I'm also a journalist, and I see the point. There are those in the movement who look down on Miss Kenney because she was a mill-girl, even though she's one of the best speakers and bravest suffragettes. I felt there might be an article in it.'

'The advertisement explains why Miss Tabor went,' said Margaret. 'She'd have assumed it was a group for shy people rather than working people. But why does Mrs Philbrook stay?'

'Not through shyness,' said Maude. 'Her husband left her terribly badly off, so she has an understanding of financial restraint even if she has enough to live on without getting a job.'

'Did he spend it all on philanthropy?'

Maude snorted. 'Only at the end of his life, to make up for what he'd been spending it on before. I sense she has a lover somewhere.'

'Hedley Tabor?'

'Each to their own. She's rather a dark horse. She—' Maude cleared her throat and straightened up. When she spoke again, her voice was louder than before and her cheeks a little rosy. 'And next time you do a talk, take me. If anyone harangues you, I shall suggest you demonstrate to the audience using their innards.'

'Er, thanks.' The abrupt change of subject was startling, and Margaret turned to see if Mrs Philbrook had entered the café. But the only change was that the short, stout man was leaving.

'Let's discuss other ideas tomorrow evening,' Maude continued.

'What's wrong?' whispered Margaret.

'I half-recognised the plump man who's just gone,' Maude murmured back. 'I swear he's been at a meeting or two, on occasions when Mrs Philbrook seemed anxious. And someone like him once followed another member after she left. I tried to catch up but she managed to evade him and he was going another way, so perhaps I was wrong. He could be Mrs Philbrook's lover and tell her I was gossiping about them, which could cause awkwardness at the soirée.'

'I'm sure he couldn't have heard.' Margaret glanced at the clock. She'd promised Nellie the afternoon off, since her mother had recently had a baby. 'Did you tell the woman she'd been followed?'

'She only really talks to Mrs Philbrook, and that rather intensely, when discussing magazines. She's rather like an angry version of Miss Tabor, and possibly as wearing. I told Mrs Philbrook, who said she'd warn her. If necessary, I'll talk to her tomorrow.'

'Tomorrow?'

'There's a meeting before Phoebe's meeting. It'll be quite the contrast.'

'It'll be quite exhausting.' Margaret looked at her watch. 'Will you cycle some of the way with me before going home? I'm sure Geoff would much rather lunch at the club than come here.' She leaned forward and whispered, 'I went into Miss Halpin's house on Tuesday evening and saw nothing untoward. Have you any idea why she was worried? Was she being threatened, like you?'

'I'm not being threatened,' said Maude, half-turning to beckon the waitress. 'It's *Athene's Gazette*. It's happening to all the suffrage papers. As for Miss Halpin ... no. And I've nothing to pin anything on: it's just a feeling. But I'm sure I'm right.'

The afternoon was hot. In the garden, Margaret rolled balls and built towers from blocks with the children until they staggered off to yank daisies from the lawn. Juniper lay stretched out in the sun, too full of sunshine to mind being decorated with mangled flowers and leaves. Margaret sat against the tree, wishing she felt as content.

Freda strode out from the house, pausing to inspect something in Edie's hand, then picking her up to pass to Margaret along with the post. 'It's nearly time for tea, ma'am, and it's too bright out here for little eyes. But in case you want them to stay out a little longer, I've come to replace the lettuce under their hats.'

'The...?'

'Keeps their heads cool, ma'am. *Everyone* knows that. Anyhow, Miss Edie has picked something up and I'm worried she'll eat it.'

'Thank you, Freda.' Margaret looked at Edie's hands and her own white blouse and decided against pulling her into her lap. 'I'll bring them inside shortly.'

'They'll need their hands washing.'

Margaret swallowed the urge to snap and turned to her daughter as Freda strode away. 'Show Mummy, Edie.'

Edie held out a yellow snail smaller than her own thumbnail. 'Pity sail.'

'Yes, very pretty,' agreed Margaret. 'Don't crush him, darling. Put him down very carefully on the tree. He's sure to be very frightened by a big girl like you.'

'Keep?'

'Snails like to be free to do as they please, but they have to do it very slowly, before anyone notices they're trying to escape. Rather like Mummy these days.'

'Mummy not a sail!' Edie giggled.

Margaret put her fingers on her head like a snail's eyes and waggled them. 'No?'

'No! You more squashy.'

'I hope that's a compliment,' said Margaret. 'Shall we sit here till it's time for your milk?'

'Wanna pay Alec.'

'Two minutes. Don't either of you put anything in your mouths. Including your fingers.'

She watched them for another few moments, then turned her attention to the mail. There were letters from Katherine and her father, in which neither mentioned a date for their return, an invitation to give a talk at a church hall in Edgware, and a letter from Phoebe, with the agenda for the suffrage meeting taking place the following evening. It was a sign of the times that she hadn't simply sent a postcard.

Margaret stood up, pocketed the post and took the children to the scullery to wash their hands. A sudden burst of muttered cursing from the hall made her cover their ears, then peer round the corner.

Dinah, the char, was bumping her way out of the store-room, dragging the new vacuum cleaner as if it was a naughty schoolboy about to be very sorry for whatever he'd done to the unidentifiable object in her other hand. 'I don't know what the missus was thinking of, getting you,' she snapped, giving the vacuum cleaner a shake. 'It'd cost her the same to hire another maid a coupla days a week, and she'd be a whole lot less trouble, even when she has her monthlies— Oh! Hello, doctor. I, er... wasn't expecting to see you here.' Dinah blushed deep scarlet.

'The children and I have been in the garden,' said Margaret. 'I thought the device might save all of you some time. What's the difficulty?'

'Well,' said Dinah, scowling, 'the thing about brooms and mops and carpet beaters and dustpans is that not a one of them has more than two parts to worry about and it's clear how to work them. Every time I empties this bl— dashed thing, I have to put it back together. Things that look like they fit don't. And things that don't fit do. I mean, it's all gotta go somewhere, and you musta spent – what – four guineas on it, so I don't want to break it.'

'You could have fooled me by the way you're dragging it around,' said Margaret, inspecting the machine and wishing she knew where to start. The children prodded it, then crowed 'Daddy!'

'Er, is everything all right, Dinah?' said Fox.

'Can't work out where this bit goes, sir.'

She waved the item at Fox, who put his head on one side, then took it from her and attached it swiftly and firmly. 'There you are.'

'Thanks, sir,' said Dinah. 'It's not often I need a man, but this thing has me beat.'

Fox nodded to her. 'Could you come, Margaret? It's important.' He left the kitchen.

She scurried after him. 'How did—'

'Sorry if I pre-empted you showing Dinah what to do.'

'Er...'

Fox raised his eyebrows, a grin forming on his lips. 'It was obvious, wasn't it?

'Yes, of course.'

He swept the children up and kissed them.

'I wasn't expecting to see you home so early,' she said.

'I'm afraid I need to pack a case, ready to leave first thing tomorrow.'

'You can't go anywhere.' Margaret tried to keep a smile in her voice. 'Your cholera belt is at the laundry.'

'I don't need it,' he said, kissing her again. 'And I'll be back on Sunday morning. I'm not going far.'

'Bikkits,' said Alec. 'Daddy, bikkit time.'

'Freda will have put milk and biscuits in the nursery,' said Margaret. 'I need to take them up.'

'Nellie can deal with that. You can help me pack.'

'I gave Nellie some time off. She has a new baby sister.'

'What number is that?'

'Eleven, I think. I'm wondering if I should have a word with her mother about ways to avoid a twelfth, but I suspect she'd think it was interfering with nature. Freda can manage till six o'clock.'

After they'd left the children in the nursery, Margaret watched Fox pack a change of clothes and his toiletries. 'Have you found the woman?'

'No, but she'd sent a letter to Queale's sister which we should have had two weeks ago. It was one of the items caught up in the Carmelo Street bomb. Not destroyed, but sufficiently scorched to take a while to decipher who it was for. When she received it, there was a letter inside addressed to Queale. The sister didn't know whether to open it or not, fearing it might distress her. It was only recently that she wondered if it might help Queale's case, which she thinks is a misunderstanding about embezzlement. Thankfully, she contacted one of us, not the police.'

'And it's coincidence that both came from Carmelo Street?'

'The handwriting is quite different to that on the parcel, what's left of it.'

'That's not an answer.'

Fox shrugged.

'So you know who the woman is?' said Margaret.

'No, but we let Queale out on a short leash again. This time, we managed to intercept his mail before a suffragette set fire to the postbox.'

'That isn't funny, Fox.'

'No, it isn't. Queale had sent identical advertisements to be placed in both *The Lady* and *The New Dorcas*. They're addressed to BLS from George, with a series of letters and numbers in between and "alt" in brackets partway along. Smith was convinced it was a code, especially since Queale's forenames are Silas Alfred, not George, but Elinor reminded him that Queale's diary is full of dragon-slaying references – the dragons being us – and said the rest were Bible verses. Naturally I knew them all by heart, but I had her write them down in case a heathen like you didn't.'

'I shan't remind you that you can barely remember the way to church.'

'Churches are stuffy.' Fox opened a piece of paper. '"The wicked plotteth against the just, and gnasheth upon him with his teeth. The Lord shall laugh at him; for he seeth that his day is coming. Their sword shall enter into their own heart, and their bows shall be broken." Then "alt" in brackets, then "I pray not that thou shouldst take them out of the world, but that thou shouldst keep them from the evil one. Discretion shall preserve thee, understanding shall keep thee. Better is the end of a thing than the beginning thereof and the patient in spirit is better than the proud in spirit. And let us not be weary in well doing, for in due season we shall reap if we faint not."' He stretched his jaw. 'My mouth hurts.'

'That's because you're gnashing upon Queale with your teeth.'

'What a revolting thought.'

'It seems easy enough to decipher,' said Margaret. '"I'm still in deep trouble but hope to get out of it. I hope you haven't destroyed the papers, simply kept them safe somewhere.'

'Agreed.'

'What did you do next?'

'Put them back in the mail so that we can watch for a reply,' said Fox. 'Elinor has her clerks going through back issues of both journals, looking for similar messages and possible replies. It's probably hopeless, given the amount of sanctimonious drivel people pay to have printed, but it's one of those digging jobs we have clerks for.'

'Maybe the rest aren't Bible verses.'

Fox grunted. 'One can only hope so, and also hope that BLS, presumably Brave Little Suffragette, doesn't act on her own initiative. The treaty is due to be signed in a week. It's just waiting and watching for the moment. Elinor and Bert are doing that.'

'Therefore you're packing for something else?'

'Not precisely.' Fox laid his case on the bed. 'Who knew where we were keeping Queale, and tried to kill him – and potentially my men – with a letter bomb? Who followed him on Monday and stirred up a panic on the underground, during which they intended to push him under a train? Does that person want him dead to stop the documents being published? Or to force the mistress's hand into publishing them, out of grief? Or—'

'Or for their own profit, if they can find them by cutting out the – for want of a better word – possessor, which puts the mistress at risk.'

'Yes: there's money to be made from war. I think this is Abney's doing. He won't care about picking a side; he'll sell to the highest bidder.'

'So you have to go to Flanders.'

'Abney's still not home,' said Fox. 'And there are plenty of agents and couriers in Britain to take a closer look at first.'

'A closer look? You know who they are?'

'A good many of them, yes. And strange as it seems, it's sometimes best to let them work, while keeping an eye on them to see where they lead. What they do share, we can often influence or intercept. It's like an intricate dance.'

'Don't make it sound less than dangerous, Fox.'

He pulled her into his arms. 'I know what I'm doing. And tonight we shall attend a soirée and forget it all. I shall be back on Sunday.'

Fourteen

The soirée, taking place in the ballroom of the hospital's greatest benefactor, was well-attended and hot. A river of tunes from a string ensemble trickled between the guests as they circulated and chatted, sharing Dorcas Free's triumphs and veering away from anything distressing. Margaret wore a new teal gown with silvery trimmings, wondering if she appeared as odd to the other female doctors, who wore a simple grey uniform to work, as they did to her. Dr Naylor was almost frivolous in a delicate dove-grey dress which revealed a little of her throat. Dr Callendar was self-conscious in a highly fashionable deep-pink frock with a narrow skirt, while Dr Howe wore a plain and somehow sensible gown of dark green.

Dr Innes walked up to Margaret with a small, bespectacled woman in her mid-thirties wearing a perfectly fitting mustard-yellow dress. He introduced her as the Honourable Daphne someone or other, the surname lost in a sudden burst of laughter from Mr Bryce who, being a local businessman, was interested in becoming a benefactor himself.

The Honourable Daphne shook hands as Dr Innes went to greet Maude and Geoff. 'Bernard says you're quite the suffragette,' she said, her voice drawling a little. 'But you helped him immensely at that regrettable incident on the underground the other day, your views notwithstanding.'

Margaret blinked. This must be Dr Southern's wife, perhaps ten years older and several rungs above him on the social scale. There was little point in arguing that he and Margaret had worked on an equal footing. Either Mrs Southern had no idea that her husband exaggerated his own importance, or perhaps she had every idea, but was too loyal and well-bred to show it. A social event wasn't the moment to find out.

'There was no bomb, suffragette or otherwise. That was a misunderstanding.'

'Oh. One doesn't read the newspapers. Only the *Poetry Review*, the *Lady* and occasionally *Athene's Gazette*.'

'The latter supports votes for women, you know.'

'One wants the vote,' said Mrs Southern. 'And one is fully in support of enterprises such as Dorcas Free. But violence is unfeminine and unpatriotic. The Empire needs women as its backbone, now more than ever. A little window and lamp-smashing is not so bad – very satisfying, and irritating without being injurious. One did that sort of thing once or twice as a young girl. Did you?' She didn't wait for an answer. 'The vote will come in due course. Speaking of the Empire, I gather your husband is a rather superior bobby.' She gave a tiny chuckle as she enunciated the slang. 'I suppose his men will be guarding the delegates at St James's Palace.'

'I really couldn't say,' said Margaret.

'I suppose not.' Mrs Southern turned towards Fox, who was speaking with Dr Gesner and Mrs Innes, as Mrs Philbrook walked towards them, her turned-out toes kicking at a wine-red skirt.

'I believe you are acquainted with my friend Sabina?' said Mrs Southern.

'I am indeed.' They shook hands.

'Sabina's late husband worked with my father to create Dorcas Free. Did you know?'

'Yes,' said Margaret. 'It's a wonderful institution and you must both be very proud.'

'We are.' Mrs Southern offered her hand again and made a slight bow. 'Delighted to make your acquaintance, Dr Demeray. One must speak with Dr Howe.'

'Delighted to make yours, too.'

'Our paths do keep crossing this week, doctor,' said Mrs Philbrook, with a warm smile. 'At least this event is relaxing and uncontentious. I've been speaking with your husband – quite the oyster, isn't he? I suppose your job has its confidential elements, too. Whatever do you talk about at home? I should be terrible at keeping quiet about what I do.'

'I don't believe that for a moment,' said Margaret. 'Every suffragette has secrets, though mine are rather old and dusty. I'm sure you're very discreet.'

Mrs Philbrook put her finger to her lips and winked. '"Self-reverence, self-knowledge, self-control; these three alone lead one to sovereign power.".'

'Sovereign power?'

'A quotation from Tennyson. Does Mrs Holbourne tell you what she is planning?'

'Apart from seeking justice for Miss Halpin and Mr Stokes, not at all.'

'I wondered if she'd thought of disrupting the royal wedding in Germany, but it seems not,' said Mrs Philbrook. 'Something seems to be on her mind.'

Margaret couldn't see Maude's face from where they were standing. She wondered if there had been another threatening letter, or if she'd been followed. She felt uneasy. 'Is your group quite safe?' she asked. 'Unbothered by opponents?'

'It's not *my* group,' said Mrs Philbrook. 'I simply attend, but we all take care of each other. Mrs Southern and I shall be at the Epsom Derby: perhaps we'll see you there. Hello again, Mr

Holbourne. I'll leave you two to talk while I reacquaint myself with Mr Bryce. He's rather refreshing.'

Geoff shook hands. 'Good evening, M. I thought you enjoyed hobnobbing. You look a little weary.'

'Busy day,' said Margaret. 'And Mr Bryce's laugh is giving me a headache, although I agree with Mrs Philbrook. There are a lot of stuffed shirts and bodices in this room. The Bryces seem more honest, somehow.'

'I wish Maude agreed. She's always complained that I'm too idle, yet when I find something to be involved with, she's angry. I don't interfere with her investments, but she doesn't seem to think I deserve the same respect. Do you know why?'

'Is it a risky investment?'

Geoff looked baffled. 'The riskiest thing I've ever done is marry Maude. I just like the theatre... Could your cousin Albert speak with her? He's rather a whizz with money.'

'I'm not sure Maude would appreciate that,' said Margaret.

Geoff stopped a waitress and took a glass of wine for himself and Margaret. 'May I be frank?'

'I'm not going to criticise Maude behind her back.'

'No, of course not.' Geoff took a sip of wine, then stared into the middle distance. 'The Valerina is very close to Carmelo Street, which someone tried to blow up, and a Miss Halpin who might have been involved was shot a few roads away soon afterwards.'

'Maude had nothing to do with that bomb.'

'She won't discuss anything related to the militant campaign.'

'She's very upset about Miss Halpin.' Margaret was troubled. Why was Maude discussing it with her and not Geoff?

'Miss Halpin was militant, wasn't she?'

'That doesn't make her guilty of bombing.' Margaret put her hand on Geoff's arm. 'You must talk to Maude.'

'I haven't been able to since she was last in Holloway.' Geoff's expression had its usual amiable vacancy, but his eyes darted as if he were chasing thoughts. 'She thinks I'm angry that she was imprisoned. I was, perhaps. The children were so upset, and she was treated so badly and came home so changed.' His voice cracked and he cleared his throat again. 'She'll be all right in the end, won't she? Her throat and her appetite and her humour and her...Maudeness? I've thought of moving us to India.'

'Maude would hate the memsahibs. She'd be too forthright and loathe club life. I bet you would, too.'

'Australia, then. She'd have the vote there. Or do I mean New Zealand?'

'Both. But Maude wants the vote here. And you have your business interests. Wouldn't you want to see them come to something?'

'Not as much as I'd like Maude back,' said Geoff. 'She's unhappy, so I'm unhappy. You're not happy about her either, are you?'

'It's not unhappiness,' said Margaret, 'it's worry.'

'That goes without saying.' Geoff mumbled into his wine. 'Unless it's something else she's trying to stop me finding out. If there's another man, I don't want to know.'

'That's absurd,' said Margaret, but Geoff had moved away and Dr Naylor was approaching with a well-heeled gentleman. She didn't know if Geoff had heard her. Even as she said it, she met Maude's eyes across the room and realised that she could no longer read her friend at all.

Fox left early the following morning. Margaret caught up on work in the afternoon then left for the meeting at Phoebe's, arriving at seven.

Mr Tabor deposited his sister but said he couldn't stay, as he had offered to drive Mrs Philbrook to a small dinner being held by Dorcas Free governors, and collect her afterwards. Something furtive about his smile suggested the intimacy Maude had hinted.

Maude herself, across the room, seemed irritable, interrupting the agenda with a blunt question. 'What has anyone actually done recently?'

Mrs Nutford said that when she'd been out for tea with Miss Tabor earlier in the month, she'd knocked off a policeman's hat with her umbrella. To her chagrin, he had assumed it was accidental. Or possibly, thought Margaret, he had decided there were better things to worry about than two small middle-aged suffragettes on a rainy day in May.

'My friend and I blocked the keyhole of a courthouse staff entrance with putty one night,' said Miss McCabe. 'Then we pasted a Votes for Women poster over it with strong glue.'

'I took a hammer to my member of parliament's window,' said Mrs Snoville-Lewis. 'I recommend a small hammer to everyone. They're quite cheap, according to my maid.'

'Did you do it in the dead of night?'

'Well, yes.'

'It's not enough,' said Maude. 'Members of parliament should be tackled directly. Their journeys to the Commons made impossible, their houses uninhabitable, their lives miserable until they accede to our request. This is not an embroidery contest. This is one battle in a long line: rebel barons, the Peasants' Revolt, the Civil War, Peterloo, Chartists, the Reform League. Women died alongside men to bring about change. Why are we sitting here as if we're organising a tea-party?'

'Mrs Holbourne is so very underappreciated,' Miss Tabor whispered to Margaret. 'How can they not see the truth of what she says? This is a war, and we must go into battle.'

Margaret tried to imagine Miss Tabor going into battle, when it was unlikely she'd ever been armed with anything more dangerous than an embroidery hoop. Out of the corner of her eye, she could see Maude coming to the boil.

Phoebe's sister-in-law Etta held up a finger. 'Anticipating you, Mrs Holbourne. Item one on the agenda: a march on parliament to—'

'No!' Maude rose. 'Other groups don't waste time with marches! Women, including several here, have endured prison for the cause. There needs to be more direct action.'

'I agree,' said Mrs Nutford. 'We marched on parliament on Black Friday. All those of us who could, that is.' She frowned at Etta. 'And look what happened.' Her voice trembled. 'We were treated appallingly and gained nothing but bruises.'

To Margaret's immense surprise Miss Tabor also stood up, her tremulous voice barely audible. ' Yes! I—'

'That was nearly three years ago,' declared Etta.

Miss Tabor cleared her throat. 'Yes, but—'

Louder voices drowned hers. Margaret, feeling sudden pity for someone who was never heard, called out 'Miss Tabor has something to say!'

The room fell silent. Miss Tabor, beetroot red, crushed her dainty handkerchief in mortification.

'Go on,' whispered Margaret.

'I— I shall never forget Black Friday, *never*. I shall support this cause until I die, but I shall not suffer another man – neither jeering policemen at the behest of the Home Secretary, nor the baying crowd – to treat me as I was treated then. Nor will I willingly be party to any *other* woman being subjected to such manhandling. When I heard that they threw Mrs Billingshurst from her wheeled chair, it showed from what depths of humanity some police are taken. Mrs Pankhurst says we should take a different approach.'

'Whenever I mention direct action, I'm shouted down by Dr Demeray,' snapped Etta.

The room turned to Margaret.

'I disagree with fire-bombs or vitriol,' she said. 'Suffragettes are being blamed for what happened at Carmelo Street post office, and also for a hoax on the underground, though neither has been claimed by anyone. The press is hinting that the death of a militant suffragette actress was in revenge. I don't want to harm anyone in the name of our cause, whoever they are.'

'You hurt quite a few policemen on Black Friday,' pointed out Phoebe. 'Your anatomical knowledge came in rather handy, as I recall.'

'If they see fit to grab us by our breasts or groins, they should expect similar in return,' said Margaret. 'That's beside the point, though. Black Friday was an unequal battle, even though *we* were vilified in the press as aggressors. And it was nearly three years ago.'

Miss Tabor was still trembling. 'I never thought the respectable press could print such lies. Those reporters stood by while women were thrown into crowds of men, to be treated as those men wished, and all they wrote of was our unwomanly behaviour when defending ourselves. I still have nightmares about that day.'

'And nothing whatsoever has changed,' said Maude. 'They play cat and mouse with us in public, as they do in prison. One minute they're considering us, then they drop us for the Irish question. The Irish question is in the ascendant now, but who knows if that'll be dropped for something else, which will cause another problem altogether. We can't trust them.'

'We should go underground,' said Phoebe. 'If we brought the country to a halt, they would *have* to listen to us.'

'I like the idea of setting fire to things, like Maude does,' said Etta airily, as if discussing flower arranging.

'Are you prepared to do it yourself?' snapped Margaret.

Etta wriggled slightly. 'It's very difficult for me to get away. The children, you know.'

Maude gave Etta a disgusted glare. 'I have children, and I generally spend a good deal more than ten minutes a day with them, but I was prepared to sacrifice that and risk prison.'

'Without setting fire to anything, we could make it hard for the whole country to run,' said Phoebe, in a loud clear voice. 'Barricade telephone exchanges, or telegraph offices, or post offices, or railway stations.'

'Good idea!' exclaimed Mrs Nutford. 'We could take it in turns for days. Just as one group is moved away by the police, another group moves in. Bring everything to a standstill without necessarily doing damage.'

The others exchanged glances. Their expressions varied from excitement to fear to misery.

'Would we get arrested?' asked a shop assistant.

'Possibly,' said Maude. 'But it's an honour, and we'd all be here for each other afterwards.'

Margaret bit her lip. Life was never that simple. 'I maintain, as I always have, that if all women everywhere, regardless of their rank or status, stopped doing what they usually do for forty-eight hours, men would see that we are neither irrelevant nor unimportant.'

Etta cleared her throat. 'I propose we discuss what could be done, then draw up a rota. If we plan it properly, it might be quite fun.'

'It's not supposed to be fun,' snapped Margaret. 'It's supposed to be effective. And what are *you* going to do?'

'I'm a busy woman, my dear, but I shall be behind the scenes, subtly orchestrating things. You won't even notice I'm there.'

Maude scowled. 'For the first time, Etta, you've said something I agree with. I'm absolutely certain we won't.' She licked her lips and took a breath. 'This is a war and there are battles to be fought, if women are brave enough. If no one in this group is prepared to do that, you will have to understand if I leave. By all means, Etta, draw up your rota. Miss Halpin and Mr Stokes were both murdered because they supported the cause. Their murderers should be brought to justice and the campaign must not lose momentum. I am for stronger action than this group proposes. That is all I'll say on the matter.' She looked round the room, meeting every person's eyes, then left.

'How can anyone reject that call to arms?' breathed Miss Tabor. 'Mrs Holbourne must feel so betrayed.'

Margaret didn't reply. Maude hadn't looked betrayed, but dangerous. She listened to the remainder of the meeting without comment and as coffee was being served, took her leave of Phoebe in the hallway. 'I'm worried about Maude,' she said.

'So am I,' said Phoebe.

'Should we telephone?'

'Best not, I think.' Phoebe sighed. 'I promised I'd take Miss Tabor home. I can't say I'm looking forward to it. All that wittering.'

'We're supposed to be going out with Maude tomorrow,' said Margaret. 'I daresay that's off.'

'Don't be too sure.'

Phoebe kissed her, then returned to the meeting as Margaret climbed into the cab which had been hailed for her.

When she reached home, the streetlights had come on, and while the hall light was still off, the lamp in the sitting room shone to welcome her. As Margaret put the key in the lock, a feeling of disquiet unnerved her. She pushed the door open and listened, just able to make out soft, indistinct chatter coming from the kitchen. The house smelled of polish, baking, and fresh flowers. She was being foolish.

She stepped forward and tripped, stumbling in the darkness and grabbing the hall stand to steady herself. The china dish on the stand slid to the floor and smashed.

The kitchen door opened, illuminating two female silhouettes. 'Doctor, is that you?' Nellie's voice.

'Yes! I caught my foot on the mat. We'll need the dustpan and brush.'

'Yes, ma'am,' said Freda.

Margaret found the switch and turned the lights on, then looked down. The mat was in its usual place, but on it was a brown-paper parcel addressed to her, with neither stamp nor postmark. It was just small enough to go through a letterbox and just big enough to trip over.

'Can someone make me some tea?' she called. 'Don't rush.'

'Yes, ma'am.'

Margaret crouched, her heart thumping. She could see no grease on the parcel and there was no odd smell. All the same, she took an umbrella from the stand and hooked its handle under the string, then took it into the front garden. Under the streetlight, it appeared innocuous. Margaret cursed herself for being oversensitive and took it into the sitting room.

Inside was a small box containing the type of small hammer Mrs Pankhurst encouraged suffragettes to keep in their handbags and a typed note saying *Keep me out of sight*.

'Good grief, Maude,' muttered Margaret. 'Is this a peace offering or a call to arms? You scared me to death.'

She balanced the hammer in her hand. She had no intention of putting it in her handbag. It was tiny and light, designed for hammering nothing bigger than a tack, but thinking of Maude's furious face and clenched hands, it unnerved her. As Nellie and Freda came down the hall, chattering, she shoved it back in its wrapping, buried it deep in the bureau and locked the drawer.

Fifteen

Margaret had expected Maude to call off the trip to St James's Park, but first thing in the morning she telephoned to arrange when she and Phoebe would collect her and the children. It was as if no angry words had been exchanged, Margaret's ideas had not been dismissed, and no hammer had been delivered as either a prompt, or worse, a taunt. Perhaps it was best to let things lie.

'I apologise if I undermined you last night,' said Margaret, once they were settled at the park and unpacking the hamper. 'It wasn't my intention.'

'I said my piece,' said Maude. 'I'll still attend occasionally to stir you all up, if Phoebe doesn't mind.'

'Please do,' said Phoebe, pouring lemonade into small cups. 'You say all the things to Etta that I can't. I'd rather retain our friendship.'

'Absolutely,' said Maude. She sipped at her lemonade and winced. 'I should have brought one of Geoff's hip flasks. I daresay even Mr Tabor has one to liven up a picnic. Although perhaps not. He and his sister are like children, so ridiculously excited about getting away from their mamma. I really can't see ours being like that, can you?' She paused. 'Could either of you change your working days next week to have Wednesday free?'

'Hardly,' said Phoebe. 'On Wednesday there's a presentation assembly for the parents.'

'I might be able to,' said Margaret. 'Why?'

'I feel we could do with blowing some cobwebs away. Shall we go to the Epsom Derby? I've always wanted to take you to a race, Demeray: you don't let your hair down enough these days. Edwards will put the bets on for us. Just us and no men. Quite modern.'

Margaret frowned. 'If you were that modern, Maude, you'd put your own sixpence on instead of asking your chauffeur.'

Maude ignored the slight. 'Are you worried your Calvinist ancestors will spin in their graves?'

'Let them,' said Margaret. 'All right, I'll ask.' She sat up straighter and watched the children. Eleven-year-old Becca was holding Edie's hand as they crouched near a sleeping duck. Maude's sons, Sam and Johnny were playing 'It' with Alec. Margaret sketched them as she sat on the grass, then looked around at the wider scene.

A dainty middle-aged woman had passed, scurrying at speed. From behind, she was sparrow-like in a smart beige costume topped by a boater with a pink ribbon, the roll of grey hair at her nape neatly pinned with a tortoiseshell comb. 'Isn't that Miss Tabor?' she said.

Phoebe followed her gaze. 'Mrs Tabor would never let her out alone. Besides, have you ever seen Miss Tabor do anything that rapid or decisive? She's of a similar build and you were just speaking about Miss Tabor. Don't you think so, Maude?'

But Maude was too busy watching the children. 'Hi!' she called. 'Stop that!' She threw the cup down and jumped to her feet. Sam was chasing a duck towards the water and Alec and Johnny were running after a squirrel. Flinging her sketchbook aside and leaving Phoebe to mind Edie, Margaret rushed after Alec.

It was easier to catch a child of eighteen months than one of nearly six, but even so, Alec's turn of speed was impressive. By the time she and Maude were settled back on the grass, Maude's chest heaving as she recovered from the effort of running, and Phoebe was tempting the children with more items from the hamper, the woman who might have been Miss Tabor was forgotten.

When Phoebe took her turn to walk the children to the water's edge, Maude said 'How did you find the soirée?'

'Headache-inducing, but hopefully also effective for fundraising.'

'I daresay you saw the Bryces.'

Margaret put her head on one side. 'Why do you dislike them so? Are you worried they'll use Geoff's money for risqué productions?'

'Bryce is too canny for that.' Maude clicked the catch on her handbag repeatedly, a sign that she longed for a cigarette.

'Have you told Geoff your concerns about Miss Halpin and Mr Stokes? If you won't go to the police with your suspicions, he could.'

'I don't trust the police and Geoff won't discuss anything political even the Balkan conference.' Maude gestured in the direction of St James's Palace. 'He probably thinks I'd try to set fire to it.'

'Would you?'

'I doubt Fox and his pals would let me close enough,' said Maude, with an ambiguous grin. 'But no. The situation in the Balkans is dreadful and something needs to be done.'

Margaret's legs had pins and needles and she shifted position. 'It would be an opportunity to make a point.'

'Don't goad me, Demeray.'

'Will *Athene's Gazette* discuss the merits of the various allegiances being made?'

Maude stared at her. 'Good God, no: I'd lose half my readership if I did. I want women to have the vote. I can't concentrate on anything else until we have it.' Her voice was hoarse again.

'Stop talking, Maude.'

'I'm afraid for you and Phoebe, and anyone who supports the cause. I'm more concerned for those who are militant than those who are not, but the average fanatic isn't very discerning about whom they select as a victim. You undertook post-mortems on Jeremiah Stokes and Lois Halpin. Couldn't you see the similarities?'

'Yes and no. How long have you been a member of that group they were in?'

'Since March. There's no apparent leader: everyone says their piece and acts according to their conscience.'

'Like a Quaker meeting with violent intent.'

'Not violence,' said Maude. 'Direct action. Arson.'

'Unless it's a ruin in the middle of a deserted island, arson always risks life.'

'I have always taken care to ensure no one was around,' said Maude. 'The only person at risk was me.'

'You kept petrol and kindling in your garden shed!' said Margaret. 'Your children or the servants could have—'

'I did nothing of the sort!' snapped Maude, then started to cough. 'If someone says that, they put it there,' she wheezed. 'It's part of a pattern. I might have been a victim myself through apparent incompetence.'

'And you're sure it's because of your political views?'

'Yes.'

'On suffrage?'

'That's all I care about.'

'What about Stokes and Miss Halpin?'

'What about them?' Maude's jaw had set and she was looking towards the children and Phoebe.

Margaret cast her mind back to Miss Halpin's inquest. Mr Bessemer had given his evidence in a strong North London accent: 'The old lady was bad enough, but Jonas Carter turned her head with even more sinful ideas.'

Mrs Bessemer, talking of her sister in a low, soft trembling Belfast voice. Tearful, barely distinct. 'She was secretive because she knew we wouldn't approve.' Had they meant immorality, irreligion, socialism, anarchy or something they considered downright treacherous?

'What was Miss Halpin like in prison?' Margaret asked.

'We barely had time to speak with each other,' said Maude. 'Besides, she was sent to the hospital wing.'

'Why?'

'The guards threw a bucket of water over her when she didn't work fast enough one morning and she fell ill. After Emily Davison, among others, nearly died last year when cells were flooded, I imagine they didn't dare risk Lois developing pneumonia. The government may not like us, but I doubt they want us to die in their establishment.'

'One hopes not.'

'Lois was keen to get married as soon as possible and distance herself from a sister she loved, but found irritating, and a brother-in-law she loathed. They disagreed on Irish Home Rule. The Bessemers are fervent Unionists, Carter and Lois republicans. I doubt they're the only family in conflict.'

'No,' said Margaret, recalling Fox's assertion that Ireland would not become free of Britain without blood.

Maude frowned. 'Oh Lord.' She stared into the distance.

Margaret waited but Maude didn't elaborate. 'Do you think there's anything in the Bessemers' assertion that Mr Carter arranged for Miss Halpin to be shot?'

'Public notice was given for a July wedding,' said Maude. 'Why set a date then murder the person you want to marry?'

Her voice was hoarse and her face anxious. 'Much as I loathe fussing over you, Demeray, not only are you a suffragette, but you did the post-mortems on those two. You'll have reached conclusions you didn't report in public. The truth is... Stokes was worried about someone and confided in Lois, and eventually she confided in me. But she wasn't clear, and she died before I could ask her to explain. All I know is that the woman they were worried about is another suffragette who's planning something stupid or is under threat. Whatever it is, she's in danger. So I have reason to worry about you as much as anyone.'

'You needn't,' said Margaret.

'Because Fox will protect you?'

'Because I can protect myself. And I'm not planning anything. Just worry about yourself and talk things over with Geoff.'

'Don't fuss,' said Maude, the moment of visible emotion past. 'Just because you and Fox are still ridiculously sentimental.'

'You and Geoff should rekindle that.'

'You should mind your own business.'

On Sunday, it felt too hot for any sort of roast lunch and the children were still too small for a restaurant, so Margaret had Freda make up a simple picnic. Leaving a note for Fox, they took it to Hyde Park.

Once they had eaten, the maids packed up the hamper as the children resisted all attempts to make them rest.

'Sam-Sam?' said Alec hopefully, peering about.

'No Sam today,' said Margaret. 'Just Mummy, Nellie and Freda.'

'And Daddy!' Alec pointed, bouncing up and down.

Fox emerged from behind a tree and swept him up. 'I was trying to surprise you all. I must be losing my skills.'

'Silly Daddy.'

'Lotta ducka!' said Edie, pointing as he picked her up too. 'Daddy catch one.'

'No, thanks,' said Fox. 'Ducks are too wet and flappy.'

'Silly Daddy. Catcha Edie!' Edie got up and hurried away with the rolling gait of a sailor.

'Me too!' cried Alec, rushing after her.

'Can't your children stay where they're supposed to?' grumbled Fox.

'I'm not the one who keeps disappearing,' said Margaret. 'It must be in the blood. Go and catch them. If they fall in the water, Nellie will make you do the laundry.'

'Can a man get no peace?'

'No.'

Margaret told Nellie and Freda to go home and take the afternoon off, then watched Fox chase the children, who crowed and giggled and looked over their shoulders to see if he was following, stumbling where the ground was uneven. Neither of them showed any signs of red-headedness so far. Both Alec's and Edie's wavy locks were white-blond. Alec had Margaret's blue eyes and Edie had Fox's green. Edie stumbled and Fox scooped her up before she fell, then tucked Alec under his other arm before bringing them, giggling and squirming, back to Margaret.

'Daddy's too old for this sort of thing,' grumbled Fox. 'He needs to lie down. Are you two going to lie down too?'

'No,' said Alec, knuckling his eyes. 'Alec a lion.'

'Edie too,' said Edie. 'Grr.' She yawned.

'You're not real lions,' said Margaret. 'Real lions always lie very still and pretend to be asleep. You can't do that.'

'Can.'

'Can too.'

Fox lay back on the blanket. The children lay down against him and after a little squirming, fell asleep.

'Well done,' said Margaret.

'I come home so that I don't have to chase anyone,' said Fox, opening his eyes. 'It's very unfair.'

'Alec was running faster yesterday,' said Margaret. 'And you're not wearing a corset.'

'Have you looked?' Fox winked, then eased his arms out from under the children to let Margaret put them in the perambulator.

'I'll check later.' Her smile faded. 'Did you have to chase anyone?'

'No. But I didn't find much out, either. Surveillance on Abney suggests he left his Flanders home at least a week ago. Elinor's wading through passenger lists and port entries.' He gestured to the blanket. 'Come and lie down. How have things been here?'

'Maude is still convinced someone is out to kill suffragettes and started with Stokes and Lois Halpin.'

Fox yawned. 'When did Stokes, whoever he is, die?'

'Easter.'

'They're moving very slowly, given all the people they have to get through. At this rate, our grandchildren will be voting before they're half done.'

'Don't be facetious.'

'It's nonsense. Maude has brain fever.'

'There's no such thing. Something's niggling me about it, something which points away from suffrage, though I'm not sure what. But Maude's stuck on her idea.'

Fox grunted. 'When did you do all this questioning? At the suffrage meeting?'

'No. That was awful and quite another story. But yesterday, she, Phoebe, the children and I all went to St James's Park.'

He opened one eye. 'Did you hear anything?'

'Nothing unusual. Why?'

'There were reports of an odd noise somewhere near the underground.'

Margaret shrugged. 'London is noisy. That's why I'm unnerved in the countryside: it's too quiet and the sounds are too spasmodic. Has Elinor found anything out from the small ads?'

'Yes and no,' said Fox. 'Quotations from Tennyson, the Bible and any number of sentimental books which boil down to "I'm sending you documents – hide them", "I've hidden them" and an awful lot more "We must meet in secret" and "When we are free to marry", and so on.'

'Coded?'

'Only Smith thinks so. I just think that, devotional texts aside, the two of them have a taste for the nauseatingly romantic. They're like a middle-aged Romeo and Juliet.'

'Maude thinks *we're* ridiculously sentimental.'

'Let her.' Fox cuddled her closer and kissed her forehead.

'Will your questioning of Queale become more, er, vigorous?'

'Not on my watch. There are subtler ways of getting information which is more likely to be true. So why was the meeting awful?'

'Maude said we were all too unmilitant, then sent me a Mrs Pankhurst-pleasing hammer. I'm not sure whether it's a goad, a reminder of my deficiencies, or she's noticed one of my pictures is askew. I didn't know how to ask without annoying her.'

Fox made a noise in response, but she feared it was instinctive as he had fallen asleep. Despite the sun and the joy of having her family around her, Margaret wondered if he'd heard her, and wondered why she still felt uneasy.

Sixteen

On Monday morning, Margaret bade farewell to Miss Lewin.

'Matron went to see my home, to be sure my mother can care for me during my convalescence,' said Miss Lewin. Her deafness was improving by the day. She was pink and seemed to be gaining confidence. 'Dr Callender says I'll regain use of my left hand to a large degree, and someone will train me in occupational craft work to strengthen it until I can go back to work.' She smiled. 'It might help calm my nerves. Everything makes me jump.'

'I'm not surprised,' said Margaret. 'But in time and with help, I'm sure you'll overcome that. You're a strong woman.'

'I was worried about my fiancé,' said Miss Lewin. 'Matron allowed one visit. I was so anxious about telling him the engagement ring had had to be cut off, but he said what did I take him for? He doesn't care about the hand, either. We're not getting married for a year or two, so I should have time to learn how to do housework and cook before I have to leave the post office. I'm going to tell everyone how kind you've all been to me.'

'That's wonderful news,' said Margaret.

'Was that address any good? I've been thinking and thinking. I reckon it was St John's Wood. The splodges of grease blurred it, but now I think of it, I'm sure.'

Margaret frowned. 'St John's Wood? Not St James's?' The sense that she'd missed something crucial returned. 'And it was addressed to S Queale, Esquire?'

Miss Lewin shrugged. 'I don't remember an Esquire, but there were splodges all over, so who knows. But it was definitely NW, not SW. Then again, people put all sorts on envelopes and half the time leave the postal code off altogether. Whoever they were, at least they weren't blown up.' She shivered, then brightened again. 'Thanks for coming, doctor. I'll write and let you know how I'm getting on after I'm home.'

On her return to the mortuary wing, Margaret opened the Stokes file again. He had lived and died in St John's Wood. His address hadn't been relevant to the post-mortem and Dr Naylor had attended the inquest alone, so Margaret hadn't heard it read out. She knew the district because she had lived there with her first husband what felt like a hundred years before. The address was on a note from the undertaker who'd brought the body to Dorcas Free: Flat 4, Russett House, Cabot Street, St John's Wood, NW.

Margaret stared at it. 'Good grief.' She flicked through the additional information provided by the police, but while other tenants were mentioned, there were no names. So Jeremiah Stokes had been shot on the landing of a building which might be connected to Queale. Perhaps it hadn't been a burglary he'd disturbed, but something else entirely. It was pointless telephoning Fox, who would be hard to reach until after the treaty had been signed. She drafted a brief telegram, asking him to send someone to meet her on the steps at two o'clock for news from a mutual friend, and took it to the desk for Miss Upton to send.

Polly appeared at her side just as she'd finished. 'You're very eager,' said Margaret. 'The anatomy lesson isn't until this afternoon. The body isn't even here yet.'

'I have something for you, doctor. I worked on it over the weekend.'

'I hope you spent more time relaxing than studying, Miss Buckram.'

'I did go out with a friend,' said Polly, as if admitting that she'd robbed a bank. 'But I worked hard on this, too. I know it's important.' She handed over a folder.

'This isn't your report on epidemic and pestilential diseases, surely? That's not due until next week.'

'No, it's the report into my research on laudanum. Will you be able to read and mark it now?'

Margaret turned the pages of neat handwriting. The report seemed fairly brief. 'I'll read it now, ask you some questions, then give you an indication on marks. Please could you ask someone to bring us tea?'

Polly grinned. 'Yes, doctor.'

The report confirmed everything Margaret had suspected. Every now and then the academic prose veered towards sentiment, but Polly had kept most of it under objective control without losing a sense of the personal. Case histories were concise, but the misery of the women behind them was more than apparent.

A, wife of a respected banker, was prescribed laudanum for the treatment of dysmenorrhea. When it no longer helped her condition, her physician increased the dosage. A became unable to fulfil a normal life, being almost constantly semi-conscious, yet found that as her yearning for the drug increased, its effectiveness decreased. She decided to stop taking laudanum and complained that the pain, sickness and distress of withdrawal felt like insanity, and was so severe that she considered destroying herself.

T, the estranged wife of a man of independent means, was encouraged to take laudanum by a 'friend' in order to counter her depression. Unable to live without it, she was drawn into the criminal world and eventually died from an overdose of chloral. She left an infant child, though it is unknown whether T took laudanum during the pregnancy. If so, the child's whereabouts being unknown, any effect on it is also unknown.

G supported her addiction through prostitution. A pregnancy, contracted while she was taking high doses of laudanum on a daily basis, continued almost to term and the child was delivered safely. It was below normal weight for its gestation, its head abnormally undersized, and reluctant to feed. The infant showed signs of addiction, suffering convulsions and arrhythmia once no longer nourished through the womb. The child perished within twenty-four hours. G's subsequent fate is unrecorded.

When Margaret asked Polly questions to see how much she'd absorbed, the young woman seemed sobered by her own report. 'I can buy as much laudanum as I want pretty much anywhere,' she said. 'It's in patent medicines, even for children. Some women keep it in perfume bottles, so their husbands don't know they're taking it. I thought it simply provided relief for the sufferer. It ought to be banned entirely.'

'As a patent medicine, yes,' said Margaret. 'But morphine can help in cases of extreme pain when nothing else can. I agree it should be more strictly controlled, along with a great many other drugs. I daresay there will come a day when cocaine's no longer put in carbonated drinks as an alternative to alcohol.'

Polly shifted in her chair. 'And, er... my mark?'

'I'll read it through again,' said Margaret. 'But I'm minded to give you one hundred per cent. Have you a copy? I'd like to send this to Inspector Silvermann, if you're agreeable. Beyond the desperate pain that made Miss Halpin take laudanum in the first place, and leaving the bullet aside, there's no way of proving whether she died by her own hand, murder or accident. However, I think this will confirm to the inspector that poor Miss Halpin might have been too insensible to know whether she'd lit the gas or not, or if someone else came in and turned it on while she was insensible. At any rate, she'd have been unconscious by the time the gas overcame her.'

'Maybe her fiancé wanted to end her suffering,' said Polly, with a sorrowful sniff. 'Although if she was so deeply afflicted, I'm surprised he proposed to her.'

'He wasn't in the country,' said Margaret. 'But thank you. This is very useful.'

At lunchtime Margaret locked Polly's report in her cabinet, changed, and went to meet Maude for lunch. She paused at the entrance to the underground, which would shorten her journey, but felt unenthusiastic about the stuffy heat of the carriages.

A man with a cane limped towards her, head down. He stopped and raised the cane, looking beyond her to hail a cab, then focused on a young woman as she passed. He was short, with grey hair, and his clothes, though good, hung loosely on his frame. His face, behind a white beard and moustache, had dropped on one side. His gaze ran down the young woman's figure, pausing at her bust, and the corner of his mouth lifted in a smirk. Then a cab pulled up and he climbed inside.

Shivering, Margaret hurried on.

Maude had ordered for both of them on the assumption that Margaret might have little time, but sat sipping wine, her food barely touched. If Margaret was showing any signs of the agitation she felt, Maude didn't notice. There was something about the way her outfit didn't quite match which suggested she hadn't thought very hard when getting dressed that morning. 'Have you heard? A bomb went off near St James's Park.'

'When?'

'Saturday, when we were there.'

'There's been nothing in the papers.'

'Yet,' said Maude. 'All the same, I've been questioned by your lovely inspector. He'll probably ask you to confirm that I was as innocent as a daisy when I was with you and the children on Saturday.'

'Well, you were. Was anyone hurt?'

'He didn't say so. But he seems determined to believe it's a suffragette bomb and wondered if I thought there was a link to Miss Tabor being reported missing by her mother. I gather that's happened before. She disappears, is reported missing, then is later reported as having returned home. Phoebe says you saw her in the park on Saturday.'

'I wasn't sure it was Miss Tabor,' said Margaret, 'and then we were chasing after the children. I can't believe she'd plant a bomb.'

'Nor can I, but the inspector said it was hinted that she might have been out with me.'

Margaret blinked. 'You?'

'Quite,' said Maude. 'Apparently Mr Tabor said his sister admires me greatly and might be distributing charity leaflets – I assume he means suffrage leaflets – on my behalf. This made things worse, since their mama felt such a request should have been made to her in writing, as if her daughter were twelve. Why would anyone think that Miss Tabor would deliver anything for me?'

'Miss Tabor is rather in awe of you.' said Margaret. 'She thinks you the most wonderful person. She was very moved by what you said at the last suffrage meeting.'

'I hope everyone was,' said Maude. 'But I'd rather people didn't have pashes on me, especially if it means police interrogation.' She grinned ruefully. 'As if I'd ask Miss Tabor to do something important. She can't do anything discreetly. Some wizened old crony of her mother's is forever spotting her skulking unaccompanied and taking her home like a naughty puppy.'

'Did the inspector tell you all that?'

'Mrs Philbrook told me about her frequent bids for freedom. She finds Miss Tabor rather spineless and we're both rather glad her membership of the more militant group was short-lived. The poor woman probably went on the lam, getting a thrill from being free for a few hours. Maybe she's managed to get further away this time. She's probably staying with Miss Brown or Mrs Nutford. I daresay she'll eventually be caught and taken home.'

Margaret sighed. 'She was nearly caught at the rally in May. I had to rescue her, and she was preparing all sorts of fibs.'

The waiter refilled their glasses and Maude raised hers. 'To Rhoda Tabor. One day, may she escape successfully! And down with all policemen who have fixed ideas.'

'To Rhoda Tabor!' Margaret sipped her wine, knowing she'd have to leave most of it. 'Was it on one of her escaping days that she went to the other suffrage group?'

'It was only once,' said Maude. 'She'd said she was visiting Miss Brown for afternoon tea and her brother called her a cab. Presumably she then asked the cabbie to go elsewhere. But perhaps it was a step too far for a snob: too many junior clerks, shop-girls, actresses and maidservants. She looked around as if she was surrounded by tigers, with no idea what to say to anyone, and clung to me. But when we stopped for tea and I went to speak with Lois, Stokes cornered her.'

'Jeremiah Stokes?' Margaret sat forward. 'Why?'

'It was his way. He'd hold forth in a whisper about his campaigning to anyone who would let him. I don't think he had many friends.'

'How did she react?'

'As if one of the tigers had her in its jaws. Mrs Philbrook rescued her, then took her to Miss Brown's. Goodness knows how she explained her lateness, but they seemed perfectly friendly next time I saw them both.' Maude shrugged and took a deep draught of wine.

'Will you be honest with me?' said Margaret. 'What do you honestly think about suffragettes planting bombs?'

'They'd argue that extreme situations require extreme measures.'

'And you?'

'It wouldn't be my choice,' said Maude. 'Anyway, enough about all that. What's wrong with you? You came in looking as if you'd seen a ghost.'

'I saw a rather sinister man on the way here,' said Margaret. 'Or possibly I misread a damaged face.' She sighed. 'Or it's pure imagination. My nerves are on edge. Probably because I'm worried about you.'

'Then tell your inspector friend to interrogate the right people before anyone else gets hurt.'

'If he asks, I intend to. I'll just have to hide that hammer, in case he searches my house and gets the wrong idea.'

Maude raised her eyebrows. 'Whatever are you talking about, Demeray?' She finished her glass of wine and beckoned the waiter for the bill.

'The hammer you put through my letterbox on Friday evening. I nearly broke my ankle on it.'

'Not I,' said Maude. 'After the meeting, I went home for a calming nightcap. Perhaps it was Mrs Snoville-Lewis. She's keen on hammers.'

Margaret returned to find Fox making his way up the hospital steps. 'Have you time for a walk?' he asked. His face was pale, and though in public he was rarely demonstrative, his hand held hers for longer than normal.

'Only a little, then I must go back. Did you get the telegram? I need to tell you something.'

His arm tensed and he looked about him. 'The noise in St James's on Saturday was almost certainly a bomb.'

'I know. Maude told me.'

'Has she been questioned?'

'Yes.'

'The treaty is due to be signed on Friday in St James's Palace. If this bomb was intended as a suffragette attack, the attacker could have walked past you and hundreds of other people. I'm horrified.'

'So am I,' she said. 'But Maude knows nothing about it.'

'It could have been intended for the underground, Wellington Barracks, Queen Anne's Gate or Westminster Medical School. Unless it was another attempt on Queale, because they don't realise we've moved him.'

'That's what I wanted to tell you. I think Alf Emery was wrong and Miss Lewin was right about that address.'

'What?'

'S Queale's.' Margaret explained what Miss Lewin had told her. 'What if it was never intended for Mr S Queale, at the address where you held him, but for *Mrs* S Queale?'

'There is no Mrs Queale. At least, not a relevant one.'

'It could be what his mistress calls herself and the address where she lives. You said he was quite respectable. Or perhaps they were married abroad.'

Fox pondered. 'It's possible. But why blow *her* up?'

'Why blow *him* up? That's not all: the address is where Jeremiah Stokes died. The man whose death Maude is worried about, because he knew a suffragette was planning something foolish. He told Miss Halpin, who told Maude. Miss Halpin was an Irish republican and Stokes was passionate about universal franchise. What if he – and therefore Miss Halpin – knew that Mrs Queale, on Queale's behalf, is trying to destablise the government? Perhaps they initially supported what she wanted to do, until their knowledge became too risky.'

'Then their murders – assuming Miss Halpin was murdered – make sense, but the letter bomb doesn't.'

'You said yourself that other people want those documents,' said Margaret. 'Perhaps they want to frighten her or stop her from talking. Perhaps they already have the documents and don't want her to tell. Perhaps that's what Stokes disturbed. And there's something else.'

'What?'

'Can you find out if Mr Abney has had palsy, apoplexy, or something like that while he has been in Flanders?'

'Why?'

'Because I think I saw him in Marylebone earlier.'

'Could you swear to it?'

'No,' said Margaret. 'If it's him, then he's been ill. But this man looked at a young woman in the way that Abney used to, and it made my skin crawl.'

Seventeen

Dr Gesner hailed Margaret on her return, his face solemn. 'There's been some confusion. A body has arrived for the lesson, but not ours, so to speak. The workhouse body went to Westminster Medical School and a body they expected came here.'

'How did they manage that?' said Margaret. 'Westminster Medical School is nearly three miles away, and the workhouse is more or less round the corner.'

'I think both were being kept in the same cold place,' said Dr Gesner. 'But they're quite dissimilar. Westminster was expecting someone who died violently, not someone who died of natural causes.'

'Will they be exchanged?'

'No, the police are coming here. They didn't want to delay it any further.' Dr Gesner grimaced. 'It is not fresh. I have dismissed the students, since we haven't time to prepare them for someone who has been dead for a while in late May.'

Fifteen minutes later Inspector Silvermann arrived with a constable, and the corpse was brought from the cold room. The stench of putrefaction was strong, whatever was under the sheet insubstantial and oddly shaped.

Margaret's heart lurched. Was it a child? It had never been easy to deal with dead children, but now that she had her own, the thought of little lives snuffed out by disease, poverty, neglect or cruelty tore at her.

'Good afternoon, Dr Gesner, Dr Demeray,' said the inspector.

'Is this a Scotland Yard case, Inspector?' said Dr Gesner. 'Wouldn't you prefer the post-mortem to be undertaken at a more established hospital?'

'It might as well stay here,' said the inspector. 'It's nasty. And it's possible that the deceased is from this area.' He frowned as Margaret reached for the cover. 'Before you do that, doctor, I ought to explain. It's unpleasant, but there's not much for you to look at. Somehow, that makes it worse.'

'A child?' She exchanged glances with Dr Gesner, his expression impassive but his face pale, and at the constables who'd borne the stretcher, one of whom was slightly green. 'Struck by a train? A murder victim?'

'Neither child nor train,' said the inspector. His expression darkened. 'An adult woman. An explosion. So either murder, culpable manslaughter or accident. Poor creature copped it good and proper.'

'An explosion?' gasped Dr Gesner. 'There has been nothing in the papers!'

'We're keeping it quiet till we know what's what, because we suspect a bomb.'

'Could this have been the bomber?' said Dr Gesner.

'If it is, I have less sympathy,' said the inspector, 'but I do have some.' He glanced at Margaret, then back at Dr Gesner. 'If it was a gas leak, we'll have to find out who's responsible. But if it was a bomb, either it went off before she could get away, she caught the bomber setting it up and was left to cop it, or she was just in the wrong place at the wrong time.' He cleared his throat. 'This is worse than Carmelo Street. Know what I mean?'

'Do you want us to confirm that the explosion killed her?' said Dr Gesner. Margaret could see from his clenched jaw that he felt no more enthusiasm for the task than she did.

'Pointless,' said the inspector. 'She must have been close to the explosion and a load of brickwork came down on her. If the explosion didn't kill her, the bricks did. I'm chiefly interested in seeing if we can identify her.'

'Where did this happen?' asked Dr Gesner.

The inspector cleared his throat. 'It's under wraps just now.'

'You can trust us.'

'Not far from St James's Park underground station. Saturday afternoon, we think.'

Margaret breathed deeply and realised that the inspector was watching her. This must be what Maude had been questioned about. And perhaps the body coming to Dorcas Free was not accidental but deliberate, so that the inspector could observe Margaret's reaction.

'What is it, doctor?' he said. 'Is there some reason why you shouldn't deal with this?'

'None,' she answered. 'But I was in the park on Saturday afternoon between about two and four with friends and our children. I heard nothing.'

The inspector sniffed, his eyes still fixed on her. 'It's a big old park and a small device might not make much noise, I suppose.'

'If she died on Saturday afternoon,' said Dr Gesner, 'why not bring her before now?'

'She wasn't found till early today,' said Inspector Silverman. 'On a sunny Saturday most people were in the park, it seems.'

'It is a busy place,' said Dr Gesner. 'Surely someone would notice something.'

'Apparently not,' said the inspector. 'She was found just inside the ladies' cloakroom of an empty restaurant which is being done up. Any noise, dust or debris would be put down to builders, only they weren't working this weekend. Maybe she was caught short and encountered a bomb planted with the intention of simply damaging a building. Or maybe, as you say, she was the bomber.'

'It's for the police to work out the whys and wherefores,' said Dr Gesner. 'But surely a woman wouldn't go into an empty building to, er...'

'There aren't many lavatories for women, but even an empty restaurant would have a cloakroom. If a woman were desperate enough, she might. Don't you agree, Dr Demeray?'

'Perhaps,' said Margaret. 'Most women would have gone to the Army and Navy Stores. They're not so far away from St James's underground station. They wouldn't go in a public house.'

'Wouldn't it depend on how desperate they were? Anyhow, will you look?'

Margaret drew back the cover, wishing she were about to reveal a treasure instead of the meagre remains of what had once been a human being. There was little enough: most of the body had been crushed and shattered by falling masonry. But strangely and pathetically, three parts were almost undamaged, though filthy with dust and blood. The lower half of the woman's left leg, including a foot in a buttoned shoe, with a pathetic shred of fine stocking embroidered with daisies dangling over the edge like froth. A hand, with its pale glove. Worst of all, the woman's head. blackened and scorched by fire. The explosion had destroyed her eyes, her skull and face were distorted, yet the greying hair was still pinned up in a hideous parody of a fashionable style.

'There's no point trying to make a likeness of the face,' said the inspector. 'Her own mother wouldn't recognise her. But if it's possible to detach that glove, we can take fingerprints. If she's a suffragette, there's a chance we can identify her from that. If not, at least we have them and we can use them if anyone is reported missing. There's a fragment of an envelope with a Paddington address and a Marylebone postmark from a few days ago, but nothing else of any use. We're still going through the debris for jewellery that might identify her. We've got this...' He pulled a tortoiseshell comb from his pocket. 'It's fancy enough; maybe an emporium will recognise it. Do you know if it's a particular make?'

Margaret shook her head, then pointed at the fragments of the body. 'How did they survive, when...'

'I'm consulting an expert,' said the inspector. 'I imagine that, depending where the bomb was in relation to the victim, it can happen. Here, hang on, lad—'

The constable fainted, caught just in time by the inspector.

'*Gott in Himmel*,' said Dr Gesner, shaking his head. 'That poor woman. I imagine her rushing along with some errand to complete, then as you say, needing a moment of privacy.'

Margaret looked down at the dainty grey shoe. 'May I see the comb?' she asked.

The inspector handed it over. 'What is it?'

'I don't know where it's from,' she said, 'but I know someone who owns something similar.'

'I see,' said the inspector.

Margaret turned the tortoiseshell comb over. She tried to visualise Miss Tabor at the suffrage meetings and rallies: the shy features of a woman she barely knew, whose personality faded into the background of confident women like Maude and Etta. She recalled Saturday afternoon and the rushing form of the person she'd wanted to look at before the children interrupted. Had it been Miss Tabor? Was this her body? If she'd hailed the woman, even if she'd mistaken her identity, would that have saved her? Margaret wanted to remember Miss Tabor, but the features of someone she found dull and annoying were foggy.

Even if they hadn't been, she knew it would take months, if not years, before she could see Miss Tabor as she should have been.

When she looked up into the inspector's face, she saw an unusual softening. 'Might it be someone you know?' he asked.

'I know someone who has a comb like this and wears similar shoes. But a good many other women do. I might not know this poor wretch at all.'

The broken cheekbones and nose, the shards of debris embedded in the flesh, the swollen mouth and the sightless sockets distorted any features that could identify the woman. One could only estimate size, race and possibly approximate age.

'These are the things that might identify her,' said Inspector Silvermann. He opened an envelope and extracted a scorched portion of another one, with part of a familiar street printed on it, and a gold and ruby earring, a mocking garnish among destruction.

Margaret heard herself gasp.

'Is it your acquaintance, Dr Demeray?' said Dr Gesner.

Margaret looked at the woman's head and after a second's hesitation, brushed the loose hair from the edges of the face. Then she took the earring and lifted it gently. She had seen it often enough. 'I fear it is.'

An hour later, Margaret sat in the back of a motor vehicle with the inspector, wishing she could have changed into something less severe than her hospital dress before meeting the Tabors.

'She's missing, all right,' said the inspector. 'Her brother says she had an invitation to spend the weekend with a friend in Marylebone.'

'That seems surprising,' said Margaret. 'Her mother is dictatorial, and Miss Tabor generally has an escort. Why stay overnight in Marylebone? It's walking distance.'

'Well, she had him hail a cab and went all the same. When she didn't come home on Sunday evening, Mr Tabor went to the friend's place and found she hadn't been invited and had not been there. He told his mother that Miss Tabor had stayed for another night, rather than worry her, but meanwhile reported his sister's disappearance to the police. That would have filtered through to the Yard eventually, but your identification of the earring and comb, together with the envelope and her disappearance, is compelling. So here we are.'

'Did he say who the friend was?'

'A Miss Pendleberry who lives in Marylebone.'

'Phoebe?' said Margaret.

'You know her?'

'Very well. Her grandmother was Mrs Tabor's friend a good many years ago, I believe. But Miss Pendleberry was with me on Saturday and said nothing about it. To be honest, it seems an unlikely thing for her to do.'

'Was she with you when you thought you saw Miss Tabor?'

'Yes, and I pointed her out, but she didn't think it was, and the woman had gone before I could tell you and besides we were chasing after children. Has anyone from the police contacted her?'

'Yes, and she denies any knowledge. How do you both know Miss Tabor when neither of you seems to like her?'

'It's not dislike,' said Margaret. 'Just a lack of things in common.'

'There must be something.'

Margaret bit her lip and looked out of the window.

'I was thinking about your father the other day,' said the inspector into the silence.

'My father?' Margaret turned back, anxious. Her father, while compos mentis, was sometimes a little vague, apt to get locked in bookshops or wander out of them reading their wares without remembering to pay first. So far, it hadn't involved the police. And surely, while he was still in Madeira, anything he did was irrelevant. 'Why?'

'It was the name. I suddenly realised there must be a connection between you and Roderick Demeray Esquire, the Travelling Gent. He used to do magic-lantern shows. I remember one about the Far East when I was a boy. He made it seem like we were there. That was him, wasn't it?'

'He writes books now.'

'His talk was very clear and informative. Detailed. Have you inherited that?'

'I think so.'

'Tell me how you know Miss Tabor. Simply because she's the daughter of the ... whoever it was?'

'Miss Pendleberry's grandmother's friend.' Tension made Margaret smile. 'It's like *la plume de ma tante* at school. *Mon amie est la petite-fille de l'amie de ma mere.*'

'If you say so,' said Inspector Silvermann. 'You don't want to hear the language I learned at my school. The teachers had enough trouble teaching us proper English. And stop side-tracking. How do you know her?'

'We're in a suffrage group run by Miss Pendleberry,' said Margaret. 'Don't you know?'

'It doesn't hurt to get you to confirm it. And a certain Mrs Holbourne is a member, too.'

'She attends, yes.'

The inspector nodded. 'I understand Miss Pendleberry's brother is an MP and her sister-in-law is group secretary. I'm surprised he lets either of them do it.'

'Percival supports them,' said Margaret.

'Best way to stop his house getting burnt down by Mrs Holbourne, I suppose.'

Margaret rolled her eyes. 'The group has nothing to do with what's happened to poor Miss Tabor. I keep hoping I'm wrong. But that earring...'

'There was a bomb and there was a suffragette. Both were by a tube station near fancy houses and a barracks, within spitting distance of the Palace and the Houses of Parliament. Not to mention a quiet little office which your husband may know.'

Margaret waited but he said nothing more, his face enigmatic. Was this the address where they'd kept Queale, or somewhere else?

'Is there anything else you haven't told me?' said the inspector. 'How involved was Miss Tabor? Was she militant? Or was a militant trying to draw her into militancy? You say you had only one thing in common with Miss Tabor, Dr Demeray, but it might be the only thing that matters. How militant would you say she was?'

'I never thought her militant at all,' Margaret said, after a pause. 'Miss Pendleberry's group isn't, particularly. I always felt that for Miss Tabor it was more about the excitement of getting away from her mother and being part of something more exciting than her usual dull routine. She lived through the activities of other members rather than doing anything herself.'

'Was she on that march in 1910?'

'Black Friday?' said Margaret. 'Yes, and thoroughly distressed at being manhandled when she'd done nothing more threatening than shake an umbrella. She was terribly worried that her photograph would get into the papers but fortunately it didn't. Her mother knows nothing about the suffrage meeting. She thinks it's a prayer group and sewing circle.'

'Miss Tabor told falsehoods, then.'

'You're speaking as if you're certain she's dead,' snapped Margaret. 'Miss Tabor would argue that Phoebe generally opens and closes with prayer, particularly if someone is arrested or in prison, and therefore it's at least partly true.'

'By *someone* you mean Mrs Holbourne.'

'I mean anyone, Inspector,' said Margaret. 'And Mrs Holbourne has nothing to do with this.'

Eighteen

The car eased to a stop outside the Tabors' house.

'How well do you know the family?' asked the inspector.

'I barely know Mrs Tabor. I've met Mr Tabor a few times. Aren't they going to wonder why I've come?'

'You're here to tell them she didn't suffer.'

'I can't say that.'

'You *will* say that.'

'But—'

'You don't know one way or another. Just tell them she didn't. That falsehood won't hurt anyone, unlike Miss Tabor's fib about where she was going. Besides, you recognised the belongings. You might be able to persuade them to give us something with her fingerprints on.'

'Neither Dr Gesner nor I are sure we can get anything to compare them with, and if the Tabors' housemaid is any good, there won't be fingerprints on anything.'

'There's always something.' The inspector handed Margaret out of the car and followed her up the steps. Curtains twitched in every window around them.

Mr Tabor, pale-faced, was waiting in the drawing room. He greeted Margaret with warmth and held her hand in his for a moment. 'I don't understand. Has there been an accident? Is she at the hospital? Hospitals aren't for people like us: they're for the poor. I'll go and bring her home. We can afford the best nurses, and she should be here to—'

'Let's all sit down, Mr Tabor,' said the inspector. 'I'm afraid we may have bad news. A woman was caught in an incident and taken to Dorcas Free. I'm sorry to say that she is dead.'

'Rhoda?' Mr Tabor took a photograph from the table beside him and handed it to the inspector. 'It's her?'

'I'm so sorry, Mr Tabor,' said Margaret. 'The nature of the incident means it's not easy to identify the body. But there's reason to believe it may be. As I knew her, the inspector asked me to come.'

The inspector and Margaret scanned the photograph. Miss Tabor in a winter dress, resting her hand on an urn in a way that suggested she needed its support. She looked every day of her age: tense, anxious, ducking her head a little. The inspector handed it back to Mr Tabor. 'As the doctor says, it's not possible to be certain from her features, but I'd say it's certainly a woman of this build and age.'

Mr Tabor swallowed hard, his jaw clenched. 'But Rhoda might simply be missing. The police need to keep looking.'

Margaret took a small parcel from her bag. 'The police brought the lady's remains to Dorcas Free. When I saw some of the deceased's belongings, I thought I recognised them. I'm sorry. I so hope I'm wrong.'

'Let me see.' Mr Tabor's voice was sharp. He took the parcel, opened it, then licked his lips. 'I gave Rhoda a comb like this,' he murmured. 'And the earring... It looks like one of a pair she wore which were our grandmother's. Rhoda was named for her. It's all bent – what happened to it?' He brushed the earring with his fingers. 'I need to see her.'

The inspector indicated some decanters on a side table. 'I'll pour you a drink, sir. Perhaps we should explain a little more before I take you to see her. It will be very distressing.'

Mr Tabor's gaze fixed on Margaret. 'What does he mean? A motor accident? Why can't she be identified? Have you seen her? Where did this woman die?'

'Near St James's underground station,' said the inspector, handing him a glass of brandy.

'What?' Mr Tabor blinked. 'Rhoda's never been on an underground train in her life. But then, she's only recently begun to show the courage to be independent.' His voice caught a little. 'If it is her, it's tragic. Just as she was starting to live, she died. On Saturday morning she was happy, excited to be going out and she said she anticipated delivering a gift. I shall be honest, Inspector: I wasn't entirely sure she was going to Miss Pendleberry's. Rhoda stretches the truth a little if she doesn't want Mother to know what she's doing. I thought she was going out alone for what she'd call an adventure in the sunshine, going to a shop to buy a gift and take it somewhere. I was happy for her. But I should have made sure of what she was doing. She doesn't know about the world. If this lady is her, I'll never forgive myself.' He downed the brandy and coughed as its heat burned.

The inspector topped up Mr Tabor's glass. He had sat nodding in sympathy during the other man's speech. 'I'm afraid it's not as simple as that,' he said. 'There was an explosion on Saturday. Before you ask, no, it hasn't been reported in the papers yet and no, I don't believe it was gas. I believe it was a bomb and the victim was nearby when it detonated. This is why you will find it upsetting to see the remains.'

Mr Tabor was staring at him, the brandy sloshing in the glass as his hand shook.

'I know your sister was in a suffrage group with Dr Demeray here,' the inspector continued. Mr Tabor's eyes turned to Margaret but he remained silent. 'Dr Demeray says that your sister was not in any way militant, and in her view, was unlikely to make or set a bomb.'

'I should think so!' exploded Mr Tabor. 'The very idea is laughable. And stop talking as if she's dead. Rhoda wants the vote, but she wants a little excitement more. Don't you agree, doctor? I don't believe for a moment that she would set a bomb – I don't believe she *could*. Her education was all literature and art. She was sentimental – kittens, puppies that sort of thing. She knows nothing about science or violence.'

'Is it possible that she might have delivered the bomb for someone else? Or that she might have been meeting someone with a different view?'

'Stop talking as if she's dead. This must be someone else.'

'Your sister has been missing for three days. Has she gone missing before?'

Mr Tabor slumped. 'Only for a few hours. I should never have let her go out on her own,' he said bitterly. 'Never. As for the suggestion that any of her suffragette friends would ask her to set a bomb in the underground, I'm sure it's not true.' He turned to Margaret. 'You've known those women much longer than I have, Dr Demeray, but I don't believe even the most vociferous of them would be unkind enough to put a timid woman like Rhoda in a situation she was unprepared for. Why does everyone assume it's suffragettes these days? Why not Russian anarchists, or Fenians? I don't know what I shall tell Mother. I—'

The drawing room opened and Mrs Tabor hobbled in on Eddison's arm. Mr Tabor and the inspector jumped to their feet.

'What are you talking about, Hedley?' she demanded. 'What is it you need to tell me? Who is this person?' She waved her stick at the inspector, then turned to Margaret. 'What is Mrs Foxcroft doing here, wearing what looks to be a prison warder's uniform?'

'Please sit down, Mother,' said Mr Tabor. 'I'm afraid there's terrible news. Eddison, pour your mistress a brandy.'

'I don't take strong drink, Hedley, no matter what the occasion. I can smell that you have, and it's barely noon.'

'Please, Mother. Sit.' Mr Tabor led his mother to a chair and settled her in it, then crouched beside her, holding her hand.

'Stop fussing,' said Mrs Tabor. 'What is so bad that you believe I need brandy? And I repeat, who is this person?'

'This is Detective Inspector Silvermann.'

'Silvermann? Is he German?'

'I don't believe so, Mother, and it's irrelevant. He's brought news of Rhoda. She's ... she's had an accident.'

'An accident? Today?' Mrs Tabor turned to the inspector. 'What sort of accident? Is she badly hurt?'

'I'm afraid it appears that she may be dead, madam.'

Eddison gasped and put her hand to her mouth. Mrs Tabor blinked. Her mouth pursed even more and she stuck out her face and gazed at her son with faded blue eyes, her crepey jowls quivering above the lace collar. She looked more like a tortoise than ever. 'Hedley, is this true?'

'I told you that Rhoda had said she was going to Miss Pendleberry's on Saturday, but she didn't go there. I must have misunderstood what Rhoda was doing. I reported it to the police, but I didn't want to worry you. I hoped everything would resolve itself, so—'

'So you could hide your falsehood and hers.' Mrs Tabor sat back. She took a glass of brandy from Eddison but didn't drink it. 'You stupid boy.'

'I'm so terribly sorry, Mrs Tabor,' said Margaret.

'Why?' said Mrs Tabor. 'Have you anything to do with this sorry state of affairs? Did you, or one of Rhoda's other modern friends, encourage her in this enterprise?'

'No. I—'

'Then why are you here?' Mrs Tabor's scowl deepened. 'Am I to understand that her body has been taken to a hospital for the poor, to be prodded at by men?'

'There are remains which might be hers, and they are being treated with the greatest respect, Mrs Tabor.'

'Dr Demeray helped to identify her,' said Mr Tabor. 'We should thank her for—'

'Fiddlesticks. Where and how did she die?'

'Near St James's underground station,' said Mr Tabor. 'Caught by a Russian anarchist's bomb which went off prematurely. Doubtless, they intended to attack the palace. There's a treaty being signed, and—'

Inspector Silvermann cleared his throat. 'I'm very sorry to ask you this, Mrs Tabor, as you must be terribly distressed. But do you have any idea why your daughter might have been there?'

Mrs Tabor looked a good deal less distressed than the inspector. Margaret noticed that she had started to sip the brandy. 'Clearly, I know nothing of my children's intentions. However, Rhoda would not have gone anywhere on her own initiative. She had none whatsoever. She must have been lured there. White slavery is constantly in the papers and the police do nothing.'

'With respect, madam,' said the inspector, 'there's—'

'You have no idea what you're talking about,' snapped Mrs Tabor. 'Everyone knows there are Russian gangs in this country, snatching girls and selling them to the Turks. No doubt this silly war they're having at the moment has spoiled their little game, which is why they're pretending to court us. Mark my words, my son is right.'

'I'm not sure that anarchists—'

'Rhoda would not have associated with an obvious anarchist, of course,' said Mrs Tabor. 'But *someone* fooled her into meeting them there.' Her voice faded and she sat back, looking into her lap. 'You must find them.'

'Mrs Tabor,' said Margaret, 'did Rhoda keep a diary?'

'I trained her to do so. She wrote down her devotions and counted her blessings.'

'Might I take it and see if there's anything in there which might help?' asked the inspector.

Mrs Tabor sniffed and contemplated him coldly. 'I would prefer that a lady read it and conveyed its contents. Eddison, tell Alma to fetch Rhoda's diary for Mrs Foxcroft. Now, you must all go while I compose myself. Hedley, see them out. Then I expect you to explain yourself before you fetch the rector. Inspector ... whatever your name is, I expect you to do your duty. Today, you say? It's unconscionable.' She waved her hand-kerchief in dismissal and her eyes began to fill with tears.

'Not today, madam,' said the inspector. 'Saturday. I'm very sorry.'

In the hallway, the inspector was ushered outside while Mar-garet waited for a servant to return with the diary. Mr Tabor stood with his arms folded tightly. 'I don't know what to do,' he said.

Margaret leaned close. 'I'm so sorry, Perhaps you could talk with Mrs Philbrook: I'm sure she—'

His eyes flashed. 'Are you suggesting the suffragette element, too? I thought you'd be adamant it wasn't that.'

'Not at all,' said Margaret. 'I simply thought you needed a friend.'

Mr Tabor sniffed. 'I can't leave Mother. But I'm sure if I tell Mrs Philbrook, she'd agree with me. It won't be anything to do with suffrage, but one of the causes the press is conveniently forgetting. One wonders sometimes if their reporting on suffrage is a deliberate attempt to divert attention from other political matters. And if one of those is responsible...'

'It may just have been an accident.'

'Would it be very terrible to see her?'

'I'm not sure it will help. I couldn't say for certain that it was her. If you believe the items identify her, the inspector will accept that.'

'She has an arrow-shaped scar on her left shin, about here.' He indicated the location on his own leg. 'Obviously I haven't seen her shin for years, but... Would that help?'

'It may. There's a lot of damage to that limb, and if she was a child when it happened, it may have faded. But I'll look.'

'Thank you.'

A maid trotted down the stairs, her eyes wide. She handed a leather-bound volume to Margaret, then retreated to the drawing room.

'Dr Demeray,' said Mr Tabor, 'can you tell me if Rhoda suffered at all?'

A brief hysterical laugh, followed by a thin, smothered wail, came from the drawing room.

'No,' said Margaret. 'I don't believe she did.'

Nineteen

As they made their way back to the hospital, Margaret turned the pages of Miss Tabor's diary. She read aloud from the spiky script of the last entry, on Saturday morning:

This morning's verse was from the Song of Solomon, chapter two, verse twelve. 'The flowers appear on the earth; the time of the singing of birds is come, and the voice of the turtle is heard in our land.' I hope it is not blasphemous to wonder about the turtle. The turtles I've seen in the zoological gardens have always been mute. Perhaps Israelite turtles in Solomon's time were different!!! I don't believe there are turtles in the Park but the rest is quite true, birds and flowers everywhere.

Today is a lovely day. I shall wear the outfit that Hedley says suits me so well: my nice beige costume, my grey kid shoes and gloves and my summer stockings with the flower embroidery. I hope it will not look frivolous for a woman my age to trim her boater with pink, but one feels youthful today.

We had bacon, eggs, kidneys, mushrooms and toast with marmalade for breakfast. Mother did not descend, so I let Hedley pour me some coffee. It made my heart race, so perhaps Mother is right that it is unsuitable for me. On the other hand, when the palpitations receded, I felt quite full of the joys of spring!!!!

How exciting it will be to collect a gift to take to the dear, wise, kind, admirable, wonderful woman I'd like to call friend.

She will doubtless invite me to tea and we shall have a lovely conversation about S. What fun!!! I shall relate all later.

'That suggests she intended coming home,' said the inspector. 'And it supports what Mr Tabor said. The clothes match, too. We'll have to go through the rest to see if anything leads up to this moment. What's S, do you suppose?'

'I think it stands for suffrage,' Margaret turned the pages and pointed at the dates of Phoebe's meetings and rallies. 'From what I can see, the diary's mainly very innocuous, but there are one or two woolly references which coincide with things we both attended.'

'Coded?' asked Inspector Silvermann.

Margaret shuddered inwardly, remembering a diary from two years before, then shook her head. 'I think they're just veiled in case her mother reads her diary, which I've no doubt she does.'

'Miss Tabor was forty-nine.'

'That doesn't stop some mothers.'

'Humph,' said the inspector. 'So which of your coven is the wonderful friend? Miss Pendleberry? You?'

Margaret frowned. 'I doubt it. She was friendly with other women who were more like her in experience and personality: Mrs Nutford is one. Phoebe will know, but she'll be terribly upset. Would you like me to come with you and—'

'No, thanks,' said the inspector, taking the diary. 'Please don't speak to Miss Pendleberry or anyone else about it until I say you may. I've already spoken with Mrs Holbourne, but I'll have to speak with her again. You may speak to your husband of course: I daresay he's already aware, and he knows when to keep silent. You can look for that scar and see if there's a chance of getting fingerprints from the hand, while I see if I can get some from this. Even the best maid won't dust inside a book. That reference to collecting a gift to give to a friend, though. Perhaps she'd come *from* the Army and Navy Stores with it... It should be possible to find that out.' He consulted his watch. 'Nearly one. Once I've taken you back to the hospital, I must return to the scene and see if there's anything else to be found.'

'You needn't take me all the way,' said Margaret. 'Could you ask your driver to stop? I'd like to walk from here.'

'It's a bit of a mixed area, this.'

'I used to work in the East End, Inspector. I can manage the poorer parts of Marylebone.'

The inspector grunted. 'Just remember what I said about not speaking with Miss Pendleberry or any of your suffragette chums till I say you can.'

'I shall.'

'All right. We'll leave you here.'

Margaret walked past the elegant buildings in Crawford Street, where ladies walked arm in arm followed by maids bearing their purchases, along Paddington Street, then turned down Northumberland Street, passing the deceptive grandeur of Marylebone workhouse, outside which a row of dispirited women and children and another of dejected men waited to be admitted.

It was barely half a mile to affluent Portland Place and the area where Maude and Phoebe lived. It was less than that to equally affluent Dorset Square, where Margaret and Fox often met at lunchtime. The wealthy preferred to pretend the workhouse didn't exist: it was a worse inclusion in the neighbourhood than a hospital. Margaret turned again onto Marylebone Road, with its elegant hotels and dwellings.

The rich might argue that their wealth endowed hospitals and schools and enabled them to work for charities without pay, which they couldn't do if they had to work for money. Dorcas

Free was testament to the fact that many understood *noblesse oblige*. Many more didn't. Would everyone having the vote be all that was required to even things out? Or was something more radical needed?

Margaret noticed the people about her: whistling delivery boys, scurrying maids, chatting pedestrians, hopeful salesmen, trotting nannies with perambulators, trundling cab drivers. A postman compared a letter's address with the buildings around him. A milkman's horse slumped in her harness as she waited for her owner.

Now that Margaret was alone, the reality of the situation overwhelmed her. Even after twenty years in medicine, she'd been shocked to the point of nausea by that mangled body. Never had the word 'remains' been more apt. And she'd known the victim. She'd sat next to her, taken tea with her, shared the weight of banners, accepted her praise for speeches and dia-tribes. Now the poor woman's own family would be unable to recognise her.

As she walked along, she knew that everything that sur-rounded her – the waiting poor, the bustling rich, the busy workmen, even the patient horse – would form a background which she would see whenever she thought of a woman whose life, no matter how thwarted, should have been lived to a natural end.

If only I hadn't thought her so dull, thought Margaret. *I was so impatient. If I'd taken time to befriend her, maybe she wouldn't have... And on Saturday... If only I'd hailed her. If only...*

She found a small tearoom and ordered croquettes, but left them uneaten. She sipped the scalding tea, holding the cup in a trembling hand, wishing its heat could burn away the imagined taste of death and wishing it were something stronger. Then she took a deep breath and returned to work.

At the hospital, Dr Gesner and Margaret spent the afternoon working on the remains, carefully extracting fragments of cloth and debris from the wounds and removing shoe, stocking and glove to see if there was any hope of identifying the victim more conclusively.

On the leg there was part of an old, faded scar where Mr Tabor had suggested it might be, but it was incomplete. While Margaret sketched it and Dr Gesner took photographs, it seemed unlikely that it could be used as evidence. The foot was small and a little misshapen, with callouses and corns on the toes, the heel looking tender and sore. It must have hurt Miss Tabor to walk, let alone in tight, fancy shoes, but Margaret didn't recall her ever limping.

Dr Gesner examined the head. It had been washed clean of debris and the hair cut close to the scalp, making it look even more like a grotesque from an old church. Small fragments of brick, porcelain and metal fixtures had been driven into the skin, and the skull was dented and partially crushed.

The inspector had described a room shattered by the explosion, with the basins, taps, doors and lavatories broken and distorted. The police had hurriedly developed the photographs of the scene and brought copies round. Dr Gesner pointed at the brass tap handle with its four spherical ends and the smooth brass-and-wood lavatory handle, then touched a circular hollow in the temple. 'One of these must have struck her. Not that it would make much difference to the poor wretch.'

The leather of the glove adhered to the fingertips and it took an hour of painstaking work with scalpels to separate them. Any chance of the police obtaining any prints worth having seemed remote.

'There's nothing more to be done,' Dr Gesner told the constable. 'We'll place it all in a coffin while you telephone your colleagues to collect you, and her.' He turned back to Margaret as the constable left. 'I'd like to take you to a hotel for a stiff drink. Would your husband mind?'

'I doubt it, but I don't really care,' said Margaret. 'Let's go.'

Shortly after arriving home Margaret received an agitated call from Mr Tabor, asking that she persuade his mother to accept that the remains of the bomb victim were her daughter's and agree to a funeral.

'I can't make her believe it, Mr Tabor,' she said. 'I can't swear they are hers. And it's not my duty to persuade her of anything.'

'But what if she refuses?'

'I imagine it will fall on the parish or the council and the remains will be buried as a pauper's.'

'That's appalling. Those things didn't belong to a pauper.'

'Maybe your sister is simply missing,' she said. 'The police will continue to seek her, I'm sure. If the remains aren't hers, they're someone's, and they will discover whom. I'm sorry, but perhaps there is hope.' She felt ashamed as she replaced the receiver but knew she could do nothing else. She retrieved the paper from the doormat, along with a letter from Katherine saying that she'd booked berths for herself and their father to sail from Funchal at the end of June. She wanted to write back telling them to stay in Madeira and she'd join them, and they could stay there forever.

She hadn't been sure if Fox would come home, given that the treaty was to be signed in only a few days, but he arrived at seven and told her he'd heard the body had ended up at Dorcas Free. 'It must have been a terrible thing to deal with,' he said, putting the last post on the mantlepiece and embracing her.

'It was dreadful,' said Margaret. 'Dr Gesner treated me to brandy in a hotel afterwards, but it couldn't erase the images, or the smell, or... The worst thing is thinking it's Miss Tabor.'

'So I heard on the grapevine, though it's not being given out. Was she related to the man we met at Maude's?'

'Sister. I know her from Phoebe's group.'

'Do you think she made the bomb?'

'I doubt she knew how to make toast,' said Margaret. 'I can't see her managing nitroglycerin: she'd never have got out of her house alive. Besides, I think I saw her on Saturday. She only had a small bag with her. If only I'd called out to her, but I wasn't sure and I didn't want to make a fool of myself. Then the children started running about, and...' She felt a bubble of emotion rise up. Poor Miss Tabor. She walked to the mantlepiece and picked up the mail, hoping for something nice to take her mind off everything. A bill. A letter from her dressmaker. A typed envelope which could be from anyone.

'You can't blame yourself,' said Fox. 'And if you're wrong and she was the bomber, then – it doesn't bear thinking about. Her bag wouldn't need to be big, and it's easier to convince people you're a fool when you're wise than the other way about.'

'I really don't think Miss Tabor had the skills or could have obtained the necessary equipment. But...'

'Is it definitely her?'

Margaret shuddered and slit open the typed envelope. 'It could have been anyone. But there were personal effects which I recognised: an earring, and an envelope fragment with her address on it – or at least, the street looked right.'

'Margaret, if you think for one moment that Miss Tabor was setting a bomb, please tell me, even if you won't tell the inspector.'

'I'm sure she wasn't,' said Margaret. 'But she's the third person from the same small group who is now dead under peculiar circumstances.'

'That's a lot of conjecture,' said Fox, frowning.

'I know, but I'm sure it's relevant. I'm going to find out what I can.' She extracted a letter from the typed envelope and unfolded it.

'While it's conjecture,' said Fox, 'and I have to put all my time and resources into protecting the treaty—'

'Fox—'

'Let me finish,' said Fox. 'If I can spare someone to look into it, I will.'

'Good,' said Margaret. 'Look at this.'

Typed on flimsy paper, the letter said: *She deserved it, as they all did. Let it lie, doctor. Leave it to the police, or maybe they'll start suspecting you.*

'Let what lie?' said Fox. 'Your only involvement has been undertaking post-mortems. There's nothing more for you to do.'

'Exactly,' said Margaret. 'Someone's made a false move. If this said *We know you're militant too and you're next*, or *You're mixing with the wrong people, watch out or you'll be next*, it would follow the pattern Maude expects.'

'And why would the police start suspecting you? You aren't militant, are you? There's nothing to link you to it, apart from some of your friendships.'

Margaret frowned. 'And maybe a hammer.'

'A what?'

She opened the bureau and handed him the small package. 'Do you remember me telling you about a hammer which I thought Maude had given me to spur me into action?'

'No.' Fox's face set in hard lines.

'I was afraid you'd fallen asleep but I wasn't sure, and it didn't seem important. Just childish.'

'And you didn't want me to accuse Maude of anything criminal.'

'You know she's broken the law in the past. I wasn't trying to hide anything.'

'All right. So how did you get it?'

'It was waiting for me when I came home, the night before we went to St James's Park. It frightened me to death, in fact. It was on the doormat. I tripped over it, then tried to disarm it with an umbrella.' Fox didn't laugh. 'Maude had suggested we were all lily-livered. I thought it was a taunt to chivy me into direct action.'

'Maude's not that subtle. She'd come round and put it in your hand.'

'I know, but she'd been behaving oddly. I did ask her about it. She said it wasn't her and thought it might have been Mrs Snoville-Lewis, since she's quite the hammer enthusiast.'

Fox closed his eyes for a second. 'Snoville-Lewis? Middle-aged smasher of politicians' windows?'

Margaret felt her face redden. 'So she's on your list.'

'It's an easy name to remember, but she's not a concern. Have you asked her?'

'I haven't had the chance, but...'

'What?'

'The Honourable Mrs Southern – Dr Southern's wife – seemed to think window smashing was jolly good fun. She said she wasn't militant, but her husband is opposed to militancy and she doesn't seem the sort to contradict him in public. Is she on your list?'

'I'll find out, and have this tested for fingerprints.'

'It'll have mine on.'

'Had you taken off your gloves at that point?'

'Oh. No. Good.' Margaret looked at the letter again. 'This is telling me to back away from investigations I have only a small part in. That suggests they don't want me – or through me, you – to confirm that these deaths are connected. Not by militancy, but something else. A "brave little suffragette" hiding papers?'

'I think so. Incidentally, though we can't confirm Abney is in this country right now, we discovered that he was afflicted with a form of paralysis last year, which links with what you told me about that man you saw.'

'Then I have no intention of letting it lie. Have you?'

'I'll increase the pressure on Queale, have someone analyse this letter, get all the evidence from the police on these three cases and look over it,' said Fox. 'For the next few days, Margaret, please try and act as if you're taking heed of that letter. From Saturday, God willing, I'm all yours. Apart from anything else, I can't have you replacing me with the inspector.'

'God forbid,' said Margaret. 'I'm much less likely to kill you.'

Twenty

W as the letter from Abney himself? It seemed too direct for someone who knew how to keep his involvement hidden.

Margaret found it hard to decide how to behave in response. The sender of the letter might guess that she'd pass it to Fox, but they had omitted to add a threat to make her do so. Let what lie, exactly? And what would happen if she didn't?

Perhaps it was a hurried mistake. But how could she show that she was heeding the letter's contents? Should she go about looking frightened or angry? She was both. She was also certain that even if Abney knew she'd married Fox, and where she lived and worked, he wouldn't harm her himself. However, that didn't stop him instructing someone else to do it.

Knowing Fox couldn't put a watch on her, Margaret cycled to work on Tuesday. The postman had arrived as she was leaving and she had taken a single letter from him with some anxiety, but it was in an unfamiliar, old-fashioned ladies' hand and postmarked from Paddington the previous evening. She opened it, saw Mrs Tabor's name and address printed at the top, and took it to work to read there. She couldn't face it at home. Besides, it might contain something useful to confirm identification.

In her office, Margaret braced herself and withdrew the contents.

Dear Mrs Foxcroft,

One must tell you that one's daughter is not dead.

One despairs more than ever at the state of the nation when one considers the incompetence of the police. They gave me to understand that she had been killed by a train or similar yesterday, when in fact they meant that they thought she had been killed in some despicable manner on Saturday. One would let them continue their investigations until they realised their mistake, but one has been led to believe that this might cause a friend of yours to be implicated, since she is acquainted with Rhoda.

Of course, your friend may yet be responsible for the death of whomever was found with an earring so like my mother's around the time Rhoda tells me someone assaulted her and snatched it from her ears. A robber is no loss whatsoever to civilised society, Even so, one cannot see why a lady should commit murder. One uses the word lady with reservations, since one gathers that this woman, you, and to one's horror, the granddaughter of an old friend – have all encouraged Rhoda in the dangerous nonsense which is the Suffragette Menace.

One hereby wishes you to understand that you are not to contact Rhoda. She is considering her iniquities with a trusted relation, to whose home she was escorted on Saturday evening.

On receipt of the news brought yesterday by the policeman and you, one assumed that she had absconded from that address and had died. One therefore telegraphed one's cousin to remonstrate – at an expense which one expects the police to reimburse – only to receive a reply that Rhoda was where she should be.

Ultimately, she will return home, and thereafter, she will remain at home unless accompanying me.

You will receive this in the morning, when one will inform Hedley, so that he can inform the police. Since he had been encouraging Rhoda in her rebellion, one had not told him of her whereabouts. One hopes that this is a sufficient lesson to all.

Yours sincerely, Mrs G. Tabor.

Mrs Upton knocked and entered with a telegram. It was from Inspector Silvermann.

A wicked old bat has strung us along for nearly twenty-four hours so someone needs to talk to a woman who's risen from the dead. Starting again, no thanks to anyone. Will be in touch.

'Any reply?' said Miss Upton.

'None that's printable,' said Margaret.

'Tea?'

'Strong enough to stand a spoon up in, please. It's going to be that sort of day, I fear.'

She explained matters to Dr Gesner and they waited for the inspector to return, but all they received was another telegram at noon, asking them to preserve what could be useful of the corpse and send the remainder for a pauper's burial.

At the end of a disagreeable day, she went home for a quiet evening with the maids and children, wishing the body had gone to the Westminster Medical School as it should have, where there would have been no one to connect it with Miss Tabor. The sting of *No thanks to anyone,* the memory of Hedley Tabor's stricken face and the thin wail of his mother disturbed her sleep. She longed to cuddle up to Fox, but all she could do was remind herself that she had done all she could with the best intentions and that at least the inspector now had no reason to suspect Maude.

She took the bus on Wednesday, and before working in the laboratory on samples from living patients she briefly reviewed the file on the St James's corpse with Dr Gesner. The scene of crime photograph was as bleak as ever and gave no further clues.

Why am I thinking of a picture that's wrong? she thought. *It's not this one.* But the morning was busy and there was no time to work things through in her mind.

At lunchtime, when she was about to go out, Dr Gesner entered her office. 'Inspector Silvermann telephoned. He asked whether we've read about Miss Halpin in the newspaper today.'

'I haven't,' said Margaret. 'My cat attacked the morning paper. I think she was expressing her views on current affairs.'

Dr Gesner blinked. 'Your cat has opinions?'

'Don't all cats?' said Margaret. 'What was I supposed to read?'

'Miss Halpin's fiancé has returned. The inspector is taking him to the house where she died and wonders if one of us could join him there. I suggested you, especially as your husband is apparently driving.'

'My...? I'm sorry, doctor, I really don't follow. What has my husband to do with it?'

'I can't speak for your husband. The inspector said that Mr Carter wants to speak with the person who performed the post-mortem, and I imagine the inspector thought the conversation could take place in the place where she died. *Zwei Fliegen mit einer Klatsche.*'

'Two flies with one, er...'

'Swatter. I mean that if Mr Carter visits the scene and hears our findings at the same time, the inspector can observe his reaction to both.'

'Surely he'd prefer you.'

'I do not know if he has a preference, but you are better at English idiom and the subtleties of conversation than I. Not to mention understanding why British cats read newspapers.' Dr Gesner smiled. 'Of course, in Germany, cats are bright enough to write them.'

'Lovely as it is to see you, I thought you were too busy for this sort of thing,' said Margaret, as Fox drove them towards Paddington. 'And it won't look as if I'm letting things lie.'

'Aren't I allowed to take my wife for lunch?' said Fox. 'If this is quick, I might make it true.'

'Let's start again. Why are either of us doing this?'

'You are for the reasons Inspector Silvermann gave. I am because while Elinor drew a blank with your letter, she started digging into Stokes's address. When I mentioned a possible link to the Halpin case, which she remembered because of its peculiarities, she worked her magic at Somerset House. Jonas Carter married Lois Halpin by special licence seven days before he left the country.'

'The last time I asked Somerset House for anything they demanded my request in triplicate, preferably in blood and with fifty years' notice. What magic does Elinor use?'

'Best not to ask,' said Fox. 'It doesn't work as well on land-lords, though. Getting information about Russett House's tenants is proving tricky and most of my men are busy keeping an eye on any number of disgruntled delegates.'

Margaret sighed. 'A secret marriage provides a motive that moves Lois's murder even further from what you're seeking.'

'Only if that's why she died. The papers lining her drawers all have messages sent between Queale and his mistress, including him telling her to pretend to destroy the documents and her confirming that she understood. I don't believe in coincidence. Lois Halpin knew something and it's possible she told Carter. I can ask questions without the inspector knowing why.'

'Three flies with one swatter.'

'Pardon?'

'Never mind. Had you heard that the body at St James's is definitely not Rhoda Tabor?'

'Yes.'

'I feel awful. It was partly because of my assumptions that the inspector took me to see the family and break the news.'

'Which is not normal police behaviour,' said Fox. 'He should have approached it a good deal more subtly and left you out of it. He's the one at fault, though it's unusual for him to mis-step that far. I suspect he wanted to gauge your reaction about Maude.'

'Dreadful man. Have you got any further with Abney?'

'He'll be operating under an assumed name, but your description is useful. We're still looking. However, let's deal with this first.'

When they arrived at the house, Inspector Silvermann opened the door, shook hands, then asked Fox if he'd keep an eye on Carter. 'I'd like a quiet word with the doctor out of anyone's earshot,' he said. 'We'll be back in no time, but I need Carter watched. My money's elsewhere, but we can't be too careful, can we?'

'We can't.' said Fox, slipping inside as Inspector Silvermann and Margaret walked slowly along the pavement.

The street was busy with postmen and delivery boys. A milkman's cart blocked the road. Women scrubbed doorsteps or shook dusters in the air. The inspector indicated the scene. 'Just as well you didn't drive. You'd never have got through.'

'We left the car on the main road,' said Margaret. 'I'm not fond of the tube at the moment.'

'Then tell your fellow suffragettes to stop leaving bombs.'

Margaret shivered. The inspector frowned. 'What?'

'I had no intention of misleading you on Monday. I'd never have made Mrs Tabor cry like that deliberately.'

'I believe you,' said the inspector. 'For what it's worth, I think the wailing was from that old maidservant who should have been pensioned off years ago.'

'Sadly, I can believe that.' Margaret took the copy of the Carters' marriage certificate from her bag. 'Going back to Miss Halpin, one of Fox's people discovered this.'

The inspector unfolded the document and swore. 'Why didn't my men find this? This gives Carter a motive. She was worth a coupla bob.'

'That doesn't mean he wanted her dead.'

'He asked to see you or Dr Gesner. Maybe he wants to see if he's in the clear, going from what you discovered.'

'I'm sorry it's me.'

'I'm not,' said the inspector. 'You'll be gentle if he asks about the post-mortem. Dr Gesner would sound enthusiastic about the challenge, which might come across a bit callous.'

'He wouldn't mean to.'

'Yeah, but much as I hate to say so, I'm glad it's you. Carter will be off his guard with a woman, so it'll be easier to gauge reactions.'

Margaret slowed her pace. 'If he wanted her dead, he could have massively increased the morphia level of the laudanum and no one would have suspected murder. How many empty bottles were there? She would need a lot to render her too unconscious to notice the gas.'

'I can't recall,' said the inspector. 'I'll find out.'

They retraced their steps, covertly watched by the housewives and a delivery boy who appeared to be the lad who'd wielded a paintbrush a few weeks before. 'What's your old man here for?' the inspector asked.

'Lois Halpin was a suffragette,' said Margaret. 'You said yourself that she was on a list.'

'I thought he hunted different fish.'

'One doesn't hunt fish.'

'One's never fished, has one?' he replied, in an affected tone. 'What if one is after a shark?' The inspector chuckled when she didn't reply. 'Keeping mum, or don't you know? Either way, let's see what Carter's got to say.'

Jonas Carter was sitting at the kitchen table with Fox. He was a short man, fair haired, pleasant-looking, slight. In his hand was the photograph of him with Lois. He rose to shake hands with Margaret, then nodded at Inspector Silvermann.

'We were married,' he said. 'I've just given your colleague our copy of the certificate.'

'Oh,' said the inspector. His dour expression flickered in a way that suggested he was attempting to feign surprise. 'Why didn't you tell us when you replied to our telegram?'

'Didn't want you arresting me till I could see the house,' said Carter. 'I could guess what you'd think. And I wanted to know if they'd found out.'

'Who?'

'The Bessemers.' Carter stroked the photograph. 'I had nothing to do with her death. Someone needs to swing for what happened. Bessemer's my top guess.'

'Why?' said the inspector, his face blank.

'Lois thought they had money troubles. If they didn't know we were married, they'd think all this was theirs. Have they been here since?'

'Not unescorted,' said Inspector Silvermann. 'And we changed the locks.'

Carter nodded. 'So you haven't discounted him.' He put down the photograph and looked at Margaret. There was sorrow in his face, but it was restrained. Any tears he might have cried, if he were innocent of murder and truly in love, must have long dried and had doubtless been wept in private. His journey home had taken enough time for that. 'If someone had to do a post-mortem, I'm glad it was a woman. Lois would have been pleased, in a way. And I think I've heard good things of you.'

'I promise we treated her body with the utmost respect,' said Margaret.

'I don't doubt it.' Carter took a cigarette from the inspector with trembling hands and lit it. Fox offered his hip-flask but Carter shook his head. 'We had an agreement, me and Lois. I was to stop drinking spirits, she was to stop taking laudanum. I think she would have had the harder time.'

'Yes,' said Margaret. 'It would have involved a lot of pain.'

Carter paced the room. 'There's all sorts of pain.' He pointed at the chair with its back to the oven. 'Is that where she was?'

'Yes.'

'She usually sat in that one.' He pointed at the one Fox was sitting in. 'Our wedding oughtn't to have been romantic, but it kind of was. Just us and two strangers as witnesses, and no sneering Bessemer to spoil things. It was exciting and sad at the same time. I don't suppose you understand.'

'Actually, I do,' said Margaret. 'My first wedding was like that. It was raining and I wore my dullest grey outfit and we had nowhere to go but a flat we'd never lived in. Although it felt adventurous, it wasn't the wedding I'd always imagined.'

'Ah,' said Carter. 'I made sure Lois had a pretty dress, doctor. And we had a lovely lunch and a night in a nice hotel. We planned to make up for it in Australia when the dust had settled.' He closed his eyes and ran his hand over them. 'She shouldn't be dead.' His voice cracked a little. 'I imagine you think this is a motive, Inspector. Marrying a woman of some means on the quiet, then having someone kill her while I was out of the country. But if I *were* going to get anyone killed, I'd be damned ashamed to hire someone who'd bodge it the way Lois's murder was bodged. Pardon my language, doctor.'

'Granted.'

'I don't need Lois's money. I have means of my own.'

'Mmm.' Inspector Silvermann remained impassive.

'I had my own house in Hammersmith, which I've sold, and added the proceeds to the savings I already had. You've probably learned that much.'

'Yes.'

'Lois was going to sell this place as soon as I came back and the proceeds would have been added to *her* savings. We wanted to keep our money separate. I suppose you think that odd.'

'No,' said Margaret and Fox, together.

Carter raised his eyebrows, then said, 'She was worried about the leech getting his hands on it. Bessemer, I mean.'

'Don't you like him?' said Margaret.

'He's a sanctimonious, joy-crushing, bigoted bully. And now it turns out he's a murderer too.'

Inspector Silvermann gave Margaret a warning glare. 'Please address any answers to me, Mr Carter. The doctor tends to forget whose job it is to ask questions.' He drew on his cigarette, eyed the remaining chair and leaned against the dresser. 'Everyone assumed your wife had died intestate. Mrs Bessemer has been trying to obtain probate, but it's not as simple for a sibling as a spouse. It would have been a lot simpler if you'd told us before arriving back in Blighty.'

'Will you all be straight with me?'

Inspector Silvermann nodded. 'As far as we can, without giving away evidence an innocent man wouldn't know... Except for what got into the blasted papers.'

Carter addressed Margaret. 'They say she was full of laudanum but died of gas poisoning.'

'That's right,' she said.

'And she was in that chair, slumped over the table. That's what the picture in the *Illustrated London News* shows. Is that accurate, Inspector?'

'Mmm,' grunted the inspector.

'I assume that's a yes.' He turned to Margaret again. 'And they say she was shot in the chest from the front, but you say she was already dead.'

'Not long dead, but yes. All the evidence says she was.'

'So why was she slumped forwards? Did it look right to you, Inspector? Because it doesn't to me.'

Twenty-One

M argaret gasped and turned to the inspector. 'I've felt all morning that something was wrong with a picture and I couldn't put my finger on what I was thinking of. It must be the photograph you showed me and Dr Gesner. Mr Carter's right. Why wasn't Miss Halpin lying backwards or sideways?'

'None of the reports about the inquest mentioned injuries suggesting her head had been forced into an oven or over a gas jet,' said Carter.

'There were none,' said Margaret. 'But I can't swear she wasn't.'

'I understand that, but where was the laudanum bottle?'

'Bedroom,' said Fox.

The inspector turned a scowl on him. 'That's right. Who's questioning who here?'

Carter sighed. 'She'd done it before, but usually when she was downstairs.'

'Done what?' said Margaret, ignoring the inspector's low growl. She sat in the seat opposite the one in which Lois had been found, willing the image of that slumped body out of her head.

'Taken too much when her pain from forcible feeding was bad, gone to do something, then fallen into a stupor before it was done. Holes burnt in the bottom of kettles, mostly. Food left in the oven to turn to cinders. I found her like that more than once; so did her sister. Lois had never turned on the gas without lighting it, but maybe it was just a matter of time. I hoped that when I got her away, when we could start again, she'd learn to manage without the laudanum and be as lively and alert as she ought to have been.'

'Her sister didn't mention any of that,' said Inspector Silvermann.

'That's no surprise. Bessemer wouldn't have let her.'

'Why not?' said Inspector Silvermann.

With his cigarette dropping ash, Carter counted on his fingers. 'He didn't want people to know, or he wanted Lois dead and would be happy for it to look like murder, or he murdered her. Take your pick. I know what I believe.'

'Someone shot him in the leg and his wife in the hand while they were trying to help her.'

Carter grunted, slumped back in his chair and exhaled towards the ceiling. 'Is there anything else you wanted to know?'

'What did your wife know about setting bombs?' asked the inspector.

Carter snorted. 'Nothing. She was well aware that she'd be at more risk than anyone else if she tried. She wasn't responsible for that post-office bomb, no matter what anyone says.'

'How well did you know her fellow suffragettes?' said Fox.

'Not at all. I supported her views, but didn't go to meetings. She changed the group she went to after reading an advertisement seeking militants from our class rather than the posher sort. I'm not sure if she'd have stayed, since some of them were as posh as usual and trying to take charge. She liked a man there: he was kind, but intense. She didn't think some of the women were what they seemed to be. There was one she disliked, and thought another a bit pitiful.'

'Do you know any names?'

Carter shook his head. 'Only someone Lois knew from Holloway – Mrs Holbourne. Runs a journal for women, Athena something. Anything else?'

'Was there anything about the group in letters she sent you?'

'None that have caught up with me yet,' said Carter. 'That could take weeks. She said she wanted to ask my advice about something when I got back, but in the meantime she'd speak to Mrs Holbourne. She thought someone was in trouble, but I'm not sure how. I assume it was to do with the campaign and she wasn't going to incriminate anyone in a letter.'

Margaret glanced around the room, imagining Lois insensible with the laudanum she took for the pain that Maude numbed with spirits. 'I'm terribly sorry, Mr Carter, but could she have been suicidal?'

'Never,' said Carter. 'She wanted to be out of pain, but not out of life. I thought the clean air in Australia and a fresh start...' For the first time, his voice trembled. He swallowed.

'Was she involved in any political organisation other than the WSPU?' said Fox. 'As secretary perhaps, keeping papers and so on.'

'The only other cause we care about is home rule for Ireland,' said Carter. 'But we don't belong to anything. We're... We were hoping it would go through without too much trouble. No one killed her for that, Inspector.'

'Do you know where she kept her private papers?' asked the inspector. 'Diaries, and so on?'

'She didn't keep a diary that I know of. Her house deeds were in the bank. Her bank books should have been in the dresser.'

'They weren't,' said the inspector.

'What about my gun?'

'What gun?'

'The revolver I left with Lois in case of burglars.' Carter rose and prodded inside the chimney. 'It should be here. Did anyone search the Bessemers?'

The inspector frowned. 'Yes. There was nothing incriminating.'

'He went for the police after she was shot, didn't he?' said Carter. 'I bet it's in a drain. You've looked into my finances, now look into Bessemer's. Mark my words, that'll show something worth knowing. I didn't need Lois's money and didn't expect it, but Bessemer—' There was hammering at the front door. 'I bet that's him.'

The inspector glanced at Fox and they went into the main room, with Margaret and Carter following. Inspector Silvermann opened the door and Mr Bessemer burst in. 'This is my wife's house! What's *he* doing here?' He pointed at Carter. 'I hope he's under arrest.'

'He's not, Mr Bessemer,' said Inspector Silvermann.

On the threshold Mrs Bessemer hesitated, her face pale and strained. Behind her, a small group of people gathered to listen.

'This is my wife's house,' repeated Mr Bessemer. 'I could ask you all to leave. I still don't understand why the locks were changed.'

'It's not your wife's house,' said Carter.

'It will be, once the police stop hindering probate!' snapped Mr Bessemer. 'Lois died intestate. There are no close relations bar Hannah, so Hannah is next of kin. This house and any savings Lois had are rightfully hers.'

'Only she isn't next of kin,' said Carter, 'so they're not.'

Mr Bessemer took a step forward, fists clenched. There was no trace of a limp. 'What are you talking about?'

'Come in, Mrs Bessemer,' said the inspector, beckoning.

'I-I don't want to,' whispered Mrs Bessemer. 'Lois's spirit... I'm afraid.'

'Don't be ridiculous, Hannah,' snapped Mr Bessemer. 'Come inside, now! We need to sort this out once and for all.'

Fox leaned close to Margaret. 'Go to the kitchen and sit in Lois's chair before she notices you.'

'Wh— Oh, I see.' She slipped into the kitchen and pulled the door to, peeking through.

Mr Bessemer dragged his wife over the threshold and slammed the door. 'Stop making a spectacle of yourself, Hannah,' he snapped. 'I repeat, Carter, what are you talking about?'

'In the first place,' said Carter, 'Lois made a will before Miss Bythell died. The old lady made sure of it.'

Mr Bessemer's mouth dropped open and he paled, leaving angry red blotches on his cheeks. 'I ... we... Hannah, did you know about it?'

'N-no,' squeaked Mrs Bessemer. 'Truly, Oswald, truly. D-did she leave it to you, Mr Carter?'

'She didn't know me when she wrote it,' said Carter. 'And she left most of it to you.'

Margaret could no longer see him, but Mr Bessemer's voice sounded as if he was smiling. 'I'm glad to hear it.'

'In trust.'

'What?'

'She left the capital in trust, with a limit on what Mrs Bessemer could withdraw each year.'

'What the—' Mr Bessemer exclaimed. 'No solicitor came forward with that information, so I assume Lois drafted it herself. It's probably not legal. However, knowing she had a will should speed things up. And Hannah *is* next of kin.'

'No,' said Carter. 'Lois and I married in February, therefore *I'm* next of kin. Our marriage invalidated the will.'

'What?' squeaked Mrs Bessemer. The were tears in her voice. 'If I'd known... If *you'd* known... What have we done?'

Mr Bessemer stepped into view as he grabbed his wife's arm and shook her. 'Shh!'

Mrs Bessemer pulled away from him. 'You've made investments based on my expectations!'

'Go and have a glass of water, madam,' said Fox. 'You've had a shock. Let your husband deal with this.'

'Oh, but—'

Margaret saw Fox take Mrs Bessemer's arm and steer her towards the kitchen. She slipped into the seat which Lois had died in, slumped on the table and hid her face in her arms. The voices in the sitting room grew louder as the door opened, then quieter as it partially shut.

Mrs Bessemer gasped. 'Lois? I keep seeing you like that! But it can't be...' Her footsteps came closer, and Margaret's shoulders were gripped and shaken. 'Wake up! This time, wake up! He's not here now.'

Margaret raised her head. 'Who's not here?'

Mrs Bessemer stepped back and collided with a dresser. She was noticeably thinner than she had been at the inquest, her face pale but for purple shadows round her eyes. 'You're the doctor that— I thought – I thought... Your hair's nearly the same colour and you're the same build, but I should have known you weren't Lois. She wouldn't wear a hat at her own table.' Tears started to run down her face. 'I haven't slept for weeks, and when I do sleep, I dream and I try to change what happened. For a moment, I thought I could make everything right again.'

'I can't imagine how terrible I'd feel if I found my sister's body in a gas-filled kitchen,' said Margaret. 'I don't know what I'd do.'

It was a lie: she knew exactly what she'd do. She'd fling open the windows, call for help and do everything to try and save Katherine.

Fox was on the other side of the door which he was holding ajar. She didn't dare look towards him and distract Mrs

Bessemer. The other woman was deep in a memory which was smothering her. It might not take much for her to relieve that pressure.

'Tell me, Mrs Bessemer,' she said, as softly as possible. 'You will feel better.'

'We came to talk her out of marrying Mr Carter and going to Australia. She'd given me a key so I could come round from time to time and see she was all right. Oswald wasn't supposed to know, but... Anyway, we found her... I lifted her to see if she was alive, even though we could barely breathe, but one look and I knew. I told Oswald to open the window and get help, but he said ... he said "It's a sin".'

'What is?' whispered Margaret.

'Suicide,' said Mrs Bessemer. 'I know she was in pain but she just needed more prayer, not to end her own life. People would talk, he said, and the insurance wouldn't pay— I mean, he wanted to save her reputation. He said we could make it look like someone killed her. I shouldn't have told him I had the key, or where she kept that gun. He made me hold her up while he ... and Oswald said we had to make it look real by shooting ourselves too. My hand, his leg. It didn't hurt, because Lois was dead and my heart was breaking. I didn't want her dead, and now it doesn't make a difference anyway.'

'What difference?' said Margaret. It was hard to feel pity any more, and her voice sounded sharp even to herself. She would never have held Katherine's lifeless form up to be shot then dropped her on the table, or allowed herself to be shot. If Fox had been the sort to think otherwise, she would have left him.

The door opened and Mr Bessemer pushed past Fox, blinking at Margaret seated in his sister-in-law's place. 'Come along, Hannah, everything's all right. She made another will in the same terms after her marriage. It's all yours. We can sell this place and contest the trust clause, and the police can continue to seek the burglar, and—'

'I'm tired of lying,' said Mrs Bessemer. 'I haven't been able to pray since you made me lie. If Lois was a sinner, so am I, for not standing up for her. And so are you, for wanting her money so bad. You shot me, Oswald – you shot me! You could have just shot yourself if you'd a mind to, but no, you had to shoot me too. If I inherit that money, I'll make a will of my own and you won't get a farthing.'

'We're all sinners,' said Margaret, standing up. 'For what it's worth, I think Lois's death was a terrible accident. But by doing what you did, you both dragged her name through the mud. And now you've done it to yourselves, too.'

After the Bessemers had been taken to the police station, Fox hailed a cab for Margaret to return to the hospital while he decided what to do next.

'I should have realised about that photograph,' she whispered, as they said goodbye. 'So should the police. I bet Carter's right about the debt.'

Fox nodded, his face grim. 'He's sort of collapsed. I think it's sinking in at last.'

'Poor man. But unless the papers you want are in the bank with her deeds, she never had them. I'm sorry, Fox, I think you've wasted your time.'

'If it hadn't been for the Bessemers trying to cover up what they thought was suicide, the investigation would have been different.'

'The inquest would probably have returned a verdict of accidental death, but...'

'The amount of laudanum doesn't add up, does it? Lois Halpin knew Stokes, and had doubts about at least one person in the group and was about to tell Maude why. Then Lois died from an overdose of laudanum and gas poisoning. Something's amiss. No one's time has been wasted – but Maude should be careful. And so should you.'

'I have every intention of doing so,' said Margaret. 'Today I shall concentrate on my job, and tomorrow I have to accompany Dr Naylor on visits for her book.'

'And on Friday?'

'I shall wait for you by the hearth like a good wife.'

'That'll be the day,' said Fox.

'And I'll review those post-mortem files again. If I missed something crucial from the photograph of Lois, who knows what else I've missed.'

Twenty-Two

By Friday, as the governments behind the delegates bickered and threatened each other, the papers reported little but the treaty. If the allegiances and treaties currently creaking under the strain held up, it would be signed around midday and the Balkan war would cease.

At home with the post-mortem files, Margaret tried to reassure herself with Fox's certainty that any attack on St James's Palace would be thwarted before it began.

She took the files to her study and read while the children played with wooden cups and balls on the carpet. She wrote *J Stokes, L Halpin, Unknown* down the left-hand side of a piece of paper, then put headings along the top: *suffrage involvement; bullet; gas; other factors*. She jotted information from each case file under the relevant heading.

After a while, she read it through. *J Stokes: militant; bullet – cause of death; gas – yes; bomb-making equipment. L Halpin: militant; bullet yes but irrelevant; gas– cause of death; excessive laudanum & allegations she'd planted a bomb. Unknown woman: view on suffrage unknown; no sign of bullet; no sign of gas; bomb, blow to head – either/both being cause of death.*

'Nonono!' shouted Edie. There was a dull thump. A wooden cup flew across the floor and hit the doorframe.

'Alec help,' said Alec.

'Nonono! Edie do it. Naughty ball.'

'What's wrong, darling?' Margaret dropped to the floor, retrieved the cup and offered it to her daughter, who pushed it away.

'Wanna *this* one!' Edie sobbed, trying to force a four-inch ball into a three-inch cup, tears welling in her eyes. 'Not do.'

Margaret lifted the little hands and hugged her daughter. 'You can't make things fit that don't, however much you try.'

'Can!'

'You can't.' She sighed, looking at the paper on the desk above. 'But it's always tempting.'

'Wanna.'

'I know,' said Margaret. 'Me too.'

Edie yawned mid-sob and knuckled her eyes. Alec put the last ball into the last cup of the right size, then toddled over to snuggle up.

At noon Maude arrived, stony faced, and after some persuasion, joined Margaret for lunch. 'You could have telephoned Phoebe and me about Miss Tabor,' she said. 'Or written, or come round, or something. I can't believe that I heard through a policeman on Monday afternoon.' She said the word with a slight curl of the lip, as if her elegant drawing room had been polluted. 'I had to deal with Hedley Tabor making vague accusations on the telephone, then the following morning I was told by a constable barely old enough to have left school that it wasn't Miss Tabor at all! Yet he hinted that I mustn't assume myself innocent, with some woolly references to ruby jewellery. I told him I only wear diamonds, which shut him up.'

'I'm surprised the sparks didn't cause a fire,' said Margaret, smiling.

'It isn't funny, Margaret,' said Maude, after Freda had placed beef before them, filled their water glasses and left. 'Hedley Tabor said you went with the inspector to break the news. Why didn't you do the same for me or Phoebe? Or at least tell us before he turned up.'

'I was under orders not to.'

Maude sipped her water, scowling. 'I really do miss you, Demeray. Once, you'd never have let a policeman tell you what to do – you'd have told *him* what to do. And you'd have come round immediately and told me what you thought had happened to Miss Tabor, even if it turned out to be someone else. We were all in the area when it happened. And how was the body misidentified?'

'It's my fault,' said Margaret. 'I thought I recognised some jewellery with the body, and because I thought I saw Miss Tabor that afternoon, I thought there was a possibility that the body was hers and felt terrible that I hadn't stopped her. And I felt terrible about not being able to tell you and Phoebe. I've told the inspector you had nothing to do with it.'

'Why would I?' said Maude. 'But there seems to be an idea floating round that I asked Miss Tabor to do something for me. I wouldn't. Miss Tabor makes me weary.'

'I hope you didn't say so.'

'One is not a complete fool,' said Maude. She took another sip of water. Her food remained barely touched.

'Someone must have asked her to do something. I imagine the inspector wants to ask each member of our group whether we know who and why. But none of that will help to discover who the victim really is. Unless he's angling to suggest that Miss Tabor is someone that one of us lured there, too.'

'Blame the suffragette,' said Maude. 'I still think you should have told me and Phoebe what you thought when you saw the body.'

'I was in a state of shock. I can't begin to explain what it was like. It's bad enough seeing remains like those and knowing they belong to a stranger. When I thought they were those of someone I knew, I was appalled. I neither like nor dislike Miss Tabor. I'm a little alarmed by her passion for your eloquence, but I daresay she's never been allowed to express strong emotion and it comes out in those meetings. Of course, you *are* wonderful.' She forced a grin.

'Of course I am,' said Maude. She grinned back, then sobered. 'But no one would wish that death on anyone.'

'No. And adding to the whole confusion about identity was Hedley thinking his sister was missing.'

'But surely he'd have known when he saw the remains? Or does Miss Tabor have a doppelganger?'

Margaret put her knife and fork down and pushed her plate away. It was not the right time to describe the body to Maude. 'He couldn't have told who it was.'

'Oh,' said Maude. 'How terrible. Apology accepted, Demeray. But I still think you should stop listening to policemen. It's bad enough that you let Fox tell you what to do.'

'Never.'

Maude rose, collected the port and two glasses from the sideboard and poured a small measure. 'Let's raise a glass to the unknown woman – even if the police think I killed her – and begin afresh.' She sipped, then cleared her throat. 'Shall we still go to the Derby? I want to blow the cobwebs away more than ever now. Geoff and I are going to the coast for a few days. to try and mend things between us, but I'll be back on Tuesday, and I can collect you Wednesday morning.'

'Any campaigning to be done there?'

'Not by me,' said Maude. 'Though I'll wear my Holloway badge. I'm not ashamed of my views.'

'Nor am I,' said Margaret. 'It'll be nice to do something normal. I'll come.'

Late in the afternoon, Inspector Silvermann arrived.

'To what do I owe this pleasure?' Margaret said, as she poured tea. 'I thought you might be busy today. Have the Bessemers been charged?'

'I am and they have,' he said. He scanned the room, then sat back and smiled at her. 'I often wonder what you do when you're not at the hospital.'

'I'm researching for a book I'm helping to write.'

'Fiction, like your father? One of those wretched detective novels?'

'It's about pulmonary disease among the working class.'

The inspector pulled a face. 'Write the thriller instead. Just don't make the average copper out to be an idiot, like authors usually do.'

'I'll bear that in mind,' said Margaret, 'To be truthful, today I've been reviewing post-mortem files and my student's report into laudanum. Here are my observations.' She handed over her notes.

'I don't recall you being recruited,' said the inspector. He pointed at the names on the paper. 'I don't follow. Miss Halpin's case is closed. Miss Unknown's case is open but wasn't gas. As for Stokes, what does his case have to do with the price of soap? Unless this is all to do with him planning to plant bombs and Miss Halpin posting one in Carmelo Street, and you're worried I'll look for a friend who's thinking of doing similar.'

'I'm not. And Miss Halpin had ingested more than one small bottle of laudanum.'

'Mmm. Well, if she was murdered, I still maintain it was someone taking justice into their own hands.' He closed his notebook and put it away. 'And I can't tell you how annoying it is when people do that, Dr Demeray.'

'If you mean me, I'm doing nothing of the sort. I'm giving you information.'

'You're giving me opinion,' said the inspector. 'I'm here to tell you not to protect people who don't deserve to be protected. And now I'm telling you to turn your observations into fire-lighters. You wouldn't like it if I started cutting up your patients, would you? Well, guess what? I don't like it when people start trying to solve my crimes. I'll see myself out.'

Cursing him, Margaret prepared to screw up the piece of paper and take it to the stove. Then she perused it again. No: she wouldn't like the inspector doing her job, but she'd accept his help if he offered it. If he didn't reciprocate, more fool him.

Fox came home at a quarter to seven.

'I read that the treaty was signed without a hitch,' said Margaret, as he sat down beside her. 'The paper says it will resolve all the tensions, provided the press in Britain and Germany stop publishing articles that stir up nationalism. I hope it's that simple, but...'

'Maybe it is,' said Fox. 'We've got this far without anything going wrong. The papers Queale stole would have been catastrophic before now, but they haven't seen the light of day. Perhaps his mistress did destroy them. The various embassies remain anxious until they have proof that the papers are either in the right hands or destroyed. So on that note, and with the intelligence you've given, do you fancy a visit to St John's Wood?'

'I was right?'

'A Mrs Queale leased the top-floor flat in Russett House for a year last December. No one, including the landlord, knows much about her. She's a cut above, he said. Respectable.'

'What does she look like?'

'Middle-aged. Nondescript.'

Margaret scowled. 'Do you mean that she's average-looking, or that because she's no longer in her youth and no particular beauty, she's not worth looking at hard enough to describe?'

Fox stared. 'Don't attack me: it's all I know. Everyone dealt with her so-called husband, who paid the year's rent in advance before he went abroad. Inasmuch as it's good evidence, the land agent recognised a photograph of Queale as the husband. Mrs Queale left for India shortly before Stokes died.'

'Then how—'

'I'll rephrase that. She wrote to the land agent and said that was what she was doing, and no one has seen her since before Maundy Thursday. It'll be why the police didn't mention her in their reports. But of course, where one says one's going and where one goes are not necessarily the same.'

'Are they definitely not married?'

'Not in Britain. I'm undecided on whether to tell Queale and see if he talks, or let him suspect we're getting closer and see what he does. Whether you're right about the reason for Stokes's death is another matter. We've obtained warrants of entry and the land agent has given us the spare keys to Mrs Queale's flat. I don't want to have to use the warrant to get into Stokes's old flat, so I'm hoping your presence will help me gain entry and ask questions in a subtle sort of way. I don't suppose you feel like being a medium who wants to exorcise Stokes's ghost?'

'No,' said Margaret firmly. 'I don't believe in ghosts.'

'You were worried about Miss Halpin's.'

'I wasn't.'

Fox grinned. Margaret picked up her notes and sighed. 'What is it?' he asked.

'Inspector Silvermann hinted that I should disassociate from Maude, preferably after I'd told him anything that could incriminate her in the death at St James's and in enticing Miss Tabor to plant bombs.'

'Ah.'

'I cannot believe that she would use a suggestible woman to do something for her, especially when it held such danger, nor that Miss Tabor would deliberately take a bomb anywhere for anyone, no matter how passionate she became about the cause.'

'Does Maude agree?'

'I don't think she wants to harm people or disrupt peace negotiations any more than I do,' said Margaret. 'She knows what's at stake. If it was intended for St James's Palace, I don't believe Maude or anyone from Phoebe's group is behind it. I wouldn't be surprised if it was another attempt on that flat.'

'So let's prove it. Shall we enter the fray together?'

'I don't have a fray,' said Margaret. 'Inspector Silverman told me to stop making up theories and concentrate on my job.'

'Since when did you start listening to Inspector Silvermann? Although there's a risk if anyone notices you're not letting things lie. On the other hand...'

'If I receive another letter, it might prove the point.'

'Exactly.'

'The police searched all the flats for signs of burglary including Mrs Queale's,' said Fox, as they drove towards St John's Wood. 'However, it seemed undisturbed, and there was no sign of forced entry.'

'How did the burglars get in?'

'The scullery window was open and the door to the backyard was unlocked. No one admitted being responsible for either, but there were incomplete muddy footprints and whatnot going up the stairs.'

'That's rather inefficient for a burglar.'

'Isn't it?'

'And Mr Abney would give better instructions.'

'He would, but that's not to suggest someone didn't act on their own initiative. Nothing was missing except some brass items belonging to the landlord, which gathered dust on one of the landing windowsills. It took a while for anyone to realise: even he didn't care about them and they're two a penny in Petticoat Lane. The muddy footprints only go as far as the floor Stoke's flat was on. Mrs Queale's is above.'

'So the police theory is that the burglar intended to go to hers.'

'Or start with Stokes's. Anyway, here we are.'

'Do the police reports describe Stokes? All I know is that Maude and Mrs Philbrook think he was quiet but passionate. Miss Halpin apparently said he was worried. Miss Tabor indicated he wasn't *one of us.*'

'Human?'

'You know what she meant.'

'Knowing what she meant doesn't stop it being offensive,' said Fox, with a scowl. 'He was a human being who wasn't a snob who died young. He was shy, a little disgruntled, a clerk who never seemed to progress. He had just enough income through investments to rent somewhere a little better than his salary would have allowed. No near relations except a fussing aunt in the countryside. No best girl or any girl, or even a close friend. He kept himself to himself, but it seems as if all the tenants do that. None of them seem to know each other.'

'This is London,' said Margaret. 'That's what it's like.'

'Which is both disagreeable and unhelpful,' said Fox. 'However, one of the neighbours said he'd once gone inside Stokes's flat and seen suffrage materials. He felt Stokes was trying to "convert" him and was concerned about what he'd seen. Reading between the lines, his demeanour suggested he told people Stokes could be making bombs.'

'When you say "reading between the lines", do you mean there's a secret code police use in reports, indicating a witness's personality or truthfulness to anyone in the know?'

'What a suggestion,' said Fox, eyes wide with innocence. 'He certainly told the landlord's agent. The agent visited to see what Stokes had, but found nothing. Perhaps it was all a misunderstanding.'

'Maude thinks so.'

'It's easy to assume quiet people sit at home doing nothing,' said Fox, 'and that their inner lives are as quiet as their demeanour. That's rarely true.'

Margaret nodded. 'Even Miss Tabor had her secrets.'

'And sometimes, people who feel they are always being overlooked hold deep resentments that may burst out in violence or nastiness.'

'Miss Tabor, or Stokes or someone else?'

'You tell me.'

Twenty-Three

R ussett House was about sixty years old, tall and elegant. Each of the four floors above street level had been turned into a flat, with a fifth below in what would once have been the kitchen, reached via the area steps. Mrs Queale's flat was beneath the empty attics and Stokes's flat below that.

The newly married couple in the latter were perhaps too in love to be surprised when Fox said the landlord had suggested they look round what had been Stokes's flat so they could recommend a similar one to a friend. Ragtime was playing scratchily on a battered gramophone.

'I imagine you heard that the previous tenant was murdered just outside the front door,' said the young man. He pointed confidently beyond the brand-new floorboards just inside the threshold.

'Does that worry you?' said Margaret.

'Nah. We're not superstitious,' said the young man. 'Don't tell the landlord that. We got him to knock a few quid off the rent in case of haunting.' He grinned and nudged his wife.

'The furniture's the landlord's,' she said. 'And the prints on the walls.' She pulled a face as she gestured at sentimental pictures of simpering girls and flowers and children with puppies. 'We hope to get a little house in a year or so and then we can get our own things. Modern. Not this old-fashioned stuff.'

'Mind if I look up the chimney?' said Fox. 'And knock on the walls to see how solid it is?'

'Be my guest.' The young man offered a cigarette and led Fox off to look round.

'I heard the murdered man was a suffragette supporter,' said Margaret.

'Good for him,' said the young woman. 'Me too. You?'

'Yes.'

The young woman nodded. 'Not that I'd set a bomb. The police took all his suffragette stuff, apparently, and his personal things went to his aunt's. We're not superstitious, like Wilf said, but I draw the line at sleeping in a dead man's sheets and using his crockery and reading his books.'

'Maybe I'll have a word with the landlord about taking those prints away and letting you put up your own.'

'That would be nice,' said the young woman. 'Thanks.'

Mrs Queale's flat upstairs was stale and dusty from three months of disuse, but it had a homely feel for somewhere that was only used occasionally. In daytime, the pleasant sitting room with a large sofa would be sunny, and the kitchen area with its paraffin stove and enamel basin had plenty of light. Floral bowls were placed to catch the light, one filled with dried petals. Margaret gave them a stir and the aroma of roses drifted, then died.

Through an open door Margaret could make out a pair of narrow beds, neatly made and covered in eiderdowns. They seemed more like the sort of thing a long-married couple might have, rather than two people in an illicit liaison. There was a bookcase and a small table with an old-fashioned glass dome containing dried flowers, next to a musical box with butterflies on narrow pins, ready to dance when it played. The prints on the walls were like those on the floor below: if anything, more sentimental: chocolate box children hugged fluffy kittens adorned with ribbon bows; young lovers shared shy kisses.

'We can look inside the picture frames,' said Fox. 'I'd like to do the same with the ones downstairs, but have no idea how.'

'I said we'd get the landlord to take them and let them put up their own. Perhaps one of your people can come to collect them.'

'You're not as daft as you look.'

'So kind,' said Margaret. 'We'd best be careful. How do we know Mrs Queale won't return?'

'I have people watching outside but I doubt she'll come back tonight, and I have no intention of turning the place upside down. Either she or someone working with her took the papers away on Easter Sunday thinking the house was empty, and killed Stokes because he saw them when they shouldn't have been there. Or she'd already taken them and the intruder was someone else trying to find them, and Stokes saw. Or—'

'What about the footprints on the stairs?'

'Possibly manufactured. They were barely visible and oddly spaced. A woman in a man's shoes – or wielding them – could have laid a false trail.'

'And the other option is that the papers are still here waiting for her return.'

'Yes.' Fox took a picture from the wall and started to remove the sticking paper. 'I'll do this. Can you look through the books and in any feminine place where they might be hidden?'

'I wish you'd stop assuming I know how every female mind works, Fox.'

'You've got more hope than I have.'

An hour later, nothing had come to light. There were no clothes in the wardrobe or drawers and every surface was well-polished. It would take hours to find any stray fingerprints.

'We'll have to go,' said Fox. 'I'll have someone come in and search under the floorboards and in the chimney breast tomorrow. But...'

'What?'

'I don't think they're here. Otherwise, why would someone try to blow the place up with Stokes's nitroglycerin, or a parcel bomb? And when we mentioned St John's Wood in passing, Queale went still for a moment, then said, with some asperity, "They're not there". I said, "But *she* is," and he frowned and shook his head. But he looked haunted.'

In a quiet restaurant, Fox read through Margaret's notes. 'The only link between these people, taking out any unknown political views about the treaty, is the suffrage group also attended by Maude. And you don't know where it is or who runs it.'

'Maude doesn't know who runs it, either. Mrs Philbrook also goes.'

'What do you know of the latter?'

'Not much. Maude says she's passionate about the cause and eager for militancy, but she seems affected to me. All Tennyson and romance. It's hard to imagine her smashing a window or setting a postbox alight. I don't believe she's even been arrested for anything, which has happened to more than half of Phoebe's group. She reminds me of Etta. I can't understand why Maude admires her so.'

'*Does* she admire her?'

'She compared me unfavourably to her.'

'Jealous?'

'Don't be ridiculous, Fox.'

'Irritated?'

Margaret speared a buttered carrot and contemplated it. 'Mrs Philbrook irritates me. But maybe I'm being unfair, having only met her a few times in social settings. We all present different personas for those.'

'Most do. Not all.' Fox swirled his wine. 'You don't. Could you ask Maude for more detail without it seeming odd? You needn't say why.'

'I tried to go to the meeting, but Maude won't tell me where it is.' Margaret looked out of the window as the world went by. Passers-by were presumably returning to homes where they felt safe and comfortable. *That's what I should be doing,* she thought. *Going home, to look after the children and mind my own business. That's what Inspector Silvermann told me to do. It's what Maude thinks I do, but I've got myself into this and now it feels as if Fox wants me to spy on her.*

'That's odd,' said Fox.

'She's being protective,' said Margaret. 'A member was fol-lowed on her way home one evening.'

'Then just ask her about Stokes again. It would be quite natural.'

'She and Geoff are away.'

'Where?'

'We don't keep note of each other's appointments, Fox. Do you know where your friends are all the time?' Even as she said it, Margaret was conscious that she had only ever known one of Fox's friends, who was now dead, and he'd never spoken of any others. She felt herself blush.

'No,' he said, without a pause. 'My friend is unpredictable even when she's supposed to be working.'

'I'm spending the day with Maude on Wednesday: I'll do it then. She'd find it very odd if I just asked, out of the blue.'

'Very well,' said Fox. 'I suppose that is a more natural thing to do.'

She could hear the disappointment in his voice. But she wasn't prepared to do anything about it.

Despite Margaret's fears, no more letters arrived to suggest that anyone knew she'd visited Russett House. Perhaps the writer thought she'd lost interest now that the truth about Miss Halpin's death was in the papers.

The days passed without incident. Fox was busy, ensuring that delegates left the country without issue and tracking the movements of known agents, while Elinor was still tracing advertisements. The newspapers had not been given the assumed name of the bomb victim in St James's and were making increasingly acerbic remarks about police duplicity. Queale had had a nervous collapse and was making little sense. His advertisements were increasingly bizarre, the responses increasingly indifferent.

'At heart, he's a man of peace,' said Fox. 'He's just going about it the wrong way. I wish I trusted the woman as he does. But if we push him any further we'll have to put him in an asylum, and then we'll never find out.'

After the staff meeting on Tuesday, a smirking Dr Southern told Margaret to enjoy herself frivolling at the races with his wife and Mrs Philbrook. She reminded him sharply that she was working on Thursday instead, to help Dr Gesner prepare for Miss Tabor's inquest and the re-opened inquest into Miss Halpin's death, but Dr Southern merely shrugged and winked. If he'd patted her shoulder it couldn't have been more patronising.

On Wednesday, Maude's chauffeur drove Margaret and Maude to Epsom.

'What a shame Phoebe's not here,' said Margaret after Edwards had parked and they were making their way towards the track.

'I've spotted several suffragettes.'

'Me too. Had you intended that we should join Mrs Philbrook and Mrs Southern?'

'Not intentionally,' said Maude. 'Why?'

'Dr Southern hinted at it yesterday.'

'Huh,' said Maude. 'Mrs Southern seems worse than Etta. I imagine that even when she gets the vote, she'll have a maid do the deed for her. What's her husband like? I only met her briefly at the soirée but I get the impression from Mrs Philbrook that it wasn't a love match.'

'I believe he has money,' said Margaret.

'And I know she has connections.'

Margaret chuckled. 'No doubt she and Mrs Philbrook are in some kind of enclave, maybe even with royalty. They're very patriotic. We'll be with the hoi-polloi.'

'I read that Lois Halpin's brother-in-law has been arrested,' said Maude. 'I knew there was something wrong about the case but I wasn't expecting that. Will they conclude it was suicide or accident?'

'The inquest will be reopened soon,' said Margaret. 'We're just trying to obtain more evidence.'

'I still maintain—'

'I know. But have you any idea what might be behind it?'

'Not so far,' said Maude, taking the betting slips from Edwards and steering Margaret towards the track.

'There's absolutely no hope that I'll win,' said Margaret. 'Aboyeur's on at a hundred to one. I've no idea why I picked him.'

'What if he did win? Think of what you could buy Fox with two pounds ten shillings.'

'Blow Fox. I'll spend it on myself.'

'I bet you'd feel so guilty you'd give it to charity. Then feel even guiltier for donating the profits of sin.'

Margaret stuck up her chin and looked around. The crowd was pushing towards the rails. 'Can we get anywhere near the finish line?'

'Possibly, if you don't mind either not seeing or being squashed flat. Somewhere just after the bend might be better.'

It was just possible to squeeze through to the rails near what was called Tattenham Corner. On either side, people pressed, pushed and strained to see, and cursed ladies' hats. There was a short period of shuffling, a shorter moment of still anticipation, and the starting gun went off.

Behind and above, more people pushed and leaned and yelled. In seconds, it was clear who was in the lead.

'Aboyeur!'

'Craganour!'

'Shogun!'

'Comet!'

'Louvois!'

'Go, Aboyeur!'

'Come on, Shogun!'

Maude yelled 'Craganour! Go for it!' with all her might. Her body was tense and hot against Margaret's. The bodies of the strangers pressing close were even hotter.

'Aboyeur!' shrieked Margaret, forgetting which colours she should look for as the leaders galloped past and in the thrill of the moment, laughing with excitement.

The shouts were like battle cries. Blood pounded in Margaret's ears, and the straining spectators pulled and pushed like waves, while the trembling in the ground increased. The air was full of passion and hunger and obsession and excitement. Margaret was yelling, even though her voice was now simply a vibration in her own skull. She waved and shouted and the thundering earthquake grew louder and her heart beat faster and the clamour became a torrent of names and... With a flash, the first horse and the second turned the bend, necks twisting as they strained against the reins and reached to bite each other, and the jockeys' whips flailed. Then the next two horses flashed past and Margaret craned to see past heads and hats to the finishing line, even though it was impossible, then turned back to watch the next cohort of horses rushing towards the bend.

The yelling deafened her and the heat grew. From above, the yells of those who could see the finishing line ricocheted and contradicted each other.

'Aboyeur!'

'Craganour!'

'Aboyeur!'

'Craganour!'

But maybe, against all the odds, one of the last four horses could still catch up. Maude clutched her arm and people shouted:

'Agadir!'

'Emily!'

'Here's Anmer!'

'No!'

'What the hell...?'

'They're coming!'

'Emily!'

'Oh my God!'

Someone – a woman – was standing on the course and reaching upwards. A horse crashed into her. Time slowed and the noise dulled. Horse, woman and jockey blurred as they fell. The other horses swerved and rushed past as the fallen horse whinnied and tried to stand up and the woman's summer hat bowled along the grass.

But the man and the woman lay still.

In the seconds before the people nearest rushed forward, Margaret thought she saw mud-and-blood-soiled silk between the dark flanks of the horse. Not the purple, red and gold of the jockey, but purple, white and green. Then her view was blocked as bystanders rushed to help.

The noises blurred and echoed in Margaret's head: the cheering of spectators looking the other way, the woman's cry, the man's yell, the horse's scream, and her own voice as she pulled at the people between her and the fallen man and woman: 'Let me through – I'm a doctor!' But there was no way through, and she could not be heard.

'She's dead!'

'Who cares? It's a bloody suffragette! She's killed the King's horse, and his jockey!'

'Are there any more about? I'll kill 'em myself!'

The crowd who hadn't seen or couldn't see were rushing towards the finish line, their voices ever louder and more excited.

'Craganour!'

'Aboyeur!'

'Craganour!'

'Aboyeur!'

And when a wild cheer arose as one of them crossed the finishing line, Margaret knew that either she or Maude had won their bet after all. But nothing could ever have mattered less.

Maude grabbed her arm. 'We have to run.'

'What?'

'*Run*. Someone just slapped a suffragette in the face. And I saw that man again – the one I told you about. Take off your badge and run to the car. *Run!*'

'Not so fast, ladies,' said a constable, grabbing Margaret's arm. 'We need to ask you a few questions.'

Fox came home at eight.

Margaret was swaying in the sitting room with Edie asleep in her arms as the gramophone played a nocturne. 'She couldn't settle,' she said. 'I thought I'd bring her down so she didn't disturb Alec. I've been meaning to take her back for half an hour, but it's... It's nice dancing with her.'

Edie was snuggled against her, soft curls silky against Margaret's throat, the scent of rose dusting powder filling the warm evening air, the slow waltz calming and hypnotic.

Fox put his newspaper on the sideboard and took her and Edie into his arms, swaying with them. Edie murmured, stirred, then turned and nuzzled into his jacket. 'I suppose ... er...' He glanced at the paper.

'Phoebe has called a suffrage meeting for tomorrow evening.'

'To pray?'

'I think so.' Margaret leaned against him. 'I should have guessed it would be in the evening papers,' she murmured.

'It's in the cinemas, too.'

'Already? How horrible. I only saw a little of it, but we had to give statements to the police all the same. I was still trying to work out what I'd seen, then trying hard to be objective. Maude knew Miss Davison... She's devastated.'

'Oh, Margaret.'

'It was supposed to be fun and take our minds off things. And I was going to ask Maude about Stokes, and then...'

Fox pulled her closer, kissed her head and started the slow waltz again.

'Is she still alive?' asked Margaret. 'What about the jockey? And the horse?'

'The jockey got away with a broken rib, cuts and bruises. He even asked after Miss Davison as soon as he regained consciousness The horse just suffered bruising: he'll be all right. But Miss Davison's skull is fractured and she's still deep under. I don't think they hold out much hope.'

'Oh God.' Margaret closed her eyes. 'I saw her knocked down. Before that – I'm not sure if I saw her step out or I'm imagining it. We were a little way away and it was all so fast.'

The record came to an end and Fox took Edie gently from Margaret. 'Shall I take her to the nursery? You look drained.'

'I'm sad,' said Margaret. 'Shocked. I couldn't get through to help, but I don't think that changed anything. Some women were attacked, and Maude thought we might be.'

Inspector Silvermann's words echoed in her head. *Is the vote worth that much to you? It wouldn't be to me.* 'I just wish she hadn't done it.'

Twenty-Four

eadlines on posters waited at every corner of Margaret's
journey to Dorcas Free. Every one was yelled out by the
vendors to passers by: *Madness! Militant! Tragedy! Outrage!
Insanity! Suffragette!*

She couldn't bear to buy a newspaper and read any more.

She answered her female teaching group's questions that
morning without saying she'd been at Epsom or giving a great
deal of her own opinion. Once she felt they'd vented enough,
she closed the conversation by insisting they concentrate on the
task in hand. They remained agitated and inattentive. Margaret
suspected they wanted to study head injury more than lung
disease and wanted even more to talk in pointless circles about
what Emily Davison had intended to achieve and what she'd
actually achieved.

Afterwards, she and Dr Gesner prepared for the inquest, time
slipping away as they worked back and forth from notes and
sketches and photographs. It was past their lunch-hour when
Miss Upton entered and gave Margaret a telegram.

My dear Margaret. Please meet LH house 1.15. With love Fox.

'Might I go to lunch, doctor?' she asked.

'My goodness,' said Dr Gesner, 'is that the time? Of course
you may.'

It should have been nice to be outside. The day was bright
and there was a fresh breeze. It was warm enough, but in the

shadows Margaret shivered. There wasn't enough time to walk and she'd have to take the tube.

The underground was busy: she was jostled and pushed. As she made her way down to the platform, the thought of bombs made her vigilant. She looked around to see whether anybody was behaving in a suspicious manner or any odd packages were lying about. There was nothing, but she moved as far away from the track as she could, allowing others to filter in front.

Eventually, the train pulled in. Passengers alighted and others boarded.

As she followed, Margaret felt herself shoved hard in the back, reigniting the pain left from the punch at the rally in March. She half turned to see who was responsible, but the tide of people behind her made it impossible. Inside the carriage, she turned. A florid man in a bowler stood behind her.

'Why did you push me?' she said.

'Who says I did?' He grabbed the rail as the train started to move and let himself sway with it, jolting against her. With an effort, Margaret managed to keep herself upright.

'Whoops,' he said, bumping her again. 'Wouldn't it be nice if these trains ran smoothly?' He grinned.

Then somebody pinched her. Despite several layers of clothes, she could feel fingers on her buttock. She trod on the pushing man's foot hard and rounded to hit the pincher with her handbag.

'Whoops,' she said.

Holding onto the edges of the seats as the train rocked, she made her way down the aisle and found a seat, turning to face the two men. They seemed unrepentant, one rubbing his sore foot and the other laughing at her. She felt people watching from behind newspapers and books.

A man leaned sideways. 'Are you another lunatic?'

'I beg your pardon?' said Margaret.

'The suffragette menace.' He stabbed at her WSPU badge, his gloved finger digging into her breast. 'Planting bombs, burning things. Chucking themselves in front of horses. What would *you* do?'

The woman next to Margaret shifted further away. Others nearby gave them nervous glances over their books and newspapers and shuffled away as much as they could.

'That's treason, that is,' snapped another woman. 'Trying to kill the King's horse. And trying to kill yourself is a sin.'

'If you mean Miss Davison, I don't think she was trying to kill anyone.'

'Dontcha? But are *you*?'

'I don't know what you're talking about,' said Margaret. 'I'm trying to travel somewhere, the same as everybody else.'

She moved towards the door as the train pulled into the next station. It wasn't her stop, but she couldn't bear any more. As she got out, the man who'd called her a lunatic pulled her back and struck her across the face with his folded newspaper. 'Don't pretend you ain't one of them,' he said. 'You've all got a screw loose and yer want locking up.'

There wasn't room to retaliate. Shaken, her face stinging, Margaret descended from the train. Instead of waiting for the next one, she walked out of the station and up to the street, then stood, trying to get her bearings. She sensed people staring and looked at her reflection in a window. She straightened her hat and neatened her hair. Then, with more purpose, she began walking the remaining half mile to Miss Halpin's house.

The street was lunchtime quiet. The house's windows were clean and the doorstep swept. It was one thirty, and Fox was nowhere to be seen. Perhaps he'd gone inside, rather than wait and risk looking suspicious. Even as she lifted the knocker, Margaret sensed the house was empty, but she knocked anyway, hoping she was wrong. Why would Fox ask her to meet him and not be there when she was only a quarter of an hour late? She pondered, rubbing the small of her back.

Across the street, a woman leaned out of a window. 'There's no one there, madam,' she called. Her accent was soft, with a country burr. 'You'll have to go to the house agents if you want to view it. I said the same to a fellow earlier.'

'What was the fellow like?' asked Margaret, glad the woman hadn't lost her country inclination to chatter.

The woman shrugged. 'I was too busy to take notice. Fairish, maybe?'

'Strawberry blond? My age? Medium height?'

'Nah – he was grey more than fair and shorter, maybe. Not a lot of light in this street. He was a gent of some kind, so maybe he just wants to buy somewhere to let out. Anyhow, he wasn't here long.'

'When was that?'

'About ten minutes ago.' The woman contemplated Margaret and a curious, rakish smile played on her lips. Perhaps she thought Margaret was there for illicit reasons.

'I was supposed to meet my husband here,' said Margaret, before the smile turned into a smirk.

'Wouldn't your husband wait?'

'Yes.' Margaret frowned: it was unlike Fox to go on without her. 'I think there's been a misunderstanding.' She reached into her bag for the telegram and realised she'd left it on her desk. 'I must have read the message wrong. Definitely not red-headed?'

'Don't think so.'

'Then I must have come to the wrong place. Which way did the man go?'

The woman pointed up the street. 'Another fellow followed right after him, mind.'

'Did you tell the police?'

The woman looked blank. 'People are allowed to walk along the street, ain't they? It's respectable here. We're too far from Paddington Station for it to be otherwise. Lois Halpin's death is the most interesting thing that's happened since the street was built, they reckon, and that was a misunderstanding. Ladies such as yourself wouldn't visit otherwise.'

'Visit who?'

'Lois. She was at the inquest all woebegone, so she musta been a friend. Anyway, I best get on, and you oughta find your hubby and get some lunch. You're looking a bit peaky.'

Margaret nodded her thanks, troubled. The 'lady' couldn't be Maude. Maude couldn't look woebegone if she was paid for it.

She headed for the main road. Footsteps came up behind her. She wasn't sure whether to turn or run. If it were Fox, surely he would hail her.

She paused near a doorway and turned. If the worst came to the worst, she could hammer on the door and hope the people inside would leave their lunch to answer. Was the man coming up behind her the man she'd seen in the theatre café? Maude said he had followed a woman from the meeting and later followed them at the racecourse. Was it him? Despite the heat of the day, he wore a silk muffler and his hat was slightly too large. His face, with receding chin and slightly buck teeth, looked both familiar and unfamiliar. She thought he might approach her, but he strode past as if she wasn't there.

Chiding herself for not remembering the man in the café's features, she followed. By the time she reached the thoroughfare, he was nowhere to be seen. Margaret tried to flag down a cab, but every one was occupied. One slowed as someone crossed the road and its occupant locked eyes with her. It was the man she'd thought was Mr Abney a few days before. She no longer doubted it. Something had altered his face – age, apoplexy, palsy – but that lascivious, sickening smile couldn't be mistaken. She backed into the throng and the taxi passed, traffic crawling behind it. She hurried to the underground station and started down the steps.

This time, there was no question that the shove in her back was deliberate.

Margaret stumbled as her weak ankle gave way. She clutched at the handrail to steady herself but failed, overbalancing and landing in a heap at the bottom of the steps. Her handbag skittered across the floor and a man picked it up as if he might use it to club her. Two men reached down to help Margaret up. People passed, watching out of the corners of their eyes, determined to keep out of it.

'What happened?' asked a young woman.

'Someone pushed her,' said somebody else.

'Who'd do that on purpose to a lady?' demanded a third person.

'You all right, my love?' said a man with whisky breath, leaning a little too close.

'She just tripped,' said an older woman. 'Look at the state of these steps. The litter some people drop! It's no wonder.'

'I saw someone push her.'

'Where is he, then?'

'I don't know. He's gone.'

'What was he like?'

'I don't know. He was with a woman in glasses. Maybe *she* pushed her.'

'Sit down, ducky,' said the old lady. 'I've got smelling salts in my bag. You look fit to faint.' She started to rummage in a portmanteau big enough to hold a small child.

A ticket inspector came up as Margaret was manhandled into a chair. 'What's happening, madam? Did you faint?'

'Someone pushed me deliberately,' said Margaret.

'Oh, I don't think so, madam,' said the ticket inspector. 'It's not that kind of place. You've slipped and banged your head. I can get you a nice cup of sweet tea, that'll help.'

'A policeman would help a good deal more.' Margaret wasn't sure which part of her hurt most.

'No need for that, madam,' said the ticket inspector. 'Now then, where are you going?'

Margaret was conscious of people hovering as others sidled past.

'Maybe someone was trying to kidnap her,' said the old lady. 'I've heard that's been happening a lot round here recently. Fresh young girls lured away on the underground.'

'That's libel, saying that sort of thing about a respectable station!' exclaimed the ticket inspector. 'No one's been stolen from here, and anyway they'd pull, not push, and that sort don't go for ladies of her...' He looked at Margaret and blushed. 'Of this lady's class and respectability.'

Everything felt wrong. Margaret stood up and tested her ankle. The people around her were losing interest, except for a few who perhaps had nowhere better to be.

'I'm going outside to find that policeman,' said Margaret. 'Perhaps he can take statements from those of you who saw someone push me.'

The remaining spectators looked at each other, mumbled that they'd seen nothing, and drifted away.

'Told you,' said the ticket inspector. 'Just an accident. Or someone bumped you because they were in a hurry and didn't want to own up. Now, do you want that tea or would you like someone to help you to the platform?'

'No, thank you,' said Margaret.

With what remained of her dignity, putting as much weight on her foot as she dared, she made her way outside. She felt the urge to keep her back to the wall, to avoid being pushed into the traffic, but then it would be almost impossible to hail a cab. With some relief she saw a policeman near by. She stepped forward with more confidence and this time, succeeded.

In the taxi, she sat with her head in her hands, trying to work out what had happened. Had it all been a misunderstanding because her nerves were on edge? Or had something happened to Fox? She needed to check the telegram he'd sent, then try and contact him.

Twenty-Five

W hen she finally arrived back at work, Miss Upton called her over. 'You look rather windswept, doctor. But it is rather breezy out today. More hatpins next time, maybe.'

Margaret went to her office to hang up her things and tidy her hair, and found Dr Gesner there. 'Ah,' he said, 'I was just collecting your model.' He indicated the upper torso with removable parts which Margaret sometimes used in lectures. 'If you don't mind my saying so, you look a little flustered.'

Margaret removed her hat and another strand of hair came down. She pinned it back, fingers awkward, before addressing him. 'I was pinched and shoved at the underground, and later pushed down some stairs. I feel a little—'

'Any injuries?'

'My ankle's sore and I have a few bruises, I expect. I'm sure it was deliberate.'

Dr Gesner raised his eyebrows. 'Did anyone mention suffragettes?'

'Obliquely, yes.'

'You were on the underground, wearing a WSPU badge on your jacket, and you have purple and white flowers on your hat, the day after Miss Davison ran onto a racetrack. Perhaps it's inevitable. I've heard of other women being assaulted so.'

Margaret frowned. 'Maybe some of it was that. The flowers are coincidental. But the push...'

'Nerves are not my speciality,' said Dr Gesner, 'but I'm sure yours are on edge. I can speak with the inspector, if you like. He asked for you, but—'

'What on earth does he want now?' Margaret rubbed her eyes. 'I'll deal with him, if he wants me so badly.'

'If you wish,' said Dr Gesner, with a kind smile. 'Incidentally, your husband came to take you to lunch. We had a brief chat and he left you this message.' He handed over a sealed envelope.

She extracted a handwritten note from Fox. *Came to speak with you but you'd gone out. See you in the den. F*

Chilled, she realised something that she'd overlooked earlier, in the rush. The earlier telegram had expressed a sentiment that Fox never did in writing, and gave specific instructions rather than something she had to work out. He hadn't sent the message she'd received at lunchtime.

'Perhaps you should rest before you speak with the inspector,' said Dr Gesner. 'You look somewhat shocked.'

He gave her a small, neat Germanic bow and left the room. It wasn't until he was gone that she realised he hadn't taken the model. Nor was the telegram she'd received on the desk where she had left it.

There was no time to try and contact Fox. A knock at the door ushered in Inspector Silvermann. He shook hands and took his seat with a proprietorial thump. He placed his hat on the adjacent chair, planted his feet firmly and folded his arms. 'Nice to meet you again.'

He sounded as enthusiastic as Margaret felt, but she responded in kind. 'Likewise, though I didn't expect to see you before the inquest. I shall be there, but I shan't be giving evidence.'

'Understood,' said the inspector. 'And I'll be asking for an adjournment. But that's not why I'm here.'

'I'm relieved to hear all of that,' said Margaret. 'But if our meeting isn't about that, what is it about?' She wondered if he knew she'd been to Miss Halpin's house not an hour before, and if so, how he'd interpreted it.

'The report your assistant made on laudanum.'

'Yes?'

'You said there wasn't enough laudanum in one bottle.'

'I'm not a poisons expert,' said Margaret, 'but I don't think so. The impression we were given initially was that there were more bottles.'

'The copper made an assumption based on the bottles in the ash can in the yard, but they'd been there some time: they were covered in muck and cobwebs.'

'So if she took more, she did it elsewhere. In which case, getting home would have been very hard for her. She'd have been near-insensible, and unlikely to turn on the gas when she got home. Or the laudanum got into her some other way. But there were no signs that it had been forced into her.' She waited for the inspector to contradict her, but he remained silent. 'If you're doubting us, then you'll need an exhumation and a second opinion.'

'Who says I'm doubting anything?' said Inspector Silvermann.

'If the Bessemers didn't manage it somehow, then you're back to hunting someone who might have a grudge about Carmelo Street Post Office and act on it.'

'A grudge?' snapped Inspector Silvermann. 'It was a bomb, not an egg smashed on the front door! The person with a "grudge" could be any postman, postmaster or postmistress in the country, starting with the ones who were nearly killed. Not to mention any of the shopkeepers down Carmelo Street, or any right-minded citizen who wants to be able to post a letter to his Great Aunt Annie without being mutilated.'

'I'm sorry. I didn't mean to sound flippant.'

'Well, you did. Did your husband know you were going to the races yesterday?'

Margaret sat back, her mind whirring. 'How do *you* know where I was yesterday? And more to the point, why do you care?'

'You gave a statement to a constable after that madwoman hurled herself at the King's horse. I have a copy of it, along with your friend's. You remember my list? I like to keep it tidy, annotated and cross-referenced with items of interest. Your day at the races is of interest.'

Margaret blinked and her stomach knotted. The moving image of the two people and the horse tangling as they crashed to the grass replayed itself. She heard the crack of Emily Davison's skull in her imagination and felt nauseous.

'It was a brief statement. And someone tried to assault us, purely because—'

'Of your membership of an accursed organisation,' snapped the inspector. 'I know. Are you going to tell me Miss Davison was pushed under that horse in revenge, too?'

'No, of course not. I believe she went out with intent: I just don't think it was intent to die. It has nothing to do with what happened at Carmelo Street Post Office.'

'Hasn't it?' Inspector Silvermann continued to contemplate her steadily.

'If you've read my statement, you'll know I saw very little,' said Margaret. 'I possibly saw her raise her arm and then... Then that poor horse ran into her and they all fell down. It was horrible.'

'"That poor horse"? You surprise me.'

'I like horses. I don't like seeing them hurt.'

'A townie like you?'

'A townie like me has country relations, learnt to ride twenty years ago and knows how to make a horse gallop without whacking it. Can you say the same?'

'My dad was a drayman,' said the inspector. 'So yes, I can. Not that you'd want a draught horse to gallop, but I know what you mean about the whip.' His expression briefly showed some respect, then closed down again. 'Does Miss Davison know horses? Doesn't she know what's likely to happen if you step in front of one going at fifty miles an hour?'

'I have absolutely no idea. I imagine she was trying to disrupt things by running across the track and timed it wrong.'

'Do you?'

'I've no other suggestion. And since you have my statement, what is there to ask me now? Besides, you're Scotland Yard. What has that division's work to do with yours?'

The inspector shrugged. 'We're brothers in arms.' He put his cup on the tray. 'What did you know about Miss Davison's plan?'

'Nothing.'

'You're sisters in arms.'

'We're sisters in *aims*,' retorted Margaret. 'We don't share views on means. And we're not mind-readers. Unless a suffragette makes a public statement of her intentions, there's no reason to assume every other suffragette knows what they are.'

'Unless they're friends.'

'Miss Davison isn't even an acquaintance.'

'Mrs Holbourne and she were in the same prison at the same time.'

'So were several women.'

'Including Miss Halpin.'

'The point about prison is that people are kept in cells. It's not a social club.'

Inspector Silvermann waved her opinion away. 'Does Mrs Holbourne generally go to races alone?'

'She's my friend, not my daughter,' snapped Margaret. 'Ask her.'

'You normally work on Wednesdays. Why did you take a day's leave to go with Mrs Holbourne?'

'I didn't. I took a day in lieu, because I'm here today, as you can see. And on the underground—'

'What do you know of Mrs Holbourne's intentions yesterday?' asked Inspector Silvermann.

Margaret stared at him. 'What do you mean?'

'Suffragette direct action, such as Miss Davison took. I know neither of you were wearing your colours, though you were wearing your WSPU badge and Mrs Holbourne was wearing her Holloway one. Hence, risking assault.'

Margaret frowned. 'It was supposed to be a day without any responsibilities or seriousness, for once.'

'Did you really think that Mrs Holbourne intended to take no action?'

'Yes. I mean no. I mean... It was supposed to be a pleasant day out to get away from things. I'd asked Mrs Holbourne if she had anything in mind. Leaflet distribution, for example,' she added, seeing the inspector's pencil poised to take note. 'She said no. If she'd said yes, I might have found an excuse not to go.'

'And Mrs Holbourne is always truthful about that sort of thing.'

'Yes,' said Margaret.

'I can see you believe that, doctor,' he said, snatching up his hat and rising. 'I'll see myself out. I hope you're not still grinding an axe while jumping to conclusions.'

'If you want an axe-grinder, Inspector,' said Margaret, 'perhaps you ought to look in the mirror.'

Inspector Silvermann paused in the doorway. 'This is partly a courtesy visit, as I feel you are unconnected with Mrs Holbourne's actions and I believe you're innocent, other than by association.'

'Innocent? Of what?'

'I thought you'd like to know before you find out from the papers. Mrs Holbourne is under arrest.'

'What for?' Margaret jumped to her feet. 'She did nothing at the Derby. She was as shocked as anyone!'

'That's as may be,' said the inspector. 'However, we have evidence that she set fire to a certain MP's property earlier in the month. And she was well acquainted with Miss Tabor, who worshipped her and was apparently asked to take a package on behalf of someone else – not that her evidence makes any sense. But Mrs Holbourne certainly stirs up loyalty. Who knows if the woman who died wasn't just like Miss Tabor, anonymous and mousy, which is why we can't trace her. Mrs Holbourne knew enough about Stokes to refer to him in her speeches. She attended Miss Halpin's inquest, ostensibly as a reporter, but has printed all sorts of nonsense about it in her rag since. Stokes was preparing bombs. Miss Halpin was suspected of the Carmelo Street bomb. Mrs Holbourne, as you will recall, studied chemistry at Oxford. It all points to a campaign of activity, which Mrs Holbourne seems the most likely to have orchestrated.'

'She would never—'

The inspector held up his hand. 'No one knows everything about everyone,' he said. 'She is under arrest for the attack on the Tyburnia property and possible conspiracy to commit arson elsewhere. Whether additional charges are added will depend on what evidence is found. Maybe you should think on that, Dr Demeray, and consider whose axes need sharpening most.'

Margaret arrived home at six, despondent. Fox was out, and she collected her mail to read alone. There was a letter from

Geoff, and inside, a letter from Maude, which she'd asked him to post if she were ever arrested. Maude's letter reminded Margaret of her promise to assist with the children and asked her to help keep the crimes in the public eye.

The front door opened as she was replacing the telephone receiver after talking with Geoff.

'What's wrong?' said Fox, hanging up his hat and kissing her.

'I don't know where to begin.'

'I'm sorry I missed you at lunch: I should have telephoned ahead. I heard you'd tried to contact me, but I didn't realise until I was about to come home. Was it urgent?'

'At lunchtime, I went to meet you at Miss Halpin's house.'

'Me?' Fox faced her, his face anxious.

'I had a telegram from you asking me to meet you there.'

'But I didn't send one, and I didn't go there.'

Margaret's last hope that one of Fox's colleagues had wired on his behalf, and that the fair-haired man had been him, gave up the ghost. 'Oh God, I was afraid that might be the case. I went and you weren't there, but I was late, so I thought you'd left.'

'You know I'd have waited. If you'd been late, I'd have worried. Don't you know that by now? Show me the telegram.'

'Here it is. Sent from a Paddington office.'

'I'd never send anything like this, and what do you mean, "what happened?"'

'I was threatened, pinched and slapped on the underground, and at one point I was pushed down some steps. Though I think the two things were unconnected. The first was probably just people reacting to what happened at Epsom. But after that, and then the steps...'

'What do you mean?'

'There was a man near the house I might have seen once or twice before, though possibly not. He just looked familiar, nondescript.'

'And you complain about me.'

'I know. I apologise, and he may simply live in the area. I'm not sure he was the one who pushed me. I didn't see him anywhere near when that happened, and if he'd run, I think the bystanders would have said so. Some of them thought it might have been a woman, but they wouldn't describe her.'

'I'll get Bert to collect the telegram.' Fox put through a telephone call, gave a series of directions, then hugged her.

She leaned her head on his shoulder. 'Maybe Dr Gesner's right and it was all because I had my WSPU badge on. Maude's been arrested for arson and Inspector Silvermann's hinting at all sorts of things. I want to visit Geoff, but he doesn't want to see us before tomorrow afternoon. He's taking the children to stay with Maude's grandmother in the country even though I'd offered to have Becca at least. He sounded awful. And I saw Mr Abney again.'

'Where?'

Margaret explained. 'He couldn't have been the one who assaulted me, but he could have instructed someone to do it. Looking back, I think he was in all that chaos the day we thought there was a bomb on the underground. Someone was whispering things to make people panic. I remember it. At the time I thought it was in my head, but it wasn't. It could have been him. I don't know if he recognised me then, but I'm sure he recognised me today.'

'So he's definitely back in the country,' said Fox. He held her tighter, but she sensed his mind working. 'And we still have a corpse to identify. Those two things together might change matters a great deal.'

Twenty-Six

E arly the following day Margaret found Polly preparing the laboratory for a lesson with Dr Gesner, who was still at the daily meeting.

'Good morning, doctor!' she said. 'I wasn't expecting to see you today. Are you here to meet Dr Naylor, or reviewing yesterday's inquest?'

'The latter,' said Margaret.

'May I help?' Polly became earnest. 'I want to learn your job, Dr Demeray. I may not pursue pathology, but I want to understand it.'

'This'll be thoroughly unpleasant.'

'I'm stronger than I look,' said Polly. 'And I know being a doctor won't all be mopping brows and taking temperatures. I have a very sensible aunt who nursed during the Boer War. I told her why the students hadn't been allowed to help at the post-mortem and she told me I should have insisted. Actually, she said "Where's your backbone, girl? One stiffens one's lip and has a cup of tea before going into battle. One can manage whatever one puts one's mind to." I told her it's difficult to drink tea with a stiff lip and she gave me a *very* hard stare.' Polly grinned.

For the first time, Margaret began to think they might get on eventually. 'I hope you won't ever have to work in a war.'

'So do I,' said Polly. 'But I won't have anyone saying I wouldn't be equal to it.'

Margaret frowned, then opened the file. She peered at the sketches and photographs with a lens, then went through her notes. 'It was only worth preserving the head, foot and hand. I wonder if we missed something they could tell us. Could you arrange for them to be brought in.'

'Yes, doctor.'

Margaret waited, pacing until Polly returned with a cloth-covered trolley bearing the three pathetic items that had once been part of a human being, now preserved in formaldehyde. Cleaned, submerged and unnatural in colour, they might as well have been made of wax.

Margaret compared the hand with the photographs and sketches, recalling how it had felt. The fingerprints had been impossible to extract and the skin was grazed, but the hand was... She looked at the photograph of the booted foot, before they'd extracted the foot. It had been a small, slender foot, but...

'They don't seem very ladylike,' said Polly, 'but not exactly rough. Is it because she was so dead? The workhouse bodies for dissection are usually quite tough and sometimes calloused. Miss Halpin's were different, because she led a different life. They were strong, but not rough. These are a little rougher than that. But we had Miss Halpin straight away, whereas Miss Tabor – or whoever it was – came a few days after the event. Could that be why? Or is my imagination getting the better of me?'

'I don't think so,' said Margaret. She bent and peered at the head. The hair had been cut short leaving the damaged remains of the face and head clear, though the features were even less human now. Margaret examined the dent on the temple which Dr Gesner thought had been caused by a tap or a handle. It was too uniform for a piece of brick or tile and it had split the skin and cracked the bone.

'What else do you deduce, Miss Buckram?'

Polly peered, then pulled a face. 'That looks just like the hole my father made in the wall when he was hanging a picture the other weekend. Perhaps the workmen left a small hammer which was caught up in the blast that hit her.'

'Perhaps,' said Margaret.

'Good morning, Miss Buckram, and— Dr Demeray, this is a surprise.' Dr Gesner and Dr Innes walked into the laboratory with a small group of people close behind. They were chiefly men, but among them were Mrs Philbrook, Mrs Southern and one or two other female philanthropists who had been at the soirée. 'Did you want to help with the subscribers' tour?'

'Er...' Margaret was conscious that every eye was on the remains in the jars. She hastily covered them with the cloth.

'Excuse me, excuse me,' Miss Upton pushed between the visitors. 'I tried to let you know, Dr Gesner, but I don't think the message got through to the boardroom. Superintendent Foxcroft has just arrived to see you and Dr Demeray. It's to do with the, erm ... most recent investigative post-mortem. The unexpected one.'

'Oh, I see. Dr Innes, I wonder if I could trouble you to take over from here. I had better assist Dr Demeray.'

'Certainly, certainly.' Dr Innes ushered the group out.

Dr Gesner came forward. 'What's happened?'

'I think the victim might have been dead before the explosion,' said Margaret. 'Miss Buckram and I have been reviewing the evidence. I think we came to the wrong conclusion.' She lifted the cloth and pointed at the skull.

'Good morning,' said Fox, walking into the room.

'I don't understand, Superintendent,' said Dr Gesner. 'What has this to do with Special Branch?'

'Given the venue, the date, and the possible cause, we have reason to be interested and may be able to identify the corpse,' said Fox. 'Is that an issue?'

'Not at all,' said Dr Gesner.

Fox reached into his inner pocket and handed over an image of what must have been the lavatory, after the remains had been removed and the debris cleared, to compare with the one taken beforehand. 'In the first photograph, you can see where the package must have been: where the body was. If she'd been standing that close to the package, it would have been at chest height, and ...'

'So she was lying down,' said Margaret. 'Perhaps already dead.'

'With Inspector Silvermann's knowledge, I've asked for the opinion of his expert. He indicated the marked difference in the effect of a bomb if held by or close to a standing woman, compared to a bomb in the room with someone who was lying down. The right kind of bomb in the right kind of place might result in what you were brought, but he thinks it's unusual. Possible, but not usual. He said he wished he'd seen the head properly. Odd as it sounds, he was surprised it was so unidentifiable.'

'It's a shame he didn't,' said Margaret.

'How so?'

'Look – we thought that the blow to her temple had been made by debris, but what if it was made with a hammer?'

'The sort you put up pictures with?' said Dr Gesner.

'Or the sort suffragettes smash windows with,' said Margaret. 'Maybe it was another revenge attack, after all. We need to compare that injury with the things that might have caused it. Agreed?'

'Agreed,' said Dr Gesner. 'I'll see if the police have the items which were cleared from that room, or can tell us the details, and perhaps we could send out for the right sort of hammer.'

'No need,' said Fox, without glancing at Margaret. 'I have one in our evidence cupboard we can use. The fingerprints were only partial and so far we haven't found a match in any records, but we didn't look for blood.'

In the afternoon Fox and Margaret travelled to the Holbournes' house, as arranged with Geoff the previous day. It seemed almost certain that the dent in the skull came from a hammer like the one Margaret had been sent, and Fox had given it to his people to look for traces of blood.

'It's not what Maude would do,' said Margaret. 'Even if she did, she'd dispose of the hammer without trying to implicate anyone. Please say you believe me. I might need you to back me up to the inspector.'

'Of course I will,' said Fox, squeezing her hand. 'And before you ask, I'm not here to gather evidence: I'm here because Geoff's my friend. I can't begin to imagine what he's going through. Incidentally, I forgot to tell you that Bert's no further forward with the telegram. The clerk can't remember who left it, and the request form was typed.'

'Unusual.'

'Not if it's from an office that keeps a stock of forms. It's what we do.'

'Damn.'

They were ushered into Maude's room at the back of the house. Geoff was standing by the open French windows. Birdsong filtered in with the scent of summer flowers. To Margaret's surprise, the Bryces were sitting in the garden drinking coffee. They gave a small wave in greeting.

Geoff shook hands. 'I thought it would be nice to sit outside,' he said. 'The sunshine will make us all feel better. And the garden's looking particularly fine just now – at least, nothing has been burned down.' He tried to smile at his own weak joke, then sighed when there was no response. He had lost weight in the short time since Margaret had last seen him and looked older, somehow. His voice had lost all the belligerence of early May. It was fearful and anxious. 'I thought you might be unable to come, Fox. I assumed that because of your role you'd have to distance yourself from Maude, and possibly Margaret would, too.'

'Whatever Maude has done or not done is nothing to do with me,' said Fox. 'And if any investigation involved a friend of mine, I would pass it on. But if it helps, I know nothing.'

Geoff turned to Margaret. 'And what about you? What have you told the police?'

'I have nothing to tell them,' said Margaret.

'Humph,' said Geoff. 'If you did know something, *would* you tell them?'

Margaret had repeatedly asked herself the same question in the small hours. Would she? Was she subconsciously suppressing something out of loyalty? She felt as if the seconds of not answering were years.

Geoff relit his pipe and threw the used match into the empty fireplace. 'Sorry, M,' he said. 'I shouldn't have asked that. You've always been an honest woman, and I probably feel the same way. I think Maude tried to protect both of us by ensuring we knew nothing that we could tell the police. Everything else is just suspicion. Will you be able to visit her?'

'I have an order for tomorrow,' said Margaret.

Geoff's face fell. 'Really? I was told I couldn't visit till Monday.'

'I'm surprised they gave me an order and not you.'

'Perhaps they think you're her physician.'

'I'll try to find out why they won't give you one. I imagine it's a misunderstanding.'

'Thank you,' said Geoff. He puffed at his pipe, frowning, and nodded towards the garden. 'I hope you don't mind the Bryces. I arranged their visit some time ago. It felt like an admission of something to cancel it. And I'm glad of something else to think about.'

'Something relaxing, I hope,' said Margaret.

'Something worthwhile.' Geoff gestured for them to go into the garden, but didn't move. 'Fox, can you tell me if this is the only charge against Maude, or whether there is anything else?'

'I truly don't know,' said Fox. 'I'm here as a friend.'

'Then as a friend, if you can find out, I'd be grateful. Now, shall we go outside? Thank you for coming. Apart from Phoebe, Maude's other friends are conspicuous by their absence.'

In the garden, the Bryces greeted them warmly.

'I'll show you round,' said Geoff, waving at the greenery, 'and then we'll have coffee.'

As was typical for the area, though the Holbournes' house was large, with several floors and well-appointed rooms, its pretty garden was small. It would not take long to go round it. All the same, Miss Bryce managed to keep Margaret back.

'It's very nice to see you again,' said Margaret, wishing she didn't have to make polite conversation. 'How is *Little Miss Llewellyn* doing? I assume there's no matinee today.'

'Oh, there is,' said Miss Bryce. 'But talking business with Mr Holbourne won't interfere with that. Besides, we want to help in any way we can. I imagine you feel the same.'

'Yes,' said Margaret. 'Geoff and Maude are two of my oldest friends.'

'We feel so very sorry for Mr Holbourne. Perhaps Mrs Holbourne doesn't realise quite how much misery she is causing him.'

Margaret bridled a little at her bluntness. 'Maude and I feel very strongly that women should have the vote,' she said. 'Maude is prepared to stand up for her beliefs in ways that she thinks fit, and if the police have evidence to secure a conviction, she will accept her punishment. Geoff has known this ever since he's known Maude. He has been to most of the meetings and many of the rallies we've taken part in. He believes in the cause. Someone must make a stand.'

'Please forgive me,' said Miss Bryce, 'I didn't mean to offend.' A slight flush showed through the powder on her face and she gave Margaret an awkward smile. 'I'm glad you're here, Dr Demeray. I didn't have the chance at the soirée to thank you for being so gentle and respectful about Miss Halpin at the inquest. I should have written, perhaps, but I'm still very upset about her. I appreciated that you did not emphasise the laudanum. It was a tragic situation.'

'Do you know if she obtained supplies other than on prescription?'

'I don't. But you don't need a prescription, do you?'

They had caught up with the men, who were peering at a rose bush. Margaret had a distinct impression that Fox was the only one of them who could have said anything intelligent about it, but even he was struggling to do so.

'I was speaking of Lois,' said Miss Bryce. 'I was thanking the doctor for the way she addressed the inquest.

Mr Bryce grunted. 'Lois was never the best actress,' he said. 'But after she started taking that stuff, she became worse and worse. She was unemployable, unless there was a part for a sleeping form or a corpse. It was just as well old Clementina left her that house. Even then, I don't know what she lived on. We had great hopes that Carter would help her stop taking it. Didn't we, Joan?'

'Yes,' said Miss Bryce. She touched the corner of her eye with a handkerchief. 'We did. But it was too late, and now we'll never know. I'll be frank with you, Dr Demeray – Lois is partly why I'm uncomfortable with the suffrage movement. It's not simply the bombs: it's how low decent women are being brought. I was so distressed when she became ill, as a direct result of fighting for something which will come about anyway. One day we *will* get the vote, because that is the natural order of things. No one – including Mrs Holbourne – should be suffering for it now.'

Twenty-Seven

O nce or twice, as a young woman, Margaret had spent time in police cells after acts of suffragette vandalism, though she'd never been formally charged.

As a doctor, she had treated minor criminals – men, women, children – inside East End police cells. She had visited suffragette friends in Holloway or greeted them on their release, as they left that building with its red-brick towers and dark turrets, tall and daunting as a workhouse. But she had never been inside the main body of a prison. All she knew was what she had been told by others, including Maude.

She was ushered into a room where Maude would be brought to meet her. She sat and waited, alone but for a wardress, wondering what the other woman was thinking and whether she felt any doubt about her job.

The wardress was a little older than Margaret, perhaps: certainly stronger and wirier. How could she bear to see the suffering she must witness every day? She stood in silence with her back to the wall, eyes focused somewhere over Margaret's head and hands clasped in front of her, almost part of the painted brickwork.

The room was cheerless and stuffy. Margaret could smell perspiration and wondered if it was her, the wardress, or ingrained in the room through fear. Through an open, barred window, she heard the distant sounds of the city and also suffragettes singing, as they often did, from the roof of a house in nearby Dalmeny Avenue. The melody cheered Margaret a little. But somehow, the room was so oppressive that it was all she could do not to turn and check the door behind her was still unlocked.

After fifteen minutes of silence but for the sounds of the prison itself – clanking, shuffling and distant voices – a senior wardress walked in. 'Good afternoon, Dr Demeray,' she said, without offering to shake hands. 'I am Matron Jack. Am I to understand that you are here to inspect us, to see a specific patient inmate, or to assist? I'm afraid the communication I received isn't terribly clear.'

'I'm here to see Mrs Holbourne,' said Margaret. 'She was brought here yesterday. However, as an interested member of the public and a physician, I would quite like to see the conditions here, too.'

'I'm not sure that will be possible without a more explicit order,' said Matron Jack. 'But the physician here would very much like your help. If you come with me, you will see at least some of the prison.'

Margaret hesitated, looking beyond the matron to the door. 'Come where?' she said. 'I'm expecting Mrs Holbourne here.'

'Mrs Holbourne is not terribly well, which is why we need your assistance. The physician is with her now. When he heard you were here, he specifically asked if you would help.'

'Unwell?' said Margaret. 'She's been here less than twenty-four hours.'

'Please come.'

Margaret felt herself tremble as she picked up her handbag. She had an irrational but deep-rooted sensation that if she went through the locked gates and doors into the main part of the prison, she might never leave. However, she followed the matron along a landing which ran round the internal edges of the prison. To her left were cell doors, each with a board declaring the occupant's name. To her right was a railing which ran around the inside of the building, except where the staircases were. It formed a barrier to prevent anyone falling to the open area two storeys below, where refectory tables and benches stood in rows.

The prison was not quiet. There were shouts and banging, but it was hard to know from which storey or door the noises came.

Margaret glanced over the barrier and shuddered, remembering what Maude had said about seeing Emily Davison throw herself from a place like this, breaking her back, but killing neither herself nor her determination.

Then there were other noises: sobs and muffled screams. Suddenly, Margaret recognised the voice. It was Maude.

In twenty-one years, Margaret had never seen Maude weep, except for tears of remorse when she had broken off an engagement. Margaret had never heard her cry out of terror. She had never heard her scream.

She hurried forward. 'What's wrong with her?'

Matron Jack slowed down, blocking her path. 'You must brace yourself,' she said. 'The doctor needs your help.'

Margaret followed her into a side room. A high window shone light on a reclining chair, to which Maude was tied. Four wardresses held her down as she trembled and shook, one covering her mouth with a large hand.

'What's happened?' said Margaret. 'Is she having a fit?' Even as she said it, she knew it was nothing of the kind. Maude was not being restrained for her own good. She was about to be forcibly fed.

Margaret tried to take a step forward, but the matron held her arm as the door closed. From the shadowed corner of the room stepped a man holding a feeding tube and a container of liquid food. It was Dr Southern.

'Ah, Dr Demeray,' he said. 'How nice of you to join us.' He smirked.

'Dr Innes forbade every Dorcas Free doctor from forcible-feeding prisoners! Does he know you're doing this?'

Dr Southern shrugged. 'Someone has to do it. Would you prefer these women to die of starvation?'

'That's an impossible question to answer,' said Margaret. 'But this particular woman can't be starving. She was only arrested yesterday.'

Maude looked over, pleading with tear-filled eyes, and Margaret pulled against the matron's grip.

'She's refusing food,' said Dr Southern, 'and she has a history of doing so. She mustn't become ill under the prison's watch. She could become severely ill or insane. Or should I say more insane?'

'No! This is cruel and barbaric. This is not the way to treat another person. Would you like it if you were treated like this? If your wife was?'

'I am not that kind of fool,' said Dr Southern, 'and nor is my wife. Perhaps, if you feel I'm incompetent, you should show me what to do.' He grabbed her wrist and forced the equipment into her hands.

Maude cried out again despite the hand over her mouth. Tears were running into her hair. The stench of her terror filled the room.

'No!' said Margaret. She pushed the items back, hoping the bottle of food would fall and smash, and strained towards Maude.

'Keep Dr Demeray back, Matron,' said Dr. Southern, catching the bottle. 'She'll just have to observe as I try to save this woman's life.'

'You cannot do this!' said Margaret. 'This is inhumane. This woman is not starving: she hasn't even been tried for the latest alleged offence. She's on remand.'

'She was on licence for another offence and she has breached the licence. She is a prisoner.'

'You must not do this. I will report you!'

'Who will care?' said Dr Southern. 'Everyone is sick to the back teeth of these women. Have you forgotten dealing with the remains of that woman from St James's? What did her death achieve? I take no pleasure from this.' His expression belied his words. 'But if it is a step towards saving her, then I have no compunction about it. Wardress, take your hand from the prisoner's mouth.' He leaned over Maude, who let out a scream as the doctor began to force the tube into her nostrils. 'Stop fighting me, woman!'

Tears poured from Maude's wide, outraged eyes. She thrashed under the hands of the four wardresses, who held her down with such force that Margaret, twisting in the matron's grip, half-expected to hear a snap of bone.

As Dr Southern started to pour the liquid food, Maude's choking became desperate. Her eyes opened wider. Her chest heaved and she panted and gasped. Her face started to go blue.

'Stop!' shouted Margaret. 'Stop! Stop! You're doing something wrong. You'll suffocate her!'

Dr Southern ignored her.

Maude gurgled. The tears had stopped. But her eyes stared at Margaret in beseeching desperation before starting to roll back.

'That will be sufficient,' said Dr Southern. He stopped pouring and removed the tube faster than he should have. His hands were trembling.

Maude began to choke and cough. She twisted her head as the wardresses loosened their hold. Foam and vomit appeared at the corners of her mouth.

One of the wardresses was crying too. 'I'm unstrapping her, doctor. I have to. She's going to be sick.'

Maude leaned over and vomited on the floor. There was blood on her mouth and she heaved as she filled her lungs with air.

Matron Jack released her grip and Margaret rushed forward. The crying wardress was wiping Maude's wet hair from her face. As she held Maude's trembling, gasping, choking form, Margaret addressed Dr. Southern. 'You utter fool! The tube went in the wrong way – not to her stomach, but her lungs. You were drowning her. She may never recover.' She turned to the matron, who stood, pale and shaking, in the doorway. 'Take me and this woman to the infirmary and get her a *proper* physician. Then take me to the governor. As for you, Dr Southern – you are entitled to your personal views, but your responsibility as a doctor is to heal, not harm. This woman was fit and healthy when she came in. I will make sure there is an investigation into this. And mark my words, someone will pay.'

After leaving Holloway, Margaret went to tell Geoff what had happened. She felt sick and clammy, wondering what she would have done if Maude had died, how she would ever have explained her failure to save Maude's life to Geoff.

'Dear God,' he said, putting his head in trembling hands.

They sat in silence for a while. The maid, entering with tea, frowned at her master slightly and turned to Margaret with a faint plea in her eyes.

'Don't worry,' Margaret mouthed. 'I'll explain later.'

Eventually, Geoff lifted his head. 'I shall write to our MP, to the Prime Minister, to the ... the rector. This is appalling. And isn't it supposed to be illegal?'

'Yes,' said Margaret. 'I'm so sorry I couldn't stop it. I'm so sorry.' Now that it was over, she wanted to cry, her words catching on sobs, her hands shaking. 'I am so angry, but I don't know what to do until there's a proper enquiry. I—' She looked away for a moment and saw a suffrage magazine in a rack near Maude's armchair. 'That's not true: I can think of something. Can you tell me how to contact Maude's deputy editor?'

Geoff's eyes were dry, but his voice was unsteady. 'Yes. Why?'

'No reputable paper would publish an anonymous letter without knowing who had written it,' said Margaret, wiping her face. 'And if I gave my details to a newspaper before the hospital board had been informed of events, it could weaken my argument. But *Athene's Gazette* is Maude's own paper. And they can do what they like.'

'I'll telephone her for you,' said Geoff. 'Make your letter as damning as you can.'

'I've got a better idea.'

Margaret met the deputy editor in the Gardenia Restaurant, knowing that if any suffragette overheard, the gossip would do its own job. Together, they wrote a brief, damning first-page article, using a sketch Margaret had drawn of Maude being forcibly fed. It was not brightly coloured, as WSPU propaganda posters were, but Margaret's simple lines were more real and raw, even to her own eyes.

It has come to our notice, the article said, *that a leading suffragette nearly died on Saturday while being forcibly fed against her will, even though she had been on hunger strike for less than a day, in direct contravention of recent legislation forbidding such practices. Where the feeding tube should have entered the stomach, an error on the physician's part meant that it entered the suffragette's lungs. Had another person not intervened, the woman would probably have died. She remains grievously injured.*

Details of the prison, the prisoner and the doctor involved are known to Athene's Gazette, but will not become public knowledge unless our hand is forced. This measure is to respect the dignity of the injured woman, to allow independent investigation, and to show the doctor the forbearance he did not show our sister. He may yet admit his error and seek to make amends. If so, we will accept his apology. We in the movement do not seek revenge, but justice, and we wish to demonstrate our fundamental belief that all should have the right to be treated equally. This terrible incident, however, proves once again how barbaric forcible feeding is, and furthermore, how dangerous. May politicians and physician take note. We remain unbowed and unafraid, but we will make public every outrage which occurs in our struggle.

It was all Margaret could do: not simply for Maude, but for any other woman in her position. Maude had not died. Margaret might have been wrong. It would be almost impossible to prove her allegation. But at least she had done something.

Twenty-Eight

On Sunday, four days after the Epsom Derby, Emily Davison died from her injuries.

The following morning, Margaret arrived at work early, her heart breaking from what she'd read in the papers she'd seen so far. The vitriol was gone from some – out of respect, perhaps – but in others it lurked under the surface of hypocritical platitudes, even when pitying Miss Davison's distraught and baffled parents.

She went directly to Dr Innes's room, and within moments was sitting opposite him as he read her report. He finished, then regarded Margaret over the top of his glasses. He placed her report on the table and passed two others to her. 'The governor of Holloway Prison pre-empted you,' he said. 'As did Dr Southern.'

'What do you mean?'

'Dr Southern came to my home yesterday morning, immediately before church.'

'I would never do that.'

Dr Innes's frown deepened. 'He presented me with what he calls a summary of what occurred on Saturday. The governor's report came by special delivery before you arrived. Dr Southern has not yet spoken to me this morning: I assume he feels he has the upper hand. Perhaps you should read them before we discuss it further.'

Margaret felt her jaw clench and turned her attention to the reports. Dr Southern's was more essay than summary:

I am occasionally asked to assist with saving the lives of prisoners, usually women, who are refusing to eat as a form of protest. This is to support my partner in private practice. My aim is to ensure the best care to the inmate while saving their life so that they can be released under the Prisoners (Temporary Discharge for Ill-Health) Act. Without intervention, these persons would die or become permanently debilitated. It is neither a pleasant task nor a welcome one, but it is a necessity and best performed by a specialist in gastric matters. I know you have expressed a distaste for this necessary role, which is why I had not informed you of my actions in this regard. However, I can furnish you with the details of each occasion on which I have provided direct nourishment to prisoners, together with evidence that on each occasion, the greatest care was given to avoid distress beyond that which was inevitable, due to the prisoner's own intransigence.

On Saturday I was asked to perform this duty on a prisoner, having been informed that she was refusing food and had fallen ill. On examination, the woman was indeed weak. She showed signs of being underweight and delirious from dehydration and malnourishment. This deteriorated into hysteria and violence when it was explained to her that intervention would be necessary. Despite her apparent weakness, it was necessary for four wardresses to restrain her. On hearing that another doctor was in the prison, and moreover that it was a colleague and a woman whom hitherto I had thought of as a friend, or at least a loyal acquaintance, I requested that she join me to help.

However, not only did Dr Demeray refuse to assist, but she actively tried to interfere in treatment. She snatched at the equipment, becoming almost as hysterical as the prisoner. This meant that the woman resisted all the more, causing her further pain and fear, which resulted in an evacuation of the food provided.

In her hysteria, Dr Demeray made unfounded, slanderous accusations that I had not administered the feeding tube correctly. If I had done as she says, the prisoner would have died. In point of fact, the prisoner recovered sufficiently to be sent home until the trial for her latest offence.

I am providing this statement voluntarily, so that you can counter any report you may receive from Dr Demeray, who was clearly influenced by her personal convictions and feminine weakness. I hope this will draw a line under the matter and enable you to support me against hysterical allegations.

'I was not hysterical at any point,' said Margaret, slamming the report on the table. 'Mrs Holbourne might have been described as such, but one can hardly blame her, and one of the wardresses wasn't much better. I have absolutely no doubt that Dr Southern—'

'Perhaps you should read the other report before you continue, Dr Demeray.'

Margaret cleared her throat and picked up a document with the letterhead of Holloway Prison.

On the previous six occasions when Dr Southern has assisted with the unpleasant but sometimes necessary process known as forcible feeding, there were no ill effects other than what is normally experienced by the prisoner: some pain, and occasionally a short period when control over bodily functions is lost. This leads to a great deal of distress for all, including prison staff. However, on Saturday, it was clear that the prisoner in question was in greater distress afterwards than is usual.

The infirmary physician can neither confirm nor deny Dr Demeray's allegation that the feeding tube was improperly applied, although he believes that liquid was inhaled by the prisoner at some point. However, this may have been coincidental, or as a result of her own agitations.

Nevertheless, I have commenced an investigation into the matter. Firstly, because the prisoner had not been protesting long enough for anyone to authorise the process, and secondly, because Dr Demeray should not have been asked to assist. She was not visiting in a medical capacity, but in a personal one. This should have been made clear before her suitability for the task was determined.

I listened to both Dr Demeray and Dr Southern on Saturday and I am interviewing my staff. I have no further observations to make in respect of the two doctors, other than to say that I no longer wish Dr Southern to undertake forcible feeding at this prison.

Dr Demeray retains the right to request an order to visit any prisoner, should she so wish, and that request will be considered on its own merits. However, I will not grant it if I feel that she is likely to interfere with the running of the prison or the treatment of the prisoners.

I will leave any disciplinary matters in relation to the two doctors, should you deem them necessary, in your capable hands.

Margaret read the letter twice and handed it back to Dr Innes. His expression was grave but not forbidding.

'I'm sorry if I caused you embarrassment, sir,' she said. 'I understand the point behind forcible feeding, but if it has to be done, there must be a less cruel way to approach it. I would never choose to do it unless I truly believed it necessary. Even then, I could not in conscience have continued while the person was in as much distress as Mrs Holbourne.'

Dr Innes contemplated her without speaking, then rose and went to his door. Margaret anticipated being ushered out, but Dr Innes spoke to his clerk. 'Please establish whether Dr Southern has arrived. If so, please ask him to come up immediately, unless there is a medical matter that takes precedence.'

He returned and took his seat. 'I'd rather discuss this with you both together,' he said, 'and preferably without the hospital board. But before Dr Southern joins us, may I urge caution in how you express yourself. Also, please consider that one swallow does not make a summer. Dr Southern is a respected specialist whose skills we need. On a pragmatic front, his family supports the hospital with regular, generous donations, and his wife's family bring it to the attention of a good many bigwigs with money and social influence.' He held his hand up. 'Please don't misunderstand me, doctor. The skills are the important thing. But we need the funds.'

There was a knock on the door, then it opened.

'Good morning, Dr Southern, perhaps you can join us.'

'Us?'

'Dr Demeray is already here.'

'Ah.' Even in that syllable, Margaret heard the hesitancy drop. Whoever he was afraid of, it wasn't her.

Dr Southern strode in. If not afraid, he was defensive. 'Good morning, Dr Demeray. I see you've arrived early to try and influence matters.'

'Good morning. I've arrived early to give my side of a sorry story.'

'Please sit down, Dr Southern,' said Dr Innes. 'I'm rather hoping this won't take long—'

'You must understand the level of hysteria in that woman,' said Dr Southern. 'It made her almost impossible to control.'

'Which woman?' said Dr Innes, sitting back with his fingers steepled. Even in his seriousness, there was a flicker of humour in his eyes.

'I meant the prisoner. But to some extent—'

'Mrs Holbourne was crying, Dr Southern,' said Margaret. 'She was crying from fear and distress. That is not hysteria. She had been forcibly fed before, twice. I daresay a man might behave in the same way, in the same circumstances.'

'If she hadn't struggled so, and you hadn't encouraged her—'

'She barely knew I was there. As a doctor, you must know that in extreme distress, the distress is the only thing the patient is aware of.'

'More to the point,' said Dr Innes, picking up the report from the Holloway governor, 'the prisoner did not need feeding that day as she'd only just been incarcerated. That should have been in the file which you would have checked before starting the procedure, Dr Southern.'

'It... I trusted the information given.'

'Mmhmm?' Dr Innes's eyebrows rose a little. 'By whom?'

'I, er... I don't recall. I was telephoned and I attended and, er, there she was.'

'I do not associate your work with inattention to detail. However, as you will see from this missive' – Dr Innes tapped the letter from the governor – 'investigation of any failings at the prison is underway and they do not wish you to assist in future.'

'But I—'

'You were well aware that I did not want any doctor from this hospital associated with the practice,' said Dr Innes. 'Therefore, I'm unsure of why you decided to do it without reference to me, and glad that I don't have to ask you to stop on Dorcas Free's account. I wonder what your wife would say.'

'My wife is in support,' snapped Dr Southern. 'She views women who are prepared to become criminals in low esteem and considers them damaging to the reputation of Britain and the Empire. I hope she doesn't transfer that view to Dorcas Free if there is unnecessary sentiment in the hospital's decision-making. As you know, I am a partner in a growing and lucrative private practice. I can withdraw my services at any time.' He turned to Margaret. 'I didn't think you sentimental, Dr Demeray: I thought of you, on some level, as a friend. I remain disappointed that you did not behave with more decorum on

Saturday. I dispute any failure on my part, but being assaulted by you didn't help.'

'You were the one trying to force the equipment on me,' said Margaret. 'I simply pushed it away. I was then restrained by the matron under your orders, which I doubt you have authority to give.'

'You were just upset because the criminal was your friend.' Dr Southern's voice was a mimicking whine.

'How do you know that?' said Margaret, frowning. 'I didn't say so in your presence at any point.'

Dr Southern's red face paled. 'I am sure you said the prisoner was your friend while you were haranguing the governor with your false allegations.'

'No, I didn't. I'd have felt the same about any prisoner, male or female, in that situation.' She locked eyes with him. 'I don't understand why you persisted when her distress was increasing, whether or not you believed she had been on hunger strike for some time.'

'I had incorrect information,' he said, dropping his gaze. 'I thought you'd behave as a professional. Perhaps I am expecting too much of a woman doctor.'

'You know that I'm opposed to the practice, and no one from this hospital is supposed to take part in it.'

'Perhaps you should read this, Dr Southern,' said Dr Innes, passing over the governor's letter.

Dr Southern perused the document with pursed lips, becoming paler than ever, then returned it. 'For my part, Dr Innes, without admitting any fault, I apologise for any professional embarrassment you may have been caused.' He sat back and folded his arms.

'As do I,' said Margaret.

Dr Innes took the letters and reports and put them in a folder. 'I suggest we leave the matter there. I would not like to lose either of you. There is no easy way of ascertaining whether Dr Southern made an error without causing more distress to Mrs Holbourne, and I'm sure you're not suggesting a deliberate act, Dr Demeray?'

Margaret looked at Dr Southern, recalling his demeanour and his expression on Saturday. Uncaring? Possibly. Careless? Perhaps. Did she really think that Dr Southern had intentionally tried to kill Maude? She shook her head. 'I don't believe it was deliberate.'

'Then we will leave it at that until the prison communicates again, if it does,' said Dr Innes. 'Dr Demeray, I believe you are expected in class: I suggest you hurry. Dr Southern, I will join you and Mr Dupré on the gastric ward round in half an hour. I'll see you both at the twelve o'clock meeting. Let this be an end to the matter.'

Margaret found it hard to concentrate.

Even at Tuesday's hospital meeting, it was almost impossible to keep from watching Dr Southern. He had either forgotten everything or was deliberately pretending she didn't exist, showing no interest when pathological work was mentioned. Dr Innes had said nothing further about whether he would take anything to the board.

She had left Maude to recover quietly at home, telephoning Geoff daily to see how she was, but that evening she would visit after work. She wondered whether anyone would see the article in *Athene's Gazette* when it came out on Wednesday, and if so, what would happen, but she was unrepentant.

She could only hope Maude understood it was all she could do.

There were no more telegrams, nothing to identify the woman who'd died at St James's, no more sensation of danger on the underground – but she still felt uneasy. And she still hadn't told Fox her faint doubt about Dr Gesner. She tried to work out why she was hesitating, telling herself that it was because Fox would form suspicions to add to the ones he already had. But deep down, she feared the suspicions were her own.

Twenty-Nine

Maude lay in her bedroom, pale against the covers, her dark hair in a loose plait. 'Thank you for coming, Demeray,' she said as she heaved herself into a semi-sitting position, waving Margaret's offer of help away. 'I was rather hoping you'd been arrested for the murder of Dr Southern.'

'Not yet.' Margaret kissed her friend's forehead and sat on the edge of the bed. 'The house seems quiet. Are the children still in the country?'

'Becca's trying to convert her great-grandmother by reading her *The Suffragette*, and Grandmama is reading her *Decorum* in retaliation.' Maude's breath rattled. She turned to her nightstand. On it was a flask of water and a small bottle of laudanum. She picked up the latter. 'I've kept off it this time, even though...'

'I'm glad.'

'The date of my trial has been put back. I'm rather sorry: I'd have liked to be in the dock explaining why I required a seat while being sentenced. Come and lie down like you used to at Oxford when you were telling me all about your conquests.'

'I did nothing of the sort,' said Margaret, reclining next to Maude and holding her hand. 'You were the one who was engaged about ten times and constantly drivelling on about it.'

'Only nine times.' Maude attempted a chuckle but her face grew serious. 'What *has* happened about Dr Southern?'

'The matter's being considered by our senior physician,' said Margaret. 'Holloway refuses to have him back, if that helps. He's denying my claim, of course. I think he's trying to make trouble between me and Dr Gesner, but Dr Gesner's no fool.'

'Good.' Maude stared at the ceiling. 'Emily Davison's dead.'

'I know. I'm sorry. I know you thought a lot of her.'

'Poor woman. It's only a few days since her death and she's already tucked away in the papers as if she didn't matter.' Maude's voice was bitter. She turned sideways on the pillow. 'I promise I had nothing to do with the death of that woman at St James's.'

'You already told me that,' said Margaret. 'I believe you.'

'I haven't told you everything.' Maude's hand trembled in hers. 'Has anything happened to you recently, apart from that man trying to make you force that tube down me? Anything worrying? Frightening? Threatening?'

'I was jostled on the underground the other day. Dr Gesner thinks it's because I'm a suffragette.' There was no point in mentioning Mr Abney. Maude might remember that he'd asked Margaret to speak at a symposium in 1910, might recall Margaret's distaste for him, but she had never known of his involvement in the case that Fox had been investigating when Margaret met him three years previously.

'Maybe it's just you.' Maude licked her lips. 'Look at what happened at Holloway.'

'Loathsome as Dr Southern's actions were, I'm sure it was coincidence. He heard another doctor was there and thought they might help. When he saw it was me he should have thought twice but didn't, because he wanted to make a point. He dislikes militancy.'

'I don't think it was coincidence,' said Maude. 'Geoff couldn't get an order to visit, yet you could. Why?'

'The governor said they thought I was your physician.'

'Nonsense. My physician's name is in my records: I've been there often enough. It was engineered. If that man hadn't made a mistake, I could see them incarcerating you and perhaps forcibly feeding you too—'

'That couldn't happen! Holloway's better regulated than that.'

Maude gave a hoarse laugh. 'One hopes so. But it only takes one little clerk making one little alteration in one little file to alter something big. Give me the right place to stand, and this paperclip can discombobulate an entire filing cabinet. Doesn't your friend Miss Edwards say that? I wonder Fox doesn't worry over what she does with his paperwork.'

'He trusts her implicitly,' said Margaret. There was only so much she could explain about Elinor's job, even though Elinor had met Maude and Phoebe a number of times and got on well with them, particularly Phoebe.

'I wasn't involved in Carmelo Street, either,' said Maude, struggling to sit up properly. 'I'm not convinced it was a suffragette bomb.'

'Stop talking, Maude, you're wearing yourself out.'

'I can't. It's important.' Maude took several deep breaths. 'The inspector says I attempted to lure Miss Tabor to where that woman was killed. In fact, he thinks I lured both of them, but I didn't. What did the inquest conclude?'

'It's tomorrow, and I doubt it'll conclude anything but murder by person or persons unknown. As for Miss Tabor, I thought she told Inspector Silvermann that she didn't actually get there.'

'Perhaps, but she intended to. I think someone played on her yearning for adventure. I'm not sure if they wanted to lay blame for the other woman's death at her feet or mine, or if they wanted to kill both of them. But someone's threatening to provide proof that I was the one who instructed them, and it's not true.'

'You said it was only *Athene's Gazette* that was being threatened.'

'I fibbed. It started with a telegram.'

Margaret felt a chill around her heart. 'When? What did it say?'

'The morning of the Carmelo Street bomb, just before I bumped into you,' said Maude. 'I thought it came from my printer. I've been worried that the government will try to stop it being printed, as they are with *The Suffragette.* He asked me to meet him at Gloucester Road tube station and travel with him to Paddington, as he had to catch a train, and if we missed each other, to meet at Paddington instead. He wasn't at Gloucester Road, so I did as he suggested.'

'It's not like you to do as you're told.'

'I should have realised it wasn't the sort of thing he'd do,' said Maude. 'But worry makes one behave out of character. You especially. Me less so, normally.'

'I'd like to argue but I shan't.'

'I completely disregarded the fact that the man's a complete ink-worm who barely leaves his print shop. Anyway, I went. I was jostled and pushed, which I put down to the busy time of day, but I felt nervous. As I was ascending the stairs, someone whispered in my ear: "Stop what you're doing or you and your friends will suffer Stokes's fate, or worse. And the truth will come out."'

'What truth?'

'I assumed they meant about burning down that pagoda. I tried to see who it was, but—'

'The flow of people forced you on.'

'Yes. Although I saw a man with a lopsided face and a particularly nasty leer.'

Mr Abney. 'Was it the man who'd whispered?'

'I don't know,' said Maude. 'Maybe I just noticed him because of his face, poor chap. When I got to the concourse I saw Geoff, who thought I was elsewhere, seeing Miss Bryce onto the Reading train.'

'Oh Maude... I'm sure it's not what it looked like. Geoff loves you dearly.'

'It didn't look like anything,' said Maude, scowling. 'You're missing the point.'

'What did you do?'

'Went over and asked if Geoff had seen the printer. Geoff said no. He didn't look remotely guilty and nor did Miss Bryce. Geoff took me home and said that Miss Bryce was travelling in respect of his investment in their business. I assumed he meant it was about opening a new theatre and said I thought he'd be better off investing in moving pictures, but he disagreed. I telephoned the printer on my return and found that he *had* gone to Slough from Paddington that morning. I made an arrangement to visit a few days later, but by then the Carmelo Street incident had happened and everything was rather fraught. The point is, he didn't send the telegram.' Maude paused and took a deeper draught of water. 'Can I trust you Demeray?'

'Of course you can.'

'Then I started receiving threatening letters. The first was after the Carmelo Street bomb, the next after Lois's death. Each one said the same: "Stokes, Halpin: you'll be next, and the truth will be told about what your husband is really doing if you don't stop.".'

'What?' Margaret sat up. 'I'm lost. What is Geoff doing?'

'I don't know,' said Maude. 'All I can assume is that it's to do with the Bryces. It made me furious. I wouldn't give into blackmail that easily, but I stopped direct action to find out what Geoff is doing. Then they can publish and be damned and we'd face it together. But he's never-endingly vague about it. Vaguer than normal for Geoff, that is.'

'Keep asking him.'

'I got sick of asking. Then I was afraid. What if it's something illegal?'

'You're an arsonist, Maude.'

'That's political. The Bryces are Irish but Loyalists. There are all sorts of rumours about what those opposed to the Home Rule Bill will do. Geoff's grandparents had an estate in Kildare and his brother has a mansion just outside Dublin. My sister's married to an Anglo-Irishman with a house almost as big. None of *them* want an independent Ireland, but *I* think it should happen. I thought Geoff did, too, but I can see it won't be simple. What if—'

'I can't see Geoff gun-running,' said Margaret, uneasy. 'He's upset enough about you smashing windows. Have you explained why you're asking?'

'I can't.' Maude put her face in her hands.

'Why not?'

'Because of the last letter. It said: "It should have been you who died in St James's, and you know it. We will prove it, and you will hang for her murder."'

'That has nothing whatsoever to do with Ireland.'

'Maybe it has.' Maude slid back under the covers. She closed her eyes, but not before Margaret saw tears forming. Her voice was muffled. 'I have a confession. The night of that meeting at Phoebe's, the night before we went to St James's Park...'

'Yes?'

'I received a telegram from Miss Tabor after I'd got home. It said to meet her at St James's Palace the following day, where it would be nice and respectable, for her to find out how she could help me with the cause. She said not to reply but she'd see me in the park.'

'You never said! And we never went near the palace.'

'I didn't want to meet her,' said Maude. 'I find her too weary-ing and boring for words, God forgive me, and I didn't want to encourage her. I thought if you two were with me and we sat somewhere in the vicinity, she might see me by chance, in which case you could help me get her to go away. Or better still, she wouldn't see us and I could say I'd missed her. That's what I thought had happened. I didn't know that you thought you'd seen her. I wrote her a polite, apologetic letter that evening, which I assume the police have.'

'That would prove you didn't meet her.'

'It proves I expected to. It could be intended as a double bluff. But I didn't, Margaret, I swear I didn't. I don't understand what's happening. Whether this is because of Ireland or suffrage I'm no longer sure. But Mrs Philbrook says she has received similar letters, and I swear it'll be no time before you do too. Someone is out to discredit and kill us, Margaret. Whatever they meant me to stop wasn't militancy: it was something else. And I don't know what.'

On the drive home, Margaret felt drained as she tried to make sense of what Maude had said.

'Geoff has the best defence advocate instructed for Maude's trial,' Fox said, as she mused. 'She might yet be acquitted. As far as he knows, there's very little real evidence linking Maude to that fire in Tyburnia, none for Carmelo Street, and very little for St James's. As long as she stays home and behaves herself until the end of June, under the terms of the licence for her earlier conviction, she—'

'Maud will plead guilty to the arson,' said Margaret.

'Why?'

'Because she is.'

Fox turned. 'She's kept that from you all this time?'

'I guessed on the day it happened.'

'You never said! Why didn't you tell me?'

'Because she's my friend and you were busy. Anyway, you keep saying it's not your concern. What if telling you my mere suspicion meant you had to tell someone else?'

'I bet it wasn't a mere suspicion,' said Fox. 'What else aren't you telling me?'

Margaret took a deep breath and outlined what Maude had told her. She felt her face burning. 'I told her I couldn't for a moment see Geoff being involved in something like that.'

'Not intentionally, no,' said Fox, after a pause. 'But he could be duped.'

'I know you're interested in potential caches of arms. If you find out that Geoff is involved because of what I've said...'

'It's a dilemma,' said Fox. 'But if the alternative is bloodshed, there's no choice. I'll see what we can establish discreetly. I'm sure it's a misunderstanding. But if Maude's being threatened, she must tell the police.'

'The police would say she brought it on herself.'

Fox grunted.

'More significantly, I asked as best I could what she knew about Stokes's upstairs neighbour. She said that Lois Halpin told her Stokes's neighbours were part of what she wanted to discuss. Maude assumed it was an allegation that Stokes was making bombs, which she's sure he wasn't.'

'That presupposes Maude really knew him, which she probably didn't,' said Fox, 'My men dismantled every damn picture from Stokes's old flat. Nothing. We managed to get entry while the couple were out. and lifted every loose floorboard there, and the flat above and in Miss Halpin's house. Nothing. If the documents aren't destroyed, where the hell are they?'

'Still nothing useful from Queale?'

'No. But we're letting him read the papers, and they're making him anxious.'

'Because the messages are in a different tone?'

'Presumably.' Fox drove without speaking, his jaw clenched.

'Any news on Abney?'

'He's been spotted from your description but he's surprisingly good at giving us the slip, for a man with a limp. There's always a cab or a motor vehicle with false plates at just the right moment. Whoever's paying him is paying a lot. They've probably rented a house or flat or suite and let him stay there, apparently with legitimacy. Unless we can follow we won't know where, but we've nearly managed it once or twice. It's just a matter of time.'

'Do you think he's behind any of this?'

'Yes. But someone else is doing the dirty work, which is all to do with transferring information from one place to another. I daresay he's here to see what the progress is, since they must have expected to have the papers weeks ago. Queale is such a wet, sentimental specimen that you'd expect him to have given in by now. But I think he grabbed his one and only moment of bravery and heroism and he won't let go easily. His misguided patriotism might cause a war. It's definitely caused more than one murder.'

'Are you certain?'

'I think Stokes was being used to make bombs. I think Miss Halpin may have been used to post one. I think someone was using them to cause disturbances which would be blamed on suffragettes, taking attention away from finding the papers before they could be published. Maude, with or without Miss Tabor, would have done the same, if that bomb had exploded where it could do more damage.'

'Do you still think there's a link to Dorcas Free? Dr Southern's wife is a patroness, as was Mrs Philbrook's husband. But the Holbournes are patrons too.'

'I know,' said Fox. His grip on the wheel tightened. 'There's something I need to tell you, too. I'm worried about Dr Gesner.'

'Why? Because he's German?'

'And he keeps taking leave of absence to go to Germany at a time when someone is trying to undermine the entente between Britain, France and Russia, who are allies against Germany and Austria-Hungary.'

'I like him. He likes me. He's good at his job.'

'That doesn't mean he isn't a spy, does it?' snapped Fox. 'It's hardly difficult to meet someone from Flanders on a journey to or from Germany.'

'What secrets could he take from Dorcas Free? Notes on Mrs Merryweather's prolapsed innards? Autopsy findings? Body parts?'

'The secrets don't have to be from the hospital itself, just passed through it. You have patients who work in any number of wealthy households, some of which are bound to be linked to Whitehall or the armed forces. Any one of them might be glad of extra money in exchange for passing over something they don't consider important.'

'Dr Gesner is a pathologist!' snapped Margaret. 'We deal in dead people, tissues, body parts and...'

'And what?'

'You're being ridiculous.' Margaret folded her arms and glared out of the window at any passers-by who seemed to be enjoying the evening. 'I don't believe it. You can't think every German is an enemy. I love Germany. I've liked or disliked the same proportion of Germans as British people. I've—'

'I can say the same,' said Fox. 'But some Germans here are spies, just as some of us are spies in Germany. It's possible that Dr Gesner's one of them.'

'Don't tell me you're tingling about him.'

Fox essayed a smile. 'No. Maybe I just don't like the fact that you admire each other so much.'

'What?' Margaret stared at him. 'Oh honestly, Fox. That's even more ridiculous. You need a holiday.' She unfolded her arms and put her hand over his. 'I like Dr Gesner, but I'm not attracted to him. Far too sensible. And punctual. And tidy.' She shuddered.

'*I'm* punctual and tidy.'

'Not by comparison. If he's a spy, he'll have neat little records. He hates things being out of order. Every time a body gets lost on the way from the workhouse, the chaos of the conflicting paperwork gives him apoplexy, albeit polite, understated apoplexy. Someone should be tracking down the woman from St James's. For all you know, the papers were with her.'

'We are,' said Fox.

Margaret sat silent for a while, watching the people outside. A girl and boy in their late teens were kissing behind a tree as a stern older woman marched in their direction, looking left and right as if seeking out a prey hidden in summer foliage. The urgency of the young people's kissing suggested that one of them expected to die imminently – possibly from lack of air – but given the hour, it was more likely that they were merely parting until the next day. Unless the stern woman caught them, of course, in which case imminent death – probably of the young man – might yet occur.

As the car passed they jumped apart, desperation in their faces. The boy mimed scribbling on his palm, then dashed off. The girl hunched a little, then straightened to face her guardian, an innocent smile on her face. Life was simple when the only thing you had to hide was a little love affair.

Margaret suddenly thought of the body from St James's. Was someone somewhere waiting for her to come home? 'Poor wretch,' she said. 'Poor anonymous wretch.'

Thirty

D r Gesner had told Margaret that she should go straight home after the inquest. His evidence had described only the shape of the blow to the woman's temple and left it open as to whether or not she had been dead before the explosion. The verdict had been exactly what Margaret had told Maude it would be: murder by person or persons unknown.

When she arrived home, just after four p.m., she expected Fox to be there as they'd discussed earlier, but the house was empty and quiet. Freda was shopping and Nellie had taken the children for a walk.

They'd lived in the house for more than nine months, but it was the first time Margaret had been totally alone there. Suddenly she realised that it felt like home, and would feel even more so when everyone else returned. And she also realised that she no longer yearned for the flat she'd owned for so long before marriage. She padded through all the rooms, feeling her mind clear, then took a glass of Freda's fresh lemonade into the garden. She sat under the tree with her sketchbook, Juniper stretched out beside her. Instead of jotting down words and phrases, she drew the people in the theatre café, the panic on the underground, the face of the prodding man on the tube train and the nosy passers-by.

She turned the page and sketched files, letters, a pretty boot, a bottle of laudanum, a bottle of nitroglycerin. Then a bomb in a parcel, a bomb in someone's hands, an ear cupped with a hand.

She hesitated before drawing Miss Tabor beetling across the park, then tumbled bricks under a broken roof. She drew Mr Abney as he'd been when she met him in 1910 and as he looked now, trying not to paint into his features guilt for the callous murders which should have convicted him.

Finally, she drew a woman slumped forward over a table, another asleep in a seat, another with her arm raised in entreaty. Rows of women marching. A banner: *Fight The Good Fight*.

The words and the tune of the hymn trickled through her thoughts. The hymn-writer surely hadn't thought of suffrage when he wrote lyrics based on words in the Bible. But for Emily Davison and perhaps many others, their fight for justice was a holy war. For Maude, it was simply a war. Maude had no time for piety.

Margaret inscribed a Q and entwined it with another, decorating one with vines and the other with flowers.

She circled the woman with the raised arm, then drew lines from her to the bottles and the boot. It made no sense. Maude knew these people, but then Maude knew lots of people. She was sociable, gregarious, wealthy.

She rubbed out the lines and tried again. This time, she circled the letters and drew lines to them all. Unless Maude was Queale's mistress, which Margaret found harder to imagine than her starting a prayer meeting, she knew nothing about the letters. And the letters had nothing whatsoever to do with suffrage, beyond the affectionate nickname Queale had given his mistress.

Maude was a catalyst, not because she knew, but because by asking for justice for Stokes and Lois Halpin, it seemed as if she knew.

The garden was becoming too hot. Margaret returned to the house, Juniper weaving in front of her, and entered the cool kitchen. She found some scraps in the pantry for Juniper and sat at the spotless table, reviewing her sketches.

The front door banged, she heard a familiar hurried tread, and Fox walked in. 'I'm sorry, Margaret. I know I said we could spend the rest of the afternoon here, but Carter contacted me. He thinks you might have a view on something. Do you want to come?'

Margaret closed her sketchbook. Sometimes ideas needed to brew before they made sense. 'Yes, of course.'

The street outside Lois Halpin's house was busy as people came home for lunch. Little children played in the street with balls and hoops, ekeing out the time until they were called in to eat.

Mr Carter ushered Margaret and Fox inside. The house seemed anonymous now that all the furniture, books and photographs were gone. Only the posters and old prints were still there, disconcertingly jolly. They followed Mr Carter to the kitchen and sat with him at the scrubbed table. One of the chairs stood in a corner.

'Put simply,' said Mr Carter, 'I've told Inspector Silvermann and given him the items, but I thought you might like to know too. I found traces of laudanum everywhere – in every bottle of cordial, fortified wine or patent medicine. Every health drink, every jar. Whatever she ate or drank, it was there. Maybe she couldn't smell or taste it, given her addiction, but it must have been set up ready. Does that make sense, doctor? Either Lois had gone very peculiar, or someone else made sure she drank so much laudanum that she could be gassed without realising it. The inspector said he'd investigate and tell you.'

'It might explain things more fully,' said Margaret, as non-committally as she could.

'A woman did it, I'm sure of it.'

'Mrs Bessemer?'

Mr Carter shook his head. 'Hannah would never harm Lois, even for the leech – even if they had the brains. It's someone else. Someone she trusted to enter the house. The reason I asked you here, Superintendent, is because this came. I told the inspector the gist of it.' He handed over a small, light piece of paper. 'It's a letter Lois sent me which has been following me the last few weeks.'

In a barely legible hand, Lois sent love and greetings and a summary of the Bessemers' latest failings, then wrote:

I need to tell you something and hope you don't get angry. I wish you were here to advise me.

Do you remember I told you about the group I joined after reading an advertisement, and how it didn't make sense? Most people seemed to be full of talk but nothing else, and some of them came and went and never said much at all, though they're all as thick as thieves with Mrs Philbrook when we stop for tea. But she's the sort who makes a point of being friendly, regardless of class. And there's the quiet, angry one who carries magazines about.

Stokes was all right, though. He never said much to anyone really, including me. I was sometimes very tired and he's very quiet and unapproachable, but I felt he respected what I'd done for the cause and listened to what I said when I did talk, so in a way we were friends. But not __that__ sort of friends, please believe me.

After the last meeting he attended before he was murdered, he asked me for my address, which I thought a little odd. But he said it was to do with a group member in trouble, whom he wanted to help, so I said yes.

The next day, his letter came. He said he wanted to tell me about a group member who was supposed to have gone abroad to be with her husband and was planning something very dangerous, and he didn't trust the police or know what to do. He asked me to write back if I was willing to meet. I didn't know what he meant at all, but said I would, provided it was somewhere public.

After that, he sent an invitation to see Major Barbara at Theatre Valerina on the Wednesday after Easter. I started to wonder if I'd misunderstood his meaning but you know I never keep letters, so I couldn't read back. I decided not to reply until I'd worked out what to do or say. Then I heard he'd been shot by a burglar and that he'd been making bombs.

But the more I think about it, the more I think Mrs Holbourne is right. His murder wasn't one of those things. She's only one of two women I trust, and I'm not sure of the other. She's asked me to post magazines and it seemed odd she trusts me when she knows about my illness. I'm going to ask Mrs Holbourne to visit. I'm not sure the police will believe either of us – we're both convicted arsonists and known admirers of Mrs Pankhurst. If Stokes was making bombs to plant with someone else, that just makes it worse.

By the time you read this, I shall have met with her. Maybe it won't get to you before you start back, but if it does, write and tell me if you can think of anything else I can do. I feel so muddled all the time. Some days it's worse than death. I so wish you were here.

'I don't follow a word of it,' said Mr Carter. 'Is it any use?'

'Yes,' said Fox. 'It is.'

'Good evening to you,' said Mr Bryce, as they were ushered into his office. 'What brings you here? I imagine you'd approve of us putting on *Little Miss Llewellyn*, Dr Demeray. It's Joan's idea, inspired by meeting you, I think. I'd rather be doing something a bit lighter. What's the point of all the politics flying about if you can't make fun of them? I wanted to put on a farce set in Holloway with suffragettes and wardresses doing a dance routine. After all the cinemas are showing a film with Mr

Edward Payne dressed up as a suffragette getting forcibly fed champagne. Hilarious! Why aren't we on the bandwagon? But Joan says no. Even after that maniac ran in front of a horse and nearly killed it the other week.'

'Good for Miss Bryce,' said Margaret, gritting her teeth. 'And the horse is fine, while the maniac is now dead and her funeral is on Saturday, so perhaps it would seem insensitive.'

Fox touched her foot with his own, a signal for her to stop talking. 'I imagine you wouldn't want to upset Mr Holbourne, Mr Bryce, when Mrs Holbourne has recently been through that experience. I imagine he might reconsider his backing.'

'There is that,' said Mr Bryce, unrepentant. 'Anyhow, here's the lady herself. Come along in, Joan. The doctor approves of the play.'

Miss Bryce entered and shook hands. 'I was sorry to hear about Mrs Holbourne, doctor. I don't approve of your views, as you know, but I don't believe she's any more guilty than Lois was.'

'We're here about Miss Halpin,' said Fox. 'I assume you heard about her sister and brother-in-law.'

'It's terrible,' said Miss Bryce. 'An accident worsened by greed. Poor Jonas. Did you assist with the arrest?'

Fox nodded. 'There's just one small thing we need to clear up, in terms of her state of mind. I know you said she wasn't employed here anymore, but did she visit?'

'Oh yes,' said Miss Bryce, without hesitation. 'We'd some-times have tea in the little café and sometimes in here. It rather depended on her ... state of health, if you understand. We were good friends once, before she—'

'Before her political views, which were contrary to yours, strengthened?' said Margaret.

Miss Bryce's face remained open and friendly. 'I want the vote as much as you do, Dr Demeray. I'm just willing to wait for it to happen naturally, as I told you before. The only other thing Lois and I disagreed on was' – she glanced at her brother – 'Ireland. But we were united in our love for it. I understand her views, I really do. Westminster is a long way from Dublin, and a good deal of nonsense is spouted in the name of religion, on every side.'

'Isn't it always?' said Mr Bryce. 'And that was the funny thing, you might say. Here's me and Joan, good Catholics, prepared to stay in the Union as long as the way Catholics are treated improves and the poor are treated better, and there was Lois, brought up Protestant, wanting Ireland's independence. Nothing's simple, is it?'

'But we're content to let things run their course,' said Miss Bryce. 'In my job, I want to make people forget the world for a while, or see a reflection of it and think. Hopefully, Home Rule will come in peacefully and the two nations can get on.'

'I'd raise a glass to that if I had one,' said Mr Bryce. 'I've no time for troublemakers, whether they're women running under horses or people setting bombs and gathering arms.'

Margaret watched them closely. Miss Bryce was an actress, but that didn't make her a liar. Everything she had said seemed heartfelt and honest. Any doubt that Maude might be right fell away. Whatever Geoff was up to, it couldn't be gun-running.

'Lois was a good woman at heart,' Mr Bryce continued. 'Passionate, and suffering for her passion. But I never saw her as a bomber. If she'd got well, she could have acted for us again. But she knew she was always welcome here. She often met friends in the café and we let them hire a box at a reduced rate from time to time, so she could watch the show and have a bite to eat and a bottle of wine with pals. Not that she had many, poor thing.'

'I was a little surprised the last time,' said Miss Bryce. 'I assume she planned some sort of consultation because she wasn't interested in other men. She was very much in love with Jonas.'

'It never happened, of course,' said Mr Bryce. 'So who can tell?'

Margaret opened her mouth to speak, then closed it again. Miss Bryce's eyes were locked with hers. She seemed poised to speak but uncertain as to whether she should. 'Perhaps she wanted to cheer herself up while Mr Carter was away,' Margaret said, eventually, hoping she wasn't pushing too soon.

'Maybe she wasn't quite the thing when she booked it,' said Miss Bryce. 'Or it might have been her friend that booked on her behalf. Either way, none of them turned up and she didn't write, which was unlike her. I didn't like to ask, since the other guests were men. But it was Easter time. Maybe they did something else, or perhaps she forgot to tell the others and forgot it herself.'

'Perhaps,' said Fox. 'It sounds as if she was quite poorly. Did you know the friends?'

'I just know the box was for three,' said Miss Bryce, frowning. 'The ledger won't say, but the letter of request may be somewhere in the files. It'll take hours to find after all these months. Is it important?'

'It might be. Could I look in the box?'

Miss Bryce turned to her brother for a response. He looked at the clock and grunted. 'If you can do it before six thirty, when people start arriving for the evening performance, and you don't leave a mess, then yes.'

'Thank you,' said Fox. 'I'll take Margaret home and come back with my best people as soon as possible.'

'I can't help,' said Margaret, as they left. 'I have to be at Phoebe's by seven, and I want to tell Maude—'

'You can't tell Maude anything.'

'I can tell her that I'm confident there will be justice for Miss Halpin. She'll understand not to ask more.'

'If you're sure,' said Fox. 'If I can be home in time to take you to Phoebe's, I will. Otherwise, promise me you'll take a cab.'

'I promise.'

Thirty-One

Only moments after Margaret had kissed the children goodnight, there was hammering at the front door.

She paused on the landing, reliving the fear she'd felt on the underground, then rushed to stop Freda from answering the door.

It was too late. Mrs Southern burst into the hall, staring as Margaret descended the stairs. She reached into her capacious handbag. Margaret pulled Freda behind her, wishing there was something more useful than an umbrella to hand.

But Mrs Southern's eyes were red from crying, and from her bag she extracted a copy of *Athene's Gazette.* She held out the sketch of Maude, terrified and struggling as a man seen from behind forced a tube up her nose. 'Is your husband here?'

'He's at work.'

'Get him. I need to confess. I didn't realise. I didn't know.' Mrs Southern shook the paper in Margaret's face. 'It's my fault.'

There was more banging at the door, then a familiar voice. 'You all right, Mrs F?'

'It's Bert,' Margaret said to Freda. 'I mean, Sergeant Ainscough. Let him in. The master must have asked him to, er, see that we're all right this evening.'

'Is he your husband's man?' asked Mrs Southern.

'Yes. What is this about, Mrs Southern? Perhaps you'd best come and sit down.'

'I'll tell this Ainscough person. If he has to arrest me, so be it. Your husband will see that I'm not treated like a common criminal, won't he? I don't care about Bernard.'

In the sitting room, Mrs Southern twisted her hands as she waited for Bert to find a notebook and pencil from an inner pocket. 'What is all this about, madam?' he asked.

'I have been protecting my husband for two years,' she said. 'He's been selling morphine from the hospital to people. Female friends, chiefly, but also to people rather lower down the social order. Actresses, and so forth. I've always known that, but it... It seemed more discreet than their having to go to a chemist or worse so that everyone would know. He sells chemicals too, I think, but I couldn't say what one might do with those. The hospital could manage the deficit, surely, Dr Demeray?'

'Hardly,' said Margaret. 'And the morphine is meant for desperately sick people who can't afford it, even from a chemist.'

'I do everything I can to raise funds,' protested Mrs Southern.

'That is very noble of you, but what has this to do with me?' asked Bert.

'Because I fear he hasn't stopped at selling morphine. Over the last few months, papers have been going missing from friends' homes, too. I don't know what they are, but I know from my friends that their husbands have become quite sick with worry. It must be Bernard. He's welcomed because of me, and by some notable men because of his profession.'

'Why would you think it's your husband, madam?'

'I discovered that he has a public liaison. A girl.' Mrs Southern's face hardened, and Margaret remembered being told that the marriage wasn't a love match. Perhaps Mrs Southern could endure discreet affairs, but nothing that made her a laughing stock. 'He was seen in public with her, arguing like common people do, and shaking her.' Mrs Southern sniffed. 'Vulgar. I was justified in going through his things to track her down, but he's put her where she can't be found.'

'I really don't—'

'Be quiet, man. I found he had quite the stash of magazines.' She blushed. 'I don't mean improper ones. A woman's magazine – not this one.' She waved *Athene's Gazette*. 'Some dreadful thing called *The New Dorcas*. Inside the top two magazines were documents in envelopes. They were from a ministry and headed *Top Secret*. They could only have come from the homes of people who trust us. Bernard must be passing them on to someone by giving them a magazine no one else would look at. And there were also desperate letters, pleading for him to stop blackmailing.'

Bert's eyes flickered briefly to Margaret. 'I see, madam. And you want to tell Superintendent Foxcroft all this.'

Mrs Southern swallowed and her eyes filled with tears. 'I wanted Bernard arrested, but I didn't want to be involved. I heard there was a recalcitrant prisoner in Holloway – I have connections, you know. He's done forcible feeding before: he is proud of saving lives and at the same time getting the better of women he considers unworthy of respect. I arranged for him to go and treat her. I knew it was against the law, and I expected him to be arrested. Then I could ensure that the police went through all his things and found out what he'd done. He went to Holloway, and came back in a dreadful state. My connection at the prison refused to say what had happened, except that you'd been there and stopped him doing something. The police didn't come. I thought it was just a matter of time.'

'Mrs Southern,' Margaret began, but the other woman held up her hand.

'I thought... I thought all the fuss about forcible feeding was just exaggeration by the WSPU. I've seen postcards, and a film in the cinema which made it look quite funny... Then I saw this sketch today. For the first time, I understood what forcible feeding really meant, and I recognised Mrs Holbourne as the victim and my husband as the man who could have killed her. And it was my fault.' She took a deep breath. 'I wanted to apologise to you first, doctor. I know you are friends with Mrs Holbourne, and I thought perhaps you could apologise to her on my behalf. And I want your husband to know that mine is selling secrets. He's a common traitor. I swear I didn't know. But if you have to arrest me, Sergeant Ainscough, so be it.'

'Much appreciated, Mrs Southern,' said Bert, closing his notebook. 'I'll just make a quick telephone call, then I'll drive you home. Chief Superintendent Hare will meet us there and do this all discreet.'

'Thank you, Sergeant.'

Margaret beckoned Bert and whispered in his ear. 'BLS must have been a man all along. I wonder what his middle name is.'

***

Margaret left her departure for Phoebe's until the last minute, hoping that Fox would come home early enough to drive her while explaining anything else she needed to know. When he didn't, she gave up and took a cab.

By the time she arrived, Maude was on the other side of the room in Phoebe's most comfortable chair, flanked by two younger women who somehow looked like acolytes. Margaret raised a hand in greeting and smiled. Maude nodded in response, her pale face serious. The room was full: it would be difficult to cross and she needed to talk to Maude where she couldn't be overheard. She sat down next to Mrs Snoville-Lewis and whispered, 'I confess I haven't used the hammer yet.'

Mrs Snoville-Lewis turned with an eager smile. 'Ooh! Have you bought one, doctor? I never expected you would. I recommend not painting the handle unless you're quite sure the paint won't come off. One of my pairs of gloves is quite ruined.'

'I shan't,' said Margaret. So that answered that. She fidgeted, trying to suppress her urge to drag Maude outside, establish that she had witnesses for the night on which the hammer was put through her letterbox, and tell her that Geoff wasn't involved in anything untoward.

Phoebe rose and Maude drummed her fingers on the arms of the chair. There were deep shadows under her reddened eyes.

'On Saturday, Miss Davison's coffin will come from Epsom to Victoria Station, where we shall be waiting,' Phoebe said. 'From there, the coffin will be preceded by a woman bearing a cross, in the hope that no one will be disgraceful enough to shout abuse, and we shall follow it to St George's in Bloomsbury, where there will be a brief service. Thereafter, we follow it to King's Cross Station, whence Miss Davison will make her final journey home to Morpeth and there be laid to rest in a private ceremony. It is anticipated that around five thousand women will follow the coffin through London, processing in ranks.'

'What should one wear?' asked Mrs Nutford.

'There are purple, white and black sections,' said Phoebe. 'We shall be in the white section, with black armbands and our usual sashes.'

'I may not be able to obtain leave,' said Miss Brown.

'That is understood,' said Phoebe. 'No one is under any obligation to march. For those who do, I need to know who wants to march as part of this group, since some of you may wish to join professional colleagues. For those who wish to march with me, I shall communicate with Miss Grace Roe, who is organising the march, and she will provide our places in the procession. May I have a show of hands for those who will march as part of this group?'

The majority of women raised their hands.

'Thank you,' said Phoebe. 'Now, the next task is to decide who will bear wreaths, which banners and standards to carry, and who will carry them for what period of the march.'

Throughout the discussion, Margaret had tried to catch Maude's gaze, but Maude kept her eyes on Phoebe, except when she closed them to cough into a handkerchief or sip from a glass of something that Margaret hoped was water. She was far too sick to be at a meeting, let alone take part in a three-mile procession. It was unlike her not to be flashing looks of amusement, concern or query.

Finally, the details were settled, 'We're glad to have you back among us, Maude,' said Phoebe. 'We're all truly sorry for what you've endured recently.'

Maude stood up and glared round the room. 'It may interest you to know that I was questioned again today in relation to murders I didn't commit.' Her eyes settled on Margaret. 'In case anyone wonders, I have not murdered anyone, planted a bomb, induced anyone else to plant a bomb, or been involved in anyone else's plans to do so. Yet *someone* gave information to the police which led them to believe I might have.'

'It was not I,' said Etta.

Maude ignored her. 'I was thinking back to Black Friday, and I remembered how easily Dr Demeray got out of that melée.'

'What are you talking about, Maude?' said Phoebe. 'Margaret was called to Caxton Hall to treat the wounded.'

'How convenient.'

'I'm a doctor,' said Margaret, baffled.

'Phoebe was right the other week,' said Maude calmly. 'The policemen you tackled were doubled up in agony, yet you weren't arrested.'

'Neither were many others. It was just luck. Maude—'

'I don't think it was luck. I think someone gave orders that no one should touch you.'

Margaret felt the blood drain from her face as she realised what Maude was implying. 'Even if that were true, how could anyone have singled me out in all that chaos? I—'

'For three years since, you have sat quietly.'

'I don't sit quietly unless I'm bored! Maude, what—'

'You manage to get into Holloway when my own husband can't, and you visit when I'm sufficiently weak not to consider what I'm telling you about direct action. Yet you haven't taken direct action yourself since at least 1909.'

'Are you calling me a coward?'

'I'm calling you a police spy.'

The room fell utterly silent.

A petal from a vase of flowers drifted onto the tablecloth. Etta's hand spasmed across her agenda and hit the bell, making it give a dull tinkle.

'If that's what you think, I'll leave,' said Margaret.

The silence burned.

'No!' said Phoebe. 'Margaret, Maude doesn't—'

'Maude can speak for herself,' snapped Maude.

'And you have,' said Margaret. 'So I'm leaving. And on Saturday, I'll march with other female physicians. I'm sorry you were questioned again, Maude: I think it's unjust. But I am not responsible for what the police do. Goodnight.'

Brushing aside Phoebe's protestations, Margaret stormed out of the house, promising to hail a cab. Once she was out of sight, though, she marched home on foot despite the uneasy exposure of the evening streets. It was an hour to lighting-up time but the skies were gloomy, throwing lanes and alleys into shadow. The fresh breeze held the promise of rain and she had no umbrella. But still she walked.

I pity anyone who tries to attack me, she thought, holding back her tears until mortification and self-pity were overtaken by fury, then confusion, and she no longer wished to cry. How could Maude believe it was Margaret's fault that she'd been questioned again? The inspector must have taken the information from Mr Carter and misinterpreted it, but that wasn't anything to do with her. And Maude didn't know that arrests were about to be made. Was she too sick to think straight? But even in illness, it was unlike Maude to be so forthright in public. Perhaps she'd meant every word.

Margaret arrived home as Fox was getting into the car. 'I was just coming to collect you. Did you send word that you were coming home a different way?'

'I didn't think,' said Margaret. 'Has anyone telephoned for me?'

'I don't believe so, but I've only been home five minutes. You should have telephoned, and stayed there till I could collect you. I need to tell you something and the drive would have been ideal.' He frowned. 'Wait a moment. Where did the cab drop you?'

'It didn't. I walked.'

'Why on earth... What if— What's wrong, Margaret? Something is.' He moved closer and touched her face. 'Your eyes are red. Have you been crying?'

'Not yet.'

'Come and tell me.' He ushered her towards the house and unlocked the door.

Freda, replacing the telephone receiver as they entered, jumped. 'I coulda sworn you'd just gone, sir. I'm afraid supper's not ready. You said half-past nine, and I was just doing it when the telephone rang.'

'Half-past nine will be perfect,' said Fox. 'Who was calling?'

'Miss Pendleberry for the mistress, sir. Asking her to telephone when she arrives. If I'd known you were just behind the door, I'd have kept her on the line. Are you all right, ma'am? You look sorta—'

'Something got in my eye,' said Margaret, removing her hat and putting it on the hall table. 'I don't wish to speak to anyone just now. Could you call her house and leave a message that I've arrived safely and may telephone tomorrow. The number is in the notebook.'

Freda frowned a little. 'Yes'm.'

'And then you can finish the master's supper.'

'Yes'm.'

Fox ushered Margaret into the sitting room. 'I need to tell you something, but I think you need to tell me something too.'

He looked drawn and tired, as much in need of someone to confide in as she was. She put her face in her hands. 'The meeting was fraught.'

In the reddish darkness of the fingers covering her eyes came Maude's cold expression as she vented her bitterness and the faces of a roomful of gawping women. Margaret tried to say more but her voice caught in an involuntary sob.

Fox stroked her back. 'This is an emotional time for you all. I'm sorry. I wish I didn't have to tell you another difficult thing.'

She managed to choke out 'What is it? What was in the theatre box? What's happened to the Southerns?'

Fox checked the hallway, then led her to sit as far from the door as possible. 'Dr Southern is under arrest but not admitting to anything except the theft of morphine and other items from the hospital. He says the woman he was seen with was no one of importance: he seems that kind of man. He appeared genuinely shocked by the documents and the magazines. I don't think it's him. I think someone is trying to make it look that way, and so does Hare.'

'But his name! Bernard Southern. BS?'

'Queale's BLS is definitely a woman, and Dr Southern's middle names are Franklin Jonathan. He's just another person who's been used. As for the theatre... There was nothing in the box, but the Bryces found the letter from Stokes. I'm afraid the third person was Dr Ernst Gesner. I'm really sorry to ask, but can you find out if Maude knows how Dr Gesner might have known Stokes and Miss Halpin?'

'She wouldn't even tell me how she wants her tea.'

'What? Why?'

Margaret curled up in his embrace, wishing she could cry like a child, whispering Maude's accusations. He held her, stroking her hair and saying nothing, making her feel safe in the haven of his arms.

She knew she should be concerned for Dr Gesner, and worried about the documents Queale had stolen. But none of it seemed to matter. Losing her best friend felt much worse.

Thirty-Two

Phoebe arrived on the doorstep at eight a.m., while Margaret and Fox were having breakfast. Freda brought her through to the dining room and went to make a pot of tea. Fox, pleading a need to do some work before leaving for the office, took his coffee and toast and went to his study.

'Does he know?' asked Phoebe, taking a seat beside Margaret, her expression pensive.

'Yes,' said Margaret. She felt the heat rise in her face. 'I'm entitled to tell my own husband why I'm upset.'

'Of course you are.' Phoebe reached for her hand, squeezed it, then sat back. 'I'm sorry it's so early, but I have to be back for morning assembly. I can't bear it when you and Maude fall out.'

'*I* haven't. She has.'

'Maude should not have voiced those views in public and I told her so. She—'

'Is utterly repentant, and I should expect flowers and a formal apology at any moment?'

Phoebe rolled her eyes. 'The difference between your temper and Maude's is that yours flares up from nowhere like a gas flame, scorches everyone – chiefly yourself – and disappears in seconds. Hers smoulders for ages then blazes suddenly, consuming everything in its path, then smoulders again until someone works out how to extinguish it. It's rather wearing. I told her she should have discussed any concerns with you in private.'

'She had plenty of opportunity on Wednesday, when I visited. She was quite a different person towards me then.'

'That's odd. I—' Phoebe broke off as Freda entered with the teapot and fresh toast, laid the place before her, and withdrew. 'Maude's not well, of course. Feverish, possibly. I think she's afraid, though I'm not sure of what. Do you know?'

Margaret stared into her cup. Maude had been afraid on Wednesday night. But then she'd asked for help, not made accusations. And she knew that Maude had been afraid before – of childbirth, of being forcibly fed, of Geoff deciding she was too exhausting and looking for comfort elsewhere. Truly, it was Phoebe who never seemed afraid. Margaret was ashamed that she'd never even thought that Phoebe's courage might be a disguise.

Just now, her friend's expression gave nothing away. 'Maybe Maude's concerned about the procession and fears that Special Branch will interfere, though I can't see why. The police have been fully involved with planning and will be flanking us against possible assault.'

'Good, but irrelevant.' Margaret folded her arms. 'Do you agree with what she said about me?'

'No,' said Phoebe, pouring herself tea. 'But you have to see her point.'

'Do I?'

'Yes. You must be honour bound to share information about the campaign with Fox, if he asks. Then he'd be honour bound to pass it on and it would be used against us.'

'He won't ask and I won't tell. I'm honour bound to you and Maude, too.'

'Be truthful, Margaret. If you knew, absolutely knew, that Maude was going to collect a bomb and use it for the cause, would you keep quiet or tell?'

'She wouldn't,' said Margaret. 'So it doesn't apply. Of course I'd say something. Wouldn't you?'

'I doubt it.' Phoebe had always been a secret-keeper – her inner feelings, Margaret's confidences, plans for campaigns. She was popular with her nephews and nieces and Maude's children because they could confide in her safely. As for her inner thoughts, she kept most of them quietly buried. A response that Margaret should have predicted was now unnerving.

'Fox has bigger things to worry about than suffragettes,' said Margaret.

'How do you know?'

Margaret shrugged as she toyed with her toast. The vision of Maude's furious face filled her mind. The expression on it reminded her of Joan of Arc: full of zeal, to the point of martyrdom. Maude, who was usually pragmatic and funny. The articles in her magazine were witty, often poking gentle fun at those with unbending views. 'I've gone out of my way to see if Maude's theories about Miss Halpin might be correct.'

'Perhaps the police are using that against her.'

'It's not my fault if they are. That's not a reason to turn on me, unless...' Had Maude suffered more than additional questioning? Had she received another threatening letter?

'Unless what?'

'I don't know,' said Margaret, rubbing her eyes.

'I don't think you're a police spy,' said Phoebe, 'but I must ask your views on suffrage. Maude was right in one respect. With the exception of Black Friday, you withdrew from direct action years ago. You agreed to be counted in the census in 1911; you have never even withheld your taxes. It's hard to know whether you're with Mrs Pankhurst or Mrs Fawcett.'

Margaret sat back. The mantle clock ticked. Phoebe's blue eyes were locked with hers. There was no judgment in them, simply query. Phoebe had always been able to guess the sadness, worries and secret joys under Margaret's façade, where Maude never troubled to look. Who was she with? Must she choose?

'There's nothing wrong with Mrs Fawcett's view.'

'I didn't say there was. I'd prefer a peaceful approach, but these aren't peaceful times. I'm following Mrs Pankhurst, even if one day my actions lose me the school.'

'I'm a doctor,' said Margaret. 'Most physicians keep themselves a little separate. It's hard not to. Besides, if you lost the school, you still have a large private income, as does Maude. Mine is tiny, like that of many doctors. And I've said all along that I would not support anything which endangered anyone. If you'd seen some of the things I have, you'd feel the same.'

'I believe you.'

'I support the cause financially. I specifically joined a hospital with a board who won't countenance any of its doctors taking part in forcible feeding, a rule Dr Southern breached. But will Emily Davison's death really make a difference? Was Maude's humiliation and injury worth it? Women in New Zealand and Australia got the vote without any of this – why can't we? Is this the right way to get what we want? What if it were a different cause – independence for Ireland, or India? Or better wages for the poor. Would you consider the violence justified then? Why does every change have to come with blood? Shouldn't women want a different way?'

'None of us want to be humiliated, hurt or imprisoned, Margaret. We just want the vote. Maybe Maude took her frustration out on you yesterday evening, thinking you'd give like for like.' Phoebe rolled her eyes. 'I swear I went into teaching as a direct result of being friends with you two: the best experience of managing ten-year-olds I could have got.' She took a final sip of tea and rose. 'Now, I must go. One of you has to grow up: we're all too old for this. I'll see you at the funeral procession. Please join our group, as you intended.'

'Thank you, but no,' said Margaret. 'I'll march with people who understand me.'

Fox descended after Phoebe had left. Margaret was skewering her hat in place, with scant attention to her scalp. 'I thought you'd gone,' she said. 'I'm going to see what I can find out from Dr Gesner.'

'I'd rather you didn't—'

'But I shall. And I want the walk.'

'Then I'll escort you,' said Fox, ushering her through the front door. 'Did Phoebe's visit help?'

Margaret considered as they walked. Phoebe was right. Her ire had faded, leaving hurt and embarrassment. When she'd first known Maude, the latter would have been more important. Now, she was older. She knew that embarrassment passed without leaving scars, but the same could not always be said for hurt. She shook her head. 'I'm angry with Inspector Silvermann for forcing a wedge between us. Angry with the person who's blackmailing Maude. And anxious about facing Dr Gesner.'

'Then don't.'

'I still can't believe he's anything other than what he purports to be.'

'Can't or won't believe?' said Fox. 'It's easy to be mistaken when you like someone. And someone under cover has to be competent at their job. If Dr Gesner weren't more than competent, you wouldn't have accepted him being appointed above you.'

'Even when he didn't...'

'Didn't what?'

Margaret stopped walking and looked about. They were passing a park, summer-vibrant with flowers. It was as incongruous as every little London park under the gaze of smut-blackened edifices, like green picnic cloths laid out among coal heaps.

Chugging and rattling drifted from Paddington Station, and the air was clear enough to hear shouts from barge owners in Paddington Basin, even if the words were impossible to make out. Smoke billowed from the station, St Mary's hospital and any number of other chimneys. It hovered high overhead, kettling the increasing heat.

'The day I received the telegram that misdirected me, I went back to the hospital for it and found Dr Gesner in my room, collecting something. We chatted and he reassured me, then left. But he didn't take the thing he'd come for.' She wasn't looking at Fox, but she knew his tension had increased. 'The telegram was in the waste-paper bin. I'd never have put it in there and not remembered: I'd have left it on the desk or put it in my bag or pocket. If Dr Gesner saw it on my desk, he shouldn't have done anything but leave it. On the other hand, if I'd dropped it on the floor by accident then he might have put it in the bin, but he *ought* to have put it on the desk. Just an oddity which I decided meant nothing.'

'But it niggled at you.'

'I like him, Fox. I don't mean that I'm attracted to him. I just instinctively like him.'

Fox sighed. 'I understand that, but it's easy to make allowances for someone you feel is a friend.'

'Unless you're Maude, apparently.'

'Then be like Maude,' said Fox. 'Be suspicious and prove me wrong.'

'By doing so, I'll prove her right.'

Fox tucked her arm into his and squeezed it as they started walking again. 'Out of context, Maude is right. You've told me things that stopped murders and helped to stop actions which could devastate the country.'

'I can't tell Maude that, though,' said Margaret. In her head, she counted the people who might have died if she – or someone like her – hadn't helped Fox. 'We've missed something. *I've* missed something. But I'm not having Maude accused of something she didn't do on the basis of what I've inadvertently suggested to the police. She could have purchased the laudanum that poisoned Lois Halpin but she had no reason to, and ... even if she had, she couldn't have delivered it just before Lois died. When I went to Miss Halpin's house, because of that telegram, the neighbour across the road said something about a lady visiting Lois. Someone who attended the inquest. It can't have been Maude. She was away. Was it the woman with the magazines who wanted Lois to deliver them for her?'

'And was one of the deliveries not magazines but a bomb, only without Lois realising? I'll have someone see what they can find out. It had better not be me or you, I think. Meanwhile, I'll ask Silvermann to give me all the evidence from the incident in St James's. I want to see the photographs of the scene and the woman's face again.'

'It won't help.'

'It might.'

Fox stopped and peered up the busy road. 'Let me know when you need to leave, and if I can't come I'll send Bert.' He turned to face her. 'Margaret, is there anything else you haven't told me? Something you're worried could implicate someone? Wouldn't you rather know the truth? Telling yourself you're not suspicious doesn't mean you aren't – but if it's not cleared up one way or another, that'll niggle you for ever too. And it could be critical. Even if it's about Maude.'

'I don't believe Maude could kill anyone.'

'Then help me prove it.'

'What if a piece of evidence has been made to look as if she has?'

'What piece of evidence?

'The hammer. Mrs Snoville-Lewis didn't give it to me and I don't believe Maude did. But I can't ask Maude for her alibi. But the evening of that meeting at Phoebe's in late May... someone else must have met that woman at St James's and then left the hammer with me to implicate Maude.'

'I'll deal with that somehow. Go home. Leave Dr Gesner to me.'

'No. You go home. I'm going to the hospital.'

'The man might be dangerous.'

'He isn't,' said Margaret. 'Let me prove it and join me when you can. What could he do to me?'

'In a hospital, surrounded by drugs and scalpels? I can't imagine.'

Thirty-Three

'Good morning, Dr Demeray,' said Dr Gesner, rising when she entered his office. 'I assume you're here to find out what's happening about your allegations in relation to Dr Southern.'

'Er ... yes.'

Dr Gesner gestured to her to sit, then seated himself. 'Late yesterday, Dr Innes informed me that the governing body had concluded that Dr Southern had breached the terms of his contract and he had been asked to resign. However, the only public announcement would be a statement in the press that this hospital does not condone forcible feeding and that any doctor taking part in it would be asked to leave. In normal circumstances, Dr Southern would fade away unnamed.'

'But...'

'The governing body accept that on the balance of probabilities, what you report is true. However, it would boil down to your word against his in a public enquiry. While I hope you believe that I know this to be unfair, the likelihood is that his word would be accepted and yours discounted or twisted because of your personal views. The hospital does not want to be disgraced in any way. More importantly, perhaps, it doesn't want you to be disgraced. You are highly valued.' He cleared his throat. 'Since then, other things have come to light. A thorough audit is being conducted which may involve our being questioned.

Ultimately, anything Dr Southern has done wrong concerning the hospital will be made public. Not yet, however.' Dr Gesner sat back and straightened the files before him.

Margaret's brain raced. What she had said to Fox was true: she'd instinctively liked Dr Gesner from their first meeting. But what Fox had said was true, too. A spy, by his very nature, needed to fit in, be personable, not appear suspicious. But Dorcas Free would be such an odd place to obtain information. The dentist in Portsmouth mentioned at Maude's dinner party was treating a naval officer who passed on files, but the patients at Dorcas Free were a different sort altogether. If the papers found among Dr Southern's possessions had been put there to incriminate him, surely it couldn't have been Dr Gesner. Dr Southern moved in the right circles because of his wife. Dr Gesner had no such connections that she knew of.

Before she could formulate anything, Dr Gesner knocked the ball into her court. 'What do you know of your husband's job?'

'He's a senior officer in Special Branch.' That was untrue. Fox was in an organisation which fell within the armed forces, but Special Branch was the cover he worked under. Margaret had stopped thinking of it as a lie three years ago.

'Rounding up republicans, anarchists, spies. That sort of thing?'

'I believe so.'

'Mmm. The British class system and the German one are different, of course. All the same, he is rather higher up the scale than the average – what do you call them – bobby.'

Margaret shrugged. 'I didn't appoint him.'

'I gather you've helped him before, where medical expertise is necessary to his investigation, but I'm not sure what that has actually involved. Dr Jordan at St Julia's seemed rather vague on the matter, but content as long as it didn't interfere with your hospital work.'

'I explain post-mortem findings and medical terms when necessary,' said Margaret, finding safe ground. 'And sometimes he asks me to question a young woman or girl: he understands that they might talk more readily to a female. Being a doctor means that I'm perceived as both professional and confidential.'

'Though you pass on what they've said.'

'They know I will.' *Police spy* echoed in her head.

Dr Gesner suddenly reached into a jacket pocket and Margaret tensed. What if Fox's suspicions were right? Could she move out of the way of a gun in time?

He extracted a small leather wallet and opened it. 'Here is a photograph of my wife, Ilse,' he said. 'I hope that one day you will meet her. Perhaps we could dine with you and your husband.' The photograph showed a pretty woman in her late twenties wearing a fashionable outfit. Her eyes were pale, her hair fair, in contrast to the near-black of Dr Gesner's. 'We have no children, but here she is with her father.' This time, Frau Gesner was standing in traditional German dress behind an elderly man slumped in a wing-backed chair. 'He is very frail and loves his country. He will not leave, and she will not leave while he lives. Germany is more progressive than Britain, and the economy is better, though a long way from catching up with the United States. However, I am concerned about the political situation. I would like to make my home here. She is too, but I cannot persuade her. I do not wish my father-in-law ill, but I wish...'

'You needn't tell me this, Dr Gesner.'

'I normally wouldn't,' he said. 'In fact, until Thursday I had no intention of telling you or anyone else.'

Margaret frowned, the memory of the underground making her shiver. 'I don't follow.'

Dr Gesner stood up and paced. 'I wanted to speak with you that lunchtime, and Miss Upton said you'd just left after receiving a telegram. I rushed out to see if I could catch you. I might have, only I saw someone hurry to catch up with you as you entered the underground. I assumed it was a friend and came back inside. When you came back and said you had been assaulted, I wished I had made sure.'

'There was no friend,' said Margaret, feeling her hands tremble. 'Was he short and grey-haired, with a palsied face and a cane?'

'No. Why?'

'I saw someone like that, er... loitering one day. He unnerved me.'

'That's concerning.' Dr Gesner sat down and picked up the Stokes file. 'But he is not the man I mean. I have seen you in the café attached to the Theatre Valerina. It is not far from where I lodge and the café is a good place for a meal. Someone very like the man who followed you is sometimes there too. In fact, he was in the café when I lunched there with Mr Stokes, the week before he died.'

'Oh.' Margaret blinked. She hadn't expected it to be this simple. 'I had no idea you were acquainted. His murder must have been a shock – and we've been so clinical about it – but what has this to do with the man you thought you recognised?'

'Stokes and I weren't acquainted and the man I saw may be irrelevant,' said Dr Gesner. 'I saw a back and didn't think much of it, putting the vague recollection aside until you came back injured. Even then, I knew I might be mistaken: one back is much like another. But your interest in these cases has not gone unremarked within the hospital. Perhaps it's known outside the hospital, too.'

Margaret felt the blood drain from her face.

'Try not to be alarmed,' said Dr Gesner. 'As I say, it may be nothing. It was simply circumstance that led to Mr Stokes and me visiting the café. In context, it could have been you, anyone or no one. You weren't here that day, and there's no particular reason why I would mention it. Not because it's secret: simply because the initial part wasn't unusual.'

'What initial part?'

'A member of the public entering the foyer and demanding to see a patient. It happens often, but that is not allowed. On that day, Mr Stokes insisted he needed to speak with a woman on C ward while I was discussing something with Dr Southern in the foyer.'

'Which patient?'

'I don't recall. He was very agitated, but in the ineffectual way of someone who doesn't often make demands. It was uncertain whether he would hit someone, burst into tears or suffer apoplexy. A tour was being given to benefactors that day, and no one wanted them to witness any unpleasantness. As it was lunchtime I offered to buy him a cup of tea, since that seems to be the English solution to most extremes of emotion.' Dr Gesner pulled a face. 'There are, as you know, many establishments close to the hospital, but he asked if I'd go to the café at Theatre Valerina, which is not far, but not close either. I'm ashamed to say that I regretted making the offer and wondered how quickly I might escape the situation.'

'But you took him anyway.' Margaret sat up straighter, trying to maintain an innocently interested expression.

'I ordered tea and waited for him to explain. He had calmed down somewhat, and I didn't want to agitate him again. He looked about him a great deal then apologised, whispering that he hadn't wanted to be too close to the hospital since the woman he sought might be out and about, watching him, and he wanted to talk to her where there were witnesses. I was beginning to wonder if he had escaped quite a different sort of establishment, but the mind is not my speciality, so I let him talk. Or rather, whisper. He asked if he could ask my opinion, as a professional man of good standing.'

'I always dread that,' said Margaret, keeping her voice light. 'There's always one woman at social events offering to show me lumps and bumps.'

'Ha ha, yes. I was about to tell him that he must visit his own physician when he asked my views on the emancipation of women, universal suffrage and social reform, which I could happily admit to supporting. Then he asked, "What would you be prepared to do to achieve them?"'

'And you answered?'

'I said that I aimed to adhere to the law and preserve life. Mr Stokes waved away the law, but seemed to agree about preservation of life.' Dr Gesner shrugged again. 'I did not know him in any way, beyond this odd little exchange. If you asked me to give my opinion, Dr Demeray, I'd say that if he was making bombs, he only intended to damage property. But in the photograph, if you recall, the nitroglycerin was on the table next to his teacup. That seems odd. You'd surely have one liquid or the other, rather than risk mixing them up. Anyway, Mr Stokes replied, "My friend would agree. Neither she nor I are happy."'

'The friend being the person in hospital?'

Dr Gesner shook his head. 'I don't think so. Firstly, because he seemed concerned about meeting that woman "out and about" in Marylebone. Secondly, because he seemed to be waiting for someone to join us, though they never did. I made my excuses and was about to leave when he clasped my arm and whispered, "Are you German or naturalised British?" I answered that it was the former, and he said, "Then I suppose you must think that we should be allies, instead of the other lot?" I said something to the effect that I hoped that no allegiance would ever need to be leaned on and stood up. He shook my hand and murmured, "You said you wanted to preserve law and life. What would you do if someone wanted you to go against that?" I said I'd tell the authorities. He thanked me with more warmth than I deserved, and I left.'

'What did you think he meant?'

'As I say...' Dr Gesner touched his head.

'Did you tell the police about the conversation when you heard about his death?'

Dr Gesner rubbed the bridge of his nose. 'It took me a while to realise it was the same man. I'd spent perhaps half an hour with him, chiefly wishing to get away, and had taken no note of his name, which is ordinary enough. His photograph wasn't in the newspaper. When I realised, and saw his connection to suffrage, then I understood what he'd been talking about. The whole conversation was the kind you have with a fanatic, apart from the German element. But even that had an inevitability about it. Just as women offer to show you lumps because you are a doctor, they express their views about Germany to me because I'm German. They tend not to blame me for German aggression to my face. Most British people hide a good deal of hypocrisy behind good manners.'

'I'm sorry,' said Margaret.

'It doesn't do to draw attention to oneself in connection with a political agitator. Mr Stokes's death was deemed, quite properly in my view, to be an unplanned murder, and the questionable items discovered in his flat were connected with the militant wing of the suffrage movement rather than German spies. I wasn't going to be the one to provide an alternative.' He didn't smile. 'To be honest, I forgot about it till you started considering his case in the light of Miss Halpin's. Perhaps she was the woman he didn't want to meet, or perhaps she was his friend. I have no idea: do you?'

Dr Gesner's face was troubled but open. Margaret decided to go by her own instinct, not Fox's. 'Someone told me they knew each other through a suffrage group. I am acquainted with the people who run the theatre: they knew Miss Halpin well. When I visited them yesterday, they said a booking had been made in her name before she died. It included two other names: Mr Stokes, and you.'

Dr Gesner stared. 'I... I was never invited to any such event, and Mr Stokes... I spoke – or rather listened to him – just that once.'

'Perhaps he had suggested you to Miss Halpin as a neutral person to speak with.'

'He didn't know me.' Dr Gesner shook his head. 'I didn't know her.'

Margaret realised her hands were clenched in her lap. 'What has this to do with the man you thought was trying to catch up with me?'

'It may be my mind playing tricks. He reminds me of a long-dead man I once knew in Germany. It took a moment to register the similarity. When I looked again, wondering if it was a relation, he'd moved off and I couldn't see his face. He was there when I visited with Stokes. He was there when you visited with your friend. I know you can't often identify someone by their back, but something about the man on Wednesday brought the man in the café to mind. Jacket, hat, slope of the shoulders? Or simply connection of ideas? You were heading towards Paddington, I thought, until you went into the underground and I realised you could be going anywhere.' Dr Gesner shrugged. 'It is not evidence. But I am concerned for you, and surprised your husband lets you wander unescorted.'

'I—'

The telephone rang and Dr Gesner lifted the receiver. He answered, then looked at Margaret. 'Yes,' he said. 'Will you show him through? Thank you.' He replaced the receiver. 'Your husband is here. I shall explain – that will save you time later.'

Fox entered the office and shook hands with Dr Gesner.

'Please take a seat, Superintendent. I have some information which may be of interest to you.' He summarised what he had told Margaret.

Fox nodded, his face unreadable. 'Thank you: I appreciate your candour. I doubt you need to concern yourself about it, but I will let you know either way.'

'If you don't mind, I must tell you that I may have seen your wife followed the other day,' said Dr Gesner. 'I feel her interest in these cases has put her at risk, though I do not know why. But if the man is a relation of the person I'm thinking of, they may be quite unsatisfactory.'

Fox exchanged glances with Margaret. 'When? Who?'

'Last Thursday,' said Margaret.

'Tell me what happened,' said Fox. 'And who you think it was.'

Dr Gesner pulled another photograph from his wallet. It was a small copy of a wedding photograph with at least twenty people in it, the faces hard to make out. 'This was eleven years ago. This is my sister-in-law' – he pointed – 'and that gentleman was her betrothed. He came home from India for my wedding, then returned to Calcutta. They were due to marry the following year.'

'He's British?' said Margaret, taking the photograph. She recognised no one but the doctor, his wife and her father.

'German,' said Dr Gesner. 'Professor Schmidt, a linguist. The older and deader the language, the better he liked it. He died in a cholera outbreak in August 1902. I was not sorry: I didn't like or trust him, though I could not say why. The man in the café was like an older version of him, but his features are not so marked.'

'It's been eleven years,' said Margaret.

'It's the impression I had,' said Dr Gesner, 'and it visited me again on Thursday. Perhaps it's simply the feeling that something is not quite right about someone. In the café, I felt he might have been trying to listen to Stokes's whispering. On Thursday, as I say, I assumed he was your friend, but feared he might not be. I should have followed. Superintendent, does this face remind you of anyone? I think you know what kind of anyone I mean.'

Fox held the photograph very still. Despite its size, Margaret was reminded of the small man she'd seen in the underground on the day that Fox and Queale had nearly gone under the train, the same man she'd noticed in the café. She became aware that Fox was tense. His face, however, was impassive, with a slight downturn of the mouth. 'May I take it with me to check against others?'

'Yes, of course,' said Dr Gesner. 'Now, I have a class to teach. Dr Demeray, perhaps you should go and rest. I imagine you will be marching behind Miss Davison's coffin, though I would prefer to know you were not, especially if you are concerned about this palsied man you spoke of. Does your husband know about him?'

'He does,' said Margaret. 'And on Saturday I'll be in full view of hundreds of policemen. I shall be fine.'

'The doctor's right,' said Fox. 'Let me take you home.' He shook hands with Dr Gesner, then steered her from the room and along the corridor.

'What are we going to do, Fox?'

'You're going home, sitting tight and picking through those post-mortem files again. The inspector's coming to speak with you. I've got things to look into, including what Dr Gesner said.'

'I'm sure it's all true.'

'That doesn't stop him being what I think he is.'

'Why are you so sure?'

'Because one of the known couriers we have under observation disappeared two weeks ago,' said Fox. 'The person who was supposed to be watching her and keeping me informed is Smith, and as I live and breathe, Smith is the man called Professor Schmidt in Dr Gesner's photograph.'

Thirty-Four

Margaret returned home to the sound of Freda and Nellie singing to the children in the kitchen. It was as if everything was normal, but it wasn't.

One of you has to grow up.

She put through a telephone call to Maude. Before it went through, there was a knock at the front door. Maude was on the step.

'I'd like to talk.'

'Come in. The children will be having naps soon, so we'll have the garden to ourselves.'

Maude hesitated, then crossed the threshold. 'All right. Have you any alcohol?'

'Just Fox's beer.'

'He won't miss one bottle.'

A few moments later, they were sitting at the garden table. Maude watched the sunlight catch her glass and didn't meet Margaret's eyes. 'How can I trust you? I was questioned because a bomb I knew nothing about killed a woman whose body your pet policeman gave you to look at.'

'I don't want to meet anyone who considers Inspector Silvermann a pet. And either drink that beer or re-cork it. Fox is more likely to hunt you down for wasting it than because of your political views.'

Maude sipped her beer and reached down to stroke Juniper's head.

'How could you call me a police spy?' said Margaret.

'Well, you *are*. You can't help it. But I shouldn't have said so at the meeting.' Maude lifted the glass of beer, contemplated it, then put it back on the table.

'I so wanted to talk to you last night,' said Margaret. 'I wanted to tell you that I'm sure the Bryces aren't remotely interested in either rebellion or resistance. Whatever Geoff's doing must be above board.'

'Really?'

'And also that Mrs Southern asked me to apologise on her behalf for what her husband did.'

'Did she?'

'She recognised you on the front of *Athene's Gazette*.'

Maude pulled a face. 'How appalling. You made me look like a gorgon.' But there was a faint smile on her lips.

'If we were Phoebe's pupils, she'd have us standing in corners.'

'She would.'

'Why did you say all that last night? You were perfectly happy to see me when I came to your house the other evening.'

'Because in the interim, I was assured that you'd told Fox your real beliefs and they'd got through to Scotland Yard.'

'Who assured you?'

'Mrs Philbrook.'

'You'd believe a woman you've only known for a few months over one you've known for twenty years?'

'It sounded plausible, the way she said it. And it made me realise that I want to put distance between us and carry on alone. Why should both of us be in danger?'

'I can choose for myself, and you could have picked a better way to do it.'

'Please forgive me, Margaret,' said Maude. 'I've always been able to read between the lines, but she blinded me with her enthusiasm for what I'm passionate about.'

'But she never actually does anything, does she?'

'No. Why didn't I notice? She's as full of plans as Etta. You wanted to come to the meeting, but she'd already made me feel you shouldn't, in case you felt you should pass things on to Fox. I didn't want you to be put in that sort of dilemma. Now she's disbanded what was left of the group, while forgetting that she always made out it wasn't hers.'

'Odd.'

'Odder still, she visits rather too often for someone who's not a close friend. Yesterday, she asked me what I would do for my country. I told her that I was fighting for the vote and that when that was achieved, I'd feel a good deal prouder of my country than I do now.'

Margaret nodded. 'I agree.'

'But then she asked, "If this country is not good enough and might never be, what would you do to help a country which was better?"'

'What?'

'I gabbled that suffrage was enough to worry about and said I thought the Home Rule bill should go through. But I had the impression that she wasn't talking about Ireland. She asked if I had anything in writing.'

'Had what in writing?' Margaret leaned forward. After all this time, had it been that simple? Had Maude been given the documents for safekeeping?

'I told her to read *Athene's Gazette*. Most of my opinions are reflected there.'

'Ah.' Margaret sat back.

'At the last meeting, just before my arrest, she asked very publicly if I'd had a nice time having lunch with Sally French.'

'Who?'

'That was my reaction, but she became all giggly and said, "You mustn't fret about admitting you meet with someone from a different class. We're all one in the movement". It was mortifying. I couldn't give a fig what class anyone's from, but I hadn't gone for lunch with Sally French.'

'Who is she?'

'I couldn't think for ages, but eventually I remembered. She's one of the members who comes occasionally and only ever talks to Mrs Philbrook. I haven't seen her for weeks.'

'British?'

Maude shrugged. 'I never spoke with her. She exchanged magazines with Mrs Philbrook a lot. The last time I remember seeing her...' Maude frowned. 'She seemed annoyed: she said she'd had enough, or something. I'm trying to recall what we'd discussed before the break, or what was in the suffrage magazines that week.'

'When was it?'

'Mmm ... end of May? Men with umbrellas and ... short skirts?' She blinked. 'What an odd thing to come to mind.'

'Wait a moment.' Margaret went inside and returned with the previous month's suffrage magazines. They flicked through *The Suffragette*, *Athene's Gazette* and *Votes For Women* until they came to the issue that *Votes For Women* had published on the twenty-third of May. Its cover depicted a row of Greek policemen in national dress, greeting British politicians in Corinth. The message was that security had been increased because of suffragettes.

'Not umbrellas, police helmets,' she said. 'Look at the date, Maude. It was the day before we went to St James's Park.'

'Could that body be Sally French?' Maude swallowed. 'What did she look like? Could you distinguish her features?'

'Not really,' said Margaret. 'But are you willing for me to be a police spy and tell Fox?'

Maude took a mouthful of beer and nodded.

'Are your children still in the country?'

'Yes.'

'Can you join them?'

'I'm not missing the funeral procession.'

'Neither am I – but tonight I'm staying at Father's. Take Geoff and go to a hotel. Don't tell even the servants where you're going.'

'Permission to be scared, Demeray?'

'Permission granted.'

An hour after Maude had gone, Inspector Silvermann plumped himself down in the sitting room, waving a dismissive hand at Freda as she tried to take his hat. Behind his back, Freda pursed her lips and narrowed her eyes. 'Shall I take the children to Nellie, ma'am? We don't want them picking up anything unsavoury.'

'Words?' said the inspector.

'Habits,' said Freda, tossing her head. 'Come along, Master Alec and Miss Edie.'

'But Feeda,' said Alec, 'wanna pay Mummy and funny man.'

'I have biscuits in the kitchen.'

'Oooh,' said Edie.

'Biscuits sound nice,' said the inspector.

'Don't they?' said Freda, sweeping up a twin under each arm and marching out.

The inspector chuckled, then sobered. 'She's right to take them. Nothing we're going to say is suitable for little ears.'

'No, it isn't,' said Margaret. 'Beginning with me very much wanting to know why you're haranguing Mrs Holbourne, and why she has the impression that I suggested you should.'

'The incident at St James's remains a conundrum. Miss Tabor's evidence suggests that she and Mrs Holbourne were to meet someone there. However, she was intercepted by her mama who, as you know, locked her up in the country for a few days. Now she has her locked up at home, the old ... besom.'

'I wish you'd take me to speak with her.'

'We got as much out of her as we were going to, and her mama made it clear that we weren't to visit again without a warrant. All we got was that Miss Tabor was most dreadfully sorry. She was horrified about the evil woman she and Mrs Holbourne had nearly met, who must be the victim. She is most definitely retiring from public life, for now.'

'Damn.'

'The old bat won't let you near her. We may never find out who the victim was.'

'Speak to Fox,' said Margaret. 'He may have a lead.'

'Yeah?' The inspector fell silent as he scrutinised her. 'Mrs Holbourne remains under suspicion, but I admit the evidence is circumstantial and I told her so by telephone half an hour ago. If she thinks anything you said led to that, I'm sorry. This is by way of being an olive branch. Though I wish you'd told me about the hammer.' He nodded at the bureau.

Margaret's hands went clammy. How could Fox have betrayed her?

'Look,' said the inspector. 'You think I've been accusing your friend of doing all this from the start, so you don't want to give me the tools to finish the job. But what if she did?'

'She wouldn't.'

'Smack someone on the head with a hammer? Not deliberately, perhaps, but in a fit of rage? I've seen her speak. Terrifying.

By accident, when swinging it? She's strong, for all she's been through.'

'She'd own up.'

The inspector contemplated her again, his face solemn. 'Maybe. If you're wondering: your husband had his own people examine the hammer, then liaised about their findings. Yeah, he could be covering something up. But I don't think he is, and he trusted me. Shame you didn't.'

Margaret felt herself flush. 'What did the hammer prove?'

'It's taken long enough and the strongest lens we could find, but there's a fleck of blood just visible where the face meets the neck. The rest of it is unnaturally clean, polished even, with smearing where it looks like someone held the handle while wearing white cotton gloves. But there's a bit of a fingerprint on it and the envelope has a few. That might not prove a thing. It might be the stationer's or a customer's – who knows? But they don't belong to any suffragettes who've been fingerprinted, including Mrs Holbourne.'

'Good.'

'This is my final bit of the olive branch. Your old man gave me a tip which means we have the description of someone who visited Miss Halpin's house the night before she died. A woman who's not Mrs Holbourne, since she was away.' He took out his notebook. 'A little taller than average. Light-coloured hair and spectacles. A little wide in the beam but flat-chested, with turned-out toes. Gawd, you women are vicious about each other. And with all the padding you put under your clothes, how can you tell if someone's really flat-chested or broad in the beam?'

'What do you know about what's under a woman's clothes?'

'Ever occurred to you that I may have a life outside the force?' said the inspector. 'Anyhow, here's a sketch my constable did which the witness says is about right, given there was only streetlight. God bless nosey neighbours, eh? Does this mean anything to you?'

Margaret took the notebook, even though she'd already guessed. 'It's Mrs Sabina Philbrook. She was in a suffrage group with Mr Stokes and Miss Halpin. And Maude. I think Miss Tabor went once. Her close friend is the Honourable Daphne: Mrs Bernard Southern who is the wife of Dr Southern, who nearly killed Maude. Oh my word! I've just remembered. The night someone put that hammer through my letterbox, the hammer that killed the woman at St James's... I swear Mr Tabor said he was taking Mrs Philbrook to a Dorcas Free Governors' dinner. I never knew if that was true. I don't know where Mrs Philbrook lives, but she knows where Maude lives.'

'And she knows where you live, too.' The inspector retrieved his notebook and stood up. 'Have you got anywhere to go tonight while we find her? Just in case we don't.'

'I've got Fox,' she said. 'And if you can't find her tonight but she doesn't know you're looking, she'll be in Emily Davison's funeral procession.'

'Gawd,' said Inspector Silvermann. 'It'd be easier finding a freckle on a leopard. We're expecting around six thousand women in that parade. I'd normally tell you to keep away, but you'll be safer there than anywhere. Between now and then, try and stay out of trouble. If you've got anywhere else to go, go there.'

'I have to wait here till Fox comes home, but then I will. I've already planned it.'

'Really?' The inspector reached to feel her forehead. 'You're being sensible? Things must be bad.'

By the time Fox came home at twelve, Margaret had told Aunt Alice that she'd be staying in her father's house for a day or so to air it for his return, but not to tell anyone as it was a surprise. She had given a similar excuse to the maids, whom she'd sent on ahead with the children.

'You should have gone too,' said Fox. 'I'd have met you there.'

'I've kept my wits about me. There's no telephone at Father's, and I might as well stay here in case the inspector says they've made an arrest.'

'They haven't. They can't find Mrs Philbrook at her own place, so the police think she's gone to ground. There was a governors' meeting on Friday 23rd May, but she arrived late, a little fraught, and left before you'd have got home from Phoebe's, pleading a headache. I think we can guess where she is now, can't we? And to prove it, the landlord reported that he'd had a telegram from the woman calling herself Mrs Queale, saying that she's returned from India earlier than intended and would prefer not to be disturbed as she's unwell. Will you come? Your being a female doctor will give us an excuse if anyone asks why we're wandering about the building. Not that the tenants seem to notice that sort of thing, and the only two we've met saw us together.'

'Of course,' Margaret snatched up her bag and hat, thinking of the hammer and wishing the latter were more substantial. 'Though what if she's—?'

'Armed?' said Fox. 'So am I. And we have the element of surprise.'

Once they were in the car, Fox said, 'You're right about Sally French. That was one of the aliases of the missing courier Smith was supposed to be watching. Not that it confirms she's the body. Nor does it explain why she's dead, if Sabina Philbrook was giving her the papers.'

'Is Smith actually Schmidt?'

'Bert and Elinor are going through our records. He was certainly at the same institution as Schmidt and they both succumbed to the same cholera outbreak – but Smith survived. Part of the reason why Hare recruited him was that prior to the outbreak, he had reported Schmidt's allegedly suspicious behaviour to the authorities in a particularly subtle way, with very detailed reasoning. It came to nothing, of course, because Schmidt died.'

'I see.'

'We have a photograph of the staff at the institution. They didn't look identical, but they did look very similar. Could Schmidt have exchanged places with Smith in the middle of an epidemic? Possibly. And don't forget that Dr Gesner only met Schmidt once some years ago, and only saw Smith from a distance.'

'You've never trusted Smith.'

'No. Yet apart from some incompetence, he's done nothing wrong. He even mentioned to me without prompting that he had seen you leaving Dorcas Free the other week, when he was on the trail of the letters under Hare's instruction.'

'Hare's?'

'Hare thought Dr Gesner might have them and didn't want to involve me too much. So Smith has been watching the hospital and following him. When he saw Dr Gesner watching you leave in what appeared to be a suspicious manner, he decided to follow you to keep you safe.'

'Someone pushed me down those steps.'

'Well, it wasn't Smith. He watched you catch your train but he was back in the office by one thirty, where he remained all afternoon.'

'But you still don't trust him.'

'No, I don't.'

'And you don't trust Dr Gesner, either.'

Fox didn't answer, tapping his fingers on the steering wheel. Margaret's blood went cold. 'What's happened to him?'

'Dr Gesner is fit and well and making his way home.'

'To Germany?'

'To Paddington.'

'So you're content that he's everything he says he is.'

Another silence as Fox turned into Cabot Street and steered round a dray.

'Fox?'

'He knows of Abney. He's concerned for you and he told me the name of a smart hotel in Tyburnia where a similar-looking man is staying. I can't believe he'd remember that unless he was interested. But I don't think Dr Gesner poses a threat to either country. That's the critical thing.'

'What does that mean?'

'It means I'm changing the subject for everyone's sake,' said Fox. 'And besides, we're here.'

As Fox had predicted, no one was in the public areas of the house. No one noticed them climb to the top flat. He glanced at Margaret to confirm she was ready, put his hand in an inner pocket where his revolver was, then knocked.

The door opened and Margaret could just make out the height of the woman behind it. She was fair, but she was not tall and wore no glasses. Her arm trembled on the frame and she gasped. 'Dr Demeray? H-how did you know?'

Margaret stepped closer, her heart racing. It wasn't Mrs Philbrook. It was Miss Tabor.

Thirty-Five

'Miss Tabor, this is my husband, Superintendent Foxcroft,' said Margaret. 'Please let us in. It'll be a lot more discreet.' She turned to look at Fox, whose usual detachment had been replaced by confusion. He removed his hand from his inner pocket.

Miss Tabor opened the door and indicated the sofa. She was wearing an old black dress, and a heavy black veil lay on a side table. She limped a little. In the light, Margaret could see that she was thinner and her hair had lost its shine. There were scratches on the outsides of her wrists and one on her left cheek.

'We understood a lady was unwell,' said Fox, as they sat down. 'I thought maybe Margaret could help. I—'

Margaret pressed Fox's foot with her own. Miss Tabor was twisting her hands anxiously but there was a familiar flickering in her eyes, a slight upturn in her mouth as she worked out what to say. She had been taken by surprise, but it wouldn't last. Soon, she'd start making things up. 'When did you marry Mr Queale?'

'Oh!' said Miss Tabor, blushing crimson. 'We haven't yet. We're just waiting for a, er ... a windfall. Oh, and you mustn't think...' She waved vaguely at the bedroom. 'It's *very* proper. But so much simpler to rent rooms if one says one's married. Not really a falsehood. An engagement is quite binding, even if not public.'

'The landlord thought you'd gone to India,' said Fox.

'That's a misunderstanding.' Miss Tabor swallowed. 'I went to Ilfracombe, with Mother and Hedley. I hoped that when we returned Mr Queale would have obtained the necessary funds for us to marry.' She rubbed at the scratch on her arm. 'Please don't tell Mother.' The sneakiness in her face had been replaced by genuine distress. The scratch started to bleed. 'I just wanted to be here for a few hours.' She looked round the room. 'I was hoping Silas could be here somehow.'

'Let me see,' said Margaret, lifting her hand and unbuttoning the cuff. 'How did this come about? Thorns? There's brick dust on your blouse. Miss Tabor, did you climb out of a window?'

'Yes.'

Margaret stared at her, struggling to see the image.

Miss Tabor squirmed. 'Hedley taught me when we were children. I haven't done it since I was thirteen. Mother's kept me confined to quarters. Even Hedley didn't know I'd come back to London for a day or so – just the maids. And they know better than to talk.'

'It's been three weeks since the incident in St James's.'

'It's been my whole life.' Miss Tabor's mouth trembled, then settled into a ghost of a smile. 'I occasionally confuse Mother as to where I'm going and who with. If she finds out, she feels obliged to confine me till I apologise. I'm kept in my room at night and in the back parlour by day, but today, I'd had enough. For one thing, I needed to send a telegram. I wore these clothes so anyone seeing me would think I was just one of Mother's dreadful cronies. Hedley was going out, but he managed to pass me some money and said he'd distract the maids so that no one would notice if I climbed out and left by the side gate. It isn't as easy as I recall, even from a downstairs window. I hurt my ankle, and I may have torn some' – she cleared her throat – 'linen. I thought Hedley might be waiting, but he wasn't. I had to hail a cab. But I'm glad.'

'Let me clean the scratches,' said Margaret. She went to the kitchenette and filled a bowl with water. Would Miss Tabor murder for a cause? And if so, which cause?

'You said you hoped to meet Mr Queale here, Miss Tabor,' said Fox. 'How would that be?'

Miss Tabor looked up as Margaret returned and her jaw hardened. 'Hope is hope, Superintendent, no matter how forlorn. And it's the one thing that even the police can't take from me.' Her voice trembled and a tear ran down her face. 'It's all been a terrible misunderstanding.'

Fox sat beside her. 'Do you understand the accusation, Miss Tabor?'

'Something tantamount to treason,' she said. 'Nonsense. He's a true blue Briton through and through. We believe utterly in the superiority of Great Britain and its Empire. It not only can, but absolutely *must* stand alone. It should not be allied to undisciplined and idle enemies who scheme and plot behind each other's backs. Silas simply wants the people of this country to know what is being done in their names.'

'And he sent you documents to prove it, which would earn—'

'We are loyal subjects of the King, Superintendent Foxcroft. Do not besmirch his endeavours with allegations of greed. He just requested a journalist's fee for his article, that was all. It was only fair.'

'I'm sure that's true,' said Fox. 'But—'

Margaret pressed his foot again. It was better to let Miss Tabor maintain her fantasy that the situation was a patriotic adventure and nothing to do with money which could free her to marry. She was more likely to speak openly. 'Did you meet Mr Queale on a day when you eluded your mother?'

Miss Tabor shook her head. 'Hedley took me to a lunchtime concert which was raising money for army widows. They performed *Land of Hope and Glory* and it made me cry. At the interval Hedley went away for a while, and the man beside me said he'd felt the same. He was a little shy, but felt so strongly about our country. We started corresponding, in a way. It's been very hard.' Miss Tabor looked around the flat. 'This is our haven.' There was a longer pause, then Miss Tabor put her face in her hands. 'I don't feel safe anywhere. I wish I'd never become involved in that group.'

Margaret exchanged glances with Fox, then turned back to Miss Tabor. 'Mrs Philbrook's group?'

'I saw it advertised in *The New Dorcas* one day. Advertisements are how Silas communicates with me, because my letters would be read. Anyway, it said they wanted the retiring type to join. I was feeling rather restless and useless, you see. And dear Miss Pendleberry's group, while very proper, is rather full of women who, er...' ·

'Don't let quieter women get a word in edgeways?'

'They make one feel invisible. Of course I don't mean *you*, doctor.'

I think you do, thought Margaret, with a sense of shame. 'And you found Mrs Philbrook's group better.'

'Not precisely,' said Miss Tabor, sniffing. 'I only went once. There were other shy sorts, but they were mostly of a much lower class than one is used to engaging with on a social level. Stokes was gentlemanlike, but he knew me as Mrs Queale. I was shocked. I told him that on no account must he tell anyone he knew me by a different name. I thought he'd betray me, but he didn't. And I... I confided in him, to an extent. He was very concerned for me. He told me to hide the papers, wait until Silas was free and not trust anyone, but said he would find a trustworthy professional to assist me. As I say, gentlemanlike.'

Margaret sensed Fox's frustration. If she hadn't bothered to listen to Miss Tabor in the past, and made her feel irrelevant and invisible, now was the moment to put that right.

Miss Tabor wrinkled her nose. 'Of course, I'd confided in Hedley too. I didn't know he'd mentioned it to Sabina Philbrook, because he only met her through my going to that meeting. But they became very close and she offered to help me – us. She knew someone who'd publish, she said. She does mix with some important people, of course, some of whom might treat the police with the disregard they deserve. But I said I'd rather follow Silas's instructions. She said, "Of course," and seemed quite content. It was a terrible shock when Stokes was killed, but they said it was just a burglary and that no one had entered this flat. I only began to wonder when Mrs Holbourne started to say that he'd been killed for a reason. Then his great friend Miss Halpin died and Mrs Holbourne said that was suspicious too. I told Sabina I was worried, but she said Mrs Holbourne was wrong and needed a proper suffragette task to get her back on track. She asked me to help. I was so pleased to be trusted.'

'The bomb in St James's?'

Miss Tabor nodded. 'I didn't realise it was a bomb.'

'Is that quite true?' said Margaret.

Miss Tabor opened her mouth, closed it, and stared into her lap. She mumbled, 'If Mrs Holbourne had agreed to join me, she could have told me what to do. But she wouldn't, so I had to manage alone.'

'Please, Miss Tabor,' said Margaret. 'Please explain.'

The older woman stood up, walked across the room to the window, and peeped out from the very edge. Then she returned and dropped into the armchair. 'Sabina said I could play my part by helping Mrs Holbourne to act, but it was imperative that it happened that day.' Even in her distress, it was clear that

Miss Tabor was so proud of being trusted with something more important than letter-writing that she hadn't wondered why Mrs Philbrook didn't simply ask Maude herself.

'What was the task?'

'I was to give Mrs Holbourne a note in person to ensure direct action took place. But Mrs Holbourne didn't reply to my calls, and I didn't feel I could just leave the note. The instruction was clear: the action had to take place that day. So... I felt justified in reading the note, then being brave and doing it myself.' Miss Tabor hugged herself again.

'What were the instructions, Miss Tabor?' asked Fox, sitting forward.

'Can I trust you?'

'I will do my best by Queale if you do.'

Miss Tabor swallowed. 'It said that the person Mrs Holbourne sought would give her what she needed on the dot of three, and she could ensure the greatest disruption.'

'Those exact words?'

'Something along those lines. It gave an address in St James's. I assumed that another suffragette would give her the means to set fire to St James's Palace. I thought it couldn't be too hard to do myself. Not simply for suffrage, but to stop the London Treaty from being signed,' said Miss Tabor, straightening up. 'That would give me time to publicise Silas's views.'

'There may be a truth that needs to be told one day,' said Fox. 'But I don't believe that's now, unless you genuinely want a war to break out. Not among countries which most British people couldn't point to on a map, but here, in Western Europe. Allegiances are always fragile, Miss Tabor. Throughout history, countries have made promises to each other that they may not intend to keep, and gone behind each other's backs. What keeps the peace, more often than not, are the little white lies they tell to pretend all is well.'

'I don't believe in falsehoods.' Miss Tabor pressed her lips together firmly, looking into the distance, but she fidgeted a little more.

'Tell me about the woman,' said Margaret.

Miss Tabor closed her eyes and rubbed them with her hands. Her voice was muffled. 'She was dead.'

'You mean the bomb had already gone off?' said Fox.

'No.' Miss Tabor's voice was barely above a whisper, her gaze unfocussed. 'I found the entrance to the place. It was gloomy and there was something lumpy on the floor, covered by a cloth. And there were flies. I-I couldn't help myself. I lifted the cloth and saw a face with blood on it. I wanted to tell myself it was a mannequin, a prank, but there was a smell and the flies were starting to settle. I felt so shocked and sick. That's when I must have dropped my earring. A package was on a ledge nearby and... It's true, doctor, I didn't know it was a bomb, but I remembered what I'd heard. I saw that it was leaking and there was a peculiar smell, stronger even than— I didn't know what to do. How could I explain to the police where I was and why? They might accuse me of the woman's murder. I wondered if I should pick up the parcel and take it to the palace myself. But my courage failed me and I hurried away, towards Victoria Street. I understand it was quite a small bomb.'

'It was big enough,' said Fox. 'You'd have killed yourself and who knows who else if you'd carried it away. If Mrs Holbourne had gone, she'd probably have died. You should have told the police about the woman.'

'I went to Sabina and told her,' said Miss Tabor. 'She was very angry that Mrs Holbourne hadn't gone, and sorry that I had put myself in such a difficult position. She said there must have been a misunderstanding about the device. She said she'd deal with things because one day we'd be sisters-in-law. I made my way home alone, and that's when Mother's friend saw me.'

'Miss Tabor,' said Margaret, keeping her voice steady, 'you must know that's not how legitimate suffragettes do things. Women – and men – take their own risks and plant their own devices. They don't ask others to do what they wouldn't do themselves. Didn't you ask who the other person was in this unlikely chain?'

'I was too upset that the treaty would be signed. Sabina said that treaties can be broken, though. She asked for the letters again and said she knew people who'd pay a good deal more than the ones Silas had gone to, because they knew their worth.'

'Enough for you and Hedley to be free?' said Margaret.

Miss Tabor squirmed again. 'Money wasn't the point.'

'Don't you understand, Miss Tabor?' said Margaret. 'You were never intended to get the blame for that bomb. Maude was.'

'Yes.' Miss Tabor rose and looked out from the side of the window again.

'When she mentioned money, was that when you realised you'd been used?' said Fox.

'No,' said Miss Tabor. She turned, and the way the light and shade fell on her face made her look decisive and courageous: the woman she might have been, perhaps. 'It was when I tried to fall asleep that night and saw the dead woman in St James's in my mind. Her face reminded me of a common-looking woman sharing magazines with Mrs Philbrook at the one meeting I attended. I was very distressed, as Mr Stokes had recognised me and I was trying to make him promise to keep quiet. When he agreed, I relaxed a little. I looked towards that woman and Stokes said something about her being a spy. At first I thought he meant someone spying on me to tell Mother, then I realised he must mean someone spying on us as suffragettes. That night, when I recalled that woman's face, I remembered how furtive that exchange had been and suddenly I suspected that Sabina isn't as nice as she seems. Hedley won't listen, though. Will I be murdered next?'

'Not before she finds those letters,' said Fox.

'Then I shan't give them to anyone. I kept them here until Stokes told me to hide them elsewhere. He didn't know where, of course. I'm glad I did, because someone's been in here, looking. Things are out of place.'

Fox glanced sideways at Margaret. She knew that of all things, he prided himself that his men could search somewhere and leave it exactly as they found it.

'Is there another set of keys to this house and this flat?' he asked.

'Hedley has some,' said Miss Tabor.

'Did you take the keys to Ilfracombe?' asked Margaret.

Miss Tabor gawped. 'Of course not.'

'Does Hedley know where you're hiding the papers?'

Her jaw set. 'It's not his secret. It's mine.'

'This secret is too big,' said Fox. 'For your sake, for Queale's, and for the sake of this country we all love so much, tell me where they are.'

'And then what will you do to me?' said Miss Tabor. 'Lock me up, as you've locked up Silas? I'm not scared – I've been locked up my whole life. Silas told me I'm a heroine. I stand by him.'

'This is the only way that you can save the country from disgrace and perhaps worse.'

'Disgrace?' Miss Tabor started to rub at her scratches again. 'And I'll be a heroine?'

'Yes,' said Margaret. 'Where are the documents, Miss Tabor?'

'Can't you guess?' said Miss Tabor. 'They're with the only woman who won't ask questions. She thinks they're love letters that Mother mustn't see. They're with Phoebe Pendleberry.'

Thirty-Six

'Mrs Philbrook has still made no move,' said Fox, when he visited the Fulham house early on Saturday morning. He looked exhausted, pacing the cluttered drawing room and cursing as he bumped into yet another piece of furniture. 'I'm not sure if she's discovered that the documents she's been given are false, or found another way to get them out of the house, but she's barely moved. And the police are tied up keeping Mrs Tabor quiet. This time she believes her daughter really has evaded her clutches, since she's apparently sent a telegram from Scotland. Miss Tabor, meanwhile, is driving our staff insane with her demands to see Queale and her attempts to escape house arrest.'

He paused to look at Margaret properly. She was wearing her simplest white dresse, with a black armband and sash. Her hat, trimmed with mauve and green was waiting on a chair. 'Are you still following Emily Davison's funeral procession?'

'Yes.'

'With Phoebe's group, not the physicians?'

'Yes.'

'There's absolutely no way I can protect you.' Fox banged his fist on the mantelpiece. 'Mrs Philbrook has left it till today so that she can make the transfer when every officer is tied up and the city brought to a standstill.'

Margaret shook her head. 'Not just that. If she wants to continue her life afterwards as if nothing's happened, as opposed to absconding, then she'll march. It's what people will be expecting her to do. I'd march with her if I could, but she'd see me. Is Elinor marching?'

'Yes. The procession has been organised like an army campaign. We might be able to find out where Mrs Philbrook will be and put Elinor nearby.'

Margaret hugged him. She wasn't sure which of them was more tense. For Fox, it wasn't simply catching Mrs Philbrook with the documents. They needed to catch the person she was handing them to so they could find Abney, then untangle Mrs Philbrook's part in the murders of Jeremiah Stokes, Lois Halpin and Sally French. Meanwhile Margaret was furious, not only for those pointless deaths, but because Mrs Philbrook had hidden behind the suffrage movement to betray her own country and several others to the highest bidder.

'Will Elinor be safe?' said Margaret.

Fox held her tightly. 'Keep your distance and pay your respects as you need to. Leave this to me.'

He saw her into a taxi before returning to central London by motorcycle and for the next two hours, Margaret's mind shifted between her part in the funeral procession and feeling angry about Mrs Philbrook. Today should be a day for solemn reflection, not avarice and treachery.

Ahead was the horse-drawn hearse carrying Miss Davison's coffin, draped in a flag covered in convict's arrowheads and piled with flowers. Horse-drawn vehicles and motor cars followed, filled with even more flowers. Behind the vehicles, two women bore a banner embroidered with the message *Fight on and God will give the victory*. Those words faced the rows of women following at a steady, solemn pace with their banners, faces proud and determined.

The procession was flanked by policemen, who for once did nothing but keep order. At junctions, the traffic was held back. On either side of the road, crowds of bystanders jostled to peer and stare. Open-topped omnibuses passed on the other side of the road, the occupants of the upper level gawping down.

Beyond the police lines, the crowds were near-silent, apart from some yelling at St George's Church as the coffin arrived for a short service before it continued towards King's Cross Station, from where Emily Davison would make her final journey home to Northumberland.

Maude marched beside Margaret with determination, in memory of a woman she'd known and admired. Phoebe was pale, silent, but professional. Any questions she had were buried, and knowing Phoebe, they'd stay that way. Behind them, Mrs Nutford walked with Miss Brown, murmuring briefly how sad it was that Miss Tabor could not join them.

The march was a statement as much as a memorial. But Margaret's grief was not only for a woman mown down by a horse while trying to make her argument better known. It was for all the women who fought for justice and change. The striking seamstresses seeking decent pay; the match girls and sweatshop girls, wanting workplaces which would not kill them; the women who would not be awarded a degree purely because of their sex; the betrayed wives who could not divorce on the grounds of adultery alone; every woman who had been forcibly fed until they would never be the same again in body or mind. All for the sake of asking for things that so many men seemed to think women didn't need – or, worse still, deserve.

At King's Cross, things changed. Over the sound of the band came shouts, bellows and whistles. Word passed through the ranks:

'People are trying to attack the coffin and drag it from the hearse!'

'The police are pushing back, but we mustn't let them fight alone.'

'Bunch forward and stand fast. Keep the faith. Do not retaliate.'

It'll be now, thought Margaret. *We were fools. Mrs Philbrook will have guessed someone would follow her. Maybe the people she's handing the documents to have started this aggression, just as they started the panic on the underground. She must be somewhere near the front.*

In the uncertainty among the women around her, Margaret moved forward through the lines. She caught sight of Elinor first: that unusual short curly hair under a plain grey hat, the tanned back of her neck. Then she saw Elinor pushed sideways, stumbling and falling as those behind her marched on. Mrs Philbrook pulled off her armband and dashed into the crowd, clasping a satchel as if her life depended on it.

Margaret followed, leaving her own sash and armband to be trampled. She could only hope someone would look after Elinor. The crowd was a jumble of people shoving each other. Too short to see properly, Margaret pushed between strangers, looking for Mrs Philbrook and her bag. She began to panic as people pushed back. She could see no one she recognised, except for the man she'd seen near Lois Halpin's house, wearing the same unseasonal muffler.

A hand grabbed her arm and she heard Mrs Philbrook's low, furious whisper in her ear. 'Are you doing your husband's job? Perhaps in the end, you can surprise him more than he's expecting. Hedley, come and help. You could prove useful.'

Margaret hooked her foot under Mrs Philbrook's, overbalancing her enough to loosen her grip on Margaret's sleeve, which started to rip. She stared frantically into the crowds for a familiar face and listened for a voice she knew in the throng. No one, and too many people were shouting for any individual voice to be heard, but she opened her mouth to shout all the same. It was clamped shut with a large, leather-gloved hand, and a strong arm encircled her, trapping her arms. She managed to turn slightly and realised that the man with the muffler was Hedley Tabor, weak and rabbity-looking without his beard and moustache.

'Is everything all right, sir?' said a man's voice behind her.

'He's a doctor, constable,' said Mrs Philbrook, 'This lady's unwell. We're taking her somewhere quiet.'

Margaret squirmed, and made as much noise as she could manage through the leather that was nearly suffocating her.

'Should you have your hand over her mouth and nose like that, sir?'

'She's hysterical and at risk of being sick,' said Mrs Philbrook. 'She nearly tripped me in her confusion. She might cause a commotion, which is the last thing you need to deal with.'

'I'll take care of her, constable,' said Mr Tabor, his voice soft. 'She just needs fresh air and a calm atmosphere. Go back to your duties. My car is parked nearby.'

'Good luck driving anywhere, sir. Here, you! Pack it in!' The policeman's voice faded, or the world did. Unable to get enough breath, her mouth full of the taste of leather, Margaret felt herself lose consciousness.

She came to in a small room filled with clerks' desks and ledgers. Her chin and the back of her head ached: she'd been struck to keep her unconscious. She felt sick at the thought that they could easily have killed her, and wondered why they hadn't. She was bound and gagged, lying in deep shadow, her hat lying on the floor beside her. Mr Tabor stood nearby, rubbing his arms and whispering to Mrs Philbrook who was pacing, still bearing the bag. 'Why did I have to do that, Sabina?'

'Just go, Hedley. Let me deal with this. She's been helping Mrs Holbourne to stop Rhoda from handing over the papers.'

'Rhoda's given them to you now. But I don't understand why the publisher wants to meet us here and Dr Demeray will tell—'

'The publisher is meeting *me*. I've arranged for Mrs Holbourne to come here after we've gone. She'll take the blame for what happens to Dr Demeray. Leave everything to me, Hedley. Go now.'

'I did that before and you said that Mrs Holbourne nearly killed Rhoda. I'll never forgive her. And I must protect you. I'm more than just your driver.'

'Stop fussing about Rhoda,' snapped Mrs Philbrook. 'I've done the work. The money is ours.'

'We promised Rhoda—'

'It's ours. Has she woken up yet?'

Margaret shut her eyes and kept still. She was aware of someone standing over her, the light lessening a little. A smoker's breath in her face, worse than the leather gloves.

'She's out for the count. I hit her too hard.'

'Mrs Holbourne will deal with her. The publisher should be in the room behind this by now. Let's go.'

Their footsteps and voices receded. Margaret struggled against her bonds, getting awkwardly to her feet. She felt sick, the gag sucking in each time she gasped for breath, and she tried to remove it with her shoulder. The rope on her hands was loose, but was it loose enough to untie? Mrs Philbrook was getting away, but perhaps she could get free of her bonds and either go after her or run for help. And if the so-called publisher was expected any moment, there might be time to see who it was and where they went.

The gag came free and Margaret used her teeth to help remove the rope on her wrists. It was so badly knotted that she wondered if Mr Tabor had tied her up, and despite his words, hadn't hit her as hard as he might have. Mrs Philbrook had wanted him to leave and let her handle things. Perhaps he was the only reason why Margaret was still alive. Which meant...

She pulled off her gloves and battled with the rope on her ankles, breaking her fingernails and grazing her fingers in the process, until she was free. She gritted her teeth as pins and needles started.

She tiptoed into a corridor. One end led to a front door with a window in it and the other into gloom. Margaret could smell old paper, ink, dust, candle-grease, a tiny amount of damp, and something else she couldn't place. Which way should she go?

Mrs Philbrook's voice came from the gloom. 'I've wound everything up. This is the last export I intend to make and I wanted to do it directly. I thought Mr Abney would be here. From now on, I—'

'Directly, huh?' said a man's voice, briskly. 'Let me see the paperwork, please.' A rustle, and the sound of papers brushing against each other. 'Twenty copies of a nauseating women's magazine and... It's taken long enough.'

'I hope—'

'That I remembered the continental women's magazines you were promised? Here they are. The contents of the middle one are quite fascinating, you'll find. Farewell, madam, until the next time.'

'Oh, but Mr Abney said—'

'An obsession with sharing paper is like laudanum, Mrs Philbrook. You think you've had sufficient, then you want more. After all, what Mr Abney offered through Sally wasn't enough, was it? And you took it out on her.'

'What are you talking about?' said Mr Tabor's voice.

'You've heard of honour among thieves, I imagine... sir. Well, believe it or not, there's honour among couriers too. We let each other get on with the job, but we remember the ones who are murdered. Mr Abney's a different bird: he doesn't need honour when there's money. He and your lady friend will get on well. He'll be in the kitchen at the back, ready to talk terms.'

'In the kitchen?' exclaimed Mrs Philbrook. 'He needs to come here. He mustn't stay there.'

'You don't tell Abney what to do – he tells you. Just hope that he doesn't make you cross paths with me again. I liked Sally.'

Margaret heard footsteps and ducked back into the room as a man strode past, then peered out again. Neither Mrs Philbrook nor Mr Tabor could be seen or heard. Had they returned to the next room or gone to the kitchen? The man who stepped into the street carrying a satchel didn't look like the man she now knew to be Smith, but she didn't know whether to be glad or not. She followed on tiptoe and peered into the street. Steam was rising into the sky and the street was full of people impeding the man as he tried to hurry off. They must still be near King's Cross, which meant Fox couldn't be far away.

With unspeakable relief, Margaret spotted Bert. His face relaxed as he saw her and he started forwards, but she pointed frantically. Casting his eyes to the heavens, Bert gave chase after the man with the satchel and motioned to her to follow, but Margaret needed to wait for Maude, to make sure she didn't get caught up in whatever Mrs Philbrook had planned. If Bert had found her, someone else would, too. If she could just slip into an alley and watch—

Someone pulled her backwards through the doorway. 'Those papers are false, aren't they?' Mrs Philbrook hissed in her ear. 'The man following the courier is your husband's man. You've signed my death warrant.'

'Sabina?' said Mr Tabor. 'What—'

'How many death warrants do you think the real thing would have signed?' said Margaret.

'If people cared that much, they should have guarded the real thing better,' growled Mrs Philbrook.

'No one would have died, Dr Demeray,' said Mr Tabor. 'Britain must free itself of its allegiance to Russia. A reputable publisher will—'

'We have to go Hedley. Hurry. But knock her out again.'

'Why?'

'Every reputable publisher has been warned off, Mr Tabor,' said Margaret. 'And Maude isn't responsible for luring your sister to—'

'Sabina! No!'

Margaret was shoved sideways. She heard a sharp noise and felt a sharper sting in her right shoulder. Stumbling against the wall, clasping it, Margaret stared at Mrs Philbrook, who was taking aim at her chest.

'Don't make it worse,' said Margaret, feeling blood oozing and trying to fight the memory of being at the other end of a gun with no qualms about what she should do.

Mrs Philbrook cocked the pistol and re-aimed. With an anguished howl, Mr Tabor struck his lover on the chin. As she lurched backwards, the pistol fired into Mr Tabor's forehead, then skittered across the floor as he collapsed and Mrs Philbrook dropped it.

'Hedley! Oh God, Hedley...' She fell to her knees and held his face in her hands. 'I didn't mean... Mr Abney! Come and help!' she yelled towards the gloomy rear of the building.

Margaret crouched beside her. 'Press the wound to stop the bleeding, Mrs Philbrook. I'll go and call for help and come back, but I don't know—'

'We have to leave. We must.'

The door from the street banged open and Fox burst in. 'What the— Margaret?' He lifted her into his arms. 'How badly are you hurt?'

'I'm all right. But I think Mr Tabor is dead.'

'No! Help me!' said Mrs Philbrook. 'I set a bomb in the kitchen for Mrs Holbourne to find. It's not supposed to go off for ages but...'

'A bomb?' Maude rushed through the entrance, hatless, with strands of dark hair slipping from their pins. 'I told Fox that you'd told me to come— Wait – those smells... There's petrol somewhere nearby, and a fuse. My God, the place is about to catch fire! And if there's a bomb... Get out! Everyone get out!'

Fox bundled her and Margaret into the street and shouted at passers-by to run away as fast as they could.

'Get out, Mrs Philbrook!' he called, then pulled Margaret and Maude flat onto the pavement. They put their hands over their ears as the door exploded into the street, in a shower of glass and shattered wood.

Thirty-Seven

In early July, Fox, Margaret and Margaret's father were invited to spend the weekend with the Holbournes at Maude's grandmother's house, where Maude had been reluctantly recuperating.

On the Saturday, regardless of their injuries, Maude challenged Margaret, Fox and Geoff to a horseback race across the fields. After a while, Margaret let the others race ahead. If Maude could ignore the damage to her throat, good for her, but Margaret couldn't ignore the pain in her shoulder for long. A gentle ride was enough to blow away the cobwebs a little.

On Monday she'd be back at work with Dr Gesner, who would pretend that he was reassured about Smith. She wasn't sure which of them was least convinced, but Dr Gesner was still at Dorcas Free, Fox seemed content to accept that, and Frau Gesner was considering whether to move to England after all. Fox said they might even have them round to dinner. Margaret was still unsure what it all meant, but just now she was hoping that the injury to her shoulder wouldn't make working difficult.

At the top of the hill, Margaret reined in her horse and leaned forward to pat his neck. He stamped a little but otherwise stood foursquare in the high afternoon sun as she looked along the meadows. He was glistening but seemed unconcerned, flicking his mane, tossing his head and letting out a soft whinny, as if the gallop had blown away some of his cobwebs too.

There was nowhere to tether the horse, and Margaret didn't know him well enough to feel confident in dismounting and letting him graze without fearing he'd run off, so she shifted position in the saddle and clicked for him to walk on. The sun warmed her face. Her hair was hot, little strands sticking to her face. She breathed in the scents of grass and meadow flowers as skylarks wheeled and dived in the clear blue sky, singing their hymn to summer. Somewhere behind was the house, and much further beyond, the grey smudge of air that indicated London. She wasn't minded to look at either and let the horse plod at his own pace, reins loose in her hand, wondering about the small settlements around and all the lives in them.

The soft clump of another horse cantering up made her turn, ready to nod a greeting. It was Geoff. He slowed his horse to a trot, then a walk, until he was alongside her. 'How do, M.'

'Very well thanks.'

'Wool gathering?'

'Just taking in the scenery.'

'I've been thinking about *The New Dorcas*,' said Geoff. 'How you suppose the editor of is managing under the onslaught of Maude's takeover?'

'He'll either cave in or resign,' said Margaret. 'Either way, it'll be a better magazine.'

'I couldn't work in an office: all that sitting.'

'Nor me. Although I suppose there's nothing quite as sittingy as horse-riding.'

Geoff laughed. 'At least I can stand in the stirrups for a change. Can you do anything similar in a side-saddle?'

'I'm not sure *I* can without overbalancing. It's more comfortable than it looks, honestly. And I can ride as fast as you, normally.'

'I know, but I've only ever seen you riding astride before.'

'I didn't know how the locals would react.'

'It's unlike you to care.'

Margaret shrugged. They plodded along for a while in silence, serenaded by wheeling birds and unseen crickets.

'Your hair will be a frightful tangle later,' he said. 'I mean, it's very pretty hanging down like that, but rather you than me doing battle with the brush later.'

'I like to imagine I look free, wild and likely to run off into the wide blue yonder.'

'Personally, if I were going to ride off into the wide blue yonder, I wouldn't choose a side-saddle and a riding habit for it, but each to their own.'

Margaret grinned. 'I'd pay good money to see you try.'

'I wanted to say thank you, M,' said Geoff, after a pause. 'Maude's coming back. I know she is.'

'She and Fox are probably miles away.'

'I don't mean horse-riding, M. I mean *her*.'

'I know what you mean, Geoff. And I'm glad.'

Over dinner that evening, Margaret's father and Maude's grandmother, who were a similar age, sat happily complaining about young people, by which they meant anyone under sixty-five. Her father was thinner and seemed older than when he'd gone to Madeira in November, but he was regaining something of his spirit. He had spent the afternoon talking about his plan to include Thirza in his next book, even though it was for children and mostly about dragons.

'Someone said the other day that the Suffragette Menace is still threatening the underground,' he said, after a while, enunciating the capitals. 'You don't think that's true, do you, Meg? You were always interested in that sort of thing. Suffrage I mean, not the underground. And there was an arson outrage not far from you in May, wasn't there? But of course, *you* wouldn't—'

'No, Father, I wouldn't. And it was more or less a shed anyway.'

'I'm very glad. Though I'm sure Fox wouldn't let you.'

Margaret bridled, wanting to say that Fox didn't control her, but Fox winked and touched his finger to his lips. Let her father dream. Margaret was heading towards forty and her father was over eighty. The time for arguing with him was long past.

By the time they retired to the drawing room to dance and play cards, the sky was a dark, smoky blue. Margaret stood in the doorway to the garden as Geoff wound up the gramophone.

'You can't really blame me for wondering about you,' said Maude, coming to stand next to her. 'Since you met Fox, half the people you've worked with have disappeared, been arrested, questioned or executed. I'm surprised you have any friends left.'

'None of my colleagues have been arrested this year. Only my friends.'

'True. Although no one has ever really explained what those documents were that Sabina Philbrook was trying to sell, other than it was something to do with the Balkans.'

'That's all there is to know, I imagine.'

'I wonder,' said Maude, then sighed. 'In the end, war has broken out there again despite the London Treaty, so it didn't really matter what she did.'

'What if war goes beyond the Balkans?'

'Pfft,' said Maude. 'No one wants that.' She took a puff from her cigarette, then a small sip of wine. It was only her second glass all evening. A lock of hair slipped loose and fell on her cheek in a girlish wave. 'I talked things over properly with Geoff and asked what he was doing with the Bryces. He was appalled at what I'd thought. Do you know what he was actually planning?'

'No idea.'

'Investing in the theatre, so they'd agree to put on *Lady Geraldine's Speech* for my fortieth birthday. He knew they're not especially pro-suffragette and thought it the best way to encourage them.'

'Oh, Maude.'

'I feel more of a fool about him than about you: it's easier to heal things with you. I think he'll take a while to forgive me for thinking he might be a gun-runner.'

'He will.'

'At least he's agreed to come on the suffrage march on the fourteenth. It will be enormous. People *must* listen.' She took another puff of her cigarette. 'It's hard to be sorry for Mrs Philbrook. All those people dead.'

'She planned to have you blamed for that explosion. I think if Hedley hadn't been there, she'd have killed me too.'

'Stop fussing, Demeray, you were merely scratched.' Maude glanced at Margaret's shoulder. The scar was just hidden by the neckline of Margaret's dress. 'Though if fashions change, you might have to have a tattoo so that the other side matches better.'

'I'm not letting a tattooist take a chunk of my other clavicle.'

'Then you won't be symmetrical.'

'I'll risk it.'

'I'm glad she was terrible shot,' said Maude, sobering. 'Then she was killed by her own bomb, along with some other poor sap in the building. They still haven't said who.'

'They think it was the person paying her,' said Margaret, with a shiver.

'Are you sure that Hedley was already dead?'

'Yes,' said Margaret. 'Both the Tabors picked the wrong people to fall in love with. I just hope Rhoda marries her fellow when they're eventually released, rather than do as her mother tells her.'

'Her mother's disowned her. But that won't stop the terms of Rhoda's father's will. If she survives prison, she'll be a wealthy woman one day. Goodness knows what she'll do then.'

'Hopefully, nothing at all.' Margaret sipped her wine and nudged Maude. 'More importantly, I'm glad they didn't send you back to prison for the arson.'

'I think the magistrates thought Dr Southern had done enough.' Maude shrugged and tucked her summer shawl closer round her throat and chest.

'Can you accept that I won't undertake any militant suffragette action?'

'I suppose so,' Maude blew a smoke ring. 'Maybe I concentrate too much on one thing. It's just that there are so many things wrong with the world. This is the one I'm trying to put right.'

'Then do it. I'll always support you.'

'Good,' said Maude. 'Here's your husband, coming to plot the downfall of the suffragette menace.'

In the garden, Fox drew Margaret into his arms to waltz to the gramophone music. 'I want to put the world right too,' he said. 'And so do you. It's what made me fall in love with you before I even knew you, when I used to go to your talks.'

'I just wish the world were better already.'

'Let's keep trying to make it so,' said Fox. 'But tonight, let's pretend we've already succeeded.'

He kissed her head gently. Warm velvety air brushed their faces as they danced under a soft moon and shy stars. A sudden, darting movement, perhaps a bat swooping over the shadowy shrubs, conducted a symphony of sounds drifting from the open doors and windows: the clatter of plates and glasses being gathered from the dining room, a maid singing in the kitchen.

Some distance away, a train gathered speed. Margaret rested her head against Fox's shoulder, pretending that the train was bearing all troubles and misery away.

'I love you too,' she said. And in that moment, she wasn't sure if she meant just Fox or the whole flawed world, and every other person who just wanted to dance under equal stars.

Newsletter and Other Books

To get news about my books and others, as well as the first chance to read Advanced Reader Copies of any new releases, please sign up for my newsletter at
https://BookHip.com/PHNKCAG

For information and links to:
THE MARGARET DEMERAY SERIES
THE MURDER BRITANNICA SERIES
THE CASTER & FLEET SERIES (with Liz Hedgecock)
THE BOOKER & FITCH SERIES (with Liz Hedgecock)
Weird And Peculiar Tales (with Val Portelli)
Plus short story Collections and audiobooks, please visit

https://paulaharmon.com/

I also have short stories in the following anthologies:
DORSET SHORTS
WARTIME CHRISTMAS TALES

About Paula Harmon and Links

Paula Harmon was born in North London to parents of English, Scottish and Irish descent. Perhaps feeling the need to add a Welsh connection, her father relocated the family every two years from country town to country town moving slowly westwards until they settled in South Wales when Paula was eight. She later graduated from Chichester University before making her home in Gloucestershire and then Dorset where she has lived since 2005. She is a civil servant, married with two adult children.

https://paulaharmon.com

https://viewauthor.at/PHAuthorpage

https://www.facebook.com/pg/paulaharmonwrites

https://www.goodreads.com/paula_harmon

https://instagram.com/paulasharmon

https://www.youtube.com/@paulaharmon7810/

https://bsky.app/profile/paulasharmon.bsky.social

Historical Note

While Margaret Demeray, Fox, their friends and enemies are all fictional, this book is set against real events and refers to or is inspired by events that happened to real people.

The First Balkan War which had been going on for some time was briefly halted by the London Treaty of May 1913 before erupting again into the Second Balkan War a few weeks later. What were then referred to as The Great Powers (Great Britain, France, Germany and Russia) made allegiances to protect what they believed needed protecting (not necessarily for humanitarian reasons). Ultimately the conflict paved the way for the First World War. A German dentist working in Portsmouth called William Klare was sentenced to five years penal servitude in March at Winchester Assizes for having attempted to procure a book on submarines and torpedoes. He had attempted to get a fellow German living in Portsmouth, Levi Rosenthal to assist, but Mr Rosenthal went straight to the police, who set up a trap using a clerk from the naval offices and arrested William Klare as soon as he had the book.

While the word 'suffragette' was coined by the press as an insult, in Britain, Emmeline Pankhurst, leader of the Women's Social and Political Union chose to 'own' it and proudly referred to herself and her followers as suffragettes (who chose militant action) to differentiate themselves from suffragists (who didn't), and named their magazine by the same name. By 1913, the suffragette campaign had become increasingly militant and dominated newspapers notwithstanding political issues. There were genuine fears that they would disrupt not only treaty negotiations but the royal wedding in Germany, not to mention everyday life. In Britain, there were over forty violent incidents involving arson or bombs in that year with some deaths and many injuries as a result, and a few near-misses where many hundreds of people could have died or been injured.

Emily Davison was a militant suffragette who suffered several times in Holloway, including being drenched with water and subsequently becoming ill, force-feeding and throwing herself from a balcony in despair from her treatment resulting in a broken back. No-one has ever determined exactly what she intended at the Epsom Derby, but she had bought a return ticket which suggests it wasn't suicide. The jockey and horse were to a large extent unharmed and the jockey did ask after her. The incident was greeted with fury in the press, and women who were obviously suffragettes were attacked in public on occasion. However, the funeral procession was massive, well-orchestrated and did indeed bring London to a halt. Moving picture footage of both Emily Davison walking onto the track at Epsom and the funeral procession can be found on YouTube.

The suffragette procession in July was even bigger.

The government did try to stop the publication of suffrage magazines and it could be argued that the militant suffragette campaign in the United Kingdom was little short of terrorism.

Several MPs houses were attacked, along with post offices and railway and underground stations. To give an idea of the scale of the campaign, please check out https://en.wikipedia.org/wiki/List_of_suffragette_bombings

The force-feeding suffered by Maude happened to many women in prison, who were denied status as political rather than criminal prisoners. At least one woman nearly died in a similar incident where the tube went into her lungs (this is described in the book by Joyce Marlow below, who quotes the letter of complaint from the prisoner's doctor. The Cat and Mouse Act was brought in to release women when they became unwell, only to re-arrest them as soon as they offended again. There really was a comedy film as described by Mr Bryce in which a male actor dressed up as a suffragette was hilariously force-fed champagne, which gives an indication of the general view of suffragette activity. The WSPU really did buy a house in Dalmeny Avenue and suffragettes would sing from it to encourage the prisoners in Holloway.

Millicent Fawcett, leader of the National Union of Women's Suffrage Societies, was non-militant as were other suffragists. It is a mistake to think that the suffragists disappeared, they were just overshadowed. By 1905, Fawcett's NUWSS had 305 constituent societies and almost 50,000 members, compared with the WSPU's 2,000 members in 1913. However, suffragists walked alongside suffragettes in Emily Davison's funeral procession.

It doesn't seem unreasonable that like Margaret some women would have felt conflicted. But there was a good deal of frustration that in other parts of the Empire, women had the vote. New Zealand had given it to all women over 21 (including Maori women) in 1893 and in Australia, state by state, between 1894 and 1908, the right to vote was extended to women. (Initially Aboriginal women were included, but in 1902, the right for Aboriginal people to vote was rescinded.)

The Home Rule Bill, the beginning of independence for Ireland, was underway, but Unionist resistance was growing and the threat of civil war was already close to the surface in Ireland with potential repercussions in mainland Britain.

Things which did *not* exist and/or didn't happen (as far as I know) include the two magazines Athene's Gazette and The

New Dorcas, an arson attack on an MP's house in Tyburnia, and diplomatic letters stolen in Sarajevo to be sold on in a foolish attempt to protect the British Empire.

Non-fiction books which formed part of my research (and if I have misrepresented or misinterpreted anything this is my fault entirely):

Crawford, Elizabeth 'Kate Parry Frye, the long life of an Edwardian actress and suffragette' (ITV Ventures)

Arthur, Max 'Lost Voices of the Edwardians' (Harper Perennial)

Hawksley, Lucinda 'March Women March' (Welbeck Publishing)

Heffer, Simon 'The Age of Decadence – Britain 1880 to 1914' (Windmill Books)

Langton-Hewer J 'Our Baby – for Mothers and Nurses' (facsimile from Tempus Publishing)

Marlow, Joyce 'Suffragette – the fight for votes for women' (Virago Press)

Newby, Jennifer 'Women's Lives 1800-1939' (Pen & Sword)

Printed in Great Britain
by Amazon